SAN MARINO BLUES

A Story About Love
And
Prevarication

A Novel
by
Gaither Stewart

Cyberwit Publishers

Cyberwit.net
HIG 45 Kaushambi Kunj, Kalindipuram
Allahabad - 211011 (U.P.) India
http://www.cyberwit.net
Tel: +(91) 9415091004
E-mail: info@cyberwit.net

Printed at VCORRE PRESS.

To

J.S.

my daughter, for what you were for me and how
you changed my life

Also by Gaither Stewart

NOVELS

Europe Trilogy:

The Trojan Spy
Lily Pad Roll
Time of Exile

The Fifth Sun
Asheville

SHORT STORIES

Once In Berlin
Signs of the Times
Icy Currents, Compulsive Course
To Be A Stranger
Voices From Pisalocca

ESSAYS

Trails of Memory
Babylon Falling
Recollection of Things Learned, Remembering
Socialism

ENIGMA

In Mexico twenty-five years ago I acquired a haunting painting which I named ENIGMA. In my novel, *The Fifth Sun,* written then in Mexico, I included an imaginary scene showing the painter's composition of the painting. Today ENIGMA appears as the cover art for this novel, *San Marino Blues*.

He peers at the empty canvas now illuminated by three lamps. The body, he thinks, is the essence of man; but how to capture that essence with colors? He thinks that since the eyes ar e the gates to the body, through those gates the essence moves back and forth. But he keeps in mind that also the mask is the man. In order to get to the essence through the ocular gateway, he must first free it. He paints one white dot on the left side of the canvas, about one-fourth down from the top: "The eye." It is open. He props a long mirror next to the easel. His image appears in the mirror. A reflection. What he sees in the mirror is illusion—full of him, though empty of him. A ghost is inside the mirror. He turns the mirror and his image vanishes. Forget the mirror and the illusion. Paint your inner self. He adds a second white dot to the right, opening a second gate. He mixes colors and applies a layer of light green from the top left downwards toward the bottom right. "My body". He smiles. He splashes diverse colors at random. He returns to the greenish hue and paints it over the reds and whites and blacks; the synthesis changes shades and colors; the green emerges from fire. Again he looks at himself in the mirror. He surrounds the white dots with slashes of black over the green over the red. Vertical drops of green appear above the black slits through which the white dots gleam. A yellowish slash separates the slits that are now eyes. He peers inside. He sees his own eyes looking out at him. Illusion? Can illusion be real? Strokes here and there. The greens turn brownish yellow. Wide bars down the sides frame a face. From behind the mask emerges a man. The man peers out as if from behind a death mask. The painter stares. The man-mask stares back. He looks into the mirror and into the slits. He sees himself. Man.

Gaither Stewart- Rome, Italy

Editor's note:

San Marino Blues has a depth that shines a light into the life experiences many have and then try to suppress the memories that refuse to fade. In this story, we follow John from the peaks to falling in love to the bottomless pits of irretrievable loss. In this story is the inner world of not just one man, but most of humanity. San Marino Blues is more a story of love than a love story in the conventional sense. There is a lyrical feel at times in this work that makes the words almost sing as you read them. This is an unexpected experience reading a novel. It speaks a deep connection to truths and emotions that must find their way into the light. Kudos to Mr. Stewart for bringing this exceptional work to life. I feel like I have walked in the shadows of a stranger's life in this book. You can't make characters much more real than that.
Rowan Wolf

An Introduction to San Marino Blues
By Christopher C. Black

When I finished reading San Marino Blues I realized that, in John Sutton, Gaither Stewart has created a character who will linger in our thoughts, not as an everyman, which in some ways he is, but as a man whose search for love and meaning, in a world where everyone wears a mask and truth is as elusive as happiness, transforms him into a hero of our times; whose journey through life, like ours, forces him to accept that life is often suffering, but who, nevertheless, cannot give up, cannot surrender to the fate which faces us all, solitude and death, who says, despite everything, life goes on, love comes and goes, and comes again.

The novel is described by the narrator at the beginning as a story about love; that's how it begins and how it ends. But it is much more than that. Writers of fiction draw on their own lives, lives which are the same as for most of us, desperate and continuous struggles to survive, to overcome all obstacles, to try to live with love in the face of hate, pleasure in the face of pain, understanding in the place of ignorance and confusion.

Many of us rely on religion to get us through, to give a sense of value and meaning to life, but writers with anything to say, like philosophers, search more deeply than others into the experience of life to try to come to terms with it and to find a purpose for it all.

For some, the answer, or so they think, is found in ideology, for some, in romance, for others, war or business, or art in all its forms; in this novel Gaither Stewart has succeeded in telling a story about one man's search for his own meaning in a prose style that is vibrant and direct, and through characters that are as vivid as they are real, but in a heightened way. Just as actors have to be able to act naturally in an imaginary setting but with more energy, so writers have to bring us characters that live more intensely than we can.

Through Sutton, he expresses ideas and feelings shared by all of us in the modern world where everything is constantly changing, the ground is always shifting, and the truth is hidden behind masks and ambiguities, behind conventions and propaganda, the 'prevarications" of the novel's subtitle. For Sutton is, like Stewart, not only a writer but also a revolutionary, but who like all revolutionaries has to face his own motivations and intentions on his own and so has to understand them, to understand himself.

The novel opens with a paragraph about change, and its constancy and says,

"…in a fictional story some things change as in real life, albeit about a life that wasn't actually lived, or a life that didn't get told. Still, the everything and the everywhere in change seem to me like my own life which is transience itself. I've never felt fixed in my life, never permanent. There are blank spaces that seem to me like that.

And,

'Romantic love for another person is revolutionary, something outside ourselves. That is life. An October kind of thing. "The reference to the October Revolution in Russia in 1917 is important because Sutton is a communist living in a society that wants to destroy communism. He refuses to be destroyed, for the idea to be destroyed, and he finds he is not alone.

To tell the story here would deprive the reader of the pleasure of the journey through it. But it concerns Sutton's relationships with three women, Martha, Maxime and Dorothea, his travels from Paris and London to San Marino, the small communist country in the middle of Italy, and his encounters with French intelligence agents, Egyptian communists in exile in Paris, Hank's Bar in San Marino, Bernard, a musician and rival, all against a backdrop of terrorist attacks or false flag operations by French secret services and the deteriorating conditions of society in Europe.

John Sutton is a young writer, who, when we meet him, has had some success and in the flush of that success he meets, by chance, as these things often happen, a beautiful woman named Martha who, has a father in London and an aunt in Paris, a student, a bit younger than himself. It's love at first sight and their lives are quickly entwined which provokes some reflection on the meaning of love, or what appears to be love. He writes that she awakens in him concepts of time and space and the awareness of the diverse roles and multiple lives he could still live, but that love is unpredictable and often unreasonable which brings him memories of the life with his father who was also a communist but forced underground during his childhood. The idea of the "underground" looms large in his mind since as a child he did not know what it really meant but induced images of darkness and shadows and when he was five, living in Rotterdam, he had dug a pit to try find the "underground."

The two spend their time when Sutton is not writing, going to Paris cafes, making love, and thinking about the meaning of it all, with interesting references to Greek mythology, then, bored with themselves, they decide to go to Mexico, leading to some stimulating observations about Mexico. A favourite of mine is this passage:

"On a dusty, windblown hill in Mexico I came to consider the cactus the symbol of solitude, and thus the symbol of Mexico. From a distance a row of cacti looks back at you uncompromisingly, smugly and yet so alone in the world. But close at hand, the cacti are quite different; what from the road might seem to be a mass of green thickets, from up close is independent life itself—throbbing, thriving, and surviving, both receiving the sun of life and giving life—but each cactus stands alone, as if by choice. They don't need anything or anyone."

From Mexico, Martha and Sutton travel to Argentina where they learn Martha is pregnant and they return to Paris. It is there they meet a character named Ivaan, at La Coupole, the famous Parisian café just before a bomb attack on French intelligence offices next door kills and wounds many, they are swept up in the aftermath and Ivaan becomes first a friend, then a comrade, then a rival for Martha. But in the meantime tragedy strikes, the relationship is broken, Sutton is watched by the secret service and, due to the tragedy that befalls them Sutton suffers a psychological reaction, develops claustrophobia causing him to want to go the Chartres Cathedral to walk the labyrinth in hope of a cure. The trip only aggravates things as he sees the first signs of a relationship developing between Martha and Ivaan, which in turn causes him to seek the help of a psychiatrist named Zetkin, who he picks out of the phone book because of his last name and the link to the revolutionary, Clara Zetkin, and through him the priest Père Francois, who in conversation with Sutton says,

"Then you believe in man—which must be the writers' disease. I think of the poor writer, struggling between good and evil, between optimism and hopefulness on the one hand and cynicism and pessimism on the other. Your path is not an easy one. In any case, since the religious instinct in man is as great as the instinct to eat, I find in my work that most people wish they could believe."

Ivaan takes him to the poor suburbs of Paris, the 9-3 district inhabited by Arab and African immigrants, where despair is the scent in the air and meets others like Ivaan, one of whom states,

'Social awareness is yet to be born in a concrete form in the West. But that first basic step is in gestation in today's pandemic crisis. Some people in America are asking why they have no public health care like in France. French people are asking: Why the wars? Social awareness should be bursting forth…to be followed by contagious rebellion against the absence of the social and against the wars. When social awareness will be born, then, perhaps, a revolution can be made.'

But while talk of revolution takes place, Martha, who repeatedly demands that Sutton never leave her, leaves him. And so, Sutton leaves Paris and travels to the town he spent part of his youth in, San Marino, and begins to write San Marino Blues, and while there meets the very interesting character of Hank who runs a local bar and café whose life in New Orleans among other places, is a story in itself, and then the sensuous Maxime, who tells him she left a man named Bernard who murdered a stranger on the street for looking at her. Or did he? For as with all the characters in the novel it is difficult for Sutton to know what is fact and what is fiction and because of that he never knows his real relationship with any of them.

When Maxime's-ex lover, Bernard, a musician, shows up in San Marino looking for her, Sutton becomes involved in more ambiguities. This excerpt perhaps encapsulates the state of affairs we face in the world,

"I will interrupt both my impromptu musings and this narration to reassure readers that the people in this story are not representative of the thirty-three thousand people of the population of the micro-Republic of San Marino. Nor are they intended to be. They *are* representative of the small percentage—the same as in every other place on Earth—of the different, of the diffident representatives of the existing social order of those who don't know where they belong or whom they represent; they are always in search of answers. They live their fragile and precarious lives in search of themselves. They err, fall, stand up, and try again. And again and again. Dissatisfied with where they started out, they go out into the world in search of answers; but then, disillusioned, they return and join others like themselves gathered at the top of barren Mount Titano in a kind of exile. In that respect, they *do* form a sort of, well, if not exactly a sect, then a cult, as Sammarinese people farther down the mountain suspect. Because of the lack of answers to our questions and doubts as to who we are and where we belong, we hold onto our mountaintop overhanging the ancient sea over which humans before us have traveled, searching and hoping to discover the secrets of the mysteries of life, time and space.'

From time to time Sutton returns to Paris in the hope of reviving things with Martha, each time his hope dashed, and then learns on his return to San Marino that he has been betrayed again, is alone again, leading to a trip to Munich and a new beginning, but not before the tragic end of Bernard, whose fate is as mysterious as his existence.

I have probably given away too much of the story, but the story is the framework on which Stewart presents his world view, using art to convey the truth of our condition or at least a portrait of our existences through the characters he has created and the experiences they have.

The prose is as rich as his imagination with reference to writers, artists, philosophers, to mythology, psychology, history, how they have interpreted the world, why they are important to us, all set against a broad canvas of the world condition, of politics and war, of peace and hope. For Sutton is, despite all he suffers, an optimist. Love, romantic love, the love of human kind, of nature, of art, of life itself, the love that makes Sutton a communist as well as an optimist, is the central theme of the novel because it is the central theme of our lives, and, so, to complete the circle, and return to the beginning, the novel is, as Stewart writes,

"A story about love, that's how it begins and how it ends.'

SAN MARINO BLUES

It is said that nothing stays the same. That everything constantly transforms and transmutes. That everything is in motion. As in nature also in life something is always developing and something always dying away. Nothing remains in one stage. Heraclitus of Ephesus insisted on ever-present change, on the "still becoming" as the characteristic feature of the world, as in the saying, "No man ever steps into the same river twice." As the writer trying to show one scene learns, even though things change in one place or for one person, in one way or another the same changing things are happening everywhere—over and over again—showing that the present is also the past and that the past is part of the present, that matter is truly eternal and space unlimited. As in real life, also in fictional stories some things change, albeit about a life that wasn't actually lived, or a life that didn't get told. Still, the everything and the everywhere in change seem to me like my own life which is transience itself. I've never felt fixed in my life, never have I felt permanent. There are blank spaces that seem to me like that fictional life not lived—or, not yet lived. On the other hand, some fundamental things must remain the same: children still come into the world in the same way and in the end people die the death alone. At the same time, we cannot live in life—the life in eternal change—without being part of it, as at times I have doubted. And then, what do we know of the future, the ripe future so filled with the changing everything now about to fall onto our heads? Though in our times capitalism is apparently headed toward extinction, life seems determined to continue. Yet we don't know what time and change may carry in our individual direction. But now I do know that it was because of my ephemeral perception of life and its fleeting nature and my notion of being temporary wherever I was that the falling in love sensation convinced me that I could never live again without her or in the same state of oblivion as before her. From the very start I was deathly afraid of losing Martha, and then, years later, parts of the same sensation of fear carried over to my feelings for Maxime, who caused the tingling of memory of the original fear of losing my first love. As I would say one night on Mount Titano in San Marino, love is truly hard: though beautiful, the most beautiful feeling the human can experience, romantic unconditional love is nonetheless not an afternoon tea party. Romantic love for another person is revolutionary, something outside ourselves. That is life. An October kind of thing. It overturns everything that was before. That is its nature. You are one person before you love; after finding love, you transmute into another. As the author of this story about love, I quote Rainer Maria Rilke who knew things about love and wrote that *love for another is both an ordeal and the highest testimony of ourselves; the supreme work of which all others are but preparations.*

Part One

1.

John Sutton and Martha

In September, I met Martha on the London-Paris high speed tunnel train on which we had adjacent across the aisle seats. By the time we arrived at the Gare du Nord, I had fallen in love with this girl wearing a multicolored scarf whose habit of continually pushing back her long blond hair as though to show her true self entranced me trying to see clearly into her green eyes, eyes that gradually, in an accumulation of views and sightings, revealed that she reciprocated my feelings of discovering love. I was twenty-two, she twenty. Until that moment in our lives totaling forty-two years we must have been looking for each other everywhere. Was it destiny that we met on that train? Or pure chance? She or I could have taken a later train. But it was not written that we missed each other. That autumn, as summer died, and on that day, at that precise hour, we were assigned those seats on that train, which later seemed the perfect arrangement for strangers destined to become lovers. Consequently, how could we deny the existence of destiny and the role of chance that brought us together at the same time and place? Philosophers have written that the wise man neglects nothing which helps him fulfill his Destiny, that great men become great because they have mastered chance, that what the vulgar call chance is inherent in Genius. However, I must admit that I sometimes feel I am a mere instrument of Providence who will use me as long as I accomplish her designs, but will desert me and crush me whenever she desires.

As we followed the porter with our luggage out of the station, neither of us knew exactly how to act or what to do or even where we were going together—now that we had fallen in love. In her mysterious elegance, her long brightly colored scarf fluttering in the breeze blowing up the platform, Martha stood taller than she had seemed under the low ceilings of the train so that her head and my shoulder continually brushed as we reached out one to the other. She took my hand. Or maybe I took hers. To touch. To feel. To confirm that what seemed to be happening was happening in reality.

She was going to the home of a French aunt where she would live while continuing her studies, and I to a hotel a London publisher had reserved for me near its Paris office. As the taxi accelerated across the ornate Russian bridge, she spontaneously put her head on my shoulder as if it were her long-sought place and whispered in a strange way:

"Don't ever leave me."

"What did you say, Martha?" I replied, perceiving the uncertainty in the air.

"Don't you ever leave me," again she whispered the same words just as we arrived at her aunt's apartment facing the Esplanade.

Dreamily she greeted *our* concierge who saw to our bags; to me she said suggestively there were other taxis…if necessary. An elevator to the third floor opened directly into luxury land where Aunt Thérèse embraced her still dreamy niece and, unfazed by my presence and as if unconcerned as to who I was or why I was there, she offered me her hand.

The marble foyer, the grey and pale blue colors of the luxurious double salons and the sweeping view of the long park outside the picture windows revealed where I was and prompted the thought that my father would have abhorred it all: the entire setting, the perfection of the world of privilege. The aunt reminded me of whose son I was: my father was an international anti-capitalist revolutionary Communist, not necessarily opposed however to the good things of life. So I go through life, trying all things and holding onto what I can. But this? The symbols of the imperialism he opposed were right here under my eyes: the riches of French colonialism, the conquests of Algeria, West and Equatorial Africa, the Maghreb, Indochina, the Indian Ocean islands, protectorates in Tunisia and Morocco, North Africa to be colonized, the sub-Saharan empire to be exploited. My father said French commitment to civilization of indigenous peoples was only the rhetoric; violent conquest, economic exploitation and social-cultural disruption the harsh reality. And later, in my times, were yet to occur the hatefully imperialistic destruction of progressive Libya and the violent murder of its leader Mohammad Gaddafi and undeclared and unrecognized war on Syria. All the wealth stolen at the ends of the earth and proudly-honorably handed down from generation to generation was under my eyes.

And today, here on the opulent Rue Fabert, in the new millennium, Aunt Thérèse still basked in luxury as though it were rightfully hers. As if it had always been hers—since countless generations it had been hers. This was no place for me. Now, no place for us. Time and again, blond and in love Martha Devall herself blushed at the sumptuousness at every turn. We had to get out of there. Quickly we had to flee.

"*Cherie*," her aunt said, "why don't you show your, ah, our guest our modest home while I arrange an appropriate dinner. Oh, you are English, are you not, John?" In speech, looks and manners Aunt Thérèse was the personification of the unchangeable, incorrigible European *haute bourgeoisie,* an exception to the rule that everything is in change. For her generation, Fascism was little more than an annoyance—an annoyance that however saved the system.

She looked funny when I said my father was English, on which she turned to Martha and announced in French the linguistic change. "You are here for that, no? And John, you do speak French, I assume?" When I answered in French that I had gone to French schools for a few years, the old lady, though pleased, looked somewhat confused; she didn't expect my affirmative answer. Embarrassed, she turned toward the picture window and gazing toward Les Invalides said that the cannons facing away from the great showcase monument toward the Seine had always fascinated her.

"Twenty of them," she said after checking the number. "The same as each time. I've studied the history of the cannons positioned practically under my front windows. Just imagine the power. We captured sixteen of them from the Ottomans, three from China and one from Indochina…that's twenty, no? And you know, most of them bear the inscription *ultima ratio regum,* the last argument of the kings. That's confusing, don't you think? Last argument of the kings. I've long wondered what that really means. Whose kings do they mean?"

I shrugged, getting the fuck out of this place on my mind. I joined Martha waiting for me at the end of the corridor where she kissed me once, leaned her head and shoulders back and examined me as if to reassure herself that I was the right one, then kissed me again, long and deep, as if she'd kissed only once before, had liked it, and now wanted the real enduring thing. "Sutton, don't you ever leave me," she repeated, again leaning back and showing me clearly this time the confusion of the lost look in the depths of her eyes. And later that night when she came to my bed, I kissed all of her. She kissed all of me. We merged into one body, as Octavio Paz suggested in his poem *Counterparts*, his deconstruction of the sexual act as the search for primordial meanings in the body of the loved one: *In my body you search the mountain for the sun buried in the forest. In your body I search for the boat adrift in the middle of the night.* In our search we found our real being, the path to which had miraculously appeared before us on the London-Paris tunnel train.

And I didn't leave her. Not then. Actually I've never left her.

In the following months and years, living our lives on the nearby Rue Saint-Dominique, I sometimes went with Martha to say hello to her aunt. The aging lady never failed to mention the twenty cannons of Invalides which I thought symbolized for her the Paris that once was but which no longer existed except in her waning memory. Algeria was gone, Indo-China was metamorphosed, the African colonies had vanished. "My time is ending, *mes enfants,*" she said each time, a faint eco of unconcerned fatality in her tone. "But it has been a far better time than yours will be." And Martha and I gazed at her in wonderment that her generation of Europeans believed in their own goodness and righteousness and a legitimacy so legitimate that the word itself was never spoken. Words like poverty and hunger, human rights and equality did not exist in the vocabulary of Aunt Thérèse.

Martha Devall had a certain mystery about her, a mystery deep in her character, which she revealed stingily, a mere morsel of a fragment at a time and, as a rule, right after one of her protracted silences during which she apparently conducted her internal battles. Her fear of aloneness shown to me that first day on the train from London, her terror of abandonment caused by her romantic wandering mother's desertion of husband, daughter and family Her insecurity in life for lack of maternal love, it came to seem, had fashioned her obsessively dependent love for me, or, I should say, her love for the entity that was us. Consequently, early in our relationship I concluded that her silent resistance to her own character was her strength; her resistance was the hidden power that she produced in her silences during which she gathered and refined and added to her elaborate defenses. For as I witnessed time and again, she emerged from each silence invigorated like a cocaine addict might after a long desired sniff. So still today, for me Martha will always be living proof that if strength is real and authentic it enhances beauty and the harmony of love. That's its magic. On the one hand, she was mine to protect and care for; on the other, I bathed in her regenerated power as a reward. And in our shared togetherness, her beauty literally flowered: she seemed to say, 'See and adore my face, but the real beauty of me will be seen only by you.' Yet, still today, I don't believe I've ever known the real her. And at times I have wondered if I failed to love her as she loved me. It was just as if her beauty and her body that contain it didn't belong to her, a beauty about which she seemed to lack any possessive feelings; it belonged to her missing mother; it belonged to her deserted father, to me, to life. In her was the ambivalence of her quiet strength and determination when she cast her stubbornly independent gaze on me just before placing her head on my chest and saying: "Don't ever leave me." I began to think that her extraordinary beauty needed its occasional signs of stubborn autarchy to protect her from the menace of abandonment in the world outside of herself.

Love

2.

A couple of months since their meeting on the London-Paris train had passed. John was lying on their bed naked and waiting and coddling his desire to return inside her…and stay there. It was midnight. A hard wind was blowing. Window shutters were banging. He was wondering if his need for her was love, passion or pure sex. And why not, he asked himself, the objective of pure passionate sexual love? His reality was that day after day their sexual life was proving to be dominant in their relationship: there was nothing else two people could do together or to each other or with each other than they had not done that evening. So he lay there, sensual and intemperate, dreamy and content with their togetherness—two beings physically enlaced one into the other like Siamese twins for a lifetime. Martha had just reacted by getting up for something or other; she'd put her mini-nightshirt back on that still showed more than it concealed; a wave of female smells, perfumes and creams, swept across the room; and in the same moment the pleasant sounds of the winter rain beating against the windows looking out over the back gardens completed his perplexed contentedness. It was no less Martha's sexuality than his own, he thought; it was magnetic and contagious and literally palpable. His thoughts for a moment roaming around in space and time, thinking anything at all and telling himself not to think, not to think, he looked at her across the room sprawled in a wide chair, leaning back, her legs with her beautiful narrow Italian ankles wide apart and looking at him as though she were still coming. Martha's orgasms, he reflected, had long aftereffects; she was never sexier than just after sex. In this moment, as John studied her unshackled physicality—her rare beauty—it was clear as day to him that she simultaneously fomented his literary tendency toward the metaphysical. He had accepted as fact that each of us is surrounded by a magnetic field and that when one field meets another similar field, the encounter is an explosive kind of touching, which changes each of them. Still, even though he didn't comprehend this mysterious realm of interaction between objects on the one hand and the metaphysical on the other, that didn't make it any more inconceivable. He had come to believe that there exist non-material links between separate human beings as a result of our common origins. But he did not venture beyond that point. Such thinking was not only useless; it was theologically dangerous, and furthermore far from his current minimum desire which was to occupy physical Martha and her realm. Martha never spoke of the 'path' or the 'journey through life;' she was a materialist in a Marxist sense too, and would have been shocked to hear him say, "I am what I have chosen to be.' Yet, surprisingly, she awakened in him concepts of time as an incomprehensible consideration and space as one of the inexplicable mysteries of earthly life and the awareness of the multiple lives they were perhaps destined to live during their allotted time. For that reason he held onto the precise moments like tonight as onto all his feelings in each of the varied moments with her—moments free of the obsession of her obsessions. He felt like the stranger he'd once believed he was in that enigmatic underground world with his father in which they had to become invisible to be safe, and he was shocked to realize that not even Martha saw the other him, the unseen him. And that even though she didn't see the real him—and maybe never would—he experienced in her unfettered sensuality not only the tumult of their love-making, but he also became aware of her search for the peace of permanence to replace the absence of her erratic mother. Moreover, John maintained a firm conviction that there was no real enduring love without the pillar of unchained, lawless sex in the initial stages of a relationship prolonged as long as the god passion permitted. 'After all,' he thought, 'we're passion's creatures…and passion saves love.'

In that post-orgasm moment when the night held only the sounds of the rain beating against their windows, he breathed softly and smiled to himself when he again isolated their love scents among the diverse scents swirling around him. Their bodies thickened and their minds free and full of love, they felt no need to actually speak of love.

When Martha then again said, 'Sutton, don't ever leave me', John swore that his could never end. Yet, in reality, both still seemed to perceive a gnawing insecurity in their togetherness, perhaps initially because of the fortuity of their meeting, but also because of their personal backgrounds: Martha feared abandonment because of that missing mother of whom she only rarely spoke and John because of the darkness in the underground political world in which he'd grown up. Yet, neither of them wanted to disturb their perfect relationship with marriage, which for them had little to do with the idea of permanence. In that respect both felt free to love, they believed, and highly moral since neither would dream of betraying their personal morality of what is decent in a relationship and the beauty of theirs. But they knew their kind of freedom was not for everyone. Like characters in John Sutton's love novel, *The*

End of a Love Affair, they did not consider themselves exceptional as persons, but in fact they were exceptional in their mutual respect one for the other. Both believed that their personal sexual love was as different from marriage as spirit is from flesh, as grace is in relation to both flesh and soul. As a result of such circumstances, he had not succeeded in separating his passion for her from his intellectual need to speak of the love he felt. Although their love brought them both immense joy, that joy was flawed by the doubt that since it had fallen to them so easily, it might well be an illusion that a mere breath could blow away, a mirage that could fade away just as quickly as it had arrived and leave behind only pain and the shadows of memory.

'Fickle love,' he thought.

'Don't ever leave me,' Martha repeated to herself.

Sometimes, he wondered to what extent love figured in their highly charged relationship. At times, their togetherness seemed based chiefly on her insatiable sexual appetite, which, he knew was the physical expression of her search for permanence, but which was but a short step to the promiscuity her mother had chosen. So was 'his' Martha, whom he was never to leave, also dedicated to the same profligacy? Was her role with him that of Martha or was it that of her licentious mother? In that early period of their togetherness, he had a strange dream: though part of him wanted her to adore and desire only him, in the dream John recognized another side of himself, a secret side that he defined as his 'jealousy'. He dreamed that Martha like her mother desired others too while they were making love—*oh, les mains, les mains, mes mains sur toi, les mains, ses mains sur toi, les mains, nos mains sur toi*—an image that fired his desire and held the promise of an extrasensory orgasm.

Awake, he felt a curious rapture at the idea.

But he knew he'd dreamed only an absurd love game.

'Ultimately, man just wants love,' John thought. 'You imagine elusive unconditional constant love; you may search for eternal love, but you will settle for real physical love for as long as it lasts.' He wrote stories about love, and had learned from his creations that love makes people so unpredictable and unreasonable that real enduring romantic love is rare. Still, it seemed to him that his was a love story; hers an obsession. Genuine love, even genuine erotic love, is relatively rare and is replaced by pseudo loves: consumerist desires, commodities, and in the world of capitalism by capital itself and the labor that drives it, pseudo loves which are just signs of the disintegration of love to the extent—the psychologist Erich Fromm believed—that real love is relegated to an inferior position and as a result man himself for the lack of real love is alienated from himself and from his fellow men. Fromm shows that modern civilization—one that still makes wars and destroys and annihilates—reduces human energy and skills to nil exchange value so that each of us remains essentially alone; even though engulfed in a world of videogames and gadgets, we are unaware of our aloneness. So alone that in feeling, thought and action, we have to stick close to the herd...anything not to be different from the rest.

John thought: modern life opposes the concept of love. In history and literature—as in real life—love is condemned to betrayal, although love itself, he firmly believed, refutes betrayal; otherwise love is perdition. But what about this thing of eternal love? Though constant love is impossible, why is eternal love so rare? Rare? Nearly as impossible as constant love, he believed. Mythological Ariadne's capacity to love one man forever became her condemnation to death; yet, he realized as did Ariadne, condemnation is not the same as perdition.

And so he told Martha sitting in the armchair in her revealing-concealing mini-nightshirt one version of the Ariadne myth: "She lived on the island of Crete and when Theseus arrived to kill the minotaur—the half man, half beast, the offspring of a woman and a bull, who lived in Daedalus' labyrinth and consumed humans for sustenance—she fell head over heels in eternal and constant love with him and gave him a ball of thread so he could find his way back out of the labyrinth and back to her. But that ungrateful son-of-a-bitch used the string, found his way back and sailed away from Crete without her. In this version of her myth poor Ariadne was so desperate that she threw herself into the sea, killing herself for love. Her love was eternal—and John suspected—also constant for that egotistic Theseus who was intent only on slaying the evil Minotaur, becoming a hero and abandoning Crete and Ariadne."

"Oh, yes. I read about Ariadne in a spy novel of a few years ago…in a discussion concerning loyalty and betrayal. The point was that the people and things you are loyal to can always betray you first. The hero preferred to speak of loyalty and values and morality, anything to avoid the one word that the spymaster never used: betrayal."

In their new life in this nebulous Paris of rain, sex and literature, they danced in tiny left bank locals unenthusiastically and sat bored to tears in warm cafés along the boulevards, playing the false role of a modern young Parisian couple, before rushing back to their apartment in Rue Saint-Dominique to make love, which was all that mattered. The more John thought about their obsession one for the other, the more he thought and the more he thought the more he thought about obsession. He had to stop thinking. No thinking. No thinking. He had to stop thinking about obsession and think about serious matters, although he was constantly conscious of the difficulty of thinking seriously about irreducible, actually unthinkable matters like not thinking. You begin thinking of serious matters and before you know it—right in the middle of the development of the idea—you think about a dental appointment that you dread. The problems of everyday life force their way back into your ceaselessly busy mind. You try to feel another's suffering and before you know it, you're back at your dental appointment. You text a TV station, thus contributing ten euros to child care in Yemen. Or you decide to think in a metaphysical direction: you think about fear—the fear of the weak. But theoretical thought about fear lasts only an instant; we can't bear it. Fear, you must conquer. Once fear has touched you and taken root, it doesn't just go away; it occupies your nature—and it remains as a way of life. But thoughts about fear make us afraid to even imagine anything that might cause it. Like the Underground 'he was going to' with his father. As a five-year old he heard they were going to Underground and he imagined the darkness under the ground. In his Rotterdam backyard he dug a hole as deep as possible to see what Underground looked like. It was black, solid black and airless with dirty water at the bottom. The blackness. The airlessness. The dirty water. That's what death must look like, there where they buried his father's friends. The blackness of death. And they had to go there, into the blackness of small, dirty, watery Underground. Into death. As he matured, that image remained among the many things that needed thinking about. Like poverty to escape from like the refugees flooding Europe had to do. You look at poverty, you look at a flimsy rubber boat on the stormy Mediterranean Sea full of refugees and you instantly turn away from it like from a beggar on the streets of Timbuktu. He often had such thoughts. Usually, he braked himself—for it can drive you crazy. He believed this: just being conscious, barely aware that you're a human being, is not thinking. Walking over the cobblestones of the Quartier Latin, he tried to think real thoughts. In the reading room at the library, he tried to try to think for real. Yet his new reality retreated from him and any new answers he came up with provoked new questions like the reasons for Martha's mother's desertion and his father's labyrinthine underground. And each day and each hour and each minute, invention, thank Zeus, intervened in his life. He saw in his written pages the positive effects of invention in the sexual realm that was reflected back into his literary life. One stimulated the other: sex-invention-sex-invention. Like Martha's imaginary promiscuity had a multiplier effect on his sexual life that charged his literary life. Point and counterpoint, sex and imagination. He was losing his fucking mind, he thought, until he admitted the exciting truth that he enjoyed her imaginary profligacy exactly like her mother's, about which his father's psychologist friend would have said that John desired it; that her imaginary promiscuity was, on the one hand, another pillar of his own sexual desire and a source of his literary creativity, on the other.

3.

Café Coupole

As the months passed, day by day, hour by hour, their two lives seemed to literally merge and become one. While Martha studied French literature, John wrote a set of decent short stories, new works set in former places of his previous lives in Italy and Germany. Yet, though their idealistic love and their perfect togetherness transformed them, something was still missing in the setting of their consummate love, making John realize how much the setting for love counts. Though in their togetherness they were carefree, their daily lives continued to reflect too much for his taste of the European bourgeois spirit, its ideological past and its vassalage to the United States, combined with its suppressed but perceptible conviction of being the rightful heirs of Europe's former planetary domination. But then, he recognized, they too were children of their age. So, as a consequence of his feelings of guilt of being where he shouldn't be and not writing what he should write and Martha's permanent security fixations and in order to get a fresh perspective of Europe, to take a break, to experience an interim existence, they searched out other airs, other winds, other lands of other colors far beyond the great ocean. To make time richer and more productive, and to flee the arrogant and greedy western world, they opted for what John grandly termed 'geographical transpositioning' to Latin America: they spent six months in Mexico in the city of Guanajuato where he wrote stories set in San Marino and Martha studied Spanish. To Mexico, they traveled a revealing route of Paris-Amsterdam-Detroit-Mexico City. John perceived the approach from the north to the geographic triangle of Mexico as a peculiar physical-metaphysical happening. After overflying the Rio Grande, the earthen mass below surged upwards toward them hovering motionless in the light air. The whole world was in movement. Change was underway. Like huge oceanic waves, five, six, seven, ten mountain ridges, swelling before narrowing toward the south, rolled toward them from western skies; they were a lonely image of abandonment among the elements; the black mountains clamped them in their grasp; the past skipped away across spinning gossamer clouds; in contrast to everyday life on earth the planet moved while the plane hung over the earth like a giant prehistoric bird; invisible worlds zoomed around them; white vapor trails crisscrossed the blue southern skies; Mexico narrowed and the sky retreated heavenwards; transient white clouds cast menacing dark shadows on the undulating green and brown fields below spaced by narrow rivers winding toward the Gulf; billowing chains of darkness approaching from the west collided with the east and together rolled southwards, and then, again climbing toward the sky, combined to form the great plateau that is Mesoamerica, the heart of Mexico. Bluish-black mountains filled the triangular plateau to form a gigantic pyramid surrounded by the seas. It was the top of the world, the center, where time stands still and, in the vacuum, you feel a sensation of enormous power.

John had expected to see a comfortable old town. Mexico City was nothing of the sort. Though familiar, Mexico City was another world. It had its own rhythm—the traffic, the noises, the masses on the streets, the way people moved, the park of the

Alamos, the arcades, the sudden vistas, the Italian style palazzos. Still, though it was the Old World in the New, the city had something universal about it, distinct from Detroit the city of the automobile.

For despite their poverty, Mexicans are the first to say: "Not by bread alone." Earthly bread is necessary but not enough for a man: universality seems to reside in the Mexican people. Immediately south of the Rio Grande everything had changed. The Mexican has been labeled a historical chameleon who changes his skin according to circumstances. Nobel writer, Octavio Paz, stressed that the Mexican is more Indio than Spanish which must have something to do with his strangeness and adaptability and his universality—perhaps also because of his venerable thirty-thousand years of age. Paz was obsessed with the differences between Mexicans and their North American neighbors: "Mexicans lie out of fantasy, desperation, or to conquer the squalor of their lives; North Americans don't lie about the true truth that is always unpleasant, but about social truth. "North Americans want to understand; we, to contemplate. Americans are credulous; we are believers. We, as their forefathers did, believe that sin and death constitute the foundation of human nature."

Since Martha and John felt at home, they concluded that the Mexican must be very European. However, Mexican nature makes one wonder if it's positive to be so universal that you can accept anything philosophically. For universality has not brought great fortune to Mexico. It seems that only ancient peoples like Sardinians are capable of being simply men. That is, real men, in whose shadows the ambitious of the world live. Real men without beguiling ambitions and who don't strive for perfection. John noted in an essay that men who just lead good lives are universal without realizing it; it makes them free, but at the same time vulnerable to the claws of the hawks.

After a week, however, the initial resemblances with Europe began fading. The light changed; eyes burned; beggars besieged the entrances to marvelous museums; the dirt and grime from the earthquake zone sullied the white walls of Palacio de Bellas Artes; the revolutionary murals of Siquieros, Rivera and Orozco didn't make the public water drinkable; the daintiness of Sanborn's famous eatery seemed precarious and anachronistic; the spring temperatures didn't freshen their smog-filled throats; the blasé rich in Zona Rosa restaurants ignored the withered women on the streets rationing tortillas to tiny children; the white-capped volcanoes, gigantic they knew only from hearsay because they were invisible. Perhaps they were mere legend.

The rich Paris that Martha and John knew seemed eons away.

Most of all John wanted to know who these Mexicans were who made this country another world from the rest of North America—a different world from the USA which it borders. In his *El Laberinto de la Soledad*, Octavio Paz explains that just as behind the Greek stood the Egyptians and behind the Romans stood the Etruscans and behind the Russians, the Varangians and Mongols, behind the Aztecs and the Spanish conquerors who formed today's Mexicans stood millennia of peoples in a long and crazy past. Eventually, they came to see Mexico as a tragic country—maybe because of those ancient origins. And also because of its solitude on its highlands and in its jungles. Paradoxically, though rich in an ancient culture and, as you see on the eighty-kilometer long Avenida Insurgentes, at the vanguard of modernity, Mexico remains a political caveman: a modern dictatorship based on corruption and retention of power and Yankee influence and manipulations. But somehow modern Mexico is not decadent as was the powerful Aztec society at the time of the Spanish arrival. John and Martha saw in Aztec society characteristics of the role of the will to power and dominion, the arrogance and disdain for others. They saw modern Mexico as a viable society, again on its way up: while its northern neighbor has passed its zenith, Mexico can still rise again.

Mexican solitude is basic for thinking about Mexico and Mexicans, John wrote in another essay: "As in an instantaneous snapshot, I see the echo of myself in Mexico City. I have just come out of my hotel and cross the Reforma near the Angel Monument. I wander into the Zona Rosa. I walk through the entertainment district, asking myself why it is in life that one cannot withdraw painlessly and enter a new life. And if you succeed, have you really left everything behind? Or does something always remain? Sometimes, in moments of solitude, there seems to be no escape and life itself appears to be a cul de sac.

"There is a lot of loneliness in everyone's life. Loneliness and also melancholy, which is not exactly the same thing. Loneliness and solitude are not the same thing either, but they are closely related and go hand in hand, perhaps one inside the other. Loneliness can also be a desire for solitude. Loneliness is familiar. It is a feeling; an emotion too. It is the sense of alienation you may feel in a crowd, at a party, in a classroom, when you feel distant from what is happening around you. Lonesomeness is intensive loneliness, but also the awareness of your state and wishing it were not so. Solitude is when you really are alone, though it is not necessarily disagreeable. You can choose solitude without feeling lonely. Solitude by choice is positive, a rock and a sign of strength. Loneliness is usually an undesired sense of dependency to be overcome and causes despondency but also the flightiness of creativity."

In the essay about the meaning of Mexico, John wrote of their friend Juan Francisco who paints lonely figures. Human, but lonely or abandoned. John found the same in the art of a Russian painter friend in the lonely images of prancing centaurs depicted on a cabinet door in his kitchen. They are sad. So sad, so alone. Like the little stone figures in his etchings, alone and abandoned. Once united with their creator in the Eden of the artist's fantasy, now separated, lonely and longing for reunion, perhaps like men vis-a-vis God.

Like Dürer's winged genius sitting in a reflective pose surrounded by his tools—a compass, scales, an hourglass and a magic square of numbers. The desperate artist languishes under the observation of a dog, a cherub and a bat holding the inscription *"Melencolia I."* John sensed that the meaning of Dürer's work concerned the relationship between melancholy (and loneliness and solitude) and creativity. His conclusion was that melancholy—and also loneliness and a striving for rejoining—were essential to creativity. What greater melancholy and solitude than that in the couple in Picasso's *"The Frugal Meal"*—the haggard man with an arm draped around the bony shoulders of his woman companion, each looking in opposite directions, each alone in their common solitude. Hopeless, yet assailed by nostalgia—perhaps Picasso's loneliness and nostalgia for another existence. A nostalgia that leads the artist back to his natural loneliness—for he knows where creativity resides. From Goya's deafness, from Dürer's meditation, from Picasso's nostalgia emerges the author's formula: solitude leads to loneliness and melancholy, which becomes desperation, whence inspiration, originality and creativity. But also the converse is suggested: sociability leads the artist to the search for enjoyment and exhilaration, whence to fashion, imitation and non-creativity.

He wrote how on a dusty, windblown hill in Guanajuato he came to consider the cactus the symbol of solitude, and thus the symbol of Mexico. From a distance a row of cacti looks back at you uncompromisingly, smugly and yet so alone in the world. But close at hand, the cacti are quite different; what from the road might seem to be a mass of green thickets, from up close is independent life itself—throbbing, thriving, and surviving, both receiving the sun of life and giving life—but each cactus stands alone, as if were by choice. They don't need anything or anyone. It is believed that some forms of cactus under certain controlled conditions could survive on the moon. Alone. In lunar solitude. It has to do with oxygen. They don't need much of it. The magueys. The agave. The noble plant. They provide needles for sewing, fiber for paper, clothing, baskets, medicine, roof thatching, fertilizer, fructose, and above all pulque, mezcal and tequila. You could construct a new human existence with the cactus. The wild plants, in their self-sufficient solitude, seem more real than human life. The cactus could be a way of life. Alone on a desolate cactus plain. Alone with a homeless soul like Juan Francisco who hangs onto Claudia's tits for salvation—the crying, searching, falling, emerging, swearing soul, in search of self-sufficient solitude.

After six months of life at "the top of the world", as John referred to Mexico, he perceived what seemed the physical sensation of being invaded by an alien being; he believed it was the two thousand meters altitude, the invisible volcanoes and the omnipotent pyramids. He warned Martha that they had to get out while they were still capable of separation from this land. Martha agreed that Mexico was truly magical and highly contagious; it had that same effect on her, on him, on everyone. In their search for a contrast, they agreed on the geographical extreme in Latin America: Argentina.

Magnificent "European" Buenos Aires was truly another matter. At first, the city with its French architecture and Italian-Argentine people seemed to them to resemble more the Europe they had left than the Latin America of Mexico, much more than it does in reality. The people of sprawling Buenos Aires consider it a city of the northern hemisphere erroneously plopped down in the south by the playful gods: Buenos Aires retains Europe in its DNA: Europe's cruelty and warlike nature. Not, however, that it is a true copy of Europe. Buenos Aires is a negative of Europe; it is the dream of Europe of the nostalgic European immigrant; Argentina is a credence, a faith, a religion and a dogma. The city is a fantasy, phantasmagoric, and yet inimitable in its variety. Expressions that at first captured John's imagination such as "the Argentinean is one who speaks Italianspanish and wants to be an Englishman" came to seem only journalistic coinage because it omits the genealogical fact that Argentinean blood also contains that of its masses of immigrants also from Bolivia and Paraguay and Peru and Uruguay, with visible traces too of the Guaraní aborigines. Even Jorge Borges, whose first language was English and who lived many years in Europe and died there too, was Argentinean to the core. Though Argentina is not an ethnic "melting pot", nor is it united behind some great ideal—besides Argentinaism—the multitude of peoples here somehow quickly became Argentineans. I, the author, have never been anywhere in the world where people make so little effort—none whatsoever—to speak to foreigners in another language but Argentinean Spanish, at the most bragging that they can *also* speak *Castellano*—Castezhano—before immediately returning to their *vos* and pronunciation of double l and y as zh. Thousands of buses race at breakneck speeds through the huge city and the people of Buenos Aires know all of their routes and, like Moscovites, everyone seems to know the whole enormous city and are incessantly in movement from one part of it to another. Incredible. For people of a much smaller central Paris where John and Martha lived, the northern parts of the city remain mysterious jungles.

Argentineans are too busy being Argentineans to stoop to playing false roles for longer than a minute at a time. *La Argentina*: it is far from stereotypes of tango and soccer and gauchos. *El Argentino*: he is so egocentric that other Latin Americans consider him snobbish, forever concerned with his appearance and manners, his beautiful and totally un-masculine women, obesity non-existent, enthusiastic consumers of every form of creature comforts, especially clothes, food and aesthetics; it is no coincidence that cosmetic surgery has reached its apogee in Buenos Aires.

In days and weeks and months of walking the people-packed canyon-like city streets and peering into lonely courtyards and staring up at French-style apartment buildings with their wrought-iron balconies and gaping at soaring super modern architecture great *avenidas,* John became conscious of his attachment to Old Europe just as are many Argentineans. The fin-de-siécle cafés, some of which are still known by the name Argentineans gave them all, *confiteria*, made him realize that we all have in us the link with what once was and is no more—except in our fantasy world. Sitting in a *confiteria* served by actors-waiters dressed in severe black is theater and you too become a participant in the search for times past. And it is a good and rewarding sensation, but hard to explain in words: the ancient cities of Paris and Rome are the past, but life in Buenos Aires is very much the present; but the physical city is both past and present and its people live with one foot in the past and one in the future. They are forever uncertain as to whether they want to let their past go and leap into the abyss of the unknown.

A fortuitous meeting in a confiteria facing the famous eighteen-story Dantesque Palacio Barolo with a Buenos Aires lawyer overjoyed to meet a young European changed the complexion of John's Argentinean adventure. And adventure it was. Though already ancient history for the criminal lawyer, Gustavo, the story of the almost mythological Operation Odessa of German Nazi bigwigs smuggled out of Europe and submarined to the Atlantic shores of Argentina after World War Two had the stuff of a Forsyth political thriller. Gustavo told the story off-handedly—everybody in Buenos Aires knew it, he said. People knew that CIA, Vatican and the Argentine Catholic Church, the Franco government in Spain, the International Red Cross and Swiss banks collaborated in the Odessa Operation to save top Nazi war criminals from prosecution in Europe—the CIA to use them; the escaping Nazis to make a comeback under the shadow of the Andes mountain chain.

"Many of them settled in the resort town of Bariloche, near the Andes, in the heart of Argentina's wine country—over one thousand kilometers from Buenos Aires. Come along with me, I'll show you the office that arranges things in Argentina."

They crossed the street and entered the eclectic Palacio Barolo that John had been admiring. "See those offices up there on the first floor. It's SIDE, Argentinean Intelligence. It's still full of Nazis. The CIA helped more than five thousand Nazis leave Europe and relocate here…from five to forty thousand reached South and Central America."

John knew the history: big Nazi and Fascist names got to Argentina. Set up transit camps. Issued phony passports under new names for mass murderers. Adolf Eichmann, Klaus Barbie—the butcher of Lyons—Erich Priebke—the murders in the caves of Rome—and the madman doctor, Josef 'Angel of Death' Mengele. From Bariloche and from Palacio Barolo in Buenos Aires they continued their life work, helping governments in Chile and Argentina to organize death squads. It was like back home in Nazi Europe. Rumors circulated: Hitler's chief aide, Martin Bormann, and SS boss Heinrich Himmler survived the Berlin debacle in 1945. Rumors circulated: even Hitler was saved and lived happily ever after in Bariloche in a villa facing a lake. Behind the scenes, Operation Odessa in 1946: 'to save Nazi leadership.' And Argentinean investigative journalist, Abel Basti, writes of "waves" of German U-boots arriving with top Nazi brass. ODESSA: the acronym for the German, *Organization der ehemahligen SS-Angehörigen*, Organization of Former SS Members, so secret that many investigators claimed it existed only in the minds of journalists. Odessa's worst crimes were carried out in Argentina, Chile and Uruguay.

But Gustavo updated the story: the sons and grandsons of those escaped Nazis and Fascists from Bariloche are bidding to buy this magnificent Palacio Barolo—with recycled Fourth Reich money—for conversion to a luxury hotel. The building, the pride of Buenos Aires, was built by an Italian architect according to a plan based on the *Divina Commedia*, eighteen floors, from Paradise to Purgatory to Hell. Those modern Nazis, the direct descendants, worked with CIA and the Argentine Church in Operation Condor, the 'dirty war', *la guerra sucia*, to eradicate Communists and left-wingers—thirty thousand *desaparecidos* in Argentina—their bodies dumped to the sharks in the Atlantic Ocean while those un-denazified Nazis opposed anything that smacked of Marxism, from Mexico to the Terra del Fuego. Like recently in Bolivia: the *golpe* that ousted left-wing President Evo Morales and installed a right-wing government was conducted by Jeanine Añez, the granddaughter of a leader of the Croatian *Ustasha*—an organization of third generation fascists. Another American protégée, she was quickly overturned by Bolivian Indios and went to jail where she today stands to get a fifteen year sentence.

They had been in Buenos Aires several months when Martha became pregnant. And that was that for their intercontinental transpositioning: her pregnancy and the sudden death of Aunt Thérèse brought them back to Rue Saint-Dominique sooner than they had expected.

"Hey, Sutton, how about dinner out tonight," Martha suggested one evening not long after their return home in Rue Saint-Dominique. "You've done a day's work and I've done those pelvic labor and delivery exercises for hours so we're as free as Adam and Eve."

"Great! So where would my princess-mother like to go?"

"Let's go somewhere new in a district we've never been in before."

"I read about a new place close to the Bataclan music hall—wherever that is. What about there?"

"Oh, I don't know. On second thought, why don't we play tourists and go to one of those big places in Montparnasse. You know, like the Coupole…all the writers used to go there. You're a writer so we'll enter in triumph, like Scott Fitzgerald and what's her name, you know. I'll wear a big floppy hat. Yes, yes, Sutton, that's just the place."

"Her name was Zelda. A little nutty, that woman. Died in an asylum. Maybe she struck the match that burned it down. Ok, the Coupole. I'll be the writer and you my pregnant mistress. The Bataclan will be there for another time. Still, I like the name Bataclan and read that your near relative the architect Charles Duval built it back in 1865 in the period of *Chinoiserie*—you know Chinese art, architecture, music. C0hinese kind of place, named for the Jacques Offenbach operetta and Ba-ta-clan. So we've got to see it."

"Ok, someday! For now it's the Coupole!"

As they readied to leave, John's phone vibrated. Gustavo! Buenos Aires not yet finished. Gustavo spoke Porteño. John didn't understand. Gustavo refused to speak Castellano. No communication possible. So is it in life, John thought, people appear, hang briefly in our orbit, and then shoot off into another, Gustavo perhaps into the cosmos toward the Southern Cross hanging over the southern hemisphere. Good flight to him!

That night, Martha displayed all her beauty in a flaming red and yellow scarf and a wide-brimmed Mexican hat that emphasized her stupendous face rather than hide it as that kind of hat did many. As always she held his arm as tight as she had throughout Latin America. Though he was wearing a sweater and heavy jacket, some die-hards occupied sidewalk tables near the entrance—to see VIPs on the way in and to be seen by all. Martha had the usual Martha effect: heads turned to view this magnificent damsel, which Martha never appeared to notice—though he already suspected that she cultivated her effect. John thought it was her need for approval and admiration as her wayward mother must need some one place in the exotic world in which she lived. But still, Martha rejected his offers to find her.

No sooner than they were seated at a wall table she approved of, a man at the next table cleared his throat and touched John's arm: "*Je vous en prie, pardonnez-moi pour le dérangement,* he began before switching to English, "but as your neighbor in Rue Saint-Dominique I have long wanted to meet you, the beautiful English couple that people in our building are so curious about. I see the lady often," he said looking toward Martha, "but you are invisible."

"That's because he's always at his desk while I'm out, doing things," Martha said.

"Oh, and what do you do at your desk that makes you magically invisible? Write reports? Predict the swings of the stock market? Run political polls?"

Despite the soupçon of irony or mockery in his tone, his excellent though accented English attracted John's attention. Curious about his neighbor, he half turned his chair to face him and the others at his table. The Coupole was buzzing. Waiters rushed back and forth through the swinging doors to the kitchens. Laughter sounded from every side. The eyes of beautiful women reflected the sparkle of the great chandeliers.

"He writes unstoppably," Martha added. "This man Sutton is a book machine. Through his magical machine he can see the future."

"Not magic. Hard work…sometimes boring work. But since I can't do anything else, I write things," John said, while examining the expressionless faces of the other four persons at their neighbor's table who hadn't spoken a word. Never before that moment had he perceived so strongly the reality that he was not what he seemed, the writer Martha too thought he was. In his high schools they'd praised his talent; they all assumed he was to be a writer. An artist. He knew differently. He knew hard work awaited him. Even as a teenager. He had no comrades. He had his father as teacher number one and hard work and Underground where he wrote only dark stories that he showed to no one.

"I see! By the way, permit me to introduce myself: my name is Amrani, Ivaan Amrani—Ivaan with two a's. And these are my friends, Parisians all," he said of the three men and a lone woman, all much younger than himself and none of whom looked particularly Parisian. Ivaan's most striking feature was his extremely pale face; nevertheless, John thought he could be Arab or Brazilian, Israeli or Palestinian, the man of the future. Enigma was his second name. Moreover, he'd never seen him in their building either. For no particular reason he had a funny feeling about him—that he would become an important figure in their future.

"And what are your books about, if I may be so bold to ask? Paris, the center of Europe? Politics? War and peace? Immigration that so stirs emotions in Europe? The rights of man? The law that possession means ownership forever and ever, amen?"

Ivaan's voice, his accent, his very tone were irritating, his words sardonic. In both word and manner he was invasive.

"In a way, yes. That is, insofar as fiction deals with real life and thus politics. Why, are you interested in literature?"

"Frankly no, Mr. Sutton, but I do try to follow the events of our times, and of our adopted country, *la douce France*."

"Which events, for example?" John asked, giving him a taste of his own medicine.

"Oh, like immigration policies, like equality on the job market, as I said earlier. Like racism. Like the wars France fights. Like police brutality. The rioting you may have witnessed on TV expresses the frustration caused by the beautiful ideal of the multicultural model and the brutal reality of the ghettoes. The Islamic minorities and the poor Arabs in the ghettoes of the *banlieue* who demand that France make good the promises inherent in the model and cure ills like discrimination, unemployment and ghettoization. That's why the riots. These are all realities to write about. And one day mere riots will not be enough. Far from enough. This is not going to end with riots in the suburbs. There are other ways to protest. Other options. Those who riot can also kill."

Martha's hand tightened on his arm, squeezing in such a way as to melt into him. Or was it a warning squeeze, cautioning him that the conversation weighed too heavy? For now, after repeated experiences with the variety of her arm squeezes, he perceived the differences. This new intensity was a red flag. He turned his chair back toward her. A harassed and hassled waiter stood by. Ivaan was speaking again with his own in Arabic. Ivaan bothered him, but he didn't understand what exactly it was that disturbed him. His English was not that of an Arab immigrant, his accent was unidentifiable and his tone that of the cynical Parisian intellectual.

"Shall I order the oysters?" Martha asked to call him back to her. Then looking at John but addressing herself pointedly to Ivaan and company, she said: "On second thought maybe we should've gone to the Bataclan to hear that Italian group. A little music would be better for baby than oysters."

"Bataclan?" Ivaan echoed, his voice rising a barely perceptible note. "Mr. Sutton, I noticed that your wife is expecting and I extend my congratulations to you both but if I were you I would never take my wife and a mother-to-be to places like the Bataclan which I do know quite well. Though oysters are good for the soul, in our world today home is the safest place for parenthood. For as you the writer must know, policemen are capable of anything."

As Ivaan chatted them up in an insinuating manner, ambiguous and at times menacing; as the silence of his commensals materialized as part of his ever craftier warnings; as Martha became more and more irritated at his suggestive interruptions; as the waiters rushed to and fro in their individual frenzies their faces reflecting the fire of the devilish cooks behind the swinging service doors; as the shouts to and from the kitchens joined in the incomprehensible chorus of the demons inside and the fallen angels outside; as the drunken buzz from table to table recounting unholy seashore adventures intensified and magnified and uncivilized laughter rose toward the crystal chandeliers; while all of that was going on, abruptly, from one second to the next, total darkness fell over the Coupole, the steady hum of things electric in the world ceased. Eardrums popped. Then the first shouts: FIRE! FIRE! One person up front yelled over and over the word, FIRE. In the darkness of the sudden power failure the civilized savages at Coupole tables leapt to their feet and for a split second the world plunged into a deafening funereal silence in a sudden candle-lit penumbra, just before the eruption of terrorized screams and warlike sounds of a great stampede toward the exits. In that precise moment, as time itself held its breath, a tremendous explosion on the exterior rocked the multicolored tiled floor of the Coupole: walls quaked, the green interior columns quivered, sculptures cracked and crashed, unfettered paintings and fragments from the cupola precipitated into the pell-mell confusion to be immediately trampled to smithereens by panic-stricken masses smothering the artistic essence of the famed café-restaurant itself. Terror hung in the air. Death was palpable. Masses of people rushed out the front doors. Heaps of crushed and shattered glass lay everywhere, and, as they later learned, also the bodies of the dead and injured. While in the front part of the restaurant, pools of blood accumulated and rippled directionless, Ivaan and his friends remained seated like spectators of the breakdown of a civilization that was not theirs. Ivaan looked up at John and with a sign of kindness in his black eyes pointed toward the rear; Martha and John left by an exit in the back. Quite suddenly what they were talking about had materialized. Terrorism had struck Paris. The Coupole and the people there that night and the people who frequent it will never be the same. Nor will Martha or John forget. That night a strange thing occurred to John. He became horribly conscious of something unchangeably wrong in the world of things. He became aware of the enduring effect on people who only by chance escape death from a completely unthinking, indiscriminate bomb. That bomb, constructed, placed and likely exploded by hand—like also countless thousands of others blindly-blithely dropped from the stratosphere—that bomb is as indifferent as God to the devastation. It kills the young and the old, the good and the evil, the black and the white indistinctly. He was only twenty-five years old that evening when that stark feeling of death entered into him and where it was to remain. One thing he learned well: you can't turn your back on death. And he was sad that even their enchanted baby sown in Martha's womb in an apartment in the barrio of La Recoleta in Buenos Aires would have reality to face in life; she had no choice in the matter.

***

John Sutton reminisced that when at the university in Munich they'd told him he had talent and he'd begun sketching stories about his life in places like the little republic of San Marino for some of which Munich newspapers paid him, he'd come to wonder if his life was to be tragedy, comedy or farce—as though he'd understood then the differences. However, since he studied Marx who wrote that history repeats itself, first as tragedy, second as farce, and he'd learned to reject the route of comedy, he stopped thinking in terms of precise classifications. Now today he faced new responsibilities and new realities: Martha and Samantha. He told himself that life itself is part of all—joy and sorrow and hate and also reward and penitence and love. Still, he liked to think that his own life should be observed like good wine—a composite of various elements. In your wine glass—as in your mirror—you glimpse your diverse selves only briefly before they fade and merge into one before you can grasp one of them individually to hold onto: bizarre, rebellious and irreverent, quick to repent, and just as quick to sin again. You see the beautiful and the ugly. You see the joy and the pain of living and of the difficulty of love. And now, after long observation, he'd come to the comforting conclusion that he was not a so-called joyous person. Here and there he'd seen with different eyes the sad persons and believed he'd learned one important truth: sad persons are the real persons. It seemed to him that the person who has more joy than sorrow cannot be true and real. Living a real life presupposes great sufferance. The person without a great flaw, the person who hasn't suffered great pain, who hasn't experienced a crucial, life-changing hurt or aberration and emerged cognizant of the personal significance of pain and suffering, a person perhaps for that reason devoid of a genuine sense of pity, a person who doesn't bear in himself the human stain of a great flaw and error haven't felt life to the full and can have no comprehension of the deeper meanings of life. 'I simply don't know how to deal with people without that flaw,' he thought. 'If you take a hard look around you and if you talk straight from the depths of your heart, how can you always be positive about what you see? On every occasion? What happens in you when you open up yourself and say what you really think, deep down? You will first start, surprised at the realization of the gulf of difference between positive and negative-thinkers. As Ivaan had suggested, there are many unpleasant subjects to be discussed and many truths to be spoken, which positive-thinkers prefer to leave unspoken. Like bombing civilians from unmanned drones: Like boys from Paris dying on the roads of Iraq or Syria. Oh, please, you will hear, no dark talk! Dark talk, John thought, should be more contagious; after youthful hints of riotous disorder, it unfortunately easily blends in with and merges into the flocks like those of the barn swallows on their systemic migration southwards in the spring. People want to hear "nice" things. Comforting things. Grand and uplifting things. The signs of wonders yet to happen in a rosy future. People turn away from criticisms and admonitions and warnings of the negative significance lurking in true things. No dark vales of gloom with their rotten and moldy earth. No, don't upset nice people with straight talk like "It's time to ban hand weapons and capital punishment" or "Why don't they give us a national health service and fair unemployment compensation." Don't raise your voice and yell, "*Government, do something for the people!*" Above all, please don't speak to us of ideology because if you do you must mean something like Socialism. In the unthinking minds of right-thinkers, doubts are blasphemy. But isn't it true that a thinking person *must* criticize? For after all diffidence is a control over power.' And so it is that in a right-think pleasure society, a truly thinking person—a negative-thinker—might come to live a secret life. But living in secret as John did in Underground is unhealthy, dangerous and corrupting. Jean Baudrillard notes in an essay "The Transparency of Evil" that "each transparency raises the question of its contrary, the secret. Still, some things," he says, "will simply never be visible. They will remain in the secret world and are shared in secret according to a kind of exchange different from that of the visible world. But since today everything happens in the visible world, the virtual world, what happens to those things that were once secret? Step by step, delving into the secret within the secret, they become occult, clandestine, evil. That which once was just secret becomes the evil that must be abolished too. The problem is one cannot destroy them because to a certain extent the secret, like myths, is indestructible. Therefore it becomes diabolic and infects the same instruments designed to eliminate it." You too want to be in the stream of life, a participant, and you feel guilty if you're not. You tremble because you see that your life is not rosy and that war is not peace, but you cannot speak about it except in secret. And so and so the thinking person is destined to sadness. And you will come to know that this is real life.

4.

Secret Service in Gros Caillou

The next morning newspaper headlines confirmed their conclusions that they'd been spectators and potential victims of a terrorist attack at the Coupole: FRANCE UNDER TERRORIST FIRE and ISLAMIC TERRORISTS ATTACK PARIS, and blurry photographs of bodies on the floor of the Coupole. It turned out that the main target of the bombing was not the Coupole at all; terrorists aimed at an office building on Boulevard Montparnasse adjoining the world-famous Café Coupole, which witnesses said everyone in the district knew that the office building contained the headquarters of the anti-terrorism section of the DGSE, the *Direction Générale de la Sècurité Interieure*, in effect the French MI5 or FBI. The ruins of the building were still smoldering. The destruction in the adjacent Café Coupole was caused by a bomb's blast wind—collateral damage—and, one reporter noted, a linked secondary explosive. At press time, the death count in the Coupole was fifteen, the injured twenty-eight.

The next morning, Martha and baby in her womb were sleeping soundly. John took a walk along their street from the Esplanade and Aunt Thérèse's former home to the Eiffel Tower speculating about the diverse destinies of the many people affected by the bombing: the chance that had placed them in the back part of the restaurant and the precariousness of life itself always hanging by the thread of chance. For the first time in his life, he was infused with something that he defined as an unidentifiable dread of the unknown. As he neared the avenue where they took the buses for the city center, he had the feeling he'd had several times that morning, that someone was following him. He told himself that the sensation was itself false, but it hung on, like an unjustified guilt complex for an uncommitted act. Nonetheless, he began imitating the secret agent being tailed by an enemy security service. He stopped in darkened doorways or he searched for reflections of suspicious looking persons in plate glass store fronts. When he finally stepped into Le Moulin de la Vierge bakery and asked for six of the advertised 'best croissants in Paris' he felt banally cynical. He would tell Martha that he'd taken a brisk morning walk like always.

When the doorbell rang that afternoon, Martha had just left for her labor-delivery exercises at Necker Hospital which she enjoyed chiefly to hear the stories of how other women faced their pregnancies; John had finished a section of a story about a woman who had such severe inferiority complexes that she felt she was guilty for her failing marriage even though her husband lived a second life in an unbroken series of extramarital relationships—the woman believed it was her fault because he found in others what she believed she lacked. It was shortly after three o'clock, a time when few people stirred in his neighborhood and no one ever came to their house anyway. Through the peephole he saw the distorted faces of two men in dark jackets, one of whom held a briefcase against his chest in a protective manner as if fearing that a terrorist with pistol in hand might open the door and fire.

"Monsieur John Sutton"? the one with the briefcase said, standing in the doorway and charmingly accenting the last syllable of Sutton. He mangled a few words in English before John said he spoke French, on which they stuck out their hands in a friendly way and identified themselves as employees of the government of France. They appeared to be in their early thirties, coarse looking, as though hardened by their work and the toil of tramping around the city on secret missions. John nodded and indicating the couch, and offered a coffee.

"*Pas besoin*," Briefcase said, sitting back comfortably.

"So what can I do for you?"

"We understand that you're a writer."

"That's right."

"So what do you write?" the silent one asked. "Politics? War and peace? Immigration that so stirs emotions in Europe? Human rights? Such stuff?"

"Just eighteen hours ago someone else asked me that same question."

"You mean at the Coupole? Was it that Arab you spoke with so intensively?"

"Well, so I was right this morning when I went out to buy croissants, someone *has* been spying on me. Like a story I once wrote of a Pole who was so disturbed that he was being spied on that he finally ended up on the psychiatrist's couch where after long analysis he was pronounced well—it turned out it was only the secret police."

"Croissants for your beautiful pregnant wife, and yes, I confess, you were followed," the one with the briefcase said.

"Me? Why?"

"By the way," asked Briefcase, "are you English or not?"

"Sort of. It's complicated."

"Sort of? What does that mean? Your passport says you're Dutch. And from your looks you could be anything—Lebanese, Russian, Iranian. We wonder who you are."

"So?

"And then there's that bunch of probable terrorists you chatted with so friendly-like at your life-saving rear table in the Coupole, like you knew something in advance. Why in the back? Why not up front where you could show off your stunning wife?"

"My wife? Wait a minute! She's not an object and your intimation is offensive. And my father was an Englishmen who took Dutch citizenship so that I was born Dutch—although I feel English."

"That is complicated," said the other.

"I apologize," said Briefcase. "I sincerely didn't mean to be offensive regarding your lovely wife. Look, we're interested in you only in so far as you seemed to be in the confidence of Monsieur Ivan Amrani. We know him quite well, but have to be careful since he has links to other agencies in our government. More importantly, we believe he's a front figure for more sinister people. And moreover, we had microphones at his table, so your voice is recorded too."

"Ugh, I hope I didn't say anything incriminating!" John said, keeping in mind Ivaan's words that policemen were capable of anything.

"Besides, we don't trust Egyptians," the silent one said. "An ambiguous people to say the least."

"So what do you want from me? It seems you've recorded all I know about this."

"We'd like for you to pursue your acquaintance with Ivan—and brief us from time to time."

"Listen, I'm a writer, not a snitch—even if I knew anything about Ivaan. By the way, he said he writes it with two a's. But no, this is not for me. Terrorism is your job; not mine. I don't even know what kind of terrorist they are—or who they are. They attacked you and your agency, unfortunately killing a mass of innocent people. Whose is the fault? Who is guilty? You gentlemen ask what I write, as if I knew answers. Anyway I write love stories but I am also anti-imperialist."

"We know—and you're also a Communist."

"It's disconcerting how much you know about me."

"We have plenty of them in France already. One more does no harm."

"Still, you're at the wrong door this time."

"Monsieur Sutton, we might see you again," Briefcase said, punching the silent one's shoulder and standing up. "There are other ways to get your cooperation."

"What timing! You guys scare me with your intimations, quasi insults and apologies, feints and withdrawals and new threats while I'm right on the verge of a happiness that you people would take away without a second thought—and then there's the slaughter at the Coupole."

John thought they looked at him from the door in a funny way, partly amused at his claims about happiness, partly regretful that he refused to spy for them. Did they know about that bomb beforehand? Or did they plant it themselves? Was the bomb at the Coupole a false flag operation? Ivaan apparently thought so. As false as the Twin Towers in New York.

5.

Ninth Month

If you didn't notice Martha's swollen belly you would never know she was pregnant with their child, the secrecy of it reinforcing John's idea that Samantha was their secret joy, while Martha sparkled with an exceptional grace—a pregnant grace, John believed, holding within herself age-old secrets and revealing only that their baby was on the way into the external world. The eighth month had passed as perfectly as in a fairy tale of the life of John and the goddess who confirmed that she too felt that her body and mind were ready to deliver their child: Samantha lay inside her, dreaming dreams only she knew and that she would never reveal, but which Martha, in some magic way shared, dream images unwinding inside the corridors of Martha's mind, reflections of which John thought she sometimes displayed purposefully in the colors and shadows in her eyes, as women do just before delivery of a child into the time of the world. Everything was ready for Samantha.

Meanwhile, after the "events" at the Coupole, the world was subjected to days and nights of non-stop media descriptions of the most 'horrendous, inhuman terrorist attack on democratic France'; the French government continued to vaunt its firmness in the face of the cowardly attacks on the foundations of democratic civilization; the European Union, NATO, the World Community of Freedom-loving Peoples and East European democracies including Kosovo rallied around France and stood shoulder to shoulder with

Paris in opposition to 'terroristic savagery'. *'Je suis Coupole'* echoed from the corners of the earth.

One afternoon a few days after the bombing, a few minutes after Martha had left for her exercises, Ivaan paid a call on John, ostensibly to learn how his wife had reacted to the unfortunate "affair" as he referred to the attack at the Coupole. The visit was short. John was curt. After the DGSE agents' visit and their insistence on his "cooperation", he didn't want to know anything more about ambiguous Ivaan Amrani. At the same time, the more lurid the details the media added about the Coupole, the greater his conviction that something was rotten in the Elysée Palace. The affair stank of false flag. Stories circulating about hooded terrorists shooting wildly inside the Coupole following the explosion were pure invention. Nor had he witnessed any attempts at hostage-taking, making the widespread tale of fifteen missing persons including two high-ranking government officials allegedly being held by terrorists somewhere in the Metropolitan area likely as false as stories of Noah's ark and Jonah in the whale. All of this combined to make the enigmatic persona of Ivaan more ambiguous, a riddle to yet unfold, and somehow linked to the visit of the DGSE agents. John could still see the image of Ivaan and his friends sitting calmly at their table, unperturbed by the turmoil of the explosion and the screams and cries and the mass precipitation toward the exits; and how despite the general hysteria inside the Coupole, the calm way Ivaan indicated to Martha and him a safe exit out of the inferno. In sum, it was no great stretch of his imagination to suspect that on that March evening Ivaan knew in advance what was to occur at the Coupole and the anti-terrorism headquarters.

"You seem invisible here," Ivaan said standing just inside the door. "I never see you around."

"Nor do I see you…around." Ivaan shrugged and smiled mysteriously.

"In any case, you do have new materials for the progression of the story you're writing. Such events can be fit in anywhere the creator desires."

"That's for sure. Such events, as you say, will certainly find their place in my story too. To think that I had in mind only the ups and downs of romantic love. My love story! But now the Coupole has turned that story upside down. What at first seemed one thing turns out to be another. Life is truly strange, don't you think?"

"Strange, yes, but it's life, Mr. Sutton. In life, things are always in change and as time goes by they become crazier and crazier. In fiction too things are in constant change but the stories go on and on and the days never end and it seems the same things happen over and over again."

"I hardly ever know what my characters will say or do next. And I say that as the creator of other persons. And though from the moment I create them I try to get to know them, I never feel that I really do…never really know them, I mean. So they talk and talk like us and the writer too listens and tries to understand them. "

"It must be discouraging for the writer to only partially know his own creatures. Like God, I suppose. He must be disheartened when he sees what He has created—if he did. But look, Mr. uh, say, may I call you John?"

"Of course, uh Ivaan."

"It's true that you don't see me here often, and I'll tell you why. But John, real life is not the same as in literature. Similar, yes, but not the same. In real life there are nuances that can't be reduced to words. As we said, things change. In our life today too much knowledge can be dangerous. For that reason I don't want you to know much about me. Nor do I want to know more about you either; not about you as a real person. But I'll tell you this: I know the two men who came to see you and I suspect they asked about me. They also asked me about you. So the less we know about each other, the less we can tell them. For they will be back. Policemen always come back. And also, John, I apologize for my behavior toward you and your wife at the Coupole that night. I was rather, er, uncouth and as you said, invasive. I did that on purpose in order to distance you from me—even though I *was* curious to get to know you the writer. Still, keep in mind that I'm more dangerous to you than you are to me. And John, I really do have a small apartment here in this building, but it's only a fake residence. In real life I still live in the Goutte-d'Or, right on the Rue Doudeauville. You'll have to visit it someday."

"But why do you tell me these things that I shouldn't know? Sudden friendship? Does that happen? And besides, Ivaan, you probably saved our lives at the Coupole. That counts."

"Yes, sometimes strange things happen inexplicably. My people believe that. My people believe in the spirit—your spirit and mine. Two spirits that sometimes meet. Some people see a kindred spirit in another person apropos of nothing. A spirit that is there...or it is not. I saw that spirit in your feelings for your beautiful wife, the mother, your family already of three."

Ivaan touched John's arm lightly, turned and left. It happened in such a way that John shivered with emotion and embarrassment and wondered that such things occurred in real life.

Their encounter in the Café Coupole that evening had seemed to him like the meeting of the savage and the civilized man; yet the eternal savage turned out to be more advanced than the white European man. Without breaking contact with the bodily of life, Ivaan was at once an integral man of the spirit who understood the real things of the earth and the beyond. He understood how to attain some form of true understanding. John thought that he was not mistaken.

Ten days later while Martha went for her last check-up and exercises at the Necker Hospital where she would deliver Samantha, John—on the one hand unable to contain his curiosity about the ill-famed Arab neighborhood and, on the other, anxious to speak more about the spiritual aspects of his people with Ivaan—went to the Goutte-d'Or to look around and hopefully see in his own element the man he'd quickly come to consider his friend. He'd read that the Goutte-d'Or—Drop of Gold—is a 'working class neighborhood of dark-skinned people of immigrant origin, chiefly of the Islamic faith.' As he walked its streets something magnetically mysterious seemed to reign over this eastern part of Montmartre and serpentine through its narrow passages that concealed many dark, non-Western secrets…secrets like those he'd seen in the Grand Socco of Tangier and in the medina in Oran: small African shops, Algerian cafés, Senegalese eateries, mosques, schools, nurseries, the Egyptian-inspired art nouveau Louxor cinema theater and a great open-air market. It was just like Ivaan— he thought—to live in the core of the *quartier* on the Rue Doudeauville cutting through its heart, at civic number 444, just opposite a wing of the Islamic Cultural Center.

There were five doorbells and names at the ornate entrance to the four-story building, most of which were written in Arabic. But there was Ivaan Amrani, second from the top—Ivaan with two a's as he'd specified— written in big golden Latin letters in Gothic script. John presumed he occupied the second floor, the noble floor, with its wrought iron balcony and elaborate stone work around the windows. Ivaan's apartment had to be on the *étage noble* and have the highest ceilings and the most elegant rooms in the building. That was Ivaan. His show!

"John! John!" he heard above him. He looked up straight into the eyes of the king of the Goutte-d'Or. "Stay there. I'll come for you."

Seconds later, the surprisingly light entrance door opened and Ivaan pulled him into a narrow hallway dimly illuminated by art deco lamps and up one flight of stairs with recessed spots spaced waist-high along the walls. His high-ceilinged apartment was truly another world. A world of light. Modern indirect lighting, the brightness mitigated by several art deco lamps which Ivaan referred to as *Liberty* in the Italian way. Though impressed by the grandeur of the stunning apartment—especially as compared to the modesty along the streets below—John was more struck by the savoir-faire of the man. Ivaan was not a big person, a head shorter than John, but by no means an ordinary man: his body seemed to conceal hidden strength and vital life force. His veined hands and his face were white in color, neither pure white nor cream white, more like ivory, tempered by a brown border at the hairline of his surprisingly thick non-Arabic blondish hair.

They sat on a plump sofa placed so that it looked through the floor-to-ceiling windows straight at the back of the Islamic Cultural Center.

While serving glasses of room temperature beer, Ivaan asked casually: "By the way, John, I'm curious as to why you are in France. You have choices like Germany or Netherlands or Italy or even London where your publisher is. But you choose to live here. Why is that?"

"Martha! She's half French. I actually came here on a book business trip but I met her on the way. So I stayed. As a writer I can live most anywhere—as I did in Latin America. Still, I'm not really at home anyplace either. So it doesn't matter."

"That is sad."

"What do you mean? What is sad?"

"That it doesn't matter. That you have no sense of your place...of a home, I mean."

"What about you then? I doubt you feel this is your home."

"No, but there are strong reasons I'm here—and now everything has changed. And John, another thing, I have my sources too who inform me that you and I are comrades."

"Comrades? You mean you too are ..."

"Yes, I'm a Communist. I had to leave my country because of my commitment. When I joined the *new* Egyptian Communist Party shortly after its formation I was twenty years old. And, yes, we were suppressed. First under Sadat, then Mubarak killed us or threw us into his notorious jails. We went underground or abroad but we're still mobilizing Egyptian workers today."

"But Ivaan, in these times who supports a Communist Party in the Islamic world? I don't mean to say that we have wide popularity here either, but we know that Communism has seen much better times everywhere."

"Well, for one, the great Cairo writer, Nagib Mahfuz, liked our ideas and supported the same things we do. The demonstration scenes in his famous Cairo Trilogy, like the one of Tahrir Square that got him the Nobel Prize, were ours."

"Just last year I read the Cairo Trilogy, a wonderful description of Egyptian life…three generations of that one big family."

"That's true. I come from such a social background and his Cairo neighborhoods are where I grew up. But his writings deal above all with politics. Sometimes he avoided love and the ups and downs of love stories but his political beliefs were always there. And John, he espoused not only anti-imperialism and Egyptian nationalism but he was most attracted by socialist ideas. I link Mahfuz to European writers like Heinrich Böll or to the French writer, Michel Houellebecq. There's a graffiti on the walls of the Sèvres-Babylon metro station that caught Houellebecq's attention—as reductive and ambivalent as it is—the slogan that 'God wanted inequalities but not injustices' still rings like a minimal warning to the capitalist class. That's Mahfuz too."

"Right, minimal…and only half right. My father was strong on the inequality part. That was the battle of his life. The problem in the West is that our so-called democracies are showing their dark side, Fascism. Equality and Communism are not a high priority. That's why my father believed that life has to become rebellion against inequalities. His slogan was that 'your very existence can become that act of rebellion, without which the rest is useless.'"

"Your father was a wise man."

"His real field was ethics and morality in which he acquired a certain renown. His great desire was to present his ideas in fictional form, yet he was uncertain how to go about it: he said he was continually bogged down in his own ideas. So at a certain point he wrote by hand a letter to Umberto Eco to discuss the matter. To his surprise, he said, Eco wrote back also by hand…and so began a correspondence between them. Strangely I never found the letters, neither his nor those of Eco. However, before my father's accident, he wrote out salient excerpts from Eco's long letters, which I still have. I think my dad was both surprised and discouraged by Eco's ideas. He….wait a second! I have a copy of the letter in my bag here—I always carry a copy with me. The quotes are from Eco's letters. I'll read you parts. Listen to the way Eco saw the art of writing which is what my father wanted to learn from:

> 'People have not yet learned that every work of art is a game played out at the worktable. Nothing is more harmful to creativity than the passion of inspiration. It's the fable of bad romantics that fascinates bad poets and bad narrators. Art is a serious matter. Manzoni and Flaubert, Balzac and Stendhal wrote at the worktable. That means to construct, like an architect plans a building. Yet we prefer to believe that a novelist invents because he has a genius whispering into his ear.
>
> 'Yet the impulse to narrate is common to us all. That's why so many scientists and philosophers and critics, too, write novels. Not only those that we

remember like Tolkien, Segal, Hoyle, Sartre, Asimov, and Harold Bloom, but many others we've forgotten. Writing is a way of revealing the contradictions of life that one would like to resolve. Writing fiction, like poetry, means simply to display those contradictions but not necessarily to resolve them. In fact, the reader, through his interpretive cooperation, decides what the story means. I wrote my novel, *The Name of the Rose,* simply because I wanted to. First comes the desire, like the desire to make love. Then one sits down at the worktable and begins to play and to construct a possible world. The first year after I got the desire, I didn't write, I designed, I made a plan of the abbey, I sketched out the list of names, I drew the faces of the characters. So I believe one writes a novel because of the desire to construct a world. And to communicate.'

"I too keep in mind also a curious part of this advice on writing techniques that Eco mentioned in one of his letters—although I have seldom used it in my little love stories: making lists. Here's what Eco wrote:

'I've always loved the technique of the list. For many years I made a collection of examples and considered writing a book on the use of lists, from classic literature down to Joyce. Moreover, the list is a typical medieval descriptive strategy. Therefore, I used the list in this book because it is so t is so medieval.

'In the tendency of the list there is something even more important: it is typical of both primitive and overly cultivated epochs. When one doesn't yet know, or no longer knows what is the form of the world, instead of describing a form, one lists its aspects. One proceeds by aggregation instead of by organization. In substance, my character Adso in *The Name of the Rose* does not understand well what is happening or what has happened; therefore, he lists what he sees or what he hears, and what he believes to have seen—and he knows only because he has heard or read other lists.'

"So to get back to my father, even though he insisted that the overturn of the system has to be managed, he said that spontaneous revolt planted the seeds of rebellion, which can mature into the overturn of capitalism. That was his legacy to me."

"Paris and the tradition of rebellion have also been good for me," Ivaan said. "I now realize how cityscapes like Parisian coffee houses palpitate with the violent ideas that have made cities like Moscow and St. Petersburg, Berlin, Munich and Budapest great—and for a brief time that happened in Cairo too."

"Cairo?"

"Cairo, yes, that's what Mahfuz is all about—planting the seeds of revolution. But John, it was here in Paris that existentialist intellectuals like Jean Paul Sartre and Albert Camus wrote the modern biography of European rebellion that was born with the French Revolution. Much of their thought was discussed in a café—the Café de Flore—not far from your home. There, those two writers re-hashed, again and again, the idea of the rebellion born in the western world after 1789 and most certainly they evaluated the year of 1848, the year Michael Bakunin and Friedrich Engels witnessed the second wave of revolution sweep across Europe, from Paris to Berlin and Vienna, wave after wave of rebellion and revolution. And then again in 1968, many of the mobile scenes passed down the boulevard in front of their café—an explosion only vaguely imagined by Sartre and Camus. That was the year that so briefly changed the world and it began right here—until the tide of reaction brought the liberal bourgeoisie back into place in the world."

During a moment of silence they watched the light gray rain falling turning the back of the Islamic Center into shadows. Trees along Rue Doudeauville danced in the sudden bursts of wind. Distant thunder rumbled from the north toward Belgium. "This is the kind of rain in Paris that lasts a week. In Cairo, when the rain finally arrives it is torrential. It whirls through the city with a terrible destructive force devastating the poorer districts. But everyone but the very poor loves it. But each of our Party cells used to organize help squads in those rain-torn areas.

"Well, you've had much more meaningful experiences as a Communist than I have! That's for sure. And when do you do all that reading, Ivaan?"

"Much of every night. I've never been a great sleeper. So I read. And today at forty years I'm even more convinced that my choice of so long ago was right—the only possible one. Anyway, John, when you think about the Middle East, keep in mind that European Communism is a different world from mine. You can't compare Egyptian Communists and the effect we have on our society with that of European parties. Out-of-power in Egypt is a dangerous place to be. Like many of our intellectuals before my time our early Communists didn't look toward France for help; they turned to Communist Russia. Mahfuz—not even a Communist himself and who hated to travel—left Egypt only for Serbia because it was Communist. And he loved the city of Belgrade in a special way."

"What a life you've had!—but still I wonder how you afford all this luxury."

"That's another story and for another time."

"Ivaan, you sound like Sheherazade! Now I'm not the King of Persia betrayed by my wife…and besides I'm the storyteller here."

"I won't even try to tell you tales. This apartment is really an embassy—the Embassy for a possible—maybe conceptual—Arab world. The story here is about how I gathered a lot of money for my Party in Libya where I lived with my Libyan wife. Gaddafi has been generous to us; after he nationalized the oil industry he had money to invest. And not only did he establish a republic in Libya, he realized many communist ideas: like free public housing and services to the poor; he piped water from the south to the north; and he modernized decrepit Libya."

"One of the best things he did was kick the foreign military bases out of his country! That really pissed off the Yankees."

"Right! And much of Europe has never forgiven him for it. Still, the idea of pan-Arabism is very dear to Gaddafi, as it is to my party, by the way: he wants to unify North Africa. That's why my people in Cairo decided to set up a European headquarters here in the heart of Europe—with Gaddafi's money, which the French know and don't know, although it's an open secret—and they sent me here to run it. I'm like an Ambassador of the Egyptian Communist Party to Europe—even though we're not even in the Cairo Parliament. So John, you have to understand that the DGSE is interested in me, not in you as such. You're no problem; the Egyptian Communist Party is. That is, it's both a problem and—we believe—an opportunity for France. We're a small party and our own government hates us, so the French have decided to link us to terrorism: blame Arabs and Communists; blame communist terrorists for bombing the Coupole and government offices and then use us as a scapegoat, as the Americans say, a patsy, for a false flag operation, so as to make tougher anti-terrorism and anti-immigration laws and at the same time justify their imperialism in the Middle East. You'll see! The official investigation commission report on the Coupole affair will blame Arab Communist terrorists for the bombing—something like what happened after the bombing of the World Trade Center in New York and..."

John's phone vibrated. His publisher. Without any preliminaries, Mr. Pub asked him to be in London tomorrow for a face to face meet about a story project set in 'his' San Marino. Would John please be in his office at three p.m. sharp. The next day. Of utmost importance. Three p.m. tomorrow. Two editorial assistants will be present. Precisely at three p.m. Click. No time to explain Martha and Samantha's situation. No time to postpone or beg off. That motherfucker. Three p.m. tomorrow. Who the fuck did he think he was? Three p.m. tomorrow, my ass. John felt the blood drain from his face. He felt paler than Ivaan looked.

"Problems?" Ivaan asked quietly.

"Three p.m. tomorrow in London, Mr. Pub dictates."

"Then get an early train tomorrow. You'll be there on time."

"It's Martha. Samantha is ready to enter the world. I have to be on hand to get her to Necker Hospital. Labor pains could start even today. She's independent but this is a very special moment for all three of us."

"If you like I can be on call and be in Rue Saint-Dominique in fifteen minutes. Look, John, I have children and I know how these things work. You or she can call me if her water breaks or when it's time and *tout de suite* I'm on my way. And John remember that London is only four hours away."

6.

Samantha

John was on the return train to Paris when Martha called with her hourly update: her water had broken, she'd had the first labor pains, she and Ivaan were in a taxi headed to Necker Hospital. On the Paris express, the temperature rose. Unseeing, he stared out the windows into the pouring rain, his thoughts on Martha and Samantha, his ideas evolving and changing from one instant to the next. An hour later, Ivaan updated him that Martha was in the delivery room. The doctor had explained that the baby's heartbeat had weakened, the umbilical cord was choking her; they would do a caesarian section. His heart pounded, his mind urged the high-speed train faster and faster. Signs for the Charles de Gaulle International Airport flashed past. The train began slowing. The rain eased. The ugly big city suburbs passed ever more slowly. August heat rose from the plaster of wide, dead-looking avenues. Suburban train stations passed. He observed the double files of parked cars, underpasses and overpasses, warehouses, funeral homes and now and then lone old men idling in front of open doorways. He sweated cold sweat, his legs weak and insensitive to the gradual deceleration on the approach to the Gare du Nord where he and Martha had arrived now three years ago. The train braked to a stop. His heart hammering in his breast, he ran the length of the platform toward the metro. Despite the rains, August in Paris had never been so hot. Thirty minutes later and his heart still pounding and his legs quivering uncontrollably, he joined

Ivaan in the waiting room just in time for the smiling doctor's news: "Samantha arrived safe and sound and the mother is fine." The news was good and he should feel relieved, but he didn't. How could he?

"As always we followed the baby's heartbeat with ultrasound but since we can't see clearly the cord around a fetus's neck, if the heartbeat weakens—as it did—we assume it's because the umbilical cord is wrapped tightly all the way around the baby's neck…and getting tighter."

"My god!" John exclaimed. "How does that happen? The womb seems like such a safe place."

"Yes, of course the woman's womb is a safe place. But the baby in there is quite active, you know, moving around a lot during the last months, getting ready for life out in the world. So sometimes baby and that very long cord get tangled and the cord ends up wrapped around baby's neck. And keep in mind, Monsieur, that the cord is also the lifeline for the baby in the womb and must be open and clear. The cord reaches from the baby's abdomen to mama's placenta through which she feeds the baby with oxygen, blood and nutrients; studies show long-term effects on the baby if the cord is too tight and lasts too long. So, John, to avoid risks we decided on a C-section, a caesarean operation. Much safer and necessary in this case."

The obstetrician's words terrified and comforted him at the same time—and how he must stink of sweat after all this August torment. But yes, yes, they were safe.

"And how is that done?" John croaked, his lips puffed, mouth dry and tongue unmanageable.

"Since last century the caesarean section is routine and safe. And by the way I don't believe it has anything to do with the legend of Julius Caesar's birth. The C-section was once dangerous when it began in the seventeenth century—chiefly for hygienic reasons. But since early last century it has become safe. Some women even choose the C-section route because it's painless and they can choose the child's birthdate…within certain limits of course."

"Of course, of course. But now it's really safe, right, doctor? No long-term problems?"

"We simply made an incision in the mother's lower abdomen, opened the uterus with another incision, and there was baby, delivered. The whole thing took about an hour."

"Oh God! Oh God! And that's all? All those incisions. Are there many stitches?" he asked, like that mattered.

"You can calm down now, Monsieur. Madame and Mademoiselle are both fine. And as soon as Martha gets back to her room you can see her breastfeed your daughter Samantha."

"Ok, thanks so much, Doctor, but I was wondering what happens if we have another child and the cord again gets tangled around the baby's neck? Can you keep doing C-sections? Over and over, cutting up Martha's beautiful stomach?"

"A good question, young man. Until, let's say, until the middle of the twentieth century it was considered dangerous to do a second caesarean. But surgery has become more refined—and medicine in general—and multiple C-sections are done. I have one patient today who's had four caesarians and asked whether she could have another! I told her emphatically no, even though I don't really know the limit."

"Her stomach must look like a battlefield."

"Surprisingly not. You hardly see scars."

"Incredible! Or are you kidding me?"

"I, kid you? I'm a surgeon, not a writer. I don't invent stuff."

Officially their daughter Samantha—mystically they'd somehow known from the start that their child was a girl—was escorted into the world at 12.45 p.m. on August 15 of the year 2010, in the Necker Hospital, Rue de Sèvres, Paris, France. She is beautiful. Today is her birthday, John muses, a day she will remember the rest of her life. An introspective kind of remembrance for some people, as it will be for Samantha. She will be a heroine who sees and contemplates her own life and the peculiarities of her own being—and not only on August 15.

In that same year, the swine flu pandemic raged throughout the world; Barack Obama began his presidency of the USA by withdrawing combat troops from Iraq but leaving 50,000 non-combat soldiers; the first IPAD was launched; suicide bombers killed forty people in the Moscow metro; Wikileaks published tens of thousands of documents about the US war in Afghanistan; Western powers upped military operations against Syria. But such events hardly entered John and Martha's minds: for them their daughter was already nine-months old and now that she was out in the exterior world they saw that she truly was as beautiful as her mother. After a few yells and a good wash in her first hours on the outside of the protective wall behind which she had lived, Samantha now lay on Martha's breast for her first independent lunch without that tight thing around her neck. She sucked greedily.

John looked closely at the visible red line visible on her throat and across her scrunched neck, partially concealed beneath her abundant blond hair; a beaming Martha however, he noted, winced at every draw the baby took.

The nurse saw what was happening and smoothly switched Samantha to the other breast; it was no less sensitive and redness formed around her nipples. Finally, Martha pulled back in pain despite Samantha's protests until a bottle arrived and she settled in for a good meal.

"It sometimes takes a few days to get used to breastfeeding," the nurse explained. "We'll wait a few hours and try again. No worry!"

"Sutton," Martha said, "you're as white as a ghost…paler than Ivaan. Why don't you go home and rest while Samantha and I get some sleep. You can tell me about London tomorrow. But first tell Ivaan to come in and see Samantha, then you two can beat it."

"Let's sit here in the shade and have a beer so you can relax and accept that Martha and baby are fine, that you're now a father and the doctors and the hospital the best."

"Ok, ok. I need it. Ivaan, I can't thank you enough for what you did for us."

"I did what an Egyptian woman did for me in Cairo when my wife had problems just getting admitted into the hospital because of her Libyan citizenship. Those people wanted to send her back to Benghazi or Tripoli when she was having labor pains every few minutes and about to deliver lying there on the waiting room floor."

"My God! Worse than my helplessness on that train. Well, anyway, it seems the only problem is that Martha's dream image of herself breastfeeding her child won't be possible…but she'll keep trying. For months she has cultivated her idea of motherhood and breastfeeding is a major part of it."

"All right, that's enough. Enough!"

Ivaan raised an arm and called to the waiter, "We desperately need, uh, two double Courvoisier's and two light beers."

It was cool inside what seemed the only café open on Rue de Sèvres this August 15, where Ivaan proposed the first toasts to Samantha…

"To hungry starving Samantha" John said.

"To Martha, the father, the doctor, the nurse, to me," Ivaan continued in his plot to get John drunk enough to sleep.

"I was stupid to follow the orders of that egotistic bastard of a publisher," John insisted.

"But you went."

"A useless meeting. It could've waited. He only wanted to impress two new distributors and when he found that most of his real writers were vacationing somewhere, he called me. I should've told the motherfucker on the phone to fuck off."

"Still, comrade, you did go to London and the train brought you back in time and everything worked out."

"You know, Ivaan, Samantha's birth has drawn you and me close. You seem like a big brother. I first felt that sense of brotherhood the time I saw you in the Goutte d'Or. And a sense of solidarity of people linked by some common cause. On the train I had the thought that subconsciously I must see much of my father in you. A model. And of course that you're the real Communist I'd like to be but that I don't realize in my writing—not in the kind of concrete action that I'll probably never know."

"Then I have a lot to live up to. And you might get the action you want someday soon. Since the Coupole, the secret agencies have been plotting. There's going to be a crackdown. It's in the air. That's why they bombed themselves and their own people. Certainly, a false flag operation. And if new protests begin, the reaction will be more violent. Everything is accelerating, It's the dialectic, you know. The perfect dialectic. First, the people in the *banlieue* protest against unemployment, unfair treatment of minorities, anti-immigration policies. The police respond by beating and arresting protesters. People respond with new violence, this time police open fire and a protester dies. And then the Coupole is bombed—but not by the protesters—who are blamed anyway. Police repression becomes ever more violent and new repressive laws are made. Thesis, anti-thesis, new thesis, accelerating, faster and faster. Today, demonstrations in the banlieue are violent. Of course they have guns. Police too are bound to die. One more arrest or one more police shooting can be the match that ignites another fire, a real conflagration this time. Fire and flames. Car burnings and broken storefronts, gas bombs and rocks, protester-police street battles, hundreds of arrests, hundreds of injured, universities occupied, the Sorbonne closed. But all that's still too little. Only a warm-up. As the great Antonio Gramsci wrote 'there are moments in history when the past is not yet finished and the new is not yet become reality which reflects the crooked course of peoples' lives.' But the dialectic is there—at work. Protest will become revolt and insurrection. Youth in general will join in, the unemployed, the socially excluded. And John, that's revolt. It's still spontaneous and leaderless but it wants to grow. It's inevitable that it will grow and spread and attract adherents as a virus spreads and finds its places in living organisms—especially now that the sons and daughters of immigrants are organizing and reaching out to others. The day such things come to pass, your job will be to document it. And while doing that you have to trace and re-trace the past: we have to learn the past like we learn a new language—and never forget it. Everybody needs reminders. We have to remember the past. John. You can remind us of the past."

"Ok, ok, but meanwhile, Samantha is here among us. And Ivaan, you're involved in a special way."

7.

Motherhood

While Samantha sucked on the bottle, she looked fixedly into Martha's eyes. Despite the nurse's claim that the baby's vision was still blurry, John felt certain that Samantha saw her mother's tears. Martha had tried one last time to breastfeed her, but the pain had become excruciating and both breasts were infected. She was on antibiotics and had had a blood transfusion. She had an intravenous analgesia pump hooked to her that sent pain-killer medicine into her arm. It worked, quickly. When she felt a wave of pain arriving, she only had to push a button for instant relief. The doctor came and told John the procedure: if the breast infection was not better by the next day, he would operate. Each time John came, he carried Samantha around the room and held her up to the window and pointed out to her the world outside and believed she would understand it at least as well as he did. Martha watched them together, smiled weakly and said: "Oh, Sutton, for a kid yourself you really know how to handle babies." It was true; he felt no awkwardness whatsoever when he held Samantha, who, he knew, saw him and examined him as he did her, at first probably wondering who he was. Her most prominent feature was her huge eyes of an indefinite color, curious and already expressive; he wondered how she saw him. And did she know what was going on. Her blond hair was long and her face less round than he'd expected, and she had her mother's decisive character. In any case, Samantha seemed quite content with the bottle and as the days passed he saw she was taking notice of her surroundings. So ten days later when they stood at the window together with his back to the wide spaces of the room, he told her things. Secret things. And yes, she knew him. He tickled her under the chin like a kitten. She smiled. When she then snuggled deeper into his arms and closed her eyes for a moment, he made a silent, unwritten pact with her: he would never leave her, his daughter, Samantha. And in a secret protocol for himself, he vowed he would never leave her mother either.

When he laid Samantha back into Martha's arms, the baby snuggled securely into her embrace as she never had before. Martha pulled the corner of the long green and orange scarf she was wearing over Samantha, sharing her world with their child.

"Martha, she returned to you as to her place in the world, the place where she has spent all these months becoming a person."

"And I can't even nurse her. Anyway, Sutton I've accepted it and it's not so bad after all. She likes her face against mine. The nurses say that in the long run, the bottle is better which I don't believe for a minute. No, not at all. During my exercises and talks right here in this hospital the experts pointed out that breast milk contains all the right nutrients for the baby and provides natural antibodies against many diseases. It raises the baby's intelligence too some believe, and reduces various diseases in later life. Besides it's good for mothers too, psychologically at least, and bonds them to their children."

"Well, my lovely lady, we had a bit of bad luck on the breast part but still we're fortunate in all other ways. The best of care and a beautiful sensitive Samantha with ten fingers and ten toes. The ugly will end soon. Either your breasts will heal themselves or the doctors will fix them."

"Right, oh, oh, here comes a new wave, she said, pushing the green button at her side. A minute passed in silence, Martha tense, fearing the pain. Then: "Thank God I caught it in time. Wow! Seems miraculous."

"Ok, Sutton, are you working in these crazy days? How's Ivaan? He should be Samantha's Godfather," she chattered, jumping from one thing to the next. "Who knows if Arabs have godfathers? Allahfathers. Sutton, I keep wanting to apologize to everyone, nurses, doctors, you. I'm afraid you might think I did it on purpose, though I know it's not true. But for a few days in the worst mad moments of a long pain spasm I even had the mad thought that Samantha did it on purpose—to my tits, I mean."

"No, of course not. Martha listen to this. I've been studying the intuitive faculties, the intuitive knowledge of new born babies, what they bring with them, straight from their world in the womb. Foucault naturally imagined childbirth as a changing relationship of power: the doctor a manager, the midwife a worker, the mother a machine and the baby as a product."

"Ridiculous!"

"Well, that's Foucault for you.

"I wonder how he classified pain."

"Maybe as the Devil's punishment. Anyway, studies at an American university show that far from the helpless creature we imagine who only eats, cries and sleeps, the baby is born with vast intuitive knowledge, even physics, like understanding very very young that if an object is not supported, it falls. So you can imagine that if Samantha intuited that she was hurting you, then she willingly switched to the less satisfying bottle…and now she snuggles with you to show that your arms and bosom is her place in the world, the place she feels secure."

A month and two days later, they returned home together in Rue Saint-Dominique. When they walked her around the apartment and showed her the room prepared for her, Samantha's eyes wandered in all directions, in apparent surprise at the sudden change in environment; she lifted her hands closed in the usual tight fists and snuggled into Martha's arms. John thought her behavior perfectly understandable. That first day at home, John decided to keep a diary in her name. His first entry would be:

September 12, 2010: Today, we moved from Rue de Sèvres to my home in Rue Saint-Dominique. I sleep in the baby's room they prepared for me. I think we will be happy here.

8.

Samantha

When John stared at parts of his composition and it stared back up at him so expectantly, his mind often wandered along paths distant from the text that waited only for him to decide what happened next in his story. His independent mind was instead intent on clarification: somehow, he had to grasp the contingences that continued to change and form the flow of his life since he and Martha met on the London-Paris tunnel train. That interruption had ended a pattern of uprootedness and solitude and alienation that in his mind was not right for Samantha. Enough is enough. Her arrival had set new paradigms, indicated new directions, inculcated new courage.

Two years have passed. I am twenty-seven. Martha is twenty-five. And Samantha is two years, one month and two days. Time has flown past in our lives. Martha long ago recognized that her inability to breastfeed Samantha in the Necker Hospital was due to circumstances out of her control; and she has re-flowered in her motherhood. Samantha began walking and talking at around nine months and I don't recall her ever just jabbering baby talk—in a way I wish she would—she still seems to speak only when she has something to say. Otherwise, she observes the things happening around her in both joy and it seems a kind of despair. No, she is not a laughing, joyous and boisterous child; she is observant and serious. So even if I keep her diary for her, I've accepted that like her dreams are only her dreams, also her memories are her memories and no longer mine—or my interpretation of what she sees or thinks. And that is a great mystery: what does Samantha think about her world? Does she dream dreams of her life—of our lives—in this world? Since dreamers are likely quiet and sad people, I observe her and wait for the telltale signs of the greatness in her displayed in her frequent moments of sadness and a certain faraway look in her eyes. I observe her moods and try to understand the swift changes that her huge eyes reflect. But I don't understand what they say to her or to us. And over and over I remind her that I will keep her diary for her only until the day she is capable of taking over the recording of her dreams and the family's passing life.

To Samantha's joy, Uncle Ivaan comes often so that she hangs onto him for it seems hours at a time and sometimes falls asleep with her head on his shoulder, stirring feelings of jealousy in Martha and me. Some evenings, Ivaan teaches Martha another Egyptian dish, adding to her growing repertoire. One evening, he introduced the secret of the preparation of a simple Egyptian dish, Koshari, rice with crispy onions and tomato sauce, while I took Samantha down to Rue Saint-Dominique for a short walk before giving her dinner, her saying her special goodnights and my putting her to bed with the usual German children's song. Then the three of us ate the Koshari with toasted Pita. Those were good evenings together with Uncle Ivaan.

I work at home in a room we bought from an adjoining apartment; I am now finishing my first real novel, *The End of a Love Affair*, and hope to deliver it to the publisher in a couple of months. By the middle of October I told myself to stop turning phrases in my manuscript as though in the search of what to put first or last and just submit the novel to the London publisher. Martha read parts of the book said she likes it, perhaps only because she supports me. No one else has seen it, and I myself no longer know if it's any good. It's just that way. Insecure people like me read their own work over and over to the point they no longer know if they have rendered their original ideas in a literary way, and, above all, in such a way that the publisher will believe the book commercially viable. Will it sell? For such is the real reality: the marketability of the book with which the author's idea is often incompatible so that the best books never see the light of day, while the less than best books are published, successfully marketed and sometimes become bestsellers and are adapted to the cinema world. Dan Brown's improbable novel, *Angels and Demons*, set in the Vatican—which became bestseller and film—is one of the worst novels I've ever read. Early this morning, before taking the high-speed train to London, I still haven't given my book a final title; I've suggested only the "working title": *The End of a Love Affair*, in memory of my mother from San Marino.

Now, in London, the act of passing the finished manuscript directly into the hands of the waiting publisher cannot be a less liberating feeling than that of the convict on his exit from a penitentiary at the end of a twenty-year sentence. Blessed freedom at last! No more waking up nights and looking for pen and paper to record a dream I just had or an idea occurring clearly in my chronic insomnia only to be incomprehensible in the morning—or worse, to find it banal and beside the point in general. Readers may think the ideas the author spouts so spontaneously in his novel are the author's prescient fruit of inspiration or his conclusions after long and perilous adventures in the jungles or on the high seas. Nothing is farther from the truth. The thoughts you read in the finished book—after the editors, assistant editors and junior editors have reorganized and rearranged and restructured the writer's original thoughts—which the writer too had rewritten, rearranged and restructured and turned many times, cutting some adjectives or adding an adverb here or there, turning phases and reversing the sentence order. In sum, many minds and hands have edited the original idea in such a way as to make it so ambivalent and ambiguous and wishy-washy cowardly that its very survival is miraculous and the submitted text might not have retained even the shadow of the original idea. I myself in this crucial moment of liberation have forgotten whether it survived or simply withered away in the process of its refinement. Maybe I should grab the whole manuscript from the publisher's hands and cancel the whole fucking paragraph—if it is even still there. Oh, the doubts! A few seconds earlier I'd felt as free as a bird flying south; and now I'm again a prisoner of my own doubts. 'Keep in mind that this is a draft,' I start to repeat to the publisher now examining me with his stern, accusatory but—I see—completely undiscerning gaze.

I rushed back to the St. Pancras station hoping to catch the hourly express about to depart for to Paris. It was pouring down rain in London, a steady rain that would be there for days. The city was wet; I was wet. Still trying to forget the novel, I hummed a few bars of *I will Always Love You* from that film love story I liked so much, but I still wondered what the final title of my novel would be—I suggested three alternative solutions none of which I really liked so that for me the book, the story I tell and the persons involved remained incomplete and therefore indistinct. My thoughts jumping from the novel to the rain and again to Samantha waiting in Paris, I was rushing down a wide flight of wet stairs when nearly at the bottom I slipped and stumbled forward, luckily catching myself on a railing, but twisting painfully an ankle. Limping toward my train, I felt the swelling underway: this ankle business, I knew, was going to be messy. To my good fortune, the first class car's hostess boarding just behind me took pity on me. She seated me where I could prop up my leg and after examining the now hugely swollen ankle, she bound it expertly with a medical elastic bandage, enough, she assured me, until I get home. In Paris, a baggage wagon drove me down the long familiar platform at Gare du Nord to a taxi for home. Though I'd been gone only twelve hours, that evening under an anomalous international rain, Rue Saint-Dominique seemed strange and foreign.

It was around seven p.m. I was sitting in an armchair with my right leg elevated on a table, the cuffs of my pants pushed up to my knees and Samantha in my lap. Later, I would remember each and every event of that evening, all of which would come to seem to bear some personal malefic significance: my doubts about the manuscript, the slipping on the wet staircase, the tremendous speed of the tunnel train, my ankle and the everlasting rain.

From time to time I looked at the downpour pounding so musically on our balcony and thought of our bright future. Martha was in and out, asking questions about the dinner she had ordered from a restaurant opposite our apartment. I told Samantha about the train and the long tunnel passing under the sea to another country to which she nodded with the usual serious expression in her eyes— tonight they seemed even bigger than usual. She said Uncle Ivaan brought her a funny doll baby; it was yellow, the color she loved.

She would show it to me later if I liked. It was all so homey, so warm, so predictable, so reassuring and secure, so my place in the world, in which one event preceded the other just as if according to a preordained plan for a well-lived life. Then, when she jumped down, my eyes followed her as in her shuffling gait, her little hands lightly punching the air and her fingers flexing she wandered again back to the kitchen where 'Mommy make cookies' while my thoughts from time to time turned back to the novel I'd put into the hands of the publisher at eleven a.m. this morning—it seemed a long time ago. For some unfathomable reason it occurred to me that I should've written in that thorny spot, "she left against her wishes," and not, "but she left anyway." It was ambiguous the way it was in the manuscript. Made no sense! It's the little things like that that count. It often depends on where you place an only: only what? Or do you mean only him? Or him only? Or only in that way, or only now? And that's not ambiguity; that only can become a lie. Oh, fuck it all! At about seven Samantha came and announced she was hungry and then go nighty-night. She touched my ankle and said: "poor Poppy." Then off she went again, somewhere or other. Usually, I followed her around the house and we played games. This evening was an exception: my sprained ankle. Later, she passed by a few times and touched my ankle again and said, "Poor Poppy." The doorbell rang: restaurant delivery. Martha took it and said to put it on our bill. Samantha said that we'll have dinner now and then nighty-night. In the kitchen Samantha wanted to sit on Mommy's lap. She was sleepy. Then silence until Martha called: "Sutton, look! Martha's not hungry, she just sits on my lap and has gone to sleep. I jumped up and stumbled to the kitchen. Samantha's eyes were closed. I called her, over and over. I shook her lightly. She didn't open her eyes. Deep sleep, I thought, watching her eyes. Martha stared. I telephoned the pediatrician at the Necker Children's Hospital. Her doctor was not there. The substitute asked what medicines she was taking. None. The doctor said to bring her there if we had doubts. I looked in her room for medicines. Nothing. I checked the bathroom. Nothing suspicious. Then our bedroom. And there they were: the small bottle of pink pills, a mild tranquilizer Martha had taken once or twice for post-partum nerves stood on a table out of reach for Samantha—we'd believed. The lid was off, a stool standing nearby made clear what happened. A few tablets were missing. Frantically unthinking we rushed downstairs to the taxi stand. The rain poured. Samantha slept in Martha's arms—deep sleep. REM? Or coma? We watched her eyes. They never moved. Never a flicker. Our terror. But she was breathing. Softly. Too softly? You think that such a moment should remind you of other bad moments in your past; we didn't say it but we both knew there had never been a more terrifying moment in our lives and that there was nothing worse in life to which this fear and terror could be compared. From the taxi I called the doctor: he should meet us at the door. An emergency. "Our baby is in a coma," I said.

The doctor and a medic met the taxi, took Samantha from Martha and put her on a trolley. As they wheeled her away full speed down a corridor, the medic began emergency treatment. A lady showed us to a kind of parlor with floor to ceiling windows and big cushioned extendable chairs and blankets. We were both suddenly freezing. We huddled on the chairs and watched the green fern plants outside dancing wildly in the wind and the rain, swaying and beating satanically against the great windows. And we held each other in a tight speechless embrace, afraid of speaking to each other for fear we might speak the thoughts we were thinking—both of us conscious of those unspoken words hanging over us as the night passed there in the penumbra.

In the early morning after it was over, the doctor said they had done all they could and that the diagnosis was still uncertain but that he believed the baby had had a severe and immediate reaction most likely to something she consumed.

We never saw her again. In the first minutes while it was happening and just after it happened, shock and total confusion and disbelief that it was happening, that it had happened to Samantha, to me, to us. The doctor stood before us with bowed head and empty eyes. September 12. He could say no more. He would never get used to it; some things no one ever gets used to.

We couldn't stay there in the penumbra where the stalks of plants continued their wild beat against the window. We went back home. Where else could we go? Martha sat unmoving in the armchair I had sat in last night with Samantha on my lap. Poor Poppy. Poor Poppy. I went from one room to the other, then back downstairs to the street, searching for reality. Trying to get back to real life.

In the afternoon, they called from the hospital about arrangements. No, we did not want to see her; neither of us could possibly bear the thought of seeing her like that. Two days later Samantha was put in a white casket and buried in the Montparnasse Cemetery in the presence of Martha and me, her father and his new companion, and Uncle Ivaan.

Martha was unable to live in Rue Saint-Dominique for even another day; she returned to London with her father for an indefinite period. I stayed there in the empty apartment, I, alone within the walls of our lives with Samantha and her untold dreams. So that as though it had waited for the opportune moment, it arrived, my pain. Inescapable, pure soul pain. The pain that destroys you on levels that you didn't know existed. Soul pain accumulates every possible kind of pain wrapped in one and then attacks your very essence in such a way that you can think only of how to stop the pain. If the pain would ease, I think I would be able to think clearly about Samantha—so that I could truly mourn her—and not myself. The second day in the house without Samantha, the third day, and the fourth passed, while the pain left no room for true sadness and despair. Life itself was about this monster living inside me. I'd never thought of pleasure as a final goal in life and had read and seen in my father that man is willing to suffer pain if he can be sure that his suffering has a meaning. But Samantha? What greater universal meaning could losing her have? This was pure satanic on the part of the gods of fate. Dreamless dead sleep was the only rare escape; but then on awakening back into everyday life, my first thought was the pain. Was it there? And it turned back on, blindingly, like a spotlight when you push the on button. Getting up was like stepping into an illuminated mine field. For brief moments I feel guilt for those pills; and that I'd failed to protect her as I had promised. How to live like this? Suffering the pain in this loneliness. And again I might—only for an instant— feel her nearness, on my lap, walking hand in hand down Rue Saint-Dominique. I know. I know. Everyone feels terrible pain at one time or another, for one reason or another; still, only I can feel this my pain. But no, I can't tell you what it is. A secret pain? Soul pain? Maybe soul pain is always secret. This is the very definition of soul pain; if you feel like this, you can be sure that it is your soul that's suffering and not your body. My loss. This my loss was this pain. This, my pain was my total loss; an unnameable part, a secret part, a psychic part was being ripped slowly, slowly from my soul causing the ceaseless pain. I read that Plato believes that we don't actually learn new things but recall things we knew before birth—I always thought Samantha knew things she couldn't yet pronounce—and those things, Plato meant, make up the soul. No mass, no space, no location, but, Plato thought, the soul was in the mind. Except that although the mind after all has different parts but is mortal, the soul is instead indivisible and eternal. So, Descates concluded Plato's inconclusive and uncompleted reasoning that the brain performs all the actions and mental activities attributed to the mysterious soul: perceives sensations, weighs ideas, makes decisions, and stores memories. But do the philosophers really know? Each person suffers his pain in his own way; only I suffer mine, as a consequence of which I ask again and again where the pain is. My pain seems to originate in my stomach, maybe that's where my soul is. A meaningless conclusion, however.

Sometimes Ivaan came and sat with me. He brought beer and we drank in silence. I was glad he was there, but try as I might I couldn't share my pain with him, my brother, Uncle Ivaan. One day I remembered my ankle—my guilty ankle. And for the first time I decided to take a good look at it. I took off the elastic bandage and found it was not even swollen. I shrugged and tossed the bandage aside. Strange. The swelling had simply vanished—as though it had been a mere Fata Morgana in a desert sandstorm.

Ivaan helped settle my affairs. He brought his real estate agent with whom I signed the sales contract for our apartment that in reality was much bigger than I'd thought. Ivaan said it was a good contract. The whole quartier was in high demand and it would 'net us a lot of money'. While the agent negotiated the sale of our apartment, for a week or so I stayed there as much as bearable as a self-imposed act of penance, I suppose, during which time I tried to write something, anything, just to occupy my mind: I never finished one single essay, short story or even short travel pieces for the German newspapers I once wrote for. Five minutes at my desk and the burning in my right shoulder became unbearable. Shoulder burnings! Who'd ever had such a phobia? Instead I began walking around the city: I walked from Neuilly to Bercy, from Montparnasse to Montmartre, as a rule often ending up at the Embassy, as I called Ivaan's apartment in the Goutte d'Or where I sometimes stayed for days at a time. I spoke with Martha several times each day to keep her abreast of events in Paris—that is the non-events and what happened in my soul—in reality however to keep up with her recovery. Maybe I should be with her in London: hadn't I promised Samantha I would never leave Martha alone?

But then the day I told her that the Saint-Dominique apartment had been sold, she revealed the bewildering news that she had inherited Aunt Thérèse's apartment on the Esplanade which I had so despised. Nevertheless, a ready home that was not the Rue Saint-Dominique apartment made Martha's return easier; she would not even see the place of her nightmare—to pacify me, she agreed that the bourgeois aunt's ancien régime furniture could be sold which again loyal Ivaan arranged. Ivaan seemed to be taking over our lives.

9.

Les Invalides

Though the change was like a new life, a second chance, abandoning the apartment in Rue Saint-Dominique was in a way like abandoning Samantha herself since it was the only home she had known in her brief time; nonetheless, though John too had reservations, he believed that for her mother's sake she would have approved. Although just around the corner from Rue Saint-Dominique, their new home on Rue Fabert was another world. The location of their building was splendid, facing the great park called the Esplanade linking the complex of Invalides that he hated—Army Museum and Cathedral and Napoleon's tomb—and the magnificent Alexandre III Bridge with its art deco lamps, which he loved. For him, the chief problem was that their monumental apartment building was still peopled by the same haute bourgeoisie of Aunt Thérèse and administrated by the same proponents of the imperialism that placed the twenty cannons of the former French empire facing down the Esplanade and looming over the city of Paris like an angel of wars to come. They would have to adjust to their fellow inhabitants by isolating themselves from the rest of the historical structure to which he would turn his back as much as possible. Also, he would still take his walks the length of Rue Saint-Dominique; he would still buy the best croissants in Paris at Le Moulin de la Vierge; he would over-tip the snotty class betrayer of a concierge but he would never say a word to him except bonjour or bonsoir, and anyway, fuck him! But one other matter still nagged him: Ivaan and their new palace apartment. Though the

Egyptian Communist had seen to the sale of the aunt's furniture and fixings, he had not yet actually seen the apartment. How would he react? A gift is a gift, but still, this palace-like immeuble, French imperialism, those twenty cannons, Napoleon's tomb was problematic. What would Ivan say to all the magnificence? The glory of *la douce France*? He still recalled the scorn, the malice, in Ivaan's voice that tragic night at the Coupole when he had snickered at his own words, la douce France, drawing out the full musical pronunciation of dou-ce Fran-ce. So it was that when Ivaan came for his first visit John was on pins and needles and one of the first things he nervously pointed out to him—as Aunt Thérèse had done now years back—were the twenty cannons of Invalides almost under the windows of the apartment. But to his great surprise, Ivaan thought the new "flat" just marvelous; "flat" he called it reductively, but still without a hint of facetiousness or irony in his tone. John examined his dark eyes closely and decided that his friend was on the level and would therefore be a regular guest after Martha's upcoming return. John felt a sense of pride that his only friend in the city of Paris was a Communist.

***

He arrived at the Gare du Nord with a taxi paid to wait and to carry Martha and him back to Rue Fabert. Traffic was so heavy in this area that taxis now avoided it like the plague but she hadn't decided what luggage she would bring. When Martha stepped out of the carriage, he was halfway down the same platform as always—the quai itself a link in the chain of painful memories: his ankle, the rain, the baggage cart, the rare taxi back to Rue Saint-Dominique, his propped leg, 'poor Poppy'. They stood immobile, face to face, looking each other in the eyes, hesitant and speechless at seeing the other in the flesh after the three months of their suffering. Still without a word they embraced, until, in an act of courage, John later thought, she spoke the same words as years before: "Sutton, don't you ever leave me," which John interpreted to mean 'let's try to overcome this'. And in that moment they seemed to believe they could make it together. However, deep down he suspected that Martha wondered about the degree of his solitary suffering, just as he speculated about hers: did she suffer less? The mental discussion passed in the fraction of a second of the time that they looked into each other's eyes searching for the answer to the unasked question as to who suffered most—or less. John knew that the question of how much pain and how long each level of pain endured was immeasurable and that because of the very nature of pain the question had to remain unanswered. He felt certain that in these months during which each of them suffered alone, Martha in London, he in Paris, and separated by that practically invisible but moody body of water, both of them had wondered if one morning they would wake and find that the pain was somehow less, or that it would return a bit later than on the endless days before. Would that progressive pain diminution continue? Would the pain spontaneously lessen gradually until one day in an uncertain and indeterminable future the pain would be gone and a shadowy sadness would replace it? Yet, whatever they did, whatever they thought, the unchangeable reality remained that Samantha was gone. For that reason, he wondered if the healing of the pain, or even the wish for the pain to cease, was a sign of too little love for her. Was it a betrayal? And was less pain and thus less love for Samantha a sign of his guilt? In any case, for the present such risky and conflicting words and considerations about the pain of each remained unspoken.

Martha had traveled with the same suitcase with which she'd left Rue Saint-Dominique. John pulled the trolley along the platform. She held his other arm tight, exactly as she'd always done, and as usual sending a charge through his body. Some things change less than others, he was thinking when in the same moment he felt a twinge of ankle pain, a reminder of the fatal events on the evening of his arrival here three months ago.

"Our loyal taxi is waiting," he said when they stepped outside into the winter fog that had settled into the city. Parked cars and trucks and buses filled every possible space on the great station square. Lines of nearly immobile traffic blocked the street beyond. The penetrating fog made everything eerie, the station behind them, their taxi and the driver who was perplexed as to how to proceed.

"John, why not the metro?" Martha said in a dead careless voice. "So much faster that way. No wonder there are no taxis here."

"Well, you didn't know how much luggage you might have," he said evasively: he couldn't admit that the metro now scared him—just stopping between tunnels as it often did and he would panic and break out in sweat and look around frantically for a way out.

"You could've asked me again."

"Yeah, I didn't think of it. You know I'm still not into cell phones much. Had this one in these months only to speak with you."

"No matter, John. We can see the Russian bridge this way…if we ever get there."

"The fog's thicker today so the lamps will be on."

"What lamps do you mean?"

"The art deco lamps on the bridge, they'll be turned on today."

When an hour later they finally crossed the bridge, darkness had fallen over the city and just as he'd said the fog was thick. Martha pressed her face against the car window and exclaimed how beautiful the lamps were, their dimmed red lights against the colorless fog and the misty river down below.

"Martha, you remember the houseboats down there, hundreds of them? Well, Ivaan has friends there and one day we were walking along the quai and he stopped at one of them just under this bridge. You'd be surprised who was there. It was one of the men at his table the night we met Ivaan the first time at the bombing at the Coupole, the men who didn't say a word. I think other Arabs live down there, some of them secretly. When I asked Ivaan about it, he just shrugged and said he didn't know any others."

"Oh, John, please let's don't speak of past times…of those years. Let's look ahead toward the future," she said as they headed directly to that symbol of the past glories of France, Les Invalides.

"Ok," he said agreeably, even though he thought Martha too dismissive of the recent past that in fact still belonged to Samantha and always would be Samantha time.

In his mind, the scenery changed dramatically, bizarrely as they approached Rue Fabert: in the fog, the Invalides appeared as ominous as their building loomed lugubrious, which John hoped Martha would see as he did.

She said nothing.

He'd seen their palace-like building with misgivings the very first time they arrived there; Martha, he knew, had seen it back then simply as her aunt's home. Actually, he shouldn't expect her to see its significance as he did, the symbol of the capitalist imperialist world his father had so hated, a spirit inculcated into John since birth.

"Bonjour, Monsieur Maurice", he said curtly to the concierge and went on to the elevator with the suitcase.

"I had it checked so I can assure you that the ascenseur is functioning smoothly," the concierge said, John thought, with a faint note of facetiousness.

"Good!"

To Martha, he explained: "I don't speak with that imperialist son-of-a-bitch…the fucking snob. Nothing he loves more than pronouncing Bonjour, Monsieur le Comte to some decrepit bastard with blue ribbons on his chest. Bonjour, Madame la Comtesse." His humiliating kowtowing to these imperialist bastards, trying to be like them or just to hang on to the very edges of their world that despises him. He's as guilty as they are— guiltier. They were born into it and don't know anything else. But he is an applicant for it, and incompetent to boot. Like the masses; they're guilty too, guilty applicants for membership in that guilty class that considers Maurice lower than the lowest."

"Oh, John, don't bother with him. But what was that about the elevator? Was it not working earlier?"

"No, Martha, the elevator was okay. I'm the problem, I fear. I'm scared it may stop between floors like the metro does between stations. I panic. I seem to have developed a bit of claustrophobia. So I usually walk down and risk the ride up. My walking down three floors irritates Maurice—hurts his pride in this building which furnishes him and his wife and daughter a cubby hole down in the cellars. You know, I..."

"John, I think everyone has reactions like yours from time to time."

"You think so? After this iron door opens—if it does—I'll tell you the rest."

When they stepped out of the elevator at the third floor and inside their mammoth marble entrance way, Martha gasped. She hadn't seen the apartment in years. "My God, this place is really huge—big enough to play rugby in. Are the lawyers certain it's ours?"

"Yours," John said.

"Ours," she repeated, looking into the two salons, one on each side of the entrance space; now practically empty. They too looked bigger than before. The movers had pushed their disparate unsold pieces of furniture from Rue Saint-Dominique into a far corner.

For a moment John held her arm as she usually did his and looked her in the eyes, more interested in what he might read there than telling her about his attack of claustrophobia in an ascenseur. "It seems to have come over me recently" he said anyway. "And strangely, all at once. I've never seen anyone else go as crazy as I did recently in a blocked elevator. I was headed for an office on the fifteenth floor in a skyscraper in La Défense. The elevator was full of people and was rising normally when the motor suddenly shut off with a clunk and the goddamned thing just stopped...between the ninth and tenth floors. Martha, I went completely bonkers. I pushed at all the buttons. I banged on the doors and yelled louder than anyone else. I broke out in sweat and my heart pounded wildly. But it wasn't fear we'd crash to the bottom; I was terrified of being locked inside that cage—but then, thank God, just as suddenly as it had stopped the fucking motor came back on and it glided up to the tenth floor and the doors opened smoothly just as if nothing unusual had happened. Everybody else filed out calmly and looked at me like I was a madman. I walked up the five more floors to the fifteenth and then later all the way down—fifteen floors."

"Oh, it's just one of those temporary phobias as such things often are. Sometimes I think we just have no idea what goes on in our head, or even who we are for matter. I don't. Not yet, but someday I hope to."

Surprised at this unknown side of Martha she had just shown him, he stared at her for a long moment and then, guiding her down the resplendent hollow hall and aware of the sound of their steps in the ghostly space, he had the thought that maybe he'd never really known her at all—not the real Martha. He realized that the saying was true that before we can begin to understand others, we have to understand ourselves. And he didn't. 'I don't know why I do and say some of the things I do,' John mused. 'I don't know why I feel certain things that I do. We lie to each other just as we lie to ourselves and then deny it—and then we deny our denial. So what about me the writer? Do I at least understand the characters I myself create? No! I don't. Actually I've always been aware that I don't really know them either. So who knows you? Man is truly like a novel, Zamyatin wrote, you just don't know how it will all end. Otherwise, it's not worth the read. I suppose he meant life itself.'

John walked her around their palace like a realty agent explaining one thing and another as to how he would re-do the whole "imperialistic showcase".

"Let's make this a home, Martha. Fuck the empire and fuck those cannons outside." As a start they would rip up all the marble floors and wall-to-wall carpeting and lay hardwood floors, for which Ivaan had proposed an interior architecture firm. Egyptians, of course. Communists, of course. Martha found their bedroom wonderful—John thought because there were no reminders there of Samantha too painful to live with. To make room for modern literature in his studio, he'd stored most of the collections of seventeenth and eighteenth century non-literary texts in a warehouse beyond the périphérique ring road together with other unmarketable stuff Aunt Thérèse had collected in her times; Ivaan had sold the heavy ancien regime library furniture along with the rest. Martha agreed with his idea of painting the studio walls a shadowy shade of red. They would furnish at least two of the five bedrooms for guests.

"And the kitchen?" Martha asked. "It can't stay the way it is. It was made for servants. Not normal people."

"Why, Martha, you sound like me. Or like Ivaan. But you're right; we can engage a kitchen architect I know in Milan. None better than Italian kitchens!"

After the tour, neither of them knew what to say, where to go, or what to do. The sprawling space had no center yet; no heart, no soul. That's the problem with excessive space. What to do with it? How to manage it? You manage space, or it manages you. Space had long bothered him. Manifest Destiny was a perilous slogan; Europe from the Atlantic to the Urals, no less. Like Paris itself, the center. You stand at the Arc de Triompfe and see the twelve avenues originating there like twelve spokes of a wheel and you might think you're at the center of…of what? Of Europe? Of the world? You set out down Avenue Wagram and if you walk far enough it simply peters out. You try another of the famed spokes and it ends within easy walking distance. They all end quickly, shorn of the pomposity and glory of their departure like Hitler's Sixth Army eventually stymied among the rats and cold of the cellars of Stalingrad. This house still lacks also duende, the elusive spirit, to make it a home that our apartment in Rue Saint-Dominique was for those magical two years and two months of time.

"Well, I think…" Martha was saying as the phone rang somewhere in the front part of the house and echoed up and down the hallway and through the salons and the still undetermined number of bedrooms, the library, the two studios, the storage rooms, the five bathrooms and the pantries and back to them in the kitchen. Since it was the first time the landline phone had rung, he hesitated as to where to answer, before running back up the hall to the only one he'd noted. On the way, he was conscious that his was an uneven hobbling and limping sort of run—maybe because of the general fatigue he'd begun feeling, suddenly appearing, easing off, reappearing, as if the tiredness were a living organism. He felt with trepidation the panic creeping up his legs and he knew it was insidious and unstoppable. The question had become how to handle this new impediment to life? He'd tried simply ignoring it but the IT—he'd begun calling the thing in him an IT—jumped to his stomach in the guise of nausea and he had to rest in strange places, crowding old ladies on the limited benches at bus stops or on street benches near outdoor markets. IT had become a ubiquitous encumbrance that pursued him like afternoon shadows on a sunny day.

It was Ivaan, straight-to-the point and purposeful Ivaan: "So, how is she?"

"Surprisingly good. All in all, better than I expected. We're reviewing this palace we now own. Man, it is gigantic."

"And you? What about those elevators and metros that stop in mid-journey?"

"I'll tell you about it later. But in the meantime, if you come tonight we'll take you to dinner. There's a good restaurant next door to us. I think I can manage that distance. That's one thing about Paris; there's always a restaurant next door."

"I'll be there before nine."

"*Alors, a toute a l'heure*. And Ivaan, don't be intimidated by our fucking concierge. Pronounce your name vigorously just to put the fear of God in his veins. Our door code is: 3089S."

No sooner had he hung up than the intercom buzzed, and Maurice —how he despised him—announced two gentlemen: "Old friends, they say. They want to greet you in your new home. Shall I send them up to you? Or will you descend?"

"No names, hmm. Yes, send them up so I won't have to walk down three floors."

No names, old friends. He suspected right off who they were. Secret service! And he was not wrong, although he was surprised that the two down-and-out DGSE agents he remembered had transformed into smooth well-dressed and clean-shaven officials. After their ceremonial formalities and condolences for the "misfortune that had struck his family", they got down to business:

"As we told you now some three years ago, Monsieur Sutton, we are associated with our country's anti-terrorism department," the apparent superior said and showed him an official looking ID with his photograph, which he quickly pocketed before John had time to read even his name.

"No, you told me you worked for the French government."

"Right! Anyway, as such we have never lost sight of you, so today we're here to reestablish our, er, our former relationship."

"Anti-terrorism! I read that now you people can break into private homes without a warrant and arrest people on mere whim." he replied in the same business-like tone. "Obvious that you never lost sight of me. Why, I haven't even yet filed our address change. And by the way, I might note that we never had a relationship that I knew of. Besides," he added, "where's your briefcase?"

The two men snickered and looked around the vast empty spaces as if looking for a place to sit. John just shifted his feet and crossed his arms across his chest, implying that anything that needed to be said could be said standing in this entrance hall paved with pale blue marble.

"No, we did not lose sight of you. And it is our business to know the whereabouts of people who interest us. In this case, I mean you. And chiefly only insofar as you are very close to Monsieur Ivaan Amrani. My colleague and I remember like yesterday your precision that he wrote his name with two a's. You can't imagine the number of file cards that had to be updated with that corrected detail."

"Now that's the bureaucracy of state machinery for you," John said with a barely concealed note of sarcasm. "I wrote something about that in a book somewhere."

"Yes," the usually silent sidekick interjected. "I read that book that you called a love story but that was not about romantic love at all—as you suggested with the title. It was about, well, I thought it was really about brotherhood and love for your fellowman. I found the story touching and also revealing."

"Revealing?" John said, his voice rising. "Revealing about what?"

"About yourself."

Staring at the man in surprise, John thanked him for his interpretation. "It's good to know that your, uh, your department has a literary critic in its ranks. Maybe there's hope for a better world after all."

"Not as long as people like Amrani's friends get away with things like the Coupole," the other said. "Which brings me to the reason for our visit just as your wife arrives. Something very big is in the air. We don't know what or where or when but our informers here and there hint of new terroristic attacks in the works. In France. In Paris. Maybe tomorrow. Maybe next year. But people like us sense it. We smell it. We know it's coming…sooner or later."

"Sorry to hear that but it's my opinion that what goes around comes around—if you get what I mean." Aware that he should keep his mouth shut, he added: "Centuries of imperialism have to be paid for—unfortunately, sometimes in blood."

The secret agents didn't answer but they regarded him grimly for a long moment during which he realized that these two men were not ignorant at all. They knew what was going on. Yet, they had no conception of the real story of France, of Europe, of the Western world. They believed in Europe's entitlement to its privileges and its stolen riches. They believed that France was inherently deserving of its extraordinary wealth accumulated through worldwide thievery, genocide, the destruction of whole nations, the theft of land itself and what lay underneath, the assassination of the greatest people of the times, the eradication of entire cultures. It was their birthright and their destiny to have homes like this one in the Rue Fabert. They saw those twenty cannons under his windows in front of Invalides with eyes different from his: for them those captured cannons exemplified that right which they were ready to defend, tooth and nail if necessary.

"We need your help in this matter," the superior functionary finally said. "You can learn things from Amrani that we cannot. Though we know your friend Ivaan, I can't say we know him well. That man has a way of talking so very glibly while revealing nothing. Nada. Rien. It's frustrating how we come away from meetings with him knowing less than before. He's a veritable clam."

"Yes, I know what you mean," John said resignedly. "Still, I think you overestimate his knowledge about that other world. He knows a lot of people as a result of his position as an unrecognized leader of a certain Arab world abroad. But I don't believe his part of that world includes terrorists. I will tell him you asked about him."

A long silence followed John's last words, which seemed to mark an end to their conversation

"By the way, gentlemen," John asked as they re-buttoned their coats and prepared to leave, "Is that motherfucker of a concierge downstairs your snitch? I wouldn't put excessive value on what he tells you about the rare comings and goings here.

Anyway, I will myself inform you before he does that Ivaan—two a's—Amrani is coming this evening to greet my wife who arrived on the afternoon express at 16:22 from London; moreover, we're taking him to dinner in the café-restaurant next door."

"Thanks for the tips," the chief agent said and laughed heartily. "Now we won't have to ask our informer at Gare du Nord about arrivals and departures; your precision is better than hers. So now if Ivaan reveals details about the upcoming terrorist attacks, please contact us at this number," he said leaving his card on a side table near the elevator door.

10.

Ivaan Amrani

Since his life had undergone a series of abrupt changes one after the other, he had come to understand much more about the way the system worked than back when it all began: his own life now seemed a perfect illustration of the dialectical method. He had lived with his parents and sister in a Cairo middle-class residential neighborhood, his life proceeding like that of his fellow Egyptians: he participated in the ceremony of that life, attending like others the same elementary schools, followed by upper level schools, and—as his father had so fervently desired—the university, which, however, turned out to be the catalyst for the interruption of the skein of order and sameness of his previous life. At the university he met and joined the Communist Party. As a result, he was expelled, his father lost his governmental position and in the end became a building administrator in their neighborhood, and the family moved from their spacious upper floor apartment to a dark and cramped cellar. The family's status demotion and his discovery of the reality of the condition of that social status generated his rebellion against the whole system. And thus followed the consequential ups and downs of his life: his marriage to a Libyan woman opposed by his family and his self-imposed exile to Libya where to his surprise his role in the Egyptian Communist Party brought him unexpected recognition and a certain fame, until Gaddafi's money and a Party decision opened the Arab Embassy in Paris and named him its ambassador.

Though Ivaan had first become acquainted with a happy and fulfilled Martha, the subsequent once-in-a-lifetime tragedy of horror turned her into a shadow of her former self; nonetheless, the spontaneous warmth of his greeting surprised all three of them: he kissed her on both cheeks and said softly how glad he was to see her back home again in the city of light. Though he was seldom embarrassed, he blushed slightly in a brief moment of awkwardness and, not knowing what to do with his hands, he draped an arm lightly around her shoulders. Martha was pleased and smiled warmly in a way she had not done since her arrival.

When John asked if the concierge had given him any problems, Ivaan replied that he must have a special way with concierges of the world because they all sooner or later came to love him. "I must not have told you that my father was a concierge in both Cairo and Alexandria, so I speak with every concierge as I would with my honored father. They respond to that."

"Yes, but ours is a police snitch."

"Many are…maybe because they're sinfully underpaid and live in cramped spaces and hate being obsequious to snobs, gangsters or politicos rich enough to live there."

In the restaurant downstairs they purposefully sat by a window giving onto the sidewalk along Rue Fabert. They were spotlighted there together—for all to see. After dinner, as they lingered over a bottle of Beaujolais, Ivaan asked about the London of today like the Edgeware Road area where he once had friends. Martha spoke of the Knightsbridge district where her father had taken her to a well-known Arab restaurant there. Ivaan said he happened to be in London during the Underground bombings a few years ago, "by chance" he emphasized—looking at John with an ironic smile—but that he didn't know the city now as he once did. John let the London bombings go and instead guided the conversation to the Seine riverboats moored near the Alexandre III Bridge.

"That day on the Seine quai when you stopped to speak to one of the men with you at the Coupole the night of the bombing, I began wondering how they afford those boats—the *péniches*. Living on the Seine is really expensive. How do immigrants afford them? And are there others like them in other boats? And who are they?"

"First of all, John, there are immigrants and there are immigrants. Some are very rich. And from hearsay I know more about the houseboat owners than I do about the people who live on them. It is rumored that a rich Saudi bought several of them years ago for friends, and you know how those things work; the friend of the Saudi rents it or lends it to a friend, and that friend rents to another, so that it's hard to know who lives in them now. But John, our police friends know these things already. I would guess that since the Coupole, Arabs living on the péniches on the Seine are the most watched and controlled Arabs in Paris."

"Yes, of course you're right. And not only because of the Coupole but I would guess in anticipation of the future. And anyway I would bet that many of them are police spies.

"How could they not be?" Ivaan muttered, scowling toward the window as if hoping someone was out there watching. "Police aren't always the most brilliant minds in the world, but they're not stupid either. Even I, the Arab Ambassador, am obligated to speak with their secret agents."

During a moment of silence, the three of them observed the veins of water sliding down the plates of completely sound-proof glass separating the world of the cold outside from the warmth inside the café. None of them had even noticed the January rain earlier; now it was pounding silently against the glass, some drops bigger than others zigzaging slowly slowly downwards. Was there not a face in that one, its paleness almost white? For a moment, John's thoughts traced the line leading from the rain in London that day pounding against the windows of the publisher's office, the taxi ride back to the station, the wide steps, his slide, the pain, the train hostess bandaging his swelling ankle, the Gare du Nord baggage cart carrying him to the lone taxi, the ride across the bridge to Rue Saint- Dominique, his hobbling, his elevated leg, 'poor Poppy poor Poppy', the bushes beating against the windows of that porch of terror at the Necker Hospital. Now he stared long at the drops, hypnotized by their slow downwards trajectory, his palm flattened and his fingers splayed on the cold glass and recited to himself: "cold and dark and dreary, it rains and the wind is never weary.' January is a sad month, he thought. Martha observed him and understood.

"Listen," John said, "how would you two like to go to see the labyrinth in the Chartres cathedral tomorrow?"

"The labyrinth in Chartres? Why that?" Martha asked.

"I want to walk it...just to see how it feels. I read that tomorrow it's uncovered. Takes only an hour by train from Montparnasse. We can go at eleven, do the walk, have lunch and be back before dark. So what do you say?"

"I'm with you." Ivaan said enthusiastically.

"Me, too," said Martha. "But tell us why you want to do it."

"Oh, I have a labyrinth in mind for a story—he half lied—or maybe a novel. You know, a metaphor for our walk through life, twisting and turning back and forth, like a rain drop making its way down a window. Walking a labyrinth is not exactly like the dialectical method, Ivaan—but nearly. Maybe we'll be able to see ourselves better afterwards."

***

When at noon they finally stepped off the terrifying train, John felt almost carefree. The reason he'd doubted the Montparnasse Station Master's assurance that there were no tunnels to speak on the Chartres route was precisely that ambiguous "to speak of". What could the station master have meant? To speak of? Either there were tunnels or there were not. Or did he mean that he didn't consider a tunnel a tunnel unless it was, say, over three kilometers long? Why, if the train stopped in a dark cavity under the earth in a two and a half--kilometer long tunnel, you could easily suffer a cardiac arrest before they rescued you; a mere one hundred meters were more than sufficient if the train had a sudden breakdown. Alertness is called for. If you hear those fatal iron-on-iron brakes, you know something is grossly wrong. Screeching brakes always mean something anomalous is happening; even a slowdown can transform into a full stop in an instant. Also the motors can shut down. The silence then is terrifying. And where the fuck would that leave him? On a shut-down train in a long tunnel and in a flash his terror would return. Those brakes were what made travel on the metro so hazardous. In fact, impossible. Though he hadn't believed the equivocal words of the station master, he'd hung his hopes onto the "no tunnels" part of his forecast, which in the end had proved to be right: during the fifty-seven minutes of travel time only underpasses had occasionally appeared, through which however you could always see reassuring light at the other end. So now, safely in Chartres, John looked around the station and began thinking of how he would handle walking the labyrinth: it was his brainy idea but he felt that the reality of the creeping debility concealed in his legs, his total exhaustion after only a few minutes on his feet and the accompanying nausea was a story independent of his will; his legs had come to seem detached from his body. They would decide the walk.

As they entered the cathedral, Martha grasped his arm tighter than usual which was not surprising for she'd always had a thing about churches—a mixture of fear and hate—that her errant Mother and loyal father had instilled in her as a child: the Devall's considered churches the devil's property. As a consequence, Martha had problems accepting churches, cathedrals, mosques, or temples as works of art. She had never even looked into the Saint Louis Church with Napoleon's tomb or even Notre Dame just to see how its reconstruction was going.

"John, for God's sake, what are we doing here? If this little maze can cure the soul or whatever it is that causes the pain, I'll follow you." But look at this thing! I thought of something huge, with walls and enclosures and little doors to secret places and all that."

"Look, Martha, you have to forget the church and concentrate on the magical labyrinth. Some labyrinthologists today say that you walk it to heal yourself; you don't dance on it and play games on it like they did in medieval times. But don't forget that

I'm a writer and I have imagination. And anyway, if this doesn't help me, then I've got to see a psychiatrist, quick. Besides this is not a maze with the secret doors and passages you have in mind. This *thing* is in fact pretty big. Look at it, it's as wide as the church nave. Nearly thirteen meters, I read. The labyrinth has no dead ends; it has only one path—this one is about two hundred and sixty meters long—and its curves and twisting turns and circles lead to the quiet place in the center, and then over one similar path back out. The one path—both in and out—is the point. Stick to the path and arrive at the heart, that kind of thing."

"Well, I didn't know you were a specialist in the esoteric."

"You mean labyrinths. And no, Martha, I'm not a specialist. Still, maybe your path too is there, inside the labyrinth…and mine…and maybe Ivaan's too. I think the main point is the idea of that one path, that twisting and curving line from here to the center and the one path back out. The thing is you don't have to be a spiritual person—or a specialist either—to take the path to the heart. They say that entering the labyrinth and following that one twisting and turning path zigzaging away from the center, then returning toward it, is much like striving toward your goals and then meeting the unexpected setbacks in your life from which you must recover and proceed like Sisyphus, on and on, from stone to stone, to finally reach the center. It's in the center of the labyrinth that you might find the necessary calm to live. Then, the specialists claim, on your way back out you find clarity and quiet. I'll follow that path and hope to find peace. Not in the labyrinth itself, I don't believe, but in the quiet of my calm self, holding to that one line back to myself and back to you, Martha."

"And are the experts convinced that you do come back out?"

"Cynics say hardly ever. So maybe there's risk involved. That is, it's not completely free."

"Oh, John, everything was once so beautiful—before. And now, just look at us here, examining an ugly labyrinth in a cathedral. My father was right. Take a wide berth around churches."

"My father didn't love them either, but I still want to try this. Somehow, I half believe. But you stay with Ivaan; he's not eager to take the walk either. Then we'll have a good lunch and drink some good wine and then enjoy the fine trip back to Montparnasse—on that scary train."

John staggered off the last stone and slumped onto the nearest bench on the east wall of the cathedral. He calculated he'd walked about half a kilometer on two hundred and seventy slippery, seventeenth century stones each about thirty-three centimeters in width which religious fools used to do on their knees—those medieval fanatics scooted five hundred meters on their fucking knees. Man! You really have to be in search of God to walk all the way to Chartres in order to torture yourself on the stones. Still, he didn't yet know if his walk had helped. Though he was not on his knees, his leg weakness meant he did suffer the painful impediment, the equivalent, he rationalized, to the pain of knee walking. Or would he have to do it on his knees too? For some reason, he believed it was a slow working medicine…maybe even shamanic. And he wondered—now cynically too—if boosters were necessary to get full protection. The panic and the urge to vomit that had overcome him in the center was subsiding; but the weakness in his legs and the nausea in his stomach and the vomit filled throat he'd felt out there were momentarily greater than the pain that lived in his guts and his burning shoulders, all of which, he felt, meant Samantha was present. Yet he couldn't believe that her spirit intentionally inflicted the pain on him. The heart of the labyrinth *was* Samantha; actually, he would have pushed along that half kilometer on his knees too if he thought Samantha demanded it. The mere thought that his beloved two-year old daughter could harbor such a devilish desire intensified his guilt feelings which probably lay at the root of his panic and terror and phobias, the symptoms of all his manias. In that moment, he felt that he should crawl the quarter of a kilometer back to the heart—which was Samantha—just to clarify. Oh, if he could only fly, fly like a bird back to the heart. Anyway, he had ascertained one thing: he knew where to find her. She would always be there, right at the heart of the matter. The heart of the matter, he thought, was there. There is where she was. And he knew the way back. The way to her. It all made sense now: the dubious, fearful travel to Chartres, his shuffling, sliding, pain-ridden trek to the heart. He sighed and peered around in order to pinpoint the location in his mind: East wall, cathedral, Chartres, fifty-seven minute train ride from Montparnasse Station, Paris. Paris, he thought, and in the same moment he realized Martha and Ivaan were still nowhere to be seen; he'd been on the eighth or maybe the ninth of the concentric circle of the path to the heart when he'd looked up and seen them going out of the main door of the church, trailed by Martha's multicolored Missoni scarf caught in the breeze from the open door. He shrugged, muttered "skeptics", and lifted his eyes toward the great rose window in the west wall entitled the *Final Judgment*, art also created in the thirteenth century—eschatologically linked to the labyrinth. It appeared as the very essence of art. The beauty of art. Beauty displayed and, as in all art, beauty partially concealed. The union of the beauty of the colors and the ugliness of man—ugliness as an intrinsic part of beauty—generates the necessary scars of beauty…like Milosz's necessary flaws in the whole man. John studied the window at length and didn't understand; he felt he was losing his hold on the portentous events he'd been experiencing. He'd read the Baudelaire-influenced critic who wrote that "the role of art is to subdue ugliness, a subjugation which is bound to appear somewhere in the masterpiece." Chartres, the masterpiece. The container of the symbolism written on the cathedrals rising across medieval Europe were messages to the illiterate peoples of the times. Lines straight out of Eco's letters to his father, he remembered. The year one thousand was a watershed for Europe, Eco wrote. The barbarian invasions ended and Europe breathed again; the city-states emerged; and a new spirit was born. A spirit of innovation. Born in monasteries, that new spirit and a new art spread to the cities; the greatest expression of the new art was the cathedral; the force with which that new art exploded from the earth was emblematic of the energy of the epoch. The energy of the collective. Such was the Middle Ages for Eco. Discretion and taste and joie de vivre, yes, but also the community spirit that gave birth to the Romanesque and Gothic cathedrals; and the setting itself of the cathedral is far removed from the broad perspectives of the pomp of Paris. The cathedral stands silently—as in John's recurring dream—at the center of the town that built it, the center of a city of streets that create the sense of intimacy of urban life.

All streets lead back to the magnetic cathedral and to the great piazza where it stands. Paved with timeworn stones like those of the labyrinth, the cathedral is emblematic of the unity of the new spirit that marked the medieval era. As in the epoch in which they built them in a frenzy of medieval energy, some select people today still unite. Le Corbusier's words about the cathedrals erected across Europe at the beginning of the Middle Ages reflect their communal enthusiasm—the spirit of the social.

11.

In The Windmills of His Mind

Back on Rue Fabert that same evening, he telephoned a psychiatrist he found on Internet. A male voice answered: "Zetkin."

"*Guten Abend,*" John said and continued in German. "I'm having some problems and am looking for a doctor."

"So why did you call me?" Zetkin replied also in German.

"Well, the main reason was that I liked your name."

"Why was that?"

"For historical reasons, I suppose. My father admired Clara Zetkin and the Spartacusbund."

"And you, do you share your father's sentiments?"

"Oh yes. Hey, this is turning into free analysis. Or an interrogation. Do you always do that to chance callers?"

"A professional weakness," Zetkin said and chuckled audibly. "Why don't you drop by tomorrow afternoon? At three sharp?"

"Ok, but just one question: Are you a Freudian?"

"Listen, just come tomorrow and we'll talk. I hate telephones. Tomorrow at three sharp. Rue Babylon 10. You can call me from the door."

The room was all peace and quiet and order. Hardwood floors, carpets here and there, light blue walls, one wall of bookcases, sets of small etchings on another, one tall brightly colored late cubist painting on the wall facing John, couches, a redwood desk in a corner and art deco lamps on small tables, big windows looking out onto a patio of trees and exotic plants protected by transparent covers. The perfect room. Filled with live objects and tranquility. Positive signs. He felt peaceful himself… and relaxed.

Karl Zetkin sat in a dark red fauteuil facing John seated in an easy chair with wide cushioned arms. Zetkin was a good-looking man, in his forties, dark longish hair, slim of build and of average height. He fiddled busily with the missing crease in his jeans and said nothing.

John squirmed and waited, cleared his throat, examined the window again, and wondered who was to speak first. This must be their system, playing cat and mouse. Was this guy really a psychiatrist? And shouldn't he at least ask my name and what my problem is?

"Uh, Doctor, *mein Name ist John Sutton und ich bin Schriftsteller.*"

"Yes," Zetkin acknowledged.

"I have problems."

"I imagined that."

"Look, should I fill out some forms or something, you know, with my address and the reasons I'm here."

"That's not necessary. You can tell me when you feel like it. You have one hour's time during which I'm at your disposition, so to speak."

"I, that is, we, Martha and I, lost our two-year old daughter nearly four months ago. So times are very hard." John watched Zetkin intent on tracing an imaginary crease in his pants and wondered about his choice of a shrink. Actually, it wasn't even choice; he just called the first German-sounding name listed.

"We met on the London-Paris tunnel train five years ago. We are—we were—deeply in love." And for some unexpected reason he told his story to this complete stranger: Aunt Thérèse, Rue Saint-Dominique, Latin America, Martha pregnant, his books, the Coupole, his friend Ivaan, Samantha, Samantha was gone. He'd promised never to leave her, or Martha either, now Samantha's absence was destroying his relationship with Martha. And he was under attack by his manias: his panic, his claustrophobia in elevators and underground trains, leg weakness, and now he couldn't write because of the fiery and paralyzing shoulder burnings.

"Yesterday I went to Chartres to walk the labyrinth. I thought that might help."

"Did it?" Zetkin asked, tearing his eyes from his jeans and looking at John with watery eyes.

John stared back at him as if the tender healer were crazy. "I worried because maybe I should've done it on my knees like pilgrims used to. Then I was so weak afterward I could hardly make it back to the train. And I was still afraid of long railway tunnels. The underpasses are ok as long as I can see the light at the other end."

"John, don't worry so much about your symptoms," Zetkin said, now looking fixedly at the clock on his desk. "They will be the first things to disappear—after we begin our work. You will soon begin to feel more confident about life. Now, you have explained your situation very well—like a writer. And I don't see that you consciously lie to yourself which is a big plus in your favor. Next time—let's say on Monday at three p.m.—we can talk more about Martha. And to answer your question, I do admire Freud and I hope you will begin trying to remember your dreams…even small pieces of them. Write them down during the night because dreams are evasive; they don't want to remain in your conscious. But remember that they are there. And they can give us a hand in uncovering important hidden parts of John Sutton."

And the next time was truly different. And the next.

"So what should we talk about today?" John said one Monday. "Strange but I don't have any new dreams to tell? I always dream. Maybe you turned off the spigot last week."

"No problem. They'll return. But last time I had the impression you wanted to talk finally about relations with Martha."

"Did I? Well, I don't understand why, but my loyalty bothers me. I mean, I feel chained to loyalty. A tenacious jailer. Loyalty to the past. Loyalty to the center. Loyalty to undeserving persons and ideas—at least less important than myself."

"And Martha?"

"Oh, no, I am not referring to her. And I am willingly loyal to her—and above all to Samantha."

"Samantha? What does she have to with loyalty to Martha?"

"Everything. Everything. They are the same. Well, nearly the same."

"Hmm. The same? Double identity?"

"That must be my innocence showing through."

"Innocence?" Zetkin said, making a mark on his notebook and looking up at John, unconcealed doubts and questions written in his eyes.

"It's true. I've always been an innocent since my greatest emotional reactions are to romance and beauty and mystery and love and betrayal of love. Like the innocence of the still undeveloped twelve-year old girl waiting for perfect love. Is that not worth at least limited redemption?"

"Redemption? Aha!"

"What? You seem to have doubts about innocence. But you do believe in redemption, I assume. Otherwise I'm in the wrong place here. Wrong therapist too."

"On the contrary, John. I think we've made a qualitative leap ahead."

"Innocence and redemption reach back to my boyhood when I lived with my father in Underground, at a time when I didn't know who I was and why I had to live in Underground, as a rule alone and always frantic and nervous because I was there and didn't know why. That's something to consider seriously, therapeutically, I mean. Now that I think about it, it's no wonder that I've never been peaceful, tranquil. The reason I always sit on the edge of my seat—look at me now! My knees turned away, halfway on my feet—ready to leap to my feet and escape, the reason I've never been comfortable in life. And why not turmoil? I was only five. Already at five I needed forgiveness and redemption even though I also felt five-year old innocent. Still, I already felt guilty too like I'd sinned and was being punished when I didn't even know what sin was. But when he took me Aboveground I saw that other people seemed scot-free. And I wanted to be free too. But maybe that's illusion and my innocence. Maybe nobody is really free."

"John, your conceptual Underground sounds like either total illusion or the most significant phenomenon I've ever heard."

"There's another related problem that I must mention so that you get the full picture, that you understand and forgive, but also so you do not forget *me* in your notes about madmen—with many underlinings and stars. For I truly want to tell everything—tell everything pressing me in this confession. This is a confession, is it not? Right? But Zetkin, Doctor, despite my cooperative memory, I probably still forget much of the most important. It's human, no? And at times—like when I'm writing—I tend to forget that I forget and end up adding confusion to confusion. Confusion, or is it maybe volition? I should ask you about that some other time when I'm not so talkative. My mind doesn't necessarily always cooperate. But the truth is I no longer know what is really the most important. Probably what I've told you already is less significant than what I've forgotten. I mean important things like words about the depths of my life. The depth of Underground like the depth of my recurrent desperation and anguish. I beseech you, Doctor Zetkin, don't press me now, it will all come out in the telling. You can have confidence in my formidable memory. It holds it all—except the forgotten."

Saturday night, a few weeks later, Martha wanted to do something distracting and uplifting; instead they watched an American film on a British TV channel, a love story between a young European and a Chinese woman which ended sadly. Both of them were tense as each evening at bed time. Each of them knew the other was thinking about the absence of the sexual in their life which had ended with Samantha. They couldn't even speak of sex. After the usual ablutions, they were lying on their backs, side by side in the huge bed, lights still on, near enough to each other to feel the warmth of the other's body.

Suddenly Martha stood up, alarmed: "Oh, we forgot to open a window. I can't sleep without air."

When she returned, John turned his head and kissed her just under her ear which had once been a signal. Her face flushed as before, weaker perhaps, but there was a flush. Thinking her opening the window symbolic, he turned on his side toward her. Seconds passed. He recalled the times—not long ago, or was it a future ago?—when there were no signals, no flushed faces, when they threw themselves at each other madly, greedily, hungrily, insatiably, day or night, bed, couch or floor—the times when they were merged. Now tears formed in her eyes, and he took her in his arms.

"I can't John. I don't even recognize myself. But I can't. I can't. What are we going to do?"

He understood that they might never be able to return to their former sexual relationship—never. Their relationship was now on another level, a non-sexual level where romantic love was truant: neither of them felt capable of absorbing that new reality.

Martha turned onto her side away from him waiting for the dreamless sleep that always came easily to her—the only time she could forget she was alive. John lay on his back looking toward the shadow images marking the darkened ceiling and again thought that if he could just let go, something in his mind would lead him to a place of freedom from pain. Freedom from his nightmares. He knew he drew conclusions eons distant from mainstream thought.

Nightmares so wild, but so free, most but not all of which he'd recounted to Zetkin. True freedom, he suspected, lies in madness. Where time is out of control and you no longer live from day to day, but from hour to hour, from minute to minute. And totally unfettered. No holds. No binds. No restrictions whatsoever. You just let go and leave all control and sanity behind you. It's an easy step. What a joy it would be to break out. Pure fantasy too, he warned himself. But not pointless. It's what many people want: drinkers, drug users, warmongers, the politicians, CEOs, financial wizards. Thinking such thoughts engendered the same physical reaction as did writing: he felt the first spark just above his right shoulder blade, its fingers reaching toward his neck. He massaged the hot place. The fire smoldered. His shoulder was ablaze. No more thoughts of the great incubus. He imagined walking the streets of a great city hand in hand with Martha. It's Buenos Aires. They circle the great plaza and he stops an elderly couple to ask directions, they are Italians who have forgotten their native language, they stand under the trees along the Avenida, still hand in hand, and at the *Once Station,* Ivaan is waiting and he takes Martha by the hand, they are departing together on the tunnel train for London. And then John was awake again. The room was in penumbra. The terrace door was wide open. He listened to the rain falling on the flagstones on the terrace outside the open door. Martha was awake, turned on her side toward him. She was watching him and crying.

Martha often cries. And John fears tunnels and elevators, has motor issues and his right shoulder burns and he trembles at specific dates: August 15, 2010 and September 17, 2012. And so it would be forever, he knew. 8/15 and 9/17 would burn forever.

Another Monday. Three p.m. It was his fifth session. After telling Zetkin about another sexual fiasco, he related a dream: "It's not a new dream; I've had it before. There's a wooden ladder leading down from a high place where I'm standing to a lower place I have to reach. The ladder stands flush against the wall, the rungs too shallow for my feet so that I can't face the wall and climb down. Others walk down the ladder like a flight of stairs; I take a few steps and know I can never reach the bottom. I manage a few more steps, leaning forward toward the chasm. Teetering and searching for a hold, I finally have to jump. At the bottom I hold my hurting knees and watch the others descend nonchalantly, all unharmed and without a scratch. Then I see the trick. I hadn't noticed a thick vine hanging from the top out in front of the ladder. All you have to do is hold onto the vine with both hands and walk down the ladder like a staircase. Why had I not seen the vine too? Why didn't they tell me? I dread the trip back up, but when it is my turn I manage to buy a safe return ticket at the price of one euro."

"Well, that's quite detailed. Seems real the way you tell it to me. So what do you think about the dream?"

"What do I think? I thought you were supposed to interpret my dreams."

"We do it together."

"Seems like a dream about fear. Fear permeates the dream. I hate that dream. I hate dreams of a fear that swallows up everything I say, everything I think—the fear that gives no simple answers."

"Actually, fear is a natural response to danger. Conquering fear is the point."

"In the dream, I don't fear physical pain. I think I fear showing signs of cowardice to my companions. By the way, that's something I don't believe I've ever even thought of in real life."

"Who were those companions?"

"I don't know. Not friends. I think just people I met along the way but I wanted to impress them."

"Along the way? What do you mean?"

"Well, I guess I mean I'd met them before. Or in Underground. Of course, it was in Underground. My family kept moving around. First of all, there's my being born as an Englishman in Rotterdam so that I ended up with a Dutch passport and I don't even speak the language. Then I lived in San Marino with my Italian mother, then I lived with my father and studied in Munich, my real home—if I have one. I miss its low skies and two weeks of non-stop rains and I prefer the föhn to the north winds elsewhere."

"Why did you say so quickly that those companions in the dream were not friends?"

"I suppose because I don't have any friends—except Ivaan."

"Do you feel lonely or out of place because of no friends— except Ivaan? Do you think you're hungry for friends?"

"That might be the reason I'm a writer. I create real friends."

"And you write love stories. Do you think that's a coincidence?"

"Most certainly I need love. Lasting love. Not promiscuous love. I tried that; it's unbearable. You don't know where you're going that way. That must be my father in me; he couldn't love any other except my mother."

"You don't know where you're going, maybe like in metro tunnels?"

"Yes, Zetkin, yes! Uh, Doctor, I mean. Like in those fucking tunnels where you can get lost and never get out again." Metro tunnels, the same world as Underground

"John, do you think moving around from place to place bothered you. Maybe you would have liked to belong in one place and be part of it."

"Yes, I suppose so. I missed not having lifetime friends. And how! Yes, I once wanted to belong. I didn't belong in Rotterdam even though I have that Dutch passport. I was sent like a package to San Marino where I felt like a foreigner, and today I don't even know anyone there. I just don't fit in anywhere. I once felt Munich was 'my place' but now I'm uncertain: I wonder if I can be drawn to some other place with the same force. And would being a Parisian or a Roman be the same as being a Münchener? I don't know, but somewhere in me there must be a penchant for fixedness, a desire to become indissolubly linked to one specific place where I believe peace lives. And now by pure chance I'm still here where I was building another life—but now Samantha is gone—on 9/17—and Martha is somewhere else and I'm still an outsider and my only friend in Paris is an outsider like me. No wonder I dream all these dreams about tunnels and impossible places! I worshipped my father who integrated everywhere because of his, uh, because of his political involvement; I inherited his political beliefs but not his integration capability. He was a true internationalist. His world was a real world. And he was part of it.

He changed countries and all he had to do was join the local Communist Party and he was in real life again. His eyes were sharp and he saw things as they really were. He was clairvoyant and saw through events, like he knew when to emerge from Underground. But I create imaginary worlds in my books that I call love stories, though they're not even love stories—they are stories about love. My characters are in the end like me—or as I would like to be. And I keep dreaming. I can't even close my eyes without dreaming. I didn't tell you that the reason I have difficulty remembering my dreams is because there are so many of them. There's too much to tell. I tell myself that the totality of my dreams is simply the life of my other self, my dream self, living in a dream world. Still, why do you think I keep dreaming about dark tunnels, fearing those dark tunnels and secret passages? Dreams like the one of a group of friends and I who have to get into this mysterious place. For some reason they're Croats. One is a slim boy of ten or eleven. You go up a ladder at the top of which opens a narrow dark tube-like tunnel and you have to scoot along it in the dark; you can't see the end— or light. I've done it before but this time I don't have the courage. The slim little boy goes first and gets the hang of it right off. And away he goes, scooting straight up the tunnel. But I can see that I don't fit anymore. No need to try. And besides I'm afraid."

"John, I'm surprised you don't get it. It's the easiest dream imaginable. That tunnel, the tunnel that you reject, is the way to yourself. You have to dig into yourself, search and explore. Surprising that your fictional characters haven't understood this."

"Some of them do understand. It's their creator who doesn't get it."

"The same dream over and over is the way people who have suffered an accident or have lost a close loved one re-live the situation over and over dream. It's the hope of finding a way to change the past, to penetrate the unknown and pass through to the other side, through the great wall separating your present from your past and to retrieve your life of then. You flail at the windmills in your mind: you can't bring Samantha back. And since she's irretrievable, you make yourself physically incapable of attempting the impossible. You can't stand on your own legs, you can't enter those dark caverns, you can't reach the place where you think you should go in order to change the brutal reality of that impenetrable wall, the wall that you have not yet recognized. And you punish yourself for your inability to perform the impossible—her resurrection."

John rubbed his knees and said: "Yes."

Walking and alternately resting on his way back to Rue Fabert, it occurred to him that he seldom thought of returning there as 'going home'. Not in a real sense, not in the sense of 'going home to Rue Saint-Dominique' was. Sitting on a stone wall and staring with unseeing eyes toward the Dome of the Invalides, the church containing Napoleon's tomb, he thought for a moment of tombs and wondered why he hadn't told Zetkin about the terror he'd felt when his father spoke of the darkness of *Underground*. He was five or six—at the time either in Rotterdam or Munich; he couldn't remember which—when for what seemed a long period of time his father spoke almost daily of the darkness of Underground where they lived and it seemed uncertain if they would ever re-emerge into the light.

Memory, he thought, is so complex, so inconclusive and so elusive. Memory is a re-visit of both joy and pain. Memory replaces what is unbearable with the bearable. He tried to employ memory to replace the emptiness remaining after Samantha, after 9/17; to mask the pain of her loss with fulfilling memories and warmth; to replace that unbearable grief with bearable sadness. He aspired to sadness. He respected sadness. All sad persons, he imagined, have some great grief buried deep inside them which they replace with their sadness. In the shadowy caverns and downward spiraling corridors of the mind that cold grief survives and at unpredictable times inexorably resurrects, inextinguishable, and gnaws voraciously into the sad person's very being. His memory that he re-lives in writing contains all that he has done, seen, hoped, desired, imagined, thought, touched prior to and following a visit of his grief. His memory is vast; it's all the places, skies, suns, winds, rains, rivers and oceans and mountains that have touched him. His memory is the container that holds the pieces of his book together.

Expecting the same fatigue, he stood up, staring at the meaningless Dome…and waited. He suddenly felt different. *Auf einmal anders.* Suddenly changed. 'And even if I've only had five sessions, Zetkin promised that the symptoms would soon vanish. Quickly, the shrink said. But not completely, he qualified. They can return. That's the way symptoms work, down in those dark caverns. You just never know. What sets off a symptom is the mystery. Those dark caverns haunt me. Like the same Underground as when I was little. Got to tell Zetkin more about Underground next time.

He nodded at the concierge and muttered 'bonjour, Maurice', undecided whether to try to walk up three flights or risk the elevator. He took the elevator. Seconds later the door opened into their entrance hall. Martha came out of her studio down the hall. He boasted that he'd felt only a twinge of doubt about the ride up and that he didn't even sweat. She smiled.

"Why don't we visit Ivaan and the Embassy," she said later. "I've never seen it and you can show off your new conquests on the metro."

"Well, I think…Ok, a good test. And you can always hold my hand if I weaken."

"Come on over," Ivaan answered his call. "There are other people here but you and Martha will fit in perfectly." John didn't ask who the other people were.

Walking to the Sèvres-Babylon metro as they used to, John's gait was sprightly and his mood for the first time in months light-hearted. On the train, he chatted about an idea for a short story set in wartime Paris and once risked a glance at the tunnel walls flashing past; then when the train brakes screeched iron-on-iron and the train slowed at the familiar sharp turn that had scared him, he took a deep breath and looked Martha in the eyes like at the anchor of a three-master whaling ship while the whalers are off in a boat killing a cetaceo. The perilously long but well-lit connecting passages at the midtown station where they transferred to the Montmartre train had lost their fearsomeness; yet, to distract himself from the dangerous reality of the underground through which they were passing, he read with feigned interest all the announcements and advertising of upcoming events and the anti-capitalist graffiti, dropped a five-euro note into the basket of a metro violinist for good luck, and above all, he avoided looking toward that fateful dark hole at the end of the corridor where there should be light. As they descended into the penumbra of the lower level, he resisted the temptation to tell Martha about Underground where he'd lived with his father, deciding that the effect would not be the same as when he spoke of it with Zetkin.

After showing Martha a bit of the Goutte d'Or and they bought her an Arab scarf in an Algerian boutique, he clicked Ivaan's door code and they passed from the pale winter sunlight into the darkened hall. Martha held his arm tight as they ascended the carpeted stairs illuminated by the recessed spots along the walls to the *etage noble*. Ivaan had spoken as though a few neighborhood friends had dropped in; instead the huge front room with the art deco lamps was packed with elegantly-dressed international-looking people. A youngish and lonely-looking priest in white collar and black suit stood near the entrance like a receptionist or a sentinel; and near one of the tall windows—John could hardly believe his eyes—the two smooth DGSE agents were engaged in observant conversation with one another; most certainly they had noted his and Martha's entrance.

After introducing John to Pére François, Ivaan guided Martha to a group of young people chattering in English. For an instant only, John's eyes followed Martha as she shook hands with them in an English manner: she looked absolutely gorgeous. However, he knew that her beauty was a thin shell harboring only the remnants of the person she once was.

"Monsieur Amrani told me about you, the young English writer and his lovely wife," the priest said. "So I am honored to make your acquaintance. In fact, I read your two books and was curious about the underlying spiritual tone in your work."

John laughed and said: "Thank you so much, Pére. I too am curious—and pleased—that you find something of the spiritual in my work for I like to think that spirituality—or morality—is a theme running through all my writing. As Ivaan might have also told you I'm a Communist like him, but even though non-religious, I do consider myself a spiritual person. I believe in sin—not only transgressions against religious laws—and redemption." Telling himself to shut up, he continued in a sudden burst of a new freedom. "I think man needs something to believe in. There's no way that they'll ever completely control the human condition without some sort of god for man. But power is the problem. A paradox, no? I mean to say that Power defends an ignorant kind of religion tooth and nail and uses it to dumb down the people, but it dismisses true spirituality which sees through power's gaslighting and its science that power uses to kill and which it sells as flawless and an incorruptible substitute for the real God—if there is one. Actually, Power considers itself the real God which the dumbed down people believe—but the spiritual man sees through this ruse."

"Then you believe in man—which must be the writers' license. I think of the poor writer, struggling between good and evil, between optimism and hopefulness on the one hand and cynicism and pessimism on the other. Your path is not an easy one. In any case, since the religious instinct in man is as great as the instinct to eat, I find in my work too that most people wish they could believe."

"Pére François, you talk more like a literary critic than a Catholic priest; you've told me in a few words more about my work than my few critics ever have."

"Just to finish the thought, I must say that I was struck by the note of sadness in the book about the end of an affair and had the thought that you were not only speaking of the love affair, but of, well, of life itself."

"Your perspective is unusual."

"Admittedly, I was looking for that direction in your books after my dear friend Ivaan told me about the tragedy in your life. I hope that spiritual context in your thinking is of some help to you and your beautiful wife."

"I hope so, but for the present the most important assistance has come to me from another direction…"

"I know. I know what you are going to say. It seems I knew you before our physical meeting and I must explain why. I have many friends in this city and one of them is a man named Karl Zetkin."

John started. "You know Zetkin? My doctor, my shrink? Well, Pére, this is astounding. You could be a character in one of my books. I mean, I believe one hundred percent in coincidences but this is stretching the role of chance. So how do you happen to know him?"

"A few years ago Karl and I attended a series of lessons on the esoteric together and have remained friends since. I live near him, so we meet frequently."

"So you met him by chance too! I was searching the Internet for a psychiatrist and found him. I called him chiefly because I liked his name for political reasons. Apparently I made the right choice because he has helped me immensely."

"So you're the person he told me about, a person with a black hole in his life."

"Hmm. Pére, what you tell me is confirmation of my belief that we are all somehow connected. That Zetkin and I, Martha my wife and Samantha—uh, my daughter—Ivaan my friend, even those two secret agents standing over there by the window—even though like most policemen they don't believe in such coincidences—and now you, that we are all connected in surprising ways. I think that kind of connection drives my work. For it seems to me that unlikely occurrences happen more frequently than we think. People who are searching—spiritual people—people looking for those unexpected occurrences make them happen. And the more you notice events all around you, the more they happen—but you still have to believe in them first! And then they make the world a magical place. That's why writers see coincidences and policemen don't."

"Then you probably know that Jung dealt in such related connections—the paranormal like extrasensory perception—and he coined the word that expresses such events: synchronicity."

"Pére François, this very conversation is an example of that synchronicity."

"Well, John Sutton, you indeed have heavy baggage to carry around with you. Meanwhile you might look into my church here in the Arab quarter where there are more believers in coincidences than policemen think. They think their life in Paris is all one great coincidence."

"And so do I. The policemen—I suppose it's because of their work—see every Arab as a potential terrorist; you and I see every Arab as a fellow human being looking for his way. And speaking of policemen, Pére, those two secret agents over there only look like diplomats but in reality they're agents of the top secret organization that terrorists attacked some years ago. You remember when terrorist bombs killed all those people at the Coupole, well, the real target was the DGSE office building adjoining it; it was destroyed. My wife and I were there that night and so was Ivaan so since then those two agents keep pestering us with questions about terrorists. They know I'm here right now and keep sneaking looks at me. Now they'll likely ask you what I said—please tell them everything I've said."

"I know the story and I know them too. Because I have my parish here they believe I know everything happening in the Parisian Arab world and from time to time they visit me also."

"They imitate MI5 and the CIA also in language and call us anything from informants to assets to mere contacts. They don't understand people like us who share many opinions and beliefs with terrorists; people who try to understand their frustrations and their motivations. But that doesn't mean we support terrorism. Today they have at least three of us here in one place—you, Ivaan and me—but they're shy about speaking to us about such things here. Anyway, Pére, I'm going over to speak to them. And when they ask you, please tell them everything."

Briefcase and sidekick seemed transformed. Since the Coupole affair and their first visit to me, they had apparently moved up the hierarchical ladder of the DGSE. I saw that when they came to Rue Fabert the same day Martha returned from London. Now they dress in Parisian finery and attend cocktail parties held in ambiguous places.

"Well, gentlemen, still on the Ivaan Amrani trail, I see, and here on diplomatic territory."

"Monsieur Amrani was kind enough to invite us. And we see you also know Pére François. *Bien, bien*, a small world, no?"

"Actually Ivaan didn't even invite me! My wife and I dropped in by chance. But why you, I wonder? You who seem convinced he's a terrorist."

"Not that he's terrorist but that he could be the puppeteer who moves the terrorists. At the very least he seems to know what is about to happen in that world before it happens."

"So it's all suspicion, the famous policeman's intuition, eh?"

"It's more than that."

"More than what?"

"More than just intuition, I assure you—although our intuition should not be dismissed a priori," Briefcase said in a new refined manner of the man of power, no longer the innocuous secret agent of several years ago. His name, he says, is Null. His colleague is Henri.

"Things do happen," Null goes on. "Again and again things happen, facts accumulate, and the same people pop up again and again, somehow involved, somehow touched, somehow and in some way moving events. Chance at work? We don't know. Still, the facts are that you were at the Coupole and Ivaan was at the Coupole when terrorists attacked France. Your presences there alone demand our attention. Imagine you were a policeman, would the presence of foreigners like you and Ivaan—Communists who hate the system the police defend—not arouse your curiosity? Of course it would."

"I was at the Coupole that night and also Ivaan was there but so were you and I assume others of yours were also at the Coupole. In this post-Coupole period the latter thought has remained fixed in me. I know I was there by a pure caprice of my wife; I don't know the reasons for your presence there."

"Nor do you know why Ivaan was there," Henri said, on which Null fixed his eyes on his vice-agent to silence him. So now I know that they believe Ivaan is the putative puppeteer who pulls the strings and they want to know who for. They must have suspicions.

The atmosphere suddenly became tight, almost airless and you had to gasp for air. Although no direct accusations had been made, despite the brouhaha of forced gaiety and sounds of loud talk and laughter here and there among this odd mixture of people with no common denominator—Europeans and non-Europeans, diplomats, policemen and spies, a Catholic priest and communists and beautiful women—yet ambiguity hung thick in the atmosphere on the noble floor of the apartment building in the Goutte d'Or. For some reason John still dwelled on the inexplicable fact that Ivaan had expressly not invited Martha and him and *did* invite the secret agents. Was it simply to belie the closeness of their friendship? Or was there more?

"As we have felt for some time in this post-Coupole era— we feel this every day—something big, something intense and enormous is in the air," Null said. "Life style is changing. People are confused. People no longer know what to believe in. Sparks of revolt are everywhere and our job is to catch the terrorists and rebels and render them harmless before those sparks become conflagration. After our gallant police suppressed the first mild protests among Sorbonne students in Paris, the rabble-rousers reacted in all of France—they were only waiting for the right occasion. Within a month the revolt infected workers and trade unions, social organizations, students' parents of the 1968 generation, high school students, teachers, professors and rectors of French universities."

"You make it sound more like revolution than the reaction of a handful of rabble-rousers. But as you say, it does recall 1968—whatever the spirit of today. I like to imagine the events of that year on Boulevard St. Germain parading by Camus and Sartre confabulating in the Café de Flore; but then, Null, those were spontaneous events that soon sputtered out under waves of the reaction you must love."

"Hmm," Null mumbled. "I wouldn't go so far as to...well, I too believe things are changing, you know."

While he searched for a real reply, John shifted his position so that he could see the center of the room where Martha had remained, silent and the usual out-of-place look on her face. He also noticed that Ivaan from his position on the far side of the room among a group of Middle Eastern types was also watching Martha. A touching sign of his care that began when he got her to the hospital in time and became godfather and Uncle Ivaan for Samantha. Was his care not a sign of the friendship thus far missing in his life? Or was there more than meets the eye?

"Still," John continued pompously, "that spontaneity must have planted seeds of rebellion, seeds that usually splinter into little rivulets and die out as soon as minor objectives are achieved. But one day an overturn of everything will happen now that there are people—not many yet—ready to manage the revolt. Such people are aware of what is happening—of the real reasons for rebellion, I mean to say—not just you and your DGSE. But yes, you must be pleased that the great majority of people are unaware of their real situation; people are simply afraid to see the truth about where we stand—or they don't want to know."

12.

Nine-Three

Silence reigns. No winds from the river. Fog swirls. And above the fog, somewhere high above it all in the infinity, storms are melding one into the other and forming one great storm. No birds hopping on the Esplanade today. The twenty cannons of Invalides are mere shadows. Stillness. Traffic on Rue Saint-Dominique at a standstill. Silence within the silence. In an end times atmosphere in the quiet air beneath the brewing storm, John heads toward the Russian bridge, from time to time peering upwards into the gray nothingness, certain that he is perceiving the sensation of a social mutation too, a transformation of being. He perceives every fiber of his body, his eyes, his weakened legs, the click-click-click of bone-on-bone in his hips and the by now merely imaginary swell of his ankle. Like every day He thinks of 9/17. He tells himself it is the creaking of his soul in tune with the changing universe: his soul is mutating. He would not be John Sutton much longer…nor would you be you. The art deco lamps on the Russian bridge emit only faint hints of light. From the balustrade he peers down at the riverboats moored along the right bank. He observes the shadowy figures—thirty, forty, fifty—darting around, and then congregating under the bridge. He hears hoarse voices rising through the fog.

Terrorists, he thinks spontaneously.

Ivaan's people?

Does Ivaan know they are there? John doesn't know what to think of them. What do Islamic terrorists themselves think they are doing? Fighting for human rights? Do they realize they're manipulated by Western intelligence? Or do they think they're making a revolution? A noble idea: Arab-Frenchmen forging the revolution that the French people should again make for themselves. The revolution that some Europeans used to dream of against their own governments, against the European Union, against their foreign masters. Slaves revolting against their foreign slave masters. The millennia old story is no longer the same. The elan is gone. The conundrum is complex. There are no guides; no guiding lines to follow; not even a theory to show the way. And he has only Ivaan. His guide. A revolutionary leader. Or was he a puppeteer? as Null suggested.

Ivaan was waiting at the Gare du Nord. The unavoidable maleficent Gare du Nord: his arrival there with Martha the first time, the one-day tunnel train trips from there to his publisher in London, the return there with his sprained ankle, the baggage cart and Samantha, Samantha, Samantha. Today, Ivaan was to meet a friend, a fellow Egyptian, Communist, and community leader in Saint-Denis in the ill-famed department 93.

They take the degraded RER train to the heart of the *banlieue*, the poor, ugly suburb on the northeast side of Paris with a million and a half people—seven hundred thousand of whom are Muslims: Aubervilliers, Villemomble, Drancy, Aulnay sous Bois. John had to see the bases of the Arab-French "terrorists-revolutionaries": how and where they lived, the effects of ghettoization and unemployment, the social realities of the lives of the terrorists who bombed the Coupole and who defy the world around them, a world they do not understand, a world that does not understand them. When their train emerged from the tunnel and crossed the périphérique ring road, they entered another world, a parallel world to the world of the Paris inside the ring road: a landscape of graffiti-covered walls, run-down shops battened down and secured against a tornado, office buildings in glass amidst closed stores and For Sale signs, piles of smoldering trash and above all, groups of twenty-story high public housing complexes, the *cités*, inhabited by Arabs and blacks. Halal shops, djellabas and hijabs and signs in Arabic everywhere. No policemen to be seen. Dreamscape! John perceived a sense of uneasiness. Everything was changing fast in the present out of control, the past erased from memory. The absences cast a black cloud over the future: things would never again be the same as before.

They met Ivaan's contact at a small café near a *cité* at around noon. The few customers were drinking coffee or beer. Ahmed—real name or not—was about Ivaan's age, affable, about John's height and had a powerful physique, spoke beautiful English like most educated Egyptians. He was pleased to meet and brief an English writer and comrade and asked if John had been in the *banlieue* before; John said only on passing express trains and that he was seeing the first *cités* today.

"You don't want to see them on the inside; you might not ever come out again," Ahmed said.

Every single one of the other customers had left. Except for the white French waitress now in the kitchen, the café was empty. And anyway she would not understand Arabic or English.

"That's what people said about the Chartres labyrinth," John said, "I got back out but it didn't do what I'd hoped for me."

Ahmed looked perplexed at Ivaan. A long explanation in Arabic followed during which John imagined his friend revealing the background to his walking the labyrinth.

"So how are negotiations with the others going?" Ivaan asked.

"What negotiations? Talks are going nowhere. And there is really nowhere to go."

Aware they spoke English about this apparently key subject for him, John asked the obvious: "What groups? And negotiations about what?"

Ivaan picked at his fingernails and looked toward the windows framing a huge apartment building decorated in graffiti up to the second floor.

Ahmed flexed his shoulder muscles under a tight wind jacket, put on glasses and read the Arabic writing on the back of an envelope, nodded at Ivaan and began:

"The social stratifications are complex out here in nine-three. Very little crossing over from one class or level to another. This is a poor area on the whole, though there are some who've made it in the older immigrations, like Italians or Spanish or even Chinese, who maintain their equanimity even here. And there are the French who have always lived here. These people are not rich—if they were they'd be in Paris or in south France—but some are comfortable and feel this is their home. We're concerned only with the Islamic immigration—seven hundred thousand of us— many of them are second or third generation and have lived their whole lives with their own people. But we, those like Ivaan and me, like you too, remember that once nine out of ten Muslims in the world were ruled by non-Muslims. Many of those Muslims are still alive. Did you know that only four Muslim countries escaped European imperialism?"

"Astounding. But still, your society here sounds like a lonely world, and that right here in Paris. Certainly a lonelier world than mine. Travel time from Gare du Nord was short but coming to Saint-Denis seemed like going abroad."

"You're right in that. Everyone here is uprooted from their past in one way or another. Keep in mind, Comrade John Sutton, that Saint-Denis is another world. It's part of Paris but many people here never "go to Paris". If you're a twenty-year old Arab or a black from Mali who speaks a crazy kind of French that Parisians don't even understand, Paris is a foreign land: mean and racist and stupid and where everybody is rich and their riches make the ignorant Arab immigrant feel lowly and vulgar, the scum of the earth. Much of the younger generation has broken with French mainstream society and values. The distance between the Champs-Elysées and nine-three is insuperable. Arab souls and French hearts are in total disaccord."

"Ahmed, that's a point of view Parisians have no inkling about. Saint-Denis and the whole nine-three department mean one thing to them: terrorism."

"Yet, we are here. We are *their* problem; Paris and France and the world are our problem."

"And that's another new point of view for me!"

"Seven hundred thousand people in the nine-three. That's a micro-society. And that society has major social divisions like in Paris, like in all of France: rich and poor, educated and non-educated, white and brown, and black and brown, conservative and progressive. For conservatives, nine-three is an egregious problem;

for progressives it should be seen as an enormous opportunity to solve greater geo-political, socio-political problems between the western world and Islam. In the micro-society of nine-three, the divisions are similar to those in Paris, but not the same. Social divisions—class and color divisions—that seem insuperable make our emergent leaders seem like a parliament—a parliament that however never meets. The lowest and the most brutal and the most hopeless and the poorest—at the very lowest rung in society—are the unemployed, uneducated, violent youth who only react to their situation, even though in fact they don't even understand their own situation. Led by a handful of ruthless organizers from Al-Qaeda and accompanied by foreign fighter returnees from Syria who fought in the anti-Assad forces, or in Libya, they think they are capable of destroying worlds. They're paid a daily wage to do the things they like best. They lash out at the enemy, Paris, killing or being killed. Sometimes, it's terrorism. But not terrorism to achieve specific goals; only revenge against the world."

"Paid by whom?" John asked spontaneously.

Ahmed looked at Ivaan. "It's ok", Ivaan said, I thought meaning that I'm safe.

"I think you know who pays. For them, a violent demonstration is just another day's work! Organized terrorism is more demanding. You need experienced fighters. Mercenaries. Recruited and paid by NATO and your French friends of the DGSE. If you've fought in Syria or Libya you don't care. You want to fight someone. It's an open secret in the nine-three. Nearly anyone can sign up—after a security check."

A moment of silence fell. John could hardly absorb what he was hearing. The situation was explosive. Though he'd once thought revolution was not hopeless, in this setting not even real revolutionaries could think of revolution. This was another world, a world distant from his.

"Comrade, look out that window!" Ahmed continued. "See that kid sitting on the wall near the entrance to that building, he's a 'watcher' for police presence, in spoken language here called a *shouf* –Arabic for 'watch'. Drug dealers pay him two thousand euros a month just to watch and police don't touch him because he's a minor. Why should he go to school? Why look for non-existent work? His future is death at an early age. Drug dealers lie outside the micro-society but they are also a major part of it. Drugs are not part of our camp but we would like to convert that generation lost to drugs to our cause."

"What do you mean, our cause?"

"I mean Communism in general and the unified Islamic world in particular."

"So what about their leaders? Are they terrorists or revolutionaries? Or both? Al-Qaeda or soldiers of the future?"

"Potential revolutionaries, yes. They are not yet completely lost. They lead the youth of that lowest level, the ones we Communists should eventually lead in a new revolution.

"The second level group uses the same violence of the first to achieve specific goals: better education for this youth that can't speak proper French, fair employment, police to control the drugs traffickers, decent housing. Those goals are laudable but they stop there.

"The third level is ours: protest has to be organized and point beyond Paris to all of France, to the rest of Europe like Germany and the Netherlands with their great immigrant communities, who instead of being the number one social problem for the countries they live in, could lead the way to social—and eventually—revolutionary change."

"Wow!" John exclaimed. "Immigration does contain the stuff of historical revolution—and no one recognizes it. But still, what about Islam? I hear the word Islamist, but seldom Islam."

"John, Comrade, the truth is that between extremists on the one end and Muslims questioning the foundations of their faith on the other stand the masses. Muslim masses, asocial and disunited, people who watch soccer games and drink alcohol. They fear the extremists and their violence, but they also fear the extermination of Islam. But the great ideological divide is between those who want to subordinate Islam to progress and those who want to subordinate progress to Islam. Most Muslims in reality want a normal country where the state defines what Islam is to be—but they have no idea of how to achieve it."

"Like Beirut," Ivaan said, "that great city is the acme of a non-Jewish, western civilization in the Middle East. And it's Arab. But Beirut is not the right model for other Arabs either. Arabs need a new path. With one eye over our shoulder at our great civilizations of the past and the other on the future, we have to renew our culture without confusing our future with our past. We have to modernize Arab lifestyle and adapt western science as the West once did ours. Just because Arabs shoot guns in the air and ride camels doesn't mean they don't have a broad Weltanschauung. Look how adaptable we are today, despite the long imperialism. The Arab can adapt easily in Europe but the European seldom adapts to the Arab world. See the Algerians in France, the Moroccans in Spain, the Iraqis and Palestinians everywhere. We

Arabs have wide horizons—but there are few Lawrences from the West today."

"But still, Ivaan, what you feel in the air here in Paris is real," Ahmed said. "Something big is going to happen. It's true. Their leaders have revealed that much to me personally. They want us, the politically committed, to join them in a united battle."

"So what is going to happen?" Ivaan asked, surprisingly in a manner foreign to him, innocent and naïve, which John knew he was not. Why that fiction? he wondered.

"Whatever you say remains with us," Ivaan added.

"Hard to be precise," Ahmed said. "I doubt they themselves know all the details but they claim it's to be the biggest attack on France since World War Two. And I believe them. France has over six million Muslims, ten per cent of the nation, one-third of Europe's Muslims. There are one thousand five hundred mosques in France, fifty of which are radical. Half of the prison population is Muslim. Though more radicalized since September Eleven, the Iraqi war and France's ban on veils in schools, the protests have not yet taken on a religious slant. Young rioters are not interested in Islam. The revolt is not about Islam. In fact, Islamic organizations forbid Muslims' participation in the violence. The real problems are social and economic. In Clichy-sous-Bois, near Paris's sleek Charles de Gaulle International Airport, 48% of young people, nearly all Muslims, are unemployed. No money, nothing to do, excluded from the moveable feast of rich Paris. So why not smash windows and burn cars and kill some people. Violence is the only means of expression left. France has aimed at a melting pot society: integration of the peoples from its former colonies into the great Republic of France is the motto. Integration to be achieved by social mobility; but the ideal of moving up the social ladder through work contrasts with the reality of unemployment and social discrimination. There are no minorities in the French government or black-skinned TV announcers. The melting pot has failed. Alienation and ghettoization of the ex-colonial peoples is the reality. Since the dawn of the new millennium some observers have had premonitions of a great revolt of the poor. Now it's here. And the underlying causes are familiar: the widening gap between rich and poor, unemployment, cuts in welfare, bad schools, and racial discrimination. Even third generation Algerians are marginalized and alienated. This is to be a major insurrection against the state, plans honed for years and sophisticated weapons and explosives collected. Besides being poor, unemployed and without incentives, the insurrectionists are Muslims because their parents are Muslim—French citizens by law. Second and third generation Muslims from former French colonies, alienated and discriminated against, they neither have the countries of origin of their parents, nor are they accepted as full-fledged citizens in France. They belong nowhere, only to themselves. They have nowhere to go. An unknown past, a shitty present and no future. For such reasons they hate. Hate the French. Especially they hate intellectuals like you, who analyze them and write about them in learned journals. They detest the world. They don't give a shit for life itself. To live or die is the same. They even scare me. Like they scare the French government that can't change its policies now—it's too late—and Paris doesn't even dare send its policemen here. The sparks of this uprising have been veiled behind zero tolerance, state of emergency laws, curfews, and blaming the parents of rioters and threats to cut off their already meager welfare, against a background of racist police, social discrimination and economic segregation. And Ivaan, the hope is that also French students and workers will join in and together they can force the government to negotiate on their social objectives. Even the police know there are plenty of arms in the nine-three but they don't seem to know much more—except that something is in the air. In any case, I heard that everything is to begin here in Saint-Denis with an attack on the huge football stadium, Stade de France, during an international game. Then, to Paris. Many pieces of the action are already in place; armed and trained people—and a big number of suicide bombers—are already hidden in apartments of trusted people, boyfriends and girlfriends, in different parts of the city—from Champs-Elysées to the Bastille. The plan is for simultaneous or timed attacks, first one place, then the other, to spread panic and terror. By the way, insurrectionist leaders joke among themselves that it will be a bad night for French music lovers! So music halls are a target! I have narrowed them to down to two: first, the Olympia—big and popular, but since it is in mid-town, near the Opera—it is better protected. So there remains the Bataclan, also big, and hence with probably less police presence. And they don't forget the experience at the Coupole that makes other big Montparnasse cafés natural targets: Le Select and La Closerie des Lilas. Then, the rail stations; I heard specifically that since Saint-Denis people hate in a special way the Gare du Nord—for them, the gateway to Paris—it is a target. Now for you, Ivaan, this is important: they asked me to help spread rumors among government officials about the huge numbers—that is, the many hundreds of insurrectionists and the very very hard to find suicide bombers-martyrs, ready to blow themselves up in the metro, in buses, crowded cafés and theaters—and that the police are insufficient, that they'll need the military to control the whole city. Imagine soldiers patrolling the streets of Paris! A great defeat for the national government.

"So, that sums up what I know or guess based on what I've been told or what I've heard. And I repeat, the leaders of this insurrection would be pleased if the part about military intervention becomes well known."

"My God, this in France," John said. "Unbelievable that this is even happening...and within Paris, the City of Light. The golden myth of the western world. If what you describe happens, the structure of the European Union itself will be shaken."

"Still, comrades, this is not our final goal. But the rebellion of the would-be working class of Saint-Denis in nine-three is a start. It's not yet revolution; but it may be one of the first stages of the process of revolution; revolt and insurrection can lead to the transformation we work for: the overthrow of the system. Now, comrades, I'll leave first. Wait thirty minutes or so before you go back to the station."

The Saint-Denis communist embraced each of them and left in the same quiet way the other café patrons had when the three of them had entered. John sat at their table, stunned, speechless, waiting for the minutes to pass; Ivaan appeared blasé—as if he'd known all along.

"Is it to be revolution?" John asked

"Not yet. No, not yet." Then, silence until they were on the RER back to the city: "Social awareness is yet to be born in a concrete form in the West. But that first basic step is in gestation in today's pandemic crisis. In America some people are asking why they have no public health care like in France. French people are asking why the wars. Social awareness should be bursting forth, to be followed by contagious rebellion against the absence of the social and against the wars. When true social awareness will be born, then, perhaps, a revolution can be made. Revolution is not a spontaneous affair, John; it is a result. The events of 2014 were semi-spontaneous and, in time, they sputtered out amidst waves of reaction. But spontaneity helps plant the seeds of rebellion, which still splinter into rivulets and die out when minor objectives are achieved. Still, something always remains. Shadows remain. But an overturn of everything that was, and still is, has to be nourished. It has to be managed. First we have to deal with the initial step. With awareness. Without awareness of our real condition every act of rebellion is infantile, like stamping one's foot and saying 'no' just to be ornery. Essential is the awareness of the real reasons for rebellion. That is where 99% of Westerners stand today: enmeshed in a cloud of unawareness of the real situation. Afraid to look into a mirror and see themselves for what and where they are."

When the train went back underground, John was looking out the window at the passing suburbs and considering Ivaan's analysis of what they'd just heard. John said uneasily: "Seems crazy now, but at least while they're trying to make the revolution, all revolutionaries feel pride and invincibility, secure and self-righteous in their beliefs."

"John, they have to. At that moment, that's all they have."

"But then they have to face up to the new reality they've created."

"And that's the hard part. But even though I'm aware of that reality, I'm no less a revolutionary."

John closed the elevator door behind him, gazed down the irritatingly endless corridor, and called 'Martha'! Then, again. A third time. The mansion-like apartment was unusually dark. The fog hadn't completely lifted today. No lights were on. The end of the corridor was as dark as it had been that day years ago when they first arrived here when they'd kissed in the black hole at the end, as dark as a metro tunnel, dark like Underground, he thought and felt the familiar twinge of anxiety on the point of transforming into blocked elevator panic. Spontaneously, his eyes turned toward the telephone table standing against a front wall on which they left door keys, mail and messages. And from several meters distance he saw what he realized he subconsciously looked for every time he returned home: an envelope of Martha's beige stationery addressed to "John". In trepidation he took out the folded sheet of matte paper and, before unfolding it, held it at waist height, at a distance from himself, and fantasized about its contents: she had re-enrolled at a French literature course and would return at around six; she was having a medical check-up in the hypothetical case they were to decide on another child; or she was shopping somewhere and why didn't he join her? Yet, the peculiar silence, a definitive kind of silence infecting their mammoth apartment told him the true truth: Martha was gone. The first words he read were: *John, don't you ever leave me.* Then: *For now I have to go. I'm returning to London, to my father's, for an indefinite period. Until I re-find myself. Until I find Martha again. I am letting you down now, but I think this is right. I know you have suffered, that you still suffer, and also because of me. You are my life. John, don't ever leave me. Yours.*

For days on end he alternately waited for her call or her return and at the same time—now, more for distraction than for commitment—he pondered the upcoming massive attack on the heart of Europe, the attack that seemed to him as certain as her inevitable return.

The days passed.

The weeks passed.

Martha did not return; she had evaded again.

Rumors were ever wilder; but nine-three terrorists did not strike.

He had a new dream for Zetkin. A psychedelic incubus. I see me. I am my phantom, mine alone. I see a great red dot. The word *massive* hangs in the thickening air. The air is white. I am the main character in what I know is a *pesadilla*. Pantomime in an incubus. Magical happenings all around me. People whispering. People asking if I am real. Am I anything at all? Or am I dead? Yet there are the remembrances! Do the dead remember how it was? I can try now that I have only time. I know turmoil is beginning.

His publisher liked his new proposal of his novel set in the Republic of San Marino, and he said to himself: *Les jeux sont faits.*

Part Two

13.

Return To San Marino

John stood on the central piazza in San Marino City perplexed as to what he should do first. A middle-sized suitcase plastered with old travel stickers—it had belonged to his father—and an attaché case stood at his feet. Though in principle it should be reassuring, return home was an ambiguous expectation; he didn't perceive the only-place-in-the-world-for-me sensation he'd imagined he would. Now that he was here again, he realized that San Marino could never be what he felt it would be at the time his publisher had accepted his proposal for a book set here in one of his former home places. As he'd experienced in Old Rotterdam, in the Hague, in Munich and in Paris, San Marino too, he feared would likely turn out to be a disillusionment, that it could never correspond to the enchanting childhood image of the hill town fixed in his deceitful memory and that in the end he would wonder what he was doing here. He'd come to believe that if you're forever uncertain whether one place or the other is your right place in the world, you're just fixated on the idea of "home" in general—home a symbol of times when things were better in the world. Yet the search for the one place that was his own was the real story of his life.

The Mexican shaman in Guanajuato had taught him that humans like animal beings need that one fixed spot on earth that is theirs. It's instinct. Yet, standing again on the familiar piazza, he doubted that San Marino could ever be his real place in the world. He'd been like one of the fortunate Galapagos baby turtles that escape the nefarious buzzards circling overhead in order to fulfill his destiny: return. In his maturity he had headed back here just as the turtle does to Galapagos. For that reason, perhaps, in life there also arrives a no less important counter-moment when you just want to strike camp and set out for new parts, hoping that people and things elsewhere will not be the same as what you've seen and experienced in your dark, jagged past; in his case, first in Underground and then in his great suffering over Samantha. Still, John had always had a metaphysical problem of his very own: what to do with his life and where to do i? For that reason he'd never been at ease. Never tranquil. That same uneasiness that bothers most men from birth: even behind the bars of the cradle men are uneasy; then in the schools and later in the public places of the world, sex and ambition drive them ahead. Thinking such thoughts, he perceived the familiar anxiety in his stomach and a tinge of the leg weakness starting from his ankle leading up to and joining the other symptoms still settled in his stomach or in some hidden synapse…or perhaps in his soul.

Nevertheless, he felt lucky on this day; he was pleased to find San Marino much as he remembered it of when he lived here with his mother. Same streets, same stone houses, even the same Bora winds that his mother had so feared—the cold northern winds regularly blowing over the tiny country clinging to the sides of a central Italian mountain.

On that first day of his return, he found the perfect apartment halfway up Mount Titano with a view toward Rimini and the Adriatic Sea, a three-room flat where he would write his *San Marino Blues* love story. That title had sold his proposal to his London publisher: a novel set in the tiny, Communist-governed Republic of San Marino. In the beginning, he spoke with Martha every day; then, when it became clear to both that their talks were perfunctory and they had less to recount about their separate lives, they spoke less frequently. She said her life was humdrum in her father's London townhouse where she spent her time reading French literature and searching for a subject for her dissertation; John spoke of his struggle with the first chapter of his love story. And from time to time, she still ended conversations with the same binding words as she had the day they first met on the London-Paris tunnel train: "*Sutton, don't you ever leave me.*"

He hadn't really gotten into the new book, when the publisher asked him—as he had all his writers—if he could provide quickly a series of short personalized articles for a new literary weekly magazine he was founding as a support for his publishing house. The new magazine was to be named: *The Conceptual World of Fiction.*

John accepted the opportunity with alacrity—anything to give him more time to get his mind wrapped around his San Marino novel. Time for time. A reprieve. Just the idea of such short pieces galvanized him into action. He felt the opportunity like the necessary creative shot in the arm to clarify his thoughts on the act of writing. How and why did it happen that he was a fiction writer anyway? What were his thoughts about the literary act? After an early morning start the next day, by mid-afternoon he had his first article ready:

"Fiction Writing "

By John Sutton

Though my personal preference for fiction over non-fiction has less significance today, I want to show some of the reasons for my preference for the former without ignoring the narrowing differences between fiction and non-fiction today.

Although not everyone loves literary fiction, since telling stories is as old as man, I believe it will always exist in some form or another. In recent years the novel has been widely debated and discussed—and also maligned—while the fictional novel itself is already fragile and sensitive to changing times and changing tastes of readers living enormously changed lives from those experienced by preceding generations. As a result, the reality that fiction writers seek has changed. For such reasons, the survival of the novel as an art form is a tricky question, yet pertinent because it is a reservoir of values and morality, and thus plays a major role in the struggle between good and evil.

However, one is right to wonder if old forms of the novel adequately describe our rapidly changing times. In an age of fast-lived lives and instant communication there is little time for the distracting detailed storytelling as during those former dusty slow rides in carriages to cover fifty miles for a cup of tea with a distant friend. Traditional fiction thus seems to some people a vestige of the past, at times a luxury that no few readers reject. On the other hand, even though a great deal of up-to-date facts and reality enter into any story, the fictional aspect of the novel nonetheless remains—the imaginary and the what-ifs of life.

Since political—as well as economic—events determine to a great extent the tenor of our lives, the novel easily transforms into "the political novel" or "factual fiction". The bare story itself is set in real places where real history is being made from minute to minute, and real political events are taking place, which for some readers of pure traditional fiction is off-putting because political reality in our turbulent times can easily overshadow the story itself—romance or adventure or pure action—so that non-fiction seems to them a more appropriate container.

Nonetheless, the invented characters of fiction, the geographic locales, the love affairs, the violence, the hate and pardon, provide the framework for the personal passions and fears, the successes and failures so necessary to flavor the story itself and provide characters and words and concrete ideas arising from daily realities with which the reader may identify more easily and, thus, be lured into the political and the ideological aspects of the novel.

Then there is the tricky and complex question of time to be resolved. E. M. Forster in Aspects of the Novel affirms that time must always be reckoned with: "... a story is a narrative of events arranged in time sequence." Events succeed one after another like the days follow one after the other. The writer is more or less compelled to follow some time sequence, even if very lightly, although some writers today find that concept old-fashioned as shown in novels in which time is largely ignored and sometimes truant, no matter the risks to probability and possibility. Still, in the search for reality, time plays a major role of truth. Not that time is necessarily constant or honest, but the clock continues to play its role in my own life.

So what happens within the time span of the story is the essence, as is above all how the invented characters feel about the occurrences. Within a certain time, passions emerge and intrigues, crimes, and war occur. And, as a result of changing times, the writer's judgments and considerations of real values and of their great container, Morality, change. Within this churning time sequence, intensity grows as layer after layer of the story itself—each layer perhaps separate and mysterious and inexplicable at the time it occurs—merge into something cohesive.

The most esteemed fiction writers whose work has only the thinnest guise of fiction are instead, let us say, philosophers who use the barest storyline as an allegory to express the most abstract feelings and subjective views of the innermost of the human being. For example, Kafka is not so highly considered, nor is his work so complex, simply because he wrote a story about a man who is transformed into a cockroach, or a man being tried on unknown charges.

I am presently reading an essay on Kafka by Walter Benjamin included in his book, Illuminations. I first read Kafka when I was too inexperienced to see the resemblance of Kafka's work to poetry, and furthermore I was blind to much of his allegory: he was writing about how life and work are organized in our society—which he relates to destiny. A sad situation for man! In a conversation about pre-World War One Europe and the decline of the human race, Kafka once said to his friend Max Brod that "we are nihilistic thoughts, suicidal thoughts that come into God's head. Our world is only a bad mood of God"...and concluded that "there is no hope for us."

In that sense, Kafka found that 'man is always in the wrong with God.' And in his renowned novel, The Trial, man is on trial by higher authorities—God, Power, Big Brother—but he never clearly understands on what charges. Therefore, Walter Benjamin (1892-1940) could write during the Nazi madness in Europe in the 1930s-40s: "I think of the modern citizen who knows that he is at the mercy of a vast machinery of officialdom whose functioning is directed by authorities that remain nebulous even to the executive organs, let alone to the people they deal with. The only hope of the accused is postponement and more postponement so that the trial proceedings do not turn into judgment. Therefore," Benjamin concludes, "Kafka's shame. Shame both for himself, the defendant, but shame also for the others, the judges. An illuminating idea indeed!

Another contemporary conclusion was Franz Kafka's views on progress: "To believe in progress is not to believe that progress has already taken place. That would be no belief." Kafka did not consider the age in which he lived as an advance over the beginnings of time. His was a prophetic deduction. Such a statement would be valid in any discussion of progress today. He, a fiction writer, but much more, predicted our current world.

It is said that Art stands still while History moves. The literary writer's art lies in the manner of the transmission to the reader of the author's passion, without which no life, no story, no novel, no non-fiction is valid. The passion! The passion from which emerges the writer's fantasies, his most intimate admissions, his insecurity, his fears of failure coupled with the hope of success, and with luck stumbling onto some magnificent prophecy that one day will justify and reward him.

John felt strength flow again hotly through his literary veins thanks to the few days of freedom from the chill emanated by the cloudy reality of his largely conceptual *San Marino Blues* novel which still had no beginning or end. During those invigorating days of freedom, even fears of the return of his symptoms were strangely absent—not even a hint of shoulder burning or leg weakness, while San Marino had neither underground metros nor elevators. At last, he was free of obsessions of even an imaginative repetition of the past—there would be no train travel to London when it rained, no running down slippery stairs, no ankle injuries, thus, he would run through the house with Samantha—and, and, and magically Samantha would be there, now five years old and ready for her first year in the elementary school down Rue Saint-Dominique near the Esplanade. Seeing his own salvation in what he thought of as his form of reality, he plunged into what seemed to himself a kind of fictional reality.

"Fiction Makes History More Realistic"

By John Sutton

As far as my own fiction about reality is concerned, I agree only partially with historians who perceive of history as a determining force that individual lives merely illustrate. Although pieces of history and much "place" decorate my own fiction, my major attention goes to fictional people who, I believe, make history not only true but also realistic. Fictional personae illustrate not only what people of the real world experience but show what they feel: the turmoil and conflicts that real people experience in their daily lives. History presents the facts. Fiction offers the reality for which most fiction writers strive. Fiction writers can reconstruct events as well as historians but also put real people in imaginary situations in a way historians cannot. Fred Weinstein in his History and Theory writes that while non-fiction gives you the facts, fiction give you the truth. History tells you what happened; fiction tells you how it felt. So readers sometimes wonder where history ends and fiction begins.

Moreover, pure history also has its limits. As in the example of the aftermath of war with which fiction writers often deal, there is no getting around the reality that the victors write the history of what has happened—their versions of history. Yet, both the victors and the defeated are living people, not just inanimate objects. Only in the very long term of the great sweep of the history of epochs can people be reduced to mere illustrators of history. After all, conquerors like Napoleon believed that 'history is the tale of the victors'. In a similar fashion, the historical significance of the Roman Empire emerges as proof that "pure" historicism has no heart. How can it have a heart when it is the history written by the victors? While the history that real people have lived challenges the imaginative capacity of historians to account for it, as Weinstein writes it is fiction that offers the heterogeneity and discontinuity that history written by historians cannot. Things exist, events occur, but will never be known unless they are revealed in words. But not everything that happens to us that can be reproduced in words can be actually said in a purely historical context.

Most novelists agree that fiction in general offers true, real and realistic history: Gore Vidal, Saul Bellow, E.L. Doctorow, Graham Greene, Norman Mailer, John Dos Passos, Robert Musil, Günther Grass, Carlos Fuentes, et al, believe that only fiction can bring readers closer to the subjective perceptions of people in history. As Nicola Chiaromonte writes in Paradox of History: Only in fiction and the imaginary can we learn something real about individual experience.

I had been thinking of a story set in postwar Germany where I once lived. I had tampered mentally with a story about the return home from the Russian front of a German veteran at the end of World War Two. My story would begin with the returnee's leap into the frenetic atmosphere of a destroyed Germany. At that time I read the wonderful historical novel, Europe Central, by William T. Vollmann, concerning chiefly Germany and Russia, two countries at the center of wide literary interests.

In my story outline, a small number of persons illustrate in a limited manner that tightly packed half century of history: the final years of World War Two, the division of both Germany and Europe into two parts, the Korean and Vietnam wars, the fall of Communist-led governments of East Europe, the NATO wars against Yugoslavia.

Simultaneously with these and other world-shaking events, also occurred the great swerve in the Western world during which peoples of Europe and the USA became acutely aware of the reality that everything, every aspect of life had rapidly changed from what it once was. So, the realities of very real people of our own times who have experienced these bewildering events crammed into such a restricted period can easily be depicted. And, as usual, it is in the fiction of writers like those mentioned above where the reality of that swerve emerges most clearly.

And three days later, again, John's third and likely last article:

"A LABYRINTH OF MISUNDERSTANDING"
By John Sutton

The unequal relationship between fictional literature and psychoanalysis has always rankled literary critics whose task it is to clarify, interpret, classify, rank and, especially in cases of political literature, bad-faith critics who grant themselves the right to brand and censor literature. While literary criticism often fails to perform positively—especially concerning the political novel—it is true that the entire realm of literature has consequently had to bow to the "scientific" authority of psychoanalysis and its claims of dominion over the mysteries of the writer's unconscious, whereby it interprets and informs what the writer, on the deepest level, is really saying with his words crafted in such a manner as to create literature from what would otherwise be just texts of connected words.

Today, perhaps due to a simultaneous tendency of literature and literary criticism to recognize the role of psychoanalysis and the tendency of the latter to step down a bit from its scientific pedestal from which, because of its "special knowledge", it has claimed a monopoly in the realm of meaningful interpretation of the body of language that is literature, the two realms show signs of drawing closer together. Meanwhile, the poor lonely writer is still squashed between literary critique, on the one hand, and scientific interpretation on the other. Just imagine the situation from the writer's point of view: the author who, in a long and lonely act has created a story from scratch and composed a text that qualifies for the denomination of literature, hopes he has produced real art that will appeal to the formidable array facing him consisting of reader and critic and in a sense, the publisher, too.

In any case, on the completion of the work, the writer's fundamental role ends. The established writer steps aside, in relief. The rest is salesmanship and exposure. The responsible publisher, who has hovered in the background thus far, should have been performing multiple crucial tasks: at the very start he chose a text he believed would appeal to many readers, a text hopefully favorable to critics and to the media and if possible to academia as well.

Literary critics will then translate, approving or sacking the poor writer's text for the benefit of the public, judging it and explaining to readers what the writer says in his work. Up to this point, the participants in the literary rodeo comprise elements directly involved in the production and dissemination of the final product.

It is here—not at a specific point in time—that a fifth component enters the scene like armed invader—the psychoanalyst—who will interpret the interpretations of the literary critics, delving into aspects of the facts, events, characters in the text and the persona of the author from which he or she draws conclusions from the unconscious (Freud) of the writer and his characters, conclusions capable of bewildering the unsuspecting creator who naively believed that only his genius had dreamed up and created the whole thing.

So how did the writer do it? The writer doesn't really know the full answer; he knows however that it involved much hard and lonely work. As a rule, memory provides the material. Childhood, life experiences with other persons and with the others encountered in a full life. Daydreams and fantasies, even those the writer is ashamed of—the use of which often results in the writer being considered naïve and childish—are treasure houses of material, also for the analyst.

Many writers use their dreams for ideas and inspiration in their literary creations. Years ago I underwent one year of therapy because of psychological problems resulting from the tragic loss of a loved one. My German therapist, a Freudian, prompted me to begin recording and making a conscious effort to remember parts of my rich and active dream life. Doing that period I became aware of how difficult it is to recount even the most vivid dream about which I had even made notes during the night. That difficulty is well-known to creators of the arts. The gap between the vivid, significant dream and the ragged bits and pieces you succeed in assembling and reproducing is a veritable morass of memory and language capacity. The words you manage to save—or liberate, according to Freud—emerge vague, gray, and dull, incommensurate with the original. It is the same as the difference between your real-life experiences, what you see or do in reality, and the deficient and pale words you find to describe in a literary fashion that experience, and what you really felt about the experience at the time.

Therefore, the materials, i.e. the emerging words the writer offers analysts, are simply too scant, too untrustworthy for analysis because deformed, distorted, perverted and corrupted in the reporting process, if not simply made up on the spur of the moment, so that the analyst searching for the thus far inaccessible in the unconscious mind of the subject is forced to accept as a given a false image of reality. As a result, the analyst too must improvise.

Imagine then the difficulty for the writer of political fiction, whose only resource is some kind of compromise between what he feels he must say and the diluted expression of the idea. For both critic and analyst will respond not only with criticism or analysis of the literary text but also with a rebuttal based on their own personal political ideas or opinions as to what the writer said or should have said, a criticism or analysis that will be more and more deformed as it passes down from hand to hand, as with, say, the philosophies of Marxism or, to cite the most deformed and maligned, Leninism.

In the final analysis, scientific/academic analysis—because of the absence of authentic information—easily deforms and corrupts instead of clarifying the writer's intentions. For me, the Socratic metaphor of the three beds will always be emblematic of the problem of the degeneration from the ideal to the banal. According to the metaphor, the first bed, made by God, is the Platonic ideal; a carpenter then makes a second bed in imitation of that ideal bed; and the artist subsequently paints a third bed in imitation of the carpenter's imitation of the ideal bed. Later imitators then capture less and less of the ideal. They might just barely graze the reality of a carpenter making a bed or of an artist painting a carpenter making a bed, but they can never attain the true ideal of the original creation.

MARXISM AND EXISTENTIALISM

These two philosophies provide a wealth of materials for the contemporary fiction writer, who, if the writer is honest, cannot even conceive of an authentic novel without them. Both Marxism and Existentialism are materialisms close to human existence. Both reveal an area in which human consciousness is not master in its own house. They present a number of common major themes: the relation of theory and practice; the resistance to false consciousness and the problem of its opposite; the role and the risk of the concept of the midwife of truth, whether analyst or vanguard party; the re-appropriation of an alienated history and the function of the narrative; the question of desire and value and of the nature of false desire; the paradox of the end of the revolutionary process, which, like analysis, must surely be considered interminable rather than terminable.

Jean-Paul Sartre in Question de Mode *sees Marxism as the dominant philosophy of his era and existentialism as a reinforcing element. According to his form of Existentialism "existence precedes essence". Existentialists from Soren Kierkegaard to the contemporaries Sartre and Albert Camus believed that philosophical thought begins with the living human subject. Its supreme values are freedom of the individual and authenticity. For Sartre, and also Camus, the existentialist attitude is one of disorientation in the face of a meaningless or absurd world.*

For that reason Sartre has a low opinion of traditional ethics which he condemns as a tool of the bourgeoisie to control the masses, thus again reinforcing Marxist thought. Nor is he enamored of Freud's unconscious which he considers a scapegoat for the paradox of simultaneously knowing and not knowing (in the conscious and the unconscious minds) the same information.

That year, spring and summer months passed in what seemed an all-pervasive kind of sadness until one day, out of the blue, Martha called to say that she was on her way to Rue Fabert to check on the apartment. John's immediate thought was that reconciliation of their separate sufferings was around the corner. Still, that question of time hung heavy. Six months of calendar time had passed since their physical separation; but in reality, he knew, they'd been separated much longer—the years since Samantha.

Consequently, the announcement of her trip to Paris seemed like an invitation, a hint that their past together—their past of before Samantha—was reawakening in her innermost self. He had to go. Their physical rejoining might prove to be easier than he'd imagined: their Parisian lives could be renewed, friendships extended beyond Ivaan, the Rue Fabert apartment—so distant from their style—sold, and moving to another area far from their former life. Travel from San Marino abroad—beyond the invisible border with Italy, a conceptual security wall he had constructed in his mind between him in San Marino and the Paris of his nightmares —signified crossing the barrier also between him and the past that he strived to relegate to its proper place in memory, on which he still dwelled more than he should. Memory, that according to Zetkin was stored loosely in the fatuous hippocampus, seemed to John too impermanent a place for memory like his to be fixed. As usual, he was straying and constructing a new future out of a merely possible meeting with his past; but at least a conceptual Martha was waiting; and he welcomed any and all distractions that led away from his fixation on uncontrollable memories, the recollections and the reminiscences that returned to torture him, the most frequent and most unbearable of which was the incubus that was Necker Hospital and Samantha. In any case, he preferred the theory that uncertain as memories are they appear in one or other of the billions of connections in the human brain—the scary synapses—and from there they float around vaguely as human memories do, at first aimlessly, before they seemed to lose their way and wander and wander until they pop up in one synapse or the other. He wanted to retrieve and retain both, the good and the bad memories: the bad, suffered-for memories by now paid for in full, but above all, the permanent memories stored safely, he hoped, in newly created synapses, those memories that would finally, in some future time, settle into a healthy sadness, far from his former phobias and manias. His future good memories would even include snippets of the future record of his return to Martha and their past together including the nineteen kilometers to the Bologna airport, the flight to Orly in Paris, and the taxi carrying him back to Rue Fabert.

After six months, lonely months, after six months of slowly passing time, the moment he stepped into the foyer again, he felt a sense of vertigo. With a hand on the nearby mail-and- keys table, he steadied himself and let the dizziness pass in the way children do in the game of spinning round and round, before suddenly stopping and as their surroundings continue to whirl, they shout gleefully that they are drunk. Return is inebriating like that, he was thinking when he heard Martha running down the hall, only to abruptly slow to a careful walk as she approached him—as though she'd momentarily forgotten their separation and had suddenly realized that something was bizarrely awry in her welcome behavior.

Both were perplexed of mind and awkward of any action at all. Six months were six months. London was London and San

Marino, San Marino. They looked at each other, each waiting for a cue as to who should do what first. When he reached for her, she fell awkwardly against him, kissed him lightly on the lips, then, like years before, stepped back and this time said in a low voice:

"How strange."

"What is strange, Martha?"

"The strange feeling I just had of meeting again someone I used to know." Her thoughts showed on her face, in her eyes, in the movement of her delicate hands: she shouldn't even be here. It was still too soon. How could she've even considered the idea of starting over again: the same sexual love, perhaps the same travels to exotic places, adventure and danger, and, and, and eventually another child. Revival of the past was her torment. A future that did not include Samantha was to place Samantha outside of time. Martha's subconscious sin of replacing her with another child weighed heavy on her conscience, as if Samantha were just a number: Samantha number one, Samantha number two; the second stealing part of the first, diminishing the original Samantha to a mere model, like John's Socratic bed in his article she saw in a London magazine.

"There's always a moment like this, Martha—after too long a time—when your body is far ahead of your spirit. But I think we'll catch up with us."

"Do you really think so? Anyway, John Sutton, I have to catch a train in just a few minutes."

"Oh, I see." Only then did he notice she had a coat on and that her hand bag stood ready near the door—reconfirmation that their separation continued.

"Still, you did the right thing to come. And Sutton, I don't want to lose you too…lose the thing that is us."

"I'll never leave you, Martha."

"That's what you wrote in the book about the end of an affair. But he did."

"They did. But that was make-believe. People in books may seem real, but they are not real in our everyday life."

"John, I wanted to see you in person—in real life—to ask you if you believe our love has endured what we are still enduring."

"I think it has. But I don't think the way we live now helps. You can ask almost anybody if people have inculcated in them a spirit of a permanent, all-enduring love, and the answer will be negative. Still, it does happen. But Martha, that kind of happiness is not our immediate problem; our problem now is our aloneness and our guilt—and also our sense of anxiety. That's when the symptoms like my phobias arrive. I assume you're doing in London as I am in San Marino: you're trying to overcome your aloneness without her. But now I can at least say to you the words I couldn't even pronounce to myself six months ago: 'how to live without Samantha.'"

Martha stood in the elevator door with her bag in her hand and looked aghast at his words. She said evenly: "Ivaan is waiting for you. You have to see him. And Sutton, don't you dare ever leave me." She repeated those last familiar words, and John wondered what it all meant.

The metro from Sèvres-Babylon that day didn't bother him as much as it once did—except for the rasping, grinding sound of iron-on-iron braking and the train's inglorious slowdown at that one great curve he remembered so well—it was unchanged. He'd heard that same sound on the train when they went to Chartres to walk the labyrinth in the great cathedral. He remembered also that he was on the ninth concentric circle around the labyrinth's heart when Ivaan and Martha left the cathedral. To go where? He never knew. He never asked. They walked out together. And he'd walked to the heart of the labyrinth.

The metro to Goutte d'Or seemed like a soundscape, the braking still echoing in one of his fleeting synapses, the sound that recalled his phobias, one of the many sounds leading inexorably back to Samantha.

"The situation is grim," Ivaan said as they stood at the tall window looking out onto the Islamic Center. "I couldn't tell you the main things by phone. Every communication is tapped these days. Ahmed says it's on for tomorrow evening—it's as he told us that day in Saint-Denis—only worse. And the puppeteers and their puppets are all in place; probably an array of patsies too. Ahmed knows things like that. He says the city is full of suicide bombers imported from Iraq and Syria and Libya. And I know that it's to be a full-blown false flag operation. They could stop it, the DGSE; but they won't. Many people will die tomorrow evening in Paris, John. And mark my words: this will be France's World Trade Center. And now you have to get out of here fast. They have your name, you were at the Coupole, you know me, you know Ahmed. That is enough to land you in a black site somewhere in Romania. So get out, now."

Again, Ivaan was warning him, like at the Coupole back then. Ivaan always knows such things. Ordinary people are doing ordinary things today, they go to work, go shopping, go to a cinema, take the car for an emissions check, with no thoughts about tomorrow. But Ivaan knows what the parallel world plans for tomorrow. It occurred to him that Ahmed in Saint-Denis was exposed; most likely he was cast as a chief patsy, which somehow cast an ambiguous light on Ivaan—and thus on him too. John realized he knew so little about this man. What is his genuine role in these events? And is he really a friend?

"I'm leaving now, Ivaan. Still, it's too bad it's not the real thing. As you've always said, what goes around eventually comes around; if you make war on other countries long enough, someone will someday make war on you---on your own soil."

"Yes, but this kind of terror is different. It's something else. Like you said, it's not real. It's a fake. No Libyans are in command here. No Syrians either. Our friends from Montparnasse run the whole show—together with those from Washington. It's worse than the real thing. A false flag in order to tighten the screws in France and Europe still more, tighter and tighter. *La douce France*! Yet people are to die. Others are to be whisked away—never to return. *Ah, oui, la douce France*!"

John stopped at the door and looked around to say good-bye to the Embassy. As he hugged Ivaan, he saw directly into the open cloakroom where hanging on a hook Martha's multicolored Missoni scarf looked back at him. In the same instant, in his mind he saw a precise image of Martha of only an hour earlier standing at the elevator door in Rue Faber in her black coat and with her small valise in her left hand. But something had been missing: her dress trademark, a Missoni scarf. Goddamned memory that stores such details.

Conscious that he was tailed, he walked to Boulevard Clichy, metroed to Chatelet, took a cab to Orly Airport, found a flight to Bologna and taxied back to San Marino. Everything had happened so fast he felt he'd never been away. He looked around the apartment that still seemed like a foreign land. After only one day away—a day that had hardly taken place—he understood that this was not his place either. Yet so much had occurred in that one day: separation confirmation, preparations for the attack on Paris, images of Paris on fire, Martha's Missoni scarf hanging in Ivaan's cloakroom. Were all these sundry events connected? And what did it all mean? The connections. The connections. The famous connections he believed in. Or was it all as disconnected as his lived life? In this moment, it seemed his life until now came down to a Missoni scarf hanging in an Egyptian cloakroom.

The next evening he had the TV news channel on, his computer set on *Corriere Della Sera*, *Le Monde* and the barely known *Le Foudre* bulletin-newspaper that Ivaan advised him to follow: "They seem to get certain kinds of news before it happens. And who knows whose newspaper it is—maybe it's the voice of the DGSE." The first news flash appeared at 21:05 on *Le Foudre Actuel* followed by continuous minute-by-minute updates, an hour before mainstream media began reporting: *Paris Brûle. Paris Is Buning. Simultaneous Terrorist Attacks From Neuilly To Bercy.* It was happening just as Ahmed told them that day in Saint-Denis, although with different sponsors than those Ahmed intended. But maybe not. Maybe Ahmed knew or suspected the truth even then. If so, his life was not worth two cents today. After 9/11 in New York, anything was possible.

At shortly after 9 p.m. tonight three Islamist suicide bombers blew themselves up at the entrance to the Stade de France in Saint-Denis in the northern suburbs of Paris during an international football match.

At the same time a group of Islamist attackers fired into crowded cafés and restaurants on the Champs Elysées according to first reports killing and critically injuring hundreds. Café de Roma, Café George V, Brasserie d'Alsace, Flora Danica.

Reports of other attacks are pouring in. Dozens of lone suicide-shooters invaded the metro stations of Chatelet, Etoile, Opera, Saint-Lazare, Centre Pompidou, Louvre, Concorde, Madeleine before blowing themselves up in the most crowded places. All rail stations are under attack: Gare du Nord, Gare de l'Est, Gare de Lyon, Gare d' Austerlitz, Gare Montparnasse.

In what now seems a diversionary attack on the Bataclan Music Hall a terrorist squad fired on spectators from the balcony. The victims are in the hundreds.

At around 9:45 the attack on the main target was unleashed on a packed concert at the Olympia Music Hall in midtown. Ten or more hooded terrorists dressed in black first threw hand grenades then fired wildly for endless minutes into the trapped crowds.

When police special forces arrived the terrorists ran in among spectators and blew themselves up. The victims in Paris today now number in the thousands, the injured tens of thousands.

France is at war.

At around eleven that evening *Le Foudre* published an analysis of the events, emphasizing that it was not over yet:

Paris: Tonight's terrorist attacks were the deadliest in France since the World War Two, the deadliest ever in the European Union. France has been on high alert since January of last year after attacks on Charlie Hebdo offices and a Jewish supermarket in Paris that killed 17 people.

The Islamic State of Iraq and the Levant (ISIL) again claimed responsibility for the tonight's attacks. The President of France said the attacks were an act of war by Islamic State. According to government sources the attacks were planned in Syria and organized by terrorist cells based in Belgium and Paris. Some of the Paris attackers were Iraqis. Some were born in France or Belgium and had fought in Syria. Some of the foreign fighters had returned to Europe among the flow of migrants from Syria.

In response to the attacks, a three-month state of emergency has been declared across the country in the war on terrorism. Special measures include the banning of public demonstrations, police searches without a warrant, house arrest without trial, and blockage of websites that encourage acts of terrorism. Furthermore the government vows to launch the biggest airstrikes ever in the Middle East against ISIL. The authorities are searching for surviving attackers and accomplices. Police are raiding residences in Saint-Denis, in the entire 9-3, in the Goutte d'Or and in other districts of large Islamist minorities in the French capital.

When Ivaan hadn't taken his call after their agreed on three rings, he clicked off, assuming the worst scenario: Ivaan would be questioned, maybe held, maybe more. Whoever was holding him saw John's call. John waited. Three days later, Ivaan returned his call. The same people had spoken with him—in depth, he said. He was back at home; free to speak—with great reservations on their part. And they would want to speak with John Sutton. A friend of their enemy was their enemy too. Ivaan emphasized the verb "to speak" each time he used it. He meant much more. John didn't ask about Ahmed; Ivaan just said that things were bleak in all of Paris and he'd agreed with their mutual friends to sit tight and stay inside the Embassy.

Ivaan was right about the DGSE. Early that evening, Null phoned; he and his associate would arrive in San Marino the next afternoon. They would be pleased to dine together at a place of his choice. Expense accounts to be padded, John thought—over the bodies of three thousand dead in Paris. The western world was disintegrating, but ambassadors and political leaders and their respective bureaucrats would be arranging conferences to accompany their lavish lunches and dinners. John knew two eating places: the simple trattoria near his apartment where he ate every day and Hank's Bar on Mount Titano where he'd never been. So, out of curiosity he walked up the hill, stopped at a bend in the walkway, took in the view of the first lights of Rimini blinking in the early night. Hank's Bar and Tavern was beautiful, but at seven p.m. still empty. A tall good-looking man greeted him with a strong *Ciao*.

"I'm Hank," he said in Italian and stuck out a big hand.

"*Buona sera*! I live just down the road and am looking for a new place to eat."

"*You* must be the writer! And you lived here in San Marino as a child. Missed your home town, did you?"

"My name's John…and how do you know about me? You have your own intelligence agency?"

"It's a small town. And since there are few places to eat in this area I wondered why you'd never been here. Besides, we also offer the best music in Europe. "

"A music hall, too, eh? Those are dangerous places in Paris! Actually I'm holed up here and trying to work. So I don't get out much."

"What are you writing, if I may be so curious?"

"Oh, it's a love story set in San Marino."

"Yes, but what's it really about?"

John looked at him, surprised. Hank's not what he seemed at first. "Hmm. Not many people ask that and I wish I knew the answer. That's my problem right now. I'm not sure. Maybe sincerity or something like that. Maybe loyalty. Loyalty not as a sense of duty but as related to love—in life too much loyalty can easily turn into a curse that makes loyalty a handicap when the people or things you're loyal to change and are not loyal to you."

"I think that must happen to many people. Suddenly you are jolted awake to discover that either you are out of joint with life or the life you are living is out of joint with you. Still, the quality of loyalty is not evil."

"Oh, not at all. Loyalty, and sincerity too, are still ethically desirable."

"Right! Too bad you didn't show up here before. I see we have a lot to talk about."

"Very gladly. Anyway, I want to bring two guys from Paris here tomorrow evening for dinner. Look, this is a very unpleasant affair: they're French secret agents…and they're investigating me. It's got to do with the events in Paris. But I swear I didn't do it."

"You want me to poison them or something?"

"Good idea. Those two have been pestering me since I happened to be at the Café Coupole when it was bombed several years ago. They think I've got something to do with Islamic terrorism. I don't. But my best friend in Paris—an Egyptian—is a leader of the Islamic community…and besides he's a Communist. So they're suspicious of me, maybe because I'm a Communist too."

"Well, you're among comrades here. You must know San Marino is a Communist town. "

"The whole town?"

"Nearly. But we have our fascists too—like everywhere. Seems almost fashionable. Swastikas and torch-light parades."

"Still, that the Islamist uprising in Paris is organized by Syria and a European revolution led by Islamic immigrants is in preparation is bullshit propaganda. Anyway, what poison do you have in mind?"

"What about boeuf bourguignon?"

Early the next evening, the two DGSE men were at his door. For a moment John gaped in sham admiration of their new-found finery; under their open crème-colored raincoats, they were both dressed in suits and ties with white French cuffs and sparkling links and wearing black shoes with pointed toes—the latter plus the French cuffs, John thought, sufficient reason for detesting them. They would make a big hit in Hank's Bar!

Hank had a booth table set for three persons and behaved so absurdly obsequious that John laughed out loud as did the few patrons at that early hour. He had draped a red cloth over his left forearm like a matador and wrote down their order with consummate care—and speaking to John and company in perfect Canadian French.

Null looked at him closely and asked if he learned his French in Quebec.

Hank paused, his hand in the air, and replied: "Algiers."

Null now stared openly at their host and remarked that the Algerians he knew in Paris didn't speak the beautiful French Hank did.

Again Hank paused for effect, then: "It's Cajun French; I learned it in the Algiers district of New Orleans."

"Oh," Null muttered, "Cajun French. I always wondered what it was."

After they'd tasted and loved the boeuf bourguignon, after the agents updated the statistics of casualties and property damages on fire night in Paris, and after a reference to the effects of the new national emergency laws, John asked naively who they thought was really behind the "attack on France".

"Assad," Null replied and shot out his white, white cuffs. "The cruel dictator ordered the attacks in response to France's moral support for the Syrian Liberation Army and the oppressed Syrian people under the yoke of Assadism and his dreaded secret police."

"And also Syrian-Iraqi terrorist headquarters in Paris," Henri added.

"As you know, the latter is in our field of activity," Null continued, constantly fiddling with his emerald cufflinks. "We know that the threads of Islamist terrorism come together somewhere in Paris, somewhere among the many Islamic cultural centers and the mosques, the so-called community leaders—

somewhere they all link up. We calculate that maybe two hundred terrorists were in action on fire night in Paris, at least twenty of them, suicide bombers. Now the government has named an official Fire Night Commission to prepare—with the assistance of our organization of course—a detailed study of the events and to pinpoint the organizers and the executors, a report which will be the basis of French Middle Eastern policies. My department's job—also the work of Henri and myself—is to identify the executors and, more importantly, their bosses as well as the so-called fellow travelers. Whether or not you are involved, Mr. Sutton, you wonder why we question you about such matters. The answer is because of your friends and because of your continuing presence at the wrong places at the wrong times—as you know we don't believe in coincidence: you were at the Coupole and it was bombed while you chatted with the suspect Ivaan Amrani; you go to Saint-Denis and meet a person you knew as Ahmed who is now under arrest...and under his real name and his real Syrian nationality. Moreover, even though you live in San Marino—the country of banks—on the eve of France's 9/11, you returned to Paris. If you were French you would most likely already be in prison, but despite your passport, we still don't even know who you are."

Null took a long drink of wine, gulped visibly, again extended his cuffs with a strange twisting jerk of his arms, leaned forward and examined closely his emerald links, and went on: "We want some explanations—if you ever hope to return to France with your wife, who we now know is maybe not even your wife and whose comings and goings are also anomalous, who—you might not know—travels back and forth between London and Paris and spends a lot of time at the Goutte d'Or Embassy. We wonder if she is a sort of courier for terrorists or someone's lover—or both."

"My wife is only trying to come to terms with the loss of our daughter," John said in a pissed voice and mentally ignoring the agents words about Martha at the Embassy. "Everything else is, well, everything else belongs to the world of others. And, yes, my presence at the wrong place at the wrong time was exactly that—coincidence. But for now I have a question for you: some people think the Paris events were part of a grandiose false flag operation precisely to permit the national emergency laws which are already in place: to stop immigration, to arrest and hold without charge undesirable persons, all of which has been achieved. And at this point, I have nothing else to say on the subject. I'm a writer and my mind is occupied with my own creations—not yours."

It was a few minutes after nine. Regulars were arriving. A musical trio was warming up on the small bandstand. His eyes again met the fleeting glance of an especially attractive woman alone at a table across the room. He raised a hand toward Hank.

"Hank, I think these gentlemen need a taxi," John muttered.

"Right away! You gentleman only have to walk down the walkway out front, down past the bend and about a hundred meters more. The taxi will meet you there where the paved street begins. I will explain that your presumed destination is Bologna. So I wish you a bon voyage."

14.

Hank's Bars

John stood outside Hank's Bar and looked in through the wide window and watched the drinking people and he thought they were no less beautiful in their inebriation than the leaded glass window itself. And after waiting outside in the darkness until its four a.m. closing time, he watched the beautiful drunken people of San Marino and their foreign brothers and sisters come out of Hank's Bar on the mountain top and return into the night. He thought there was a rare, strange beauty about drinking people, something soulful, something mildly sad on their contented faces— apparently satisfied with their night at Hank's—that indefinable something for which others envy good drinkers, but don't understand. They are, say, inebriated on themselves, looking at themselves in mirrors and liking what they see, something so secret and so precious that they know this is a unique moment in their lives, the memory of which must be preserved. Their beauty is not gratuitous; it requires conscious effort and will, but the rewards are unimaginably great: John felt certain that many of those beautiful persons had suffered great pain and that they had learned lessons of love. They reminded him of the man he'd crossed paths with walking the Chartres labyrinth, he on the arrival path, the other on the exit journey with the same besotted expression on his face, content with his walk to the heart of things. And he'd envied that spiritual traveler as he envied the ones now descending Mount Titano who in this moment also looked like spiritual travelers. In that moment, John perceived the special effort the beautiful drunken people make to live lives worth living and he hoped to one day emulate them and become one with them. And because he recognized them, he felt he was already a small part of them as they made their way down the trail of Mount Titano and after the great bend vanished into the lingering early morning darkness; yet, he also recognized the reality that he was still the outsider, not one of the beautiful people of Hank's Bar. Standing at the top, alone in the fading darkness he perceived his lonesomeness and the absence of someone with whom to share himself. Maybe Hank would prove to be such a person—his San Marino Ivaan.

After John's first evening at Hank's Bar, he made an entry in his writer's diary:

San Marino, September 15. Samantha's birthday passed, September 12 arriving. Hank's Bar on its mountain top is truly a special place, but the odd thing is that when you enter the tavern the first time you think it is much like other places you used to go, but you soon learn that it is not. It could never be the same. It is the other side of the moon from any bar or tavern or pub or café you might have ever known in your wanderings around the world. When you open its great oaken door and hear Hank's Ciao, you stop, look around, and you feel the after-hours speakeasy atmosphere and you realize that you love in a special way the kind of people who frequent late night places like Hank's, and you realize that this is much better than the places you used to go. You remember the all-night bars-taverns-cabarets like Simplicismus and you know right off the bat that Hank's is a different world. Another cosmos. Where at around three a.m. if you are lucky and have drunk well you pass into a kind of afterlife, an hour in Eden that you don't want to lose. For that hour you are in an afterlife. And they come from near and far, its nocturnal inhabitants, to feel the same sensations. Hank's Bar has the magical capacity to transform space into a perfect nighttime eternity, like its imposing handmade mahogany bar long enough for three bartenders to work and the smooth hand-carved high stools standing like the pillars of Hercules in front. And behind the bar sultry Juanita runs the drinking show in the same languages of polyglot Hank whose tavern and music hall near the top of rocky Mount Titano in the micro-Republic of San Marino is truly international.

Venice's Harry's Bar? No, thanks, John thought. 'I'll leave that for the American tourists over to Europe for the wedding of a prince or the funeral of a monarch and keeping an eye out for traces of Hemingway'; aware tavern cultists of the nocturnal world head for Mount Titano and Hank's. Art deco lamps and dark red wooden walls and leaded windows and heavy oaken tables for drinking and eating tavern boeuf bourguignon.

. He had begun frequenting Hank's Bar a few times a week, at first for dinner and the music—each time leaving before midnight. As time passed, he met regulars climbing the hill at the same time he was headed homewards. Consequently, he re-arranged his work schedule for the days following a night at the tavern: Hank's for dinner at around midnight, music and moderate drink until closing time, sleep till noon or early afternoon, and work and sundry chores until evening. Some nights, he and Hank had dinner together and continued their always surprising conversations. Juanita—who ran his renowned bar—served them; Juana or Nita, was once the queen of Santiago de Cuba where Hank met her. John said she reminded him of a unique well-cut diamond he'd once used in a short story set on the Munich-Paris train, and that her eyes reflected the view he imagined of dark Haiti across the shark-infested waters on a clear day.

***

"Hank" Gamper disliked his real name, Modesto, named after Grandpa Gamper. But he'd loved the man and accepted family usage of Modest which later in life he came to think of as Modest in Mussorgsky. His Tyrolean father, Albert Gamper, abandoned his Italian wife and Modesto in her home in San Marino so long ago that Hank never thought of searching for him as a son or daughter might look for their father, even though he would have been easy to find since Gamper was an omnipresent name in Alto Adige-South Tyrol: Grandpa Gamper once led the struggle for South Tyrolean independence. Though Hank returned to San Marino from time to time—and always near the top of Mount Titano which he considered his ur-home—he spent his early youth wandering around the world from north Russia to New Orleans to Cuba until at the age of thirty-five he returned home and again settled on Mount Titano to open his bar that had gradually acquired world-wide fame.

Modest "Hank" Gamper had a proclivity for opening Hank's Bars in unexpected but exotic places in the world. He loved the harmonious medley of the search for perfection to proffer his people of the night: the creation of the seductive décor and the discovery of the provocative music you hear nowhere else. In his striving to create a place where strangers meet, meld one into the other and fall in love with Hank's Bar—or eventually with each other—he secretly aimed at generating an unforgettable interstice of time between discovery of Hank's and what happens in your life afterwards.

One evening as activities on Mount Titano dwindled down and the music faded, he told John the story of the opening of his first Hank's Bar in swampy Louisiana in the rainy month of September. He was twenty-five years old when he arrived in New Orleans—the polyglot Communist claimed in order to experience in its birthplace 'pure anti-war, anti-capitalist, pro-liberation, revolutionary jazz, the jazz born out of oppression, out of the enslavement of black people— and to experience Cajun French in its purest form.' Though he'd been warned that the beautiful Algiers district of the city of music was one of the most dangerous places in the world, he settled in that renowned criminal quarter anyway, just across the Mississippi River from the touristy French Quarter run by the rich Bourbon Street Creole bourgeoisie. Bourbon Street was Bourbon Street but Algiers across the river was another matter: he felt he got to the heart of Cajun life there, an endeavor for which he'd risked all of his capital and years of time. He said that on the streets of Algiers he learned both to look over his shoulder and the importance of genuine friendship. With his savings, a small inheritance from Grandpa Gamper, and with a sense of satisfaction mixed with justified trepidation he opened his first Hank's Bar in the heart of Algiers just six months after his arrival in the old part of the New World. Only afterwards did he become aware of the protection money organized crime there would demand—which to him sounded like the Sicilian *pizzo*. He recounted that he learned from two members of the Fisher Fools

Gang that they got a percentage on business transactions in Algiers, criminal business handled quite openly—no ifs or buts—and that his tavern was on the list for protection. Such an arrangement made him doubly conscious of the terrestrial distance separating Cajun-Creole Algiers from lofty Mount Titano and its stillness in the middle of the night which always nestled in his mind. That early morning, recounting his years in Algiers, Hank said wistfully that since you can also adjust it a bit, edit out unpleasantness or dress it in fine clothes, memory is no less appealing than the real present or even a conceptual future.

Hank Gamper is a big man, muscular, dark and bearded, and though a white man, John thought there was truly something Cajun about him—even though he'd never known a Cajun before. He thought Cajun must mean the something Southern that he'd perceived in Mexico. As they spoke, John thought there was also an unsettling air about Hank and Juanita: Hank always looked at her fondly and though he sometimes called her Nita or Juana, he preferred her full name, Juanita, perhaps in order to intensify her self-esteem despite her aura of the displaced person who had suffered and for that reason was not a woman to be bullied easily.

Hank said when he asked the two Cajuns how much the hypothetical gangsters wanted for protection, they laughed and said 'no problem', that they were just messengers and that the Fools' accountants would drop in one day to examine his accounts, after which they would assess his monthly fees that when paid would guarantee him and his business affairs total security. In their colorful language they said that 'a shroud of prosperity and happiness would surround Hank's Bar.'

According to Hank, he laughed in their faces; he hadn't asked for protection, but he did know he could do without their shroud of joy and happiness. Afterwards, when from time to time the two hoodlums popped in to ask how business was going, they never mentioned the *pizzo* again. He told them honestly that Hank's Bar had no business yet; he was still trying to create the atmosphere he wanted his bar to emanate, but that he enjoyed their meetings and looked forward to them, which was true. The Algiers gangsters—when not busy breaking heads somewhere, Hank imagined—took a liking to him also: the two native Algerines encouraged his linguistic efforts and taught him colorful Cajunisms and Cajun music and Hank served them drinks and admired their sophisticated manners. And the accountants never bothered coming. On leaving, after their pleasant exchanges, Hank's messengers-accountants-pals always saluted with a joyous: *'Laissons les bons temps rouler.'*

Algiers. Hank depicted his trans-Mississippi quarter as secretive, mysterious and enigmatic, dangerous and violent, a world of shadows framed in darkness with only nervous streaks of light linking it to the great city across the river.

Algiers. The district was peopled with criminals, separatists and dissidents. Hank's morose and triste Algiers displayed no pretenses of joy and happiness and seemed unrelated to the bustle of convention-oriented New Orleans on the other side of the great river. But Hank loved the boisterous part of New Orleans anyway, bright and illuminated, romantic flickering candles in luxurious restaurants, young boys tip-tap dancing on Bourbon Street and the drink-happy stragglers zigzagging behind brass marching blues bands. Algiers instead was silent, in part mean, in part innocent…but naïve in its meanness.

Algiers Point, National Heritage area. Exposed to southern sun and rains and powerful winds. Noble winds, Hank said, recalling the winds of huge Lake Garda. The Pelèr blowing mornings from the north and the Ora arriving from the south. The Algiers gangsters smiled in disbelief at his description of local Garda people's claim of twenty different winds blowing over their lake; a few minutes of such talk and Hank felt a tick of nostalgia for his home country. He found the Algiers winds cowardly and bodiless—unlike the powerful Bora winds of Mount Titano. You can't fight Algiers winds; you run at them—and then through them—but they are still there. In any case, Hank mused to John, there is something glorious about winds that come from any direction to clean the Earth's skies of incomprehensible clouds, winds that in Louisiana transmute into murderous hurricanes coming from the Caribbean. How unlike the powerful winds blowing from China filmed in *The Story of Wind* by the documentarist Joris Yvens, from Nijmegen, whom he'd met in the filmmaker's Paris studio. Hank said he still perceived a bond between himself and Yvens because of The Flying Dutchman's world travels and his mystical relationship with the Chinese Communist Party—a friendship so close that Chinese journalists still today travel to Nijmegen seeking the roots of the man who produced his major works in China. John thought that Hank's friendship with Yvens resembled his own feelings for Ivaan Amrani, the Egyptian Communist in Paris.

Hank reminisced that Algiers Point was the entrance into the exotic mystery of the world of the Cajun peoples. In his early morning tales, he re-lived his experiences in Algiers. He reconstructed the day he strolled leisurely along the levee at the Point to observe a storm in arrival from the south and while standing vis-à-vis the Vieux Carré across the Mississippi. He recounted how the wet wind growing behind him felt on his neck while an eerie murky light invaded the Point. Clouds blackened the doleful heavens over Algiers though still sparing New Orleans and created a Caravaggesque chiaroscuro against Louisiana skies. The erratic southern winds intensified, this time resembling the *tramontana* blowing from the north over Mount Titano in San Marino. Lightning struck the spires of the cathedral across the river and a second later a thunderous explosion shook the Algiers earth under his feet. The blackness of the storm reached the city of light, underlining the ghostly whiteness of its great cathedral, colorless standing there facing the swirling directionless winds—and the river oblivious to such atmospheric events. He said he felt the coldness running down his back. And when he heard the first drops of rain on old Algiers, he stood under a shed and watched the storm front slowly, slowly passing and in that moment he realized it was time to return home.

Algiers Point. The Algiers plain of great houses and stunning architecture and colors looks across the great river at New Orleans with longing, Hank imagined. Or with scorn. Or envy. Or with hate. Forever the temptation has lived in Algiers, the temptation to join American New Orleans and put its French origins behind. For there the city-monument stands, inviting, just a stone's throw in distance and time across the grand old Mississippi River. Take the ferry to that other world across to the death-like other-worldly whiteness of the cathedral with its blindly smiling face engraved on its façade, face à face with sinful unrepentant Algiers, beckoning to its pure French Cajuns, the children of the massive French immigration of the eighteenth century, the poor Acadians, who became the Cajuns, some of whom fall for the lure and take the ferry. But most genuine Acadians never cross their River Styx. Only the fearless criminal gangs go back and forth between darkness and light—for business and the *putes*. They don't resist the great crooks' bureaucracy; they penetrate it and suck it dry just as the bureaucracy did the Roman Empire whose government, military forces, police, and business sector it controlled. As then, so now, organized crime existed as a parallel government—as all bureaucracies eventually do.

For Hank it was a different story. He was searching for the music. The special music. At first, he'd thought that over there on the other side of the river the original soul jazz lived in secret places, but that life style in which it existed was not what he was seeking. A convention or a Mardi Gras on Bourbon Street supported his belief that the origins of the real, non-commercialized New Orleans jazz was not there in the city after all; its embers lay somewhere in the heart of Algiers among the excluded and the oppressed. The trans-Mississippi quarter of "Algiers" so named because of the snobbery of earlier French settlers and Spanish occupiers who called the newcomer French Acadian scum "a bunch of Algerines": the Creoles of French and Spanish heritage speaking the Cajun French, the Cadienne of Algiers. Nearly pure French. The French of the Acadian peasants of central France recruited by Paris as instruments of French imperialism in the Americas.

In his first *Hank's Bar* in their Algiers, Hank had always been glad to see Roland and Marcel—perfect Acadiens-Cajuns, pure French and fuck the Creoles—. The three of them were about the same age and the two Fools more curious than mean. Hank recalled how the two gangsters liked sitting at an oaken table sipping Pernod and complaining of the incoherence of the incomprehensible world they lived in. And Hank understood that whatever their Fools work, the force of money had no undue influence on them personally. They did their job and were paid for it. Their roles seemed written in stone for them: Roland, affectionate and severe—though no less in the dark about the real world outside than his protégé—sometimes drank too much and the three years younger Marcel—Marcel with his unusually large head and skin as chocolate as that of a Trinidad native—soothed a drunken coal-black haired Roland and humored him into drinking coffee and slowly walked him back to his colorful wooden house to his wife and little daughter. Hank too took to visiting Roland, bearing flowers and each time kissing his wife Marie on both cheeks Italian fashion and swinging two-year old Pauline around a couple of times. A pleased Roland would watch and smile and play Cajun music—and sometimes they danced.

Hank reminisced how he and his best pal Marcel roamed over the streets of gangster-ridden Algiers, checking into cafés, bars and taverns, drinking a drink, noting the good and the bad, things to keep in mind. Hank said that at first he was apprehensive about being seen with a mobster but that Marcel continually surprised him in language and thoughts and with small acts of generosity and love for his friend Roland. In fact, Marcel's whole easy, happy-go-lucky presence was infused with careless pleasure at his surroundings, almost innocently convivial; he was the noble savage still unused to the restrictions of the civilized world and its criminal off-shoot and apparently immune to its hypocrisies and deceits. Though he was part of a criminal money-making mob, he never let that life interfere with his sense of benevolence. He was the most unlikely criminal in all of Algiers-New Orleans, always ready to bare his very soul while he drew Hank toward him into what in Hank's world would have been a strange friendship. And besides all his moral merits, Marcel had the physical constitution of a mountain bear; he would leap out of bed at four in the morning if Hank called him to come over at his closing time just to enjoy the kid gangster's optimism. Marcel seemed to love anything that kept him out of bed and outside and free in the night. His wide-ranging nocturnal life was dominated by a general anticipation of the unexpected. And apparently the world continually surprised him: he acted like he wondered how it would all turn out.

"His life sounds like a story I would like to write," John remarked, at which Hank just waved a hand distractedly, intimating: it was too complicated for literature.

But then one day the gangster was sad; Hank was leaving. They were saying their goodbyes. It was mid-morning. Rain was in the air. They were walking around the fish market, Marcel humming and singing in a low voice random bits of a sad song, now in French, now in English, Hank feigning distraction but listening intently…"*like the circles you find, da, da, da in the circles of your mind, da, da, da, les moulins de mon coeur…les moulins de mon coeur.*"

"*Marcel, c'est quoi … ce que tu chantes?*"

"*Ah ça, ça c'est seulement une vielle chanson francaise que nous chantons dans une boite que je connais…*but I forget all the words. It's a special place too…the *boite*. I'll take you there when you return."

"And you sing it in English! You speak the language much better than I do anyway," he said as though Algiers were a foreign country.

"Well, I *am* American after all, and anyway everybody in Algiers my age knows both Cajun and English. But we speak Cajun together—otherwise we wouldn't know who we really are. Still, some old people speak only Cajun and many of them have never even been across the river into what is our city too."

"I wish I knew the answer to that myself," John commented.

"Answer to what?"

"To know who I really am."

"Oh, John, who knows the answer to that? My problem was that Algiers Cajuns didn't come to Hanks Algiers Bar either. So I had too little revenue and too much time on my hands. I liked wandering around the city with Marcel but he knew my funds were running out and that I had to move on. The Fisher Fools would not miss me, he said, but he and Roland would. And believe it or not, they found a successor for my bar who paid me back my investment which was a good deal for Marcel and Roland too; the new proprietor was one they could milk as they were expected to do and redeem themselves with the Mob.

"Anyhow, John, Algiers was a unique experience and I did get some good songs for my secret list, some that you hear often here on Mount Titano. My last night there Marcel took me to a *boite* where a big name in Zydeco music was playing, some recordings of which I have and treasure. Maybe you've heard it without realizing it but what a treasure the recordings are for me."

"Zydeco?"

"Zydeco is rather new. A mix of traditional Acadien-Cajun music with blues and more modern rock n'roll, using drums and electric guitars but keeping the usual washboard and accordion. We'll listen to them one evening. My one great regret is that I never learned to dance Cajun—Zydeco too."

15.

Night People

I've always loved the night. Yet, I'm wary of it. It's at night that the most unpredictable things happen. Night is the time when you may become aware of the thing that will change your life, after which nothing will ever be the same again. Your epiphany waits for you in the darkness around the next corner; you sense that something unexpected is about to happen—one of the big moments of your life.

Here and there around the stone building, dim yellow lights blinked and flickered. Down the hill, total darkness. It was three o'clock in the morning. From outside the window, I watched her alone at her table. Her head was bent over her glass; maybe her eyes were closed. Although she looked solid and secure in her aloneness, in that apartness she seemed sad. Yet her independence from others cast her in a sublime light and I thought her melancholy possessed a sense of nobility; her separateness made her seem free of social demands and deceits and I believed she was one of those truly rare persons—rare in her inner freedom. I watched the way she drank in small sips, regular, methodical, cumulative sips, yet she never showed pleasure or inebriation like most drinkers at that hour. Actually, hers was a dangerous sort of drinking, the steady drinking of a sad person holding her every thought secret—maybe also from herself—concealed deep down in the tunnels of her mind. But if such were her reasons, then why drink alone in the middle of the night at Hank's Bar? For solace?

Or to display her sadness publically and to feel sorry for herself? Or, perhaps, she secretly hoped for the chance meeting with someone like me, I thought…or someone like herself too? Or was it simply the aesthetic idea of drinking at Hank's? I think many people come here with that same idea in their minds: drinking at Hank's, drinking and at the most getting a little tipsy at Hank's. But most likely such persons are also looking for love and the peace love sometimes brings. In that moment, I knew that someday I would reminisce about the twisted mysteries and what seemed like the splendor of such memories of you. Yet I hate such contorted, such ambivalent and unpredictable memories, the deeply-rooted kind of memories that offer no succor and leave no epitaphs, but only regrets for the things I should have done but instead left undone. I thought that if there were only some way to preview my memories—if memories had trailers—so that I could select only the pleasant pre-Samantha ones: to hear again the whistle of a rare river barge back where I once came from—after Rotterdam—to smell the still stagnant waters along the banks of small streams, to inhale the vapors rising from grilled sausages on busy downtown streets, sensations and noises to lose myself in. In such memories, I might find release. But my secret self knew that kind of peace for me was never to return.

Drinking at Hank's Bar on Mount Titano with you belongs to my most pleasant though indefinable memories and images of our early togetherness that I hazily fantasize about today, memories which I hold close in me even though everything has changed in too short a time to be comforting. The way you laughed silently when I sometimes called Hank's the "Red Bar". And you repeated that drinking at Hank's is famous among the late night drinkers who detest nightclubs and discoteques. And we agreed that Hank's Red Bar is truly different.

***

Farther down toward San Marino City, down the twisting cobblestone pedestrian street running along the narrow crest from the summit, the Titano Bar—Hank's minor competitor—had been dark for hours. The few scrawny trees pressed against the walls lining the pedestrian way seemed lonely and anachronistic considering San Marino's two millennia of age, but tonight they appeared to me as the surviving essence of displaced, under-privileged trees, deprived of any other support from their world of nature. Here and there an empty bench jammed against those stone walls along the walkway leading up to the darkened castle at the top at a soaring 739 meters seemed frightened by the encroaching masonry of forgotten epochs. Faint yellowish lights spotting Rimini in the distance recalling the highway lamps lining fog-shrouded Dutch highways flickered in the late night. And the rest of San Marèin farther down its slopes was quiet. Soon the sun would peek over the horizon of the green Adriatic and illuminate first Mount Titano and San Marino and then Rimini and the Grand Hotel on the seashore to the East. Inside the bar, Hank's angular shadow moved jerkily but gracefully against internal walls like a figure in Chinese shadow theater. Deciding on the spur of the moment just before he had time to lock up, I pushed open the heavy door and stepped into the penumbra as I had done countless times before. Since the low time in my life after I moved to Monte Titano, I permitted myself such indiscretions—depending on the circumstances of my fragile existence. At this hour, I'd had enough sleep anyway and "Red"

Hank welcomed the excuse to stay a while longer. For him four a.m. was still tonight.

"Ciao, Jack, I sensed you would show up. But I have to lock the great door. This ridiculous curfew! Four a.m. Back in old Santiago they would snicker, silly gringos!" Hank talked in a succinct streaming, his voice powerful, not loud but expressively emotional, and I liked his calling me Jack—the only one who used his nickname. In the semi-obscurity, Hank's eyes had the compelling stamp of a person doing exactly what he desired to do in life. Spontaneously, he added that Maxime hadn't spoken during the hours she'd sat stonily at her wall table, drinking—though not excessively.

"Obsessed, that woman. She kept looking toward the door. Waited to the end. Maybe for you, Tovarisch. She still rejects all advances. No one dares to try any longer. So maybe she *is* waiting for you."

"I can't figure out why you think so. Anyway I was just checking. Now she's gone anyway. And I have stories to write. All waiting for me in my lonely computer—and maybe in my sick head too. So I'll try to work now while I'm as fresh as I will be today."

"Tonight, Jack".

"But when tonight really comes I'll be back here too."

Suppressing an enduring yawn, Hank said: "That's tomorrow, Jack."

On that same evening—tomorrow evening for Hank—I, John Sutton, fake Englishman, fake Dutchman, fake German, fake novelist, a fake in life, was sitting under a low-hanging Art Deco lamp at a wall table on the opposite side of the room from where Maxime always sat—by an unspoken accord always left free for her like a *Stammtisch* in a German Gastätte—and I feel a frown cross my face when instead of an image of her, I perceive an undesired sense of pleasure with my new car, an acquisition that had freed me from the complications of public transportation to the Grand Hotel and Rimini where I go many afternoons …twenty-seven kilometers distance from our republic. Pleasure from a fucking automobile! I feel rather silly about even thinking about a car. Proof that you just can't control the mind; like water, it goes where it wants. A car excites me? Goddammit, when will she arrive? Will our lives never coincide? There, right over there across the room she'd sat, drinking and waiting for something or someone while I stood outside looking at her distorted picture self through the window and I had the thought that I'd always liked drinking women. And instead of entering and going to her I'd looked down at San Marino and the blinking lights of Rimini and thought of stories of the passing centuries until I saw her pass me by, again going out, out, out of my life like the night before. Night before? Night or day? Day or night? Is life only night like it felt in Underground—when I was five? Even on days under the burning sun of Rimini beaches it would also be night. Mad thoughts crashing one into the other and thrashing inside my skull. Mad thoughts, including visions of my new shiny black car. That it is there. A reminder of how it used to be climbing aboard a train in the last second and the conductor observes you and sees you naked, stripped of the anxiety of nearly missing the train of your life. The conductor, the experienced observer who draws conclusions from the way you literally throw your bag onto the overhead rack and settle into your seat, red-faced and sweaty and hassled by the mad rush for life, so that the good observer that the conductor is will get a revelatory look into your life and character—drinker, reveler, or frustrated searcher-thinker—that you spend much of your life trying to mask and disguise.

The next day a cold northeast wind whirling loudly in space had swept over the tiny Republic of San Marino and driven away the dark clouds and insistent thundershowers and sent most of the remaining sunbathers at the Adriatic resorts back to Bologna and Milano. The night was chilly when I pushed open the heavy oaken door and heard Hank's Munich-acquired *"Grüss di' Gott, Tovarisch."* He elbowed me lightly in the ribs at the irony of Bavaria's god, as he said, wasted on two sons of Lenin.

"Only two sons? I thought this whole country was Communist."

"Tovarisch, it is, it is. All thirty-three thousand of us Sammarinesi are Reds. We're born red. You see our redness in our progressive laws. Why, after only two centuries we just voted for legal abortions despite the admonitions of that foreign pope down in Rome."

"Every single one voted?" It came to mind that all of them, all thirty-three thousands of them, related by ideals, according to Hank by a common desire to change things in the world, were linked securely also in their mundane world that contained the same intrigues and bank loans granted or rejected, the same raised rents, the same stopped up toilets and sewers and morning traffic jams, the same neighborhood gossip, suffered the same illnesses and mourned the same deaths and funerals as everyone elsewhere.

"What about the bunch of city counselors who voted no to abortion?" Juanita interjects, smirking evilly. "Those fascist bastards should be exiled."

"Bah, them! Fascists have short political lives in San Marino, Juana amor. Anyhow, remember that in 1789 exile was only one of the options. There was that new invention: the guillotine. That was the mother of all options. Well, yes, there always will be a handful of dissidents but they might as well be in Nazi Ukraine. No one here pays them the slightest attention."

Leaving Hank and his girlfriend to squabble about the fate of San Marino dissidents, the same invisible fate-guided stage director invites me to sit down at Maxime's fearsome table ready to play my plot-changing role in an ensuing high tragedy. Feeling like Hamlet, I peer around the room doubtfully. And yet, circumstances tonight induce me to perform this role of challenger in the delusion that it's my freewill choice arrived at after long meditation. Still, another part of me has doubts: What if she sees me occupying her table and turns around and walks out? Where would we be then?

"*Keine Sorge, Tovarisch. Sie kommt etwas später heute abend,*" Hank, silently on my heels, says in his philosophical manner that I should not worry and that this is the way things are supposed to happen—in stories and in life and this evening too.

"She's coming later tonight," Juanita explains secretively like a person in the know. "And Hank's just warming up his German for the annual Sammarinese October Beer Festival. Decorated beer horses pulling wagons loaded with kegs up and down our hills. He does it every year. Speaks German to everybody. He's a Tyrolean, you know, a native German speaker."

"It's the highlight of civic life up here on Mount Titano. *O, du lieber Augustin, Alles ist hin! Geld ist weg, Mädl ist weg, Alles ist hin…* "

Then, just to confuse me Hank adds, *"The greatest secrets are always hidden in the most unlikely places."*

While Hank speaks with the trio of tonight playing songs few drinkers ever heard of—or remember—I keep my eyes on the great oaken door. Patience, patience, patience. Until at the stroke of midnight the door swings open. Maxime, of course. The force of her decision to come to me. That's written in the story too. When she sees me at her table, a hint of a smile passes like a shadow across her lips and I hope through her heart. She comes in a straight line toward me in a sensual, hip-swinging gait…and erotically unsmiling. I stand and ask if I should leave. She has that special look on her face and repeats Hank's words that things take place like this also in real life.

"I felt lonely waiting," I begin.

"I miss you when…" Maxime mutters, I believe, in an unintended non-sequitur, but taking me totally by surprise.

"When…when…what?… Aren't we skipping over many steps," I croak when the saliva returns to my mouth. "Is that the story that's unfolding here?"

"Life is unfolding here. Those in between steps happened but they happened in our minds. I knew from the first instant what was happening and I think you did too." Her voice is a song, a gentle song, mild, but sad and full of despair. Maybe mourning too. Would mourning bring clarity? Would mourning explain all? Both of us mourning our losses and pains and sorrows and death?

We're speaking English. It's like that at Hank's, all those languages. Hank speaks six counting the local dialect. Another reason some Sammarinese people down in the valley suspect Hank himself of dissidence too. Where did he learn those languages?

He's in his fifties and has had this bar long enough to become famous. So where and how did he learn Turkish, of all languages? People down there think of Hank as a charlatan and the international crowd at Hank's Bar as a sect that holds late night sessions on Mount Titano to listen to strange music, dance strange dances, celebrate magical rites and decide on mysterious matters of the world. All that occurring up here in the clouds of Mount Titano.

"Words are important, no?" I mutter. "You don't waste them, do you?"

"The right words are everything—or otherwise nothing."

"Maxime, you and I will never waste words, right?"

"No, we must never waste words, or time."

"Because things and people too *can* change."

"Yes," she said sadly, "people change."

This is one of those rare moments when I feel harmony between my emotions and the wordless things of my existence, even though the great dichotomy remains, the divide between brain and heart for which I have no word since Samantha. And I don't conceal my dependence on words, I don't even try. But fixed in *nowtime,* this is one of those moments when I need words: I know my life is about to change. Still, there is so much to say to each other, so much to explain, why we did the things we did and above all why we did not do the things we should have done, never said those many things that so very easily remain unspoken. I don't know how to explain in words that I feel that I'm by necessity already *merging* into her, and she into me, and that all those things will eventually be spoken. To explain coherently, imagination and subtlety are also necessary. And our words, hers and mine—when spoken—will be the same words all lovers speak. Despite the inactive presence of Martha still inside me—permanently it seems—I must have active, even if limited love. I don't say surrogate love, mendacious love. Eventually I will say thousands of I love you's and we will make endless love to each other; yet the words to establish the exact point where we are in the present, in *jetzt-zeit—nowtime,* as Benjamin wrote—will likely forever elude me: like the precise point at which what in life or thought at first was merely incompleteness, after repetitions and the fall of limits, the incompleteness of love transforms into loss, then sometimes into evil. Or, like the circumstances in which prudence becomes cowardice, which happened to me, circumstances that leave wounds, soul wounds, which no penitence or atonement can heal, fade away.

Maxime's eyes bore into mine, an inbred and cultivated boldness marking her expression. And she waits. She waits. What is she waiting for? For me to mention Martha? I don't even breathe her name. The evasive and deceitful word still eludes me. Or it evades me. The question now is: What does she expect? What will she expect from me when we have merged? Can I allow her to count on me considering my broken promises and the betrayal that continue to torture me? The crux of my life of all these years. That I still try to explain and detail and justify—and overcome.

While in silence we pose one to the other the critical ontological question of why, just as I hear one of the trio—not even the vocalist—recite the song's words I've since learned—*Like a circle in a spiral, like a wheel within a wheel…like the circles that you find In the windmills of your mind!*—in that critical moment, Hank lovingly intervenes: "I hereby exonerate you from your ordinarily obligatory presence until closing time, and wish you happy journey—you both need love, sleep and time. And then tomorrow the live musicians will be back with more new old songs—and so you too, with a new song."

Maxime's weak smile fades as something never ending in her resurfaces. She takes my hand. I tell her that no other tavern in the world would give drinkers in love such a sendoff. Like zombies we move toward the great door while Hank explains to someone that we are two of the just. Hank being Hank, he means Reds. Approval sounds from a table near the mahogany bar. On the cobblestones outside we reach for each other, and enlaced one into the other we make our way down the hill toward the first houses.

At Hank's, high on Mount Titano, you may come to think that nothing else exists beyond the barren mountain and its crumbling castle. But it's not like that at all. Not at all. At a bend in the cobblestone walkway, we stop for the spectacular view of the lights of Rimini provided by the *tramontana* winds that have magically cleared the cosmos out there where infinity lies. Mount Titano is like a small island—our island—elevated to somewhere in the immensity between end time and infinity. We look over the parapet and shudder at the abyss, a drop straight down of hundreds of meters to a level marked by jagged, sharply pointed rocks and a complete family of four oak trees—male, female and their two children—looking upwards at us. Life on the rock. A whole life unfolding on that nearly barren level on the side of a barren mountain only minutes from a beautiful green sea. I feel that we two people of the entire human race are invisible and drunkenly I tell her of how after the north wind blows over Rome for its three days of life you can see the ski slopes of Mount Terminillo perfectly clearly. Perfectly clearly.

"If you believe in magic", I begin.

"Shh, shh," Maxime whispers. "It is magic, the magic of life." She kisses me in her way and we speak no more. Thoughts too fly away. Only feelings exist and the sensations of love. Mere sounds express all. Let it all come down as it may. We will speak words another day.

***

Sunrays inch their way across their room, illuminating Maxime's serene sleeping face in gold. Its sad look is no longer there. "Memory of memories falling on our heads," John mutters to himself. "First, there is the original event when it happens," he recites from the text of the book he is writing. "In the instant of its occurrence, the authenticity of that happening shows forth, unmistakable, genuine and real, as described by our old friend, Wordsworth. Second, then, comes the remembrance of an eye witness of the happening. Then, in sequence like in the telephone game of persons standing in a circle, one whispering a phrase into the ear of the next, until at the end of the circle another story emerges. As you can imagine, passing time too dilutes that first remembrance into an elusive recollection of the happening, which has gradually become a reconstruction of the now vague remembrance of the event. Like the New Testament. Like Jesus Christ. The original happening has been transformed: it dwindles and dwindles on its way to becoming legendary. It may be remembered as grander and more glorious than it was when it happened; or, in the same way in gray reality infamous and loathsome."

Maxime stirs and half smiles.

John recalls: "In the same way, memory of the end of a love affair first becomes a remembrance; then a less precise recollection of the break with the love that once was. Finally, as the years pass, your recollection has become a hazy reconstruction of what happened or may not have happened. Vagueness and gradual amnesia and self-deception have had their way: you've become convinced of the infidelity of the loved one or the disloyalty of an ideal to which you've been loyal. Your reconstruction is your subjective adjustment of how things happened and how they played out: you believe you've remained loyal but that the object of your love or your beliefs has betrayed you. Until finally, with time and reason, you accept that your perception of the reality of the loved one or of the belief was misconceived from the beginning."

"Maxime, you know those things too, don't you?"

Again she smiles, her eyes still closed. Did she or did she not hear? He thinks: 'That's the dilemma of the protagonist of a love story as he tries to come to terms with the great moment of his life and with the beliefs he once held dear. But he accepts that his memory—remembrances, recollections and reconstructions—will never coincide with what really existed or with what really happened. Did Samantha really return to me with my leg propped on the chair and say, Poor Poppy? Twice? Or maybe three times? It is important to remember which. Perhaps he will never grasp the true reasons of why or of the manner in which the great fracture in his life came about. For in the passing of time his perceptions and conceptualizations warped and altered his remembrance of the reality of what was and of what occurred. The defensive task of the brain must be the accommodation of the needs and instincts of your own frangible being in order to make them bearable so that you do not blow your brains out on a daily basis.

He will try again. It now sometimes seems that the last time he was still uncertain. He feels that he has always been uncertain, tentative, conjectural, blindly tap, tap, tapping his way in the darkness. His uncertain way—since Samantha. The diffident way he has been following since the beginning with Martha. Yet he believes he now knows something new: more than an attempt to rediscover a certain past. No more failures allowed. No more futile chases. Most likely he'd only imagined he'd truly sought homelessness and believed he'd found it on Mount Titano—before Maxime. But finding her came more expensive than he'd calculated; he now knows that nothing comes for free. The price to be paid is the adaptation to substitutes for the original. The original? Martha? What is he thinking of Martha? Fixed word images have accompanied him since back then—back at midway. His search companions have been words and the goal of a final return and his indecipherable dream words 'come crashing through'. Return? Though few get the chance, return is an immeasurable, irreplaceable possibility. And to achieve return he had 'to come crashing through'—as Arendt noted: *Fearlessness is what love seeks*. Zetkin, the Freudian, in his expansive studio in Paris had insisted he dream definite describable dreams about it and that he repeat them to him. Write them down, the shrink advised. But what else has he been doing but writing down his dreams?

In his mind, September melancholy showed forth. The seventeenth of that fatal month passed. The sadness that could enhance the necessary inner harmony he sought and the affinity with the mainstream that he'd never experienced—he'd been too long in Underground. He thought of the solitude of Schiller's poor King Philip II in his play, Don Carlos, in which the Marquis Posa betrays the King, who then weeps and weeps in his sadness because he was always so alone and unloved and then when he finds a friend, the Marquis, the friend betrays him. Yet, the point is that during the writing Schiller was deeply interested in political idealism and in 1785 wrote the *Ode of Joy*, proclaiming the brotherhood of man and endorsing the notion of a higher force guiding humanity towards freedom, a spirit which infects Schiller's work. It was the summer's end, John mused. Such thoughts flashed across his mind, snippets of ideas never developed. Summer's end was a sad time of the year, the time when he was most aware of the great pain that had lain in ambush for him when he finally surfaced from Underground. The pain—and the accompanying solitude and passions and the vice of the thus far incurable omnipotent prevarication that inhabited him—the price to be paid for the unspoken, unmentioned fame that he sought. Unspoken, unimagined, rejected but nevertheless dreamed of fame. And besides, he rejected the belief that development is destiny, as some great intellects affirm. How, he asked himself, could art depend on destiny? Art itself, is an entity; art enhances life, enriches it. A career of fame quickly fades; art flowers for centuries.

End time sensations overcome him in September. But this September, Maxime is there in all her beautiful flesh and glorious form. And she changes everything. Everything except September sadness and melancholy; her presence lightens his sense of loneliness but only brushes his melancholy. Oh, Maxime! Are you my home? Or only a country inn for the weekend?

October approaches. The days dwindle down. And mornings, the cowardly day light arrives ever more distant from Hank's closing time while the late September days wane and wither like the bourgeois state for the people of San Marino. The days, the still warm September days, wane and dwindle as does the world itself. And he wonders if they can block time.

The two lovers descend deeper into each other. Much deeper than he'd imagined possible. We're no longer two, in-love-with-love. We're now one, as Isolde sings to Tristan. And illuminated by the most egotistical of Adriatic skies they cling to waning September, in their upside down life loyal to Hank's 'midnight until the approach of dawn.' On some dwindling afternoons they go to the beach at the Grand Hotel in Rimini and Director Norris comes out to greet them personally—John Sutton the San Marino writer. And today, a fine crisp day, he tells Maxime the story of Fellini-Roma-Rimini and the Grand.

"Remember the Rimini boys in AMARCORD dancing on the wide steps of a great seashore hotel on a dark winter's night? Remember them, Maxime? That was the Grand. That image marked indelibly this town and this hotel where we grab the last rays of summer sun stands like an elegant symbol of times past which is actually what Fellini's cinema is all about: Memories. Memories, Maxime. Memories. Fellini told me so! For him the Grand expressed the province's search for the beautiful world far away and was a monument to the Rimini Belle Époque that skipped over San Marino. Rome was far away. Europe was distant. Rimini and this hotel where you and I lie on the sandy beach conditioned his art, his view of life as seen in his images of the epoch, itself symbolized by the Grand Hotel where he stayed on his visits back in his home town. The manager once told me that Fellini in Rimini became a quiet, simple man without pretensions in contrast to his boisterous Rome image."

"John, did you know Fellini in Rome?"

"No, but I interviewed him once and he said the Grand Hotel for him was a ray of light from the world beyond the railroad tracks, in contrast to the boredom of the provinces still so isolated in those days. For that reason his principle film characters were immersed in a desolate interior solitude. Just across the rail tracks from the Grand lies the 2,300 year old town—the streets and piazzas of Fellini's cinema. A Roman town with amphitheater and Augustus' Triumphant Arch of 27 B.C. But superimposed on the antiquity is Fellini's Medieval-Renaissance town where Brunelleschi worked. This narrow strip of land between the sea and the north-south railroad tracks was a beacon to Rimini youth, a place where in the night they felt physically the passing of great express trains and ocean liners. The contrast between the provincial town on one side of the tracks and the wide world on the other became the center of his art.

"The scene in AMARCORD of the boys of the provinces dancing together an old-fashioned dance, slowly and silently, on the steps of the Grand Hotel and the passing in the night fog of the mysterious ship, the REX, underlines that contrast, the reality of their yearning and the symbolism of the REX in the night—in the distance, intangible and evanescent. He said that for forty years he'd been trying to explain something he couldn't explain. For forty years he'd been asked questions he couldn't answer. He said usually only a character or a shadow of a memory offered him a saving hand. You know, Maxime, that's why watching a Fellini film is like walking along the narrow edge of an abyss during an earthquake. You grasp for meanings.

"Fellini's explanations were useless because he was such a liar. He had to be. Whatever information about one film or the other wrung from its symbolist author was necessarily a lie. One of the few truths he ever uttered was that he was always autobiographical, even if he was telling the story of the life of a fish. The Maestro was always trying not to answer any questions about AMARCORD set in his native Rimini. He said that AMARCORD is a harmony that intrigues that seduces, like the alluring name of an aperitif, but that he'd only wanted to portray a real Italian province. Maxime, Fellini was a dreamer. A wanderer and a follower of circuses, the observer of life, and caricaturist. This town on the Adriatic Sea—your sea too, I believe, not mine— was the point of departure and a subtle point of reference for all his cinematographic works, for his 'scribblings' as he defined his films. Rimini, right here under us, over us, inside us too, was the base of all the Felliniana."

Lying on the sandy seaside in front of the Grand Hotel with Maxime's head against his, he mused that AMARCORD marked Fellini's return to his ur-home in Rimini: Fellini had something in his spirit missing in his own. "I need a home too, Maxime. San Marino is not home, nor was Paris a home. The thing about Fellini is that he never really deserted this complex town. The Roman-Medieval Rimini on the one hand and the typical provinces and the world of tourism on the other remained in his blood."

16.

Maxime

Maxime Novak has shoulder length light brown hair with blondish meche on one side, wide set bluish eyes, the high cheek bones of her Slovene father, of average height, the wide hips, narrow waist and ankles of her Italian mother and a spectacular figure. 'But who is this woman inside whom I now live?' John wonders. Maxime, who in this miniscule country teeming with accidental revelations and irrefutable cries for help, for some inexplicable feminine passion or on an arbitrary impulse responded to the call of John's desperate maleness; his salvation appeared to be her task in life. John felt that though he was merged securely in her, he was still less free of final commitments than she imagined. He had the thought that even if his was a good heart as Ivaan and Père François believed, he knew he had an egocentric soul—he sometimes felt he was the only one to continue suffering for Samantha. '*A wheel within a wheel*', he hummed distractedly. '*Like a tunnel that you follow to a tunnel of its own.*'

No matter his good heart. No matter his egocentric soul. For here on his shoulder lies Maxime, silent and mysterious Maxime, integral Maxime. And as Hank says 'that woman will never be part an European bourgeois." Considering her story, how could she be? But was that enough to live a life? Her father was a Communist activist during the Cold War, near the end of which she was born in San Marino a few years before they moved to Vienna where she attended bilingual schools, Italian and German, neither of which she was—like John and his Dutch passport. And like him, Maxime, with her extravagant name and her background, was forever the outsider.

"John!"—she often said his name first when she spoke to him—"John, yes. John, oh! John, please. Why? For you are John. It's not the same thing if you are Novak."

"You're right, Maxime. Names change things. It would not be the same at all if my name were William or Georg or Hans, would it? No, it would not be the same. Do you like your name, Maxime?"

"I don't like it at all."

"But it's a wonderful name. It is you. It says you. It expresses you. What name would you like then?"

"I've always wanted to be named Tiziana."

"Tiziana! Why on earth that frivolous name? It's a silly name."

"Tiziana is a happy name, John, and I want to be happy."

"Well, I've never considered happiness a goal in life. No, Maxime is strong, expressive, to the point. Maxime says it all. You can hear your force in the Latin roots of your name."

"Maxime is a sad name, John. Sad, not happy. It's the past. Maybe Tiziana is the future"

"Yes, Maxime is sad. Thank God. I like a sad, serious name. Names are unique to humanity. A name establishes identity," he said, preachy as ever. "It's an identifier and it has a meaning and a relationship to the person bearing it. Shows the importance of language for personal names which are symbols for the individual—like Maxime is for you. Maxime means the best, the most. And John is the servant. Maxime and John, I love the sound."

"John the servant and sad Maxime! Much better a servant than a sad mortal Maxime. Maxime and sadness make me think of death. John, I love life and I love you but I would love you more if I were Tiziana. I love...John, have you ever loved before?"

"Once, but not like this?" John knew her question was serious and that he was prevaricating.

"What happened?"

"It ended. I was a coward and we separated," he simplified.

"That is sad."

"And you, Maxime? Have you loved before?"

"No, never. I tried. I really tried. I've always looked for love. But I never found it. But there is a man—a crazy man—who thinks he owns me. He thinks that I belong to him because I did live with him for a while. And I did care for that strange man; but John, that's not love."

"Belong to him! Care for him! No, Maxime, that's not love. I hate such words. Like in love songs. You know the kind I mean. 'I belong to you and you belong to me.' No-o, there's no love without freedom, that's for sure. It's curious that this conversation is so much like the story I'm writing that if I continue it now I'll be influenced and in the end I'll plagiarize myself. When a publisher asked me for another story about the end of a love affair, I thought right off of a story this time set in the Republic of San Marino that people still think of as a dinky little inland offshore with many banks to handle dirty mafia money—which of course goes into the story—despite all Italian and European Union efforts to erase the nasty image. This book won't bring me fame, that's for sure.

Fame? For the writer of *such* stuff? It will send me to the bottom ring of Dante's hell. Oh, just to create a good love story, something unique and solid and meaningful—something unclassifiable. So that critics could write: *'Is he a novelist?' 'No, not exactly.' 'A commentator then?' 'No-o-o. Sutton's simply unclassifiable!'*

"But John it *is* true that love affairs end. You know that. That's sad, but love stories have a start and an end. But I don't think a love affair is real love. Real love doesn't just end. Still, what if my feelings for you, or yours for me, turn out bad?—that's another reason I'm sad."

"Somebody said that sadness doesn't know where to go but downwards. And that that's why love seeks fearlessness."

"Maybe that's true. Those words sound about right…because of my fear. Sadness makes me think of death and I hate the feeling that death is stalking me. The word is ugly. And scary. And I'm afraid. I think we need a new word just to ease its finality. I mean, all around us people are dying, just passing on. First, cremation. Then they're only ashes. They no longer exist—at least not as we knew them. Why, it's like we live only to die. And that's horrible."

"Well, I saw in Mexico that people there feel differently. For them the dead still exist. Mexicans feed them, leave food for them on holidays. They live with the dead—on good terms with *la muerte*. It comes back like a visitor; they believe its departure is only temporary."

"But not *der Tod*. German death crushes and smashes its victims without pity. That's what's so horrible, the pitiless final death of the loved one. And the ashes that the wind just carries away. And that's the end of life. Whssst, and it's gone. But, John, I run the risk: I love. A paradox, no?"

"Well, yes, because in reality and as far as love is concerned, you're fearless. At least I think of you that way. Am I right?"

Maxime hesitated, looked off into the depths of the room, momentarily absent and said in a low voice: "Not exactly." I didn't understand that 'not exactly' but I didn't pursue the subject though later I thought I should have.

"But still the death part, *muerte* or *Tod,* however you see it and how you live with it is a matter of culture. Realistic or romantic or fatalistic," John said carefully, Maxime's hypothetic fear of death hanging between them like Samantha's death hung between Martha and him: the reason for not telling her of Samantha; it would change their relationship forever.

"In my novel I have to face the question of death. The grandfather of one of the main characters says that you just have to accept the idea of death—your own death, that is— you have to talk about it, reason about it, so that it gradually becomes more familiar. His point is that you just have to get used to the idea. Still, the real death of another, your own daughter for example, is something else."

At that hypothetical point, John stopped. He decided not to involve her in his own mourning. But he thought about it. Or did he? It seemed so much of his life turned on that point: mourning. Was sharing his suffering with others mourning? Mourning must be in silence, in oneself, he decided: indivisible, unutterable, beyond words, beyond verbal description. But he knew what his mourning meant. He knew. He knew the names of death in different languages but he couldn't pinpoint the proper word for mourning for a departure of a loved one into the world of death. Attitudes of scorn, or respect, or resignation make a parody of real mysterious death about which we know nothing, making life absurd and the end of life banal. Why live at all? the philosopher asks. No, how to live best? others rebut. Life's a circus, they say. Only a Fellinian dream, and we are readers of dreamed lives. And we can speculate, even though John doesn't understand if he can speculate that he is speculating and that therefore he exists. Actually, everybody fears some aspect of death: first of all the act of dying, then the Afterlife—or a third aspect, Afterdeath. The last two domains seem about the same—but maybe they're not. An artist like Klee with his Angelus Novus thinks more about the Afterlife. For when a person dies, one way or the other he has to cross the famous underworld river separating the world of the living from that of the dead. That's the gloomy voyage of the ultimate traveler. A stern face and meek gaze and an expression as terrorized by that world as strange and unknown to the newly dead as is the world of whales to the living. But then, so is said, the eyes of the new dead quickly adapt to the darkness and become part of it and are still able to see—the sexless new dead is still in a process of disintegrating. *It* is falling into pieces. *It* already looks like Lego pieces: to be put together and taken apart again. The compassion we the living may feel for the dead person is of course also compassion for ourselves because the inevitability of death doesn't muffle the fear of the tragedy of our own mortality. So we resist. Some, to the very end. Then off we go down the scary river Styx, shattered by the very materiality—the disintegration—of dying. Already a mere trace remains, not even an echo of the materiality of life. No! He shouldn't even allow his mind to think such thoughts. No, never! But his mind had a brain of its own. A will of its own. And after all his mind was still mourning. Still, maybe we try to follow it, him, her—the face may be horrified and astonished at its disintegration, but not his or her soul, which still keeps its spiritual equanimity and looks at us with its memories alive—still remembering how it was and how it became. For artists like Klee capable of existentializing everything through imagination, the future is not an exercise in ignoring death—but a living, still remembering after-death experience.

***

Maxime has begun saying that 'whatever' our relation is, it can last only one year. The first time she said that, I smiled. A time limit on love? Hers and mine? To be honest with myself and what I felt, I should say my *love* for her, but her *fondness* for me. What more could I honestly expect from her when I haven't spoken openly to her of Martha or even mentioned Samantha and my mourning not-yet-become sadness? I did say that the one year limit sounded to me like a practice in the world of Zamyatin's utopist novel, *We*, in which every step of existence is timed and regulated. But in her colorful language Maxime insists on that 'one fucking year'. Two months have already passed and she still won't say why. Just that it has to end after one year: the reason she's now sadder than earlier, the reason she resists what she calls fate— which is something else we don't share since my views on fate leave at least some hope for us—at least a loophole. So I hammer my views into her. "Nonsense," I repeat. "Fate, destiny, chance, it's only helpless man trying to rationalize his mortality. Besides in literature and in philosophy, the terms Destiny and Fate are used interchangeably. Some philosophers believe Destiny implies that our future is the will of one intelligent force; others that it is the predetermined outcome of the laws of nature. Neither of which seems to fit us. And then there is Jung and his shadow life. You've heard Hank use the Russian *sud'ba* often—he loves that word—and he claims Russians live by it. He thinks my return to Mount Titano was pure destiny at work. For Chrissakes, he thinks we are all helpless playthings of destiny. Too reductive for me! I deal with pure chance."

I recall but don't dare reveal to Maxime the ancient Etruscan belief that nothing happens by chance, nothing at all—like our paths crossing on a high barren mountain in San Marino. Superstitious as they were, the Etruscans removed the whole idea from the present; they believed everything that happens is to announce a future event, or is the realization of a sign the gods had sent earlier—not as a portent or the foreshadowing of a future evil—but instead they regarded such events as the fulfillment of an evil already presaged. Facts as such were not important because they happen but because they arrive in order to have a meaning in the future.

For Chrissakes, Maxime's acceptance of some man's claim to her is not fate; it's her own obsession. Makes me think I should just walk away, for that woman is going to cause me a lot of pain someday, maybe even worse pain than the other time.

During the six months after I met Martha briefly in Rue Fabert and then saw her Missoni scarf hanging in the cloakroom at

Ivaan's, we continued speaking by phone and finally agreed to meet at Orly for lunch at the airport restaurant. Again there, she did what she did in Rue Fabert; this time she had to break off quickly to catch her return flight. Then, again, a year later I returned to Paris, this time uncertainly, to meet her in Rue Fabert: together we visited Samantha in the Montparnasse cemetery—the devastation still lived in us. Another August 15 had passed, then September 17. That evening, at one point during dinner in the downstairs restaurant she repeated the familiar refrain: "Sutton, don't you ever leave me." We stayed the night there in the apartment—once ours, now hers. She was traveling with a big suitcase this time, apparently for a long stay. And I slept in the guest room, alone. I left the next day without seeing Ivaan at the Embassy. I'm uncertain why but certainly it had to do with the Missoni scarf hanging in his cloakroom. A minute matter perhaps in a whole lived life, yet so meaningful for my role in my own existence. And I still wonder what it all means.

***

We're driving in my shiny black car up the Adriatic coastal highway to see the rain falling on Venice and Piazza San Marco under water. And to see if the MOSE water barriers out in the lagoon really block the high water from the Adriatic as the modern Venetian Doges, aristocrats and officialdom claim. We're still an hour from Venice and the tropical marshland that Northerners imagine they will find there, a city of water under a steaming southern sky, a prehistoric world with its islands and watery canals. The car rocks and swerves, a plaything of the gusts and bursts of a northeastern wind arriving from Hungary and the steppes of Russia so that the rain comes at us almost laterally. Suddenly Maxime takes my arm and cries, "John, John, here! Stop here! And I'll tell you the secret."

As alarmed as curious, I stop along a boardwalk facing the Adriatic Sea to the East. The sky is gray, the wind strong and humid. Thunder rumbles around the sea, the waves farther out from shore look cold and white and malicious. Nature seems to hold everything in jeopardy. Not a living soul is to be seen. I look at Maxime in trepidation. Will she tell me she's pregnant? Or will she reveal she has some terminal disease?

"It was like this that day in Beirut…"

"Beirut? What day in Beirut? Well, a missing chunk of your biography emerges. You were in the Middle East?"

"I went there with him. With Bernard. He's a musician, you know. You could have seen him at Hank's years ago. After hanging around me for a while he asked me to go with him to Beirut where his band had an engagement. I did. But I didn't love him. I just wanted to get away from San Marino. Start my life over somewhere else. Anyway, the first months went by fast in Beirut and life was exciting and different. Except for his obsessive jealousy, my life was peaceful and I studied Arabic. Then, on a day something like this we were walking on a street along the sea front. He was holding my arm tight as always, so that I didn't run away— as I wanted to at times. Only a light rain was falling. The streets were empty. No cars. No people. Until suddenly a tall elegant man appeared coming toward us along the sidewalk. He was smiling at me. He was a teacher in the language school I went to. Bernard dropped my arm and stopped. The other man made some remarks to me in Arabic and ignored Bernard. Then it all happened so fast that I—a naïve twenty-three year old girl from San Marino—hardly understood what was going on: Bernard pulled a small black pistol from his pocket—he always carried a pistol, always—and immediately shot the man three times right in the chest. I was stunned, far from canny; it seemed the world was suddenly transformed into a dream-like state and I was either losing my mind or seeing my own life through a distorted perspective. Then he took me by the arm again and we walked on, pretending that nothing had happened. Now keep in mind that he's a psychotically jealous man, but he'd twisted his problem into mine: he said my problem was narcissistic sociopathy and that I was unable to love. Once he fired a member of his band for flirting with me and slapped me for "letting it happen". He said the lesson to that man on the sidewalk was wasted since he was dead but that it was a lesson to me too…if I tried to leave him. With a terrorized look in his eyes at what he'd just done, he said I had to accept the reality that I belonged to him. But right then I had the feeling that wasn't the first time he'd killed. So on the spot I decided to leave—to escape, I should say. I came home, back to San Marino. Then shortly after—long before I met you—he came to San Marino hoping to take me back to Beirut and again asked Hank to engage his famous band. Hank just laughed in his face and sent him packing and warned him not to show his face in San Marino again."

The thought that she *belonged* to someone else drove me crazy, as crazy as the idea of my still belonging to another—but that he was a killer and back here to get her seemed absurd.

***

The planks were laid out in a mystical pattern of precise squares and ninety degree angles intersected by diagonals racing unimpeded the full one hundred and eighty meters of the Piazza straight onto the mosaics of the Cathedral. The bewildering structure looked like a creation of modern alchemists, those who also experimented with the transmutation of stone into immortality: the obsession of historians of esotericism and psychologists, philosophers and spiritualists today impacting us puny artists. What might have been the *magnus opus* of the earliest Venetians appeared as architectural poetry to us. The scheme of the crisscrossing boards laid out on barrels so that you could literally walk on water had a magical effect: it changed my whole perspective of Venice's absolute flatness and created a new enthusiasm for this land of nature's water and man's ingenuity rising everywhere out of the depths of the water. The mathematical precision of the crisscrossing patterns and the landlessness of the unfettered water and chilling noiselessness of its spellbinding rise from the depths created a sensation of something disturbing, indefinite and incomplete, a new perspective so distorted as to transmute into the grotesque—but, at the same time, it seemed, showing that there is an aesthetic in all things, mathematical or enigmatic.

"To erect those MOSE high water barriers out there in the lagoon to save Venice from flooding they spent billions and twenty years while corruption ran wild," I reminded her. "Now look at this! Piazza San Marco under water! A landless water world. All these magnificent structures, the splendid palace, the cathedral of San Marco, the Bridge of Sighs, the columns of the lion and the saint, the tower and the clock that the former Republic of Venice erected to awe seafarers arriving from the edges of the empire and from the distant corners of the world. Today, the planners must finally accept the reality that you can't really stop the terrifying force of water; it goes where it wants. The barriers rise mysteriously out of the agitated waters of the lagoon as they're supposed to do but we still have to walk on the boards if we want to have a cocktail in the Florian."

"John, I get dizzy just watching people tottering along these planks," she said and stepped up bravely on a boardwalk running along the Grand Canal side of San Marco. "For heaven's sake, everybody seems to enjoy it this way."

"They say you get the hang of board-walking quickly."

"Like walking a tight rope over an abyss," she said, plunging ahead.

"Or walking the Chartres labyrinth," I said, recalling how I teetered and tottered on the internal concentric rings of the maze in the great cathedral.

"I'll never get sea legs," Maxime repeated.

We were nearing the Campanile tower when Maxime looked up, lost her balance on the board and fell into the water landing on her feet in what turned out to be only about twelve inches deep floodwater. Wet to her knees, she crawled back on our board, and in a haltingly drenched gait, in Indian file, we arrived at the Caffé Florian where a squad of tuxedo-clad waiters covered her legs with a huge beach towel while we indulged in their gin specials.

"A little water won't hurt us and besides that red and gold blanket complements perfectly your daring purple jacket and silky black scarf—all dry—and you are beautiful." Beautiful, I thought, but never had she looked so vulnerable, which was not a condition my Maxime relished. In that moment, for the first time, I wondered if I contribute to her sense of vulnerability. I, the most precarious of the precarious, have already proved with Martha that I am not an anchor to hold onto.

"Makes me almost glad I fell in, all this attention from the waiters and you."

"I believe you'll always have plenty of attention."

"*His* attention too might be my death," she said unable to let Bernard go.

There are odd times in life, usually when multiple occurrences convey to you the real perils of your life, even death itself, that you are inclined to joke and make light of everything so as not to fall into depression and almost wish it were all over and done with—if you just didn't have to face the act of dying. This was one such time.

"Or mine," I added.

"That too, and you have to take his threat seriously. Bernard's a killer, you know."

To divert her and myself from that recurrent theme, I told her that the flooding is actually paradoxical in its positive effect on Venice's tourism industry. People come to see the natural disaster. Or experience it. Like visiting Vesuvius before the eruption! Despite the damage the high water does to the city and the havoc it causes—the flooded San Marco Square and sightseeing from the boards crisscrossing the piazza—that unique alchemist experience delights visitors who can say back home, 'I saw Venice under water and I walked on the boards on Piazza San Marco', as though saying I saw Venice before it sank into the waters like Atlantis—

that rich and wicked island that sank and now maybe rests on the deep sea bottom in the Atlantic Ocean. Venice, the city on water, under water. Venetians say that water has a magical quality: it is omnipresent. Take any *calle*, any alley, any canal, turn to the left or to the right, and you end up in water. Water, water, water. The most absent-minded wanderer or the writer sunken in his reveries steps out of his hotel to see the city and by instinct he ends up at some body of magical water. His every automatic step is waterward. What do Italians of today and yesterday dream of all winter long? They dream of bodies of water. They think of vacation, they think of water. And that is all right. Venetians are like that as are all Italians. So with Maxime and me. With halting steps, we tottered a bit more on the elevated over-the-water boards; we glanced at the hydrous mosaics inside an abandoned San Marco cathedral and again I thought Chartres and then, Zetkin. Ah, the connections, the connections. If I could only connect all the dots, all those isolated, sometimes lonely dots of a life, things like my own life might make sense. We looked into a couple of shops where yellow-booted proprietors stood knee deep in water; and again, we leapt down off the boards into the 17th century Caffé Florian for another round of cocktails before we—both of us by then watery-eyed—boarded the boards leading over the water back to the Hotel Prince to our big room with its high ceilings and tall windows and with its perfect view of the lagoon. And so it came about that to the sounds of pouring rain on our wide balcony and against the windows looking out over the lagoon to the Lido and the putt-putt of nearly empty *vaporettos* traveling across the lagoon between the San Marco landing station and the Lido and while the MOSE barriers and the Adriatic water invading the city of water rose and fell, we two water-soul searchers from Mount Titano in the San Marino Republic shacked up at the Prince for three days and three nights of love and talk in our search—as Octavia Paz wrote—in each other's body and mind for something we'd both lost somewhere along the way, or for a hitherto unrevealed secret—for our being in the middle of what for me has too long been non-being.

Maxime. Maxime. Maxime. The trilogy of her. Maxime, sad. Maxime, obsessed with death. Maxime lost and confused in love and in fondness. In my loneliest moments I feel sorry for myself too and have the mad thought that I have only Maxime in my life—and her only in part. No one in the Netherlands to which I no longer belong—to which I really never belonged despite my passport. No one in Germany where I was deserted by my few friends when I adopted foreign ideologies and I began writing of matters and of events to them foreign. No one real in Paris since Samantha and Martha left my life—except, well, Ivaan and Zetkin. Now I know that only part of Maxime exists for me. When she asks where love lives—as though I of all people knew the answer—I say it lives in our minds and our bodies. Sad Maxime says it's a gift that lives in us in many different ways and manners of expression and is always changeable and unpredictable and that it may be taken away from one instant to the next; I thought then she meant by death—but now I'm not sure that is all she thought at the time. And I think about Samantha and realize that enduring love lives also—maybe chiefly—in memory. And, memory, as you know, is not a tea party. Memory means re-visiting the grief you flee, or at least, deceive. It's the hurt, the ceaseless pain, the emptiness of life that *she* had made all joy and love. Memory holds tight the echoes of Samantha's laughter. And memory, for me, means the nothingness that has remained after she left.

The next day, rain. All day, pouring rain. Lying in bed and the eternal rain. Breakfast in bed and the everlasting rain. And under our balcony the sound of gondolas, *thap-swish, thap-swish, thap-swish*, as the gondoliers in their unique, coffin-black conveyances push valiantly and somewhat lawlessly ahead in the rain, stroke by stroke in denial of the existence of the tourism-enhancing rain: for them the Venice-Venezia Venedig rains never were, no more that the pestilence raging in Thomas Mann's *Der Tod in Venedig* and Luchino Visconti film, La *Morte a Venezia* ever existed. Visconti. Rain and rain. I lay in bed and thought of the coincidence of Mann's pestilence arriving from Asia in Europe's ports and spreading throughout the world.

At the beginning of June the pesthouse of the Ospedale Civico had quietly filled; there was not much room left in the two orphan asylums, and a frightfully active commerce was kept up between the wharf of the Fondamenta Nuove and San Michele, the burial island. But there was the fear of a general drop in prosperity. The recently opened art exhibit in the public gardens was to be considered, along with the heavy losses that in case of panic or unfavorable rumors would threaten business, the hotels, the entire elaborate system for exploiting foreigners—and as these considerations evidently carried more weight than love of truth or respect for international agreements, the city authorities upheld obstinately their policy of silence and denial. The chief health officer had resigned from his post in indignation, and been promptly replaced by a more tractable personality. The people knew this; and the corruption of their superiors, together with the predominating insecurity, the exceptional condition into which the prevalence of death had plunged the city, induced a certain demoralization of the lower classes, encouraging shady and antisocial impulses that manifested themselves in license, profligacy, and a rising crime wave. Contrary to custom, many drunkards were seen in the evenings; it was said that at night nasty mobs made the streets unsafe. Burglaries and even murders became frequent, for it had already been proved on two occasions that persons who had presumably fallen victim to the plague had in reality been dispatched with poison by their own relatives. And professional debauchery assumed abnormal and obtrusive proportions such as had never been known here before, and to an extent that is usually found only in the southern parts of the country and in the Orient.

Our Venice Days, in this modern Atlantis, passed rapidly as unoccupied time does. Visible from our balcony, rain, falling rain. The only sounds were of water smacking against stone and the passage of the invisible *vaporettos* in the Grand Canal and, just under our window looking out to the rain world, the regular, determinant strokes of a mysterious gondola headed God knows where creating in watertown Venice the atmosphere of apprehensiveness and growing uneasiness. Were *vaporettos* and gondolas escaping? If so, why? Fleeing from what? And where was left to go? You think you might as well give in to your own desires and just let go as Zetkin did in the end, but not before turning me away from the flight he chose, which that madman was certain was lurking in my subconscious.

"Rain makes me think of death," morbid, death-obsessed Maxime murmured over the breakfast tray. "Especially mornings. Makes me sad. Actually, John, I think about death constantly. My first thoughts of the day concern death. Like walking on the boards of life and the boards of death at the same time. And with death, the final definitive loss of the possibility of love."

Resisting the temptation to tell her about Zetkin, I said instead that, "Rain is better than some of the summer sea air so inimical to your health. Definitely preferable to the scirocco blowing from the Libyan deserts, across the Mediterranean, up the whole peninsula into unsuspecting tourists from North Europe out on the Lido. Saves you from the thrill of walking through the sultry narrow streets noting all the carven lions on the ever ageing buildings of the old city and the sad façades of centuries old business shields. The rain spares you the torture of some gondolier forcing you out of his conveyance to see some glass-blowers establishment from whom he hopes for a sales commission. Ah, Venice, the queen of the seas! Maxime, the problem is that once you see Venice you are infected with its uniqueness, you never forget it and you have to go back, again and again."

17.

Visitors

From our balcony I followed a small island of sunlight floating across the Adriatic skies out beyond the Lido, high above the tumbling and indecisive clouds from time to time emitting droplets into the now tranquil and receding lagoon—the menacing lagoon that I would soon be missing. Hank had just called to inform me that Maxime's old friend, Bernard, had returned and was nosing around looking for her and that he was again begging for an engagement for his San Marino Blues Band. Moreover, the day before, Hank's two Algerian mobster friends of long ago had arrived in San Marino on business. Algerian friends meant those New Orleans gangsters he'd so loved. He said the joy he felt seeing them again was only slightly overshadowed by the troubles they brought. I told him we were returning home today and that the Bernard story would work out. And that as Maxime says, all things begin and all things end.

Our *motoscafo* raced toward the car parking area. Wind blew across the lagoon and down the Grand Canal. The rain had declined to a melancholy drizzle and from San Marco to Rialto the waters were receding. When we set out southwards down the coastal highway, it was still a grey, gloomy morning; yet a timid transition to a trusty sunny Italian autumn was underway. Maxime, the rain and the water, the symmetry of the walking boards, the strange silent sounds of gondolas passing under our windows in the unceasing rain, and now with each kilometer southwards the sensation of inexorable change in the air intensified my satisfaction with *that* Venice, as new to me as it was to Maxime. I took her hand and placed it on my leg, wondering if the watery Venice was a temporary phenomenon, or was it as enigmatic Robinson Jeffers suggested: "There is no reason for amazement: surely one always knew that cultures decay, and life's end is death". Surprising, I thought of Jeffers, claimed by the Right, who clarified that he favored the whole over the individual, that often-used escape clause that philosophical rightists hold in reserve. Or was Venice a flatland Atlantis after all. I, naïve and full of hope and trust, wondered if it is possible that we will ever find that Atlantis again. Actually and more realistically, in this moment of transition, Venice appears in my fresh memory as a potential Kitezh, the legendary Russian city beneath the waters of Like Svetolyar in the Nizhny Novgorod Oblast . On that thought, the disappointment of when I released her hand for a driving maneuver, she quickly removed it from my leg.

I looked at her askance. She didn't understand what I was thinking.

"Maxime, have you too thought it a strange phenomenon, the many incredible coincidences and extraordinary meetings in a life," I said, thinking aloud, "like our meeting in Hank's Bar at the isolated top of Mount Titano, or now the surprising arrival in the micro-state San Marino of Mafiosi from distant Algiers-America and that in the same moment of time, similar or maybe the same events are occurring in many places in the world—like chance meetings on the street with persons you dreamed of the night before—and that same person tells you he/she dreamed of you the night before. Maybe it's true that time as we think we know it doesn't exist at all. Life—and time too—are like that. Maybe the gods are confused. After all their miscegenations and distracted by their own problems, they forget the time thing—creating the historical confusions generating our slipshod relation to time today. Like those Islamic people I met in Paris who have no idea about when and where they are. Perfectly willing, it seems, to push a button or pull a wire and blow themselves to kingdom come. Who knows why? Many are not a bad lot at all. Just crazy. One of their leaders told me they just don't give a shit. Incredible! And now the return of Bernard."

The rain had ceased. From time to time a southern sun peeked through the tumbling gray clouds hanging from the azure skies. The green Adriatic was still seething. The tips of the riotous rolling breakers were white and capriciously menacing. There's nothing like a stormy sea to remind you that water covers two-thirds of our planet, a relatively unknown world, the true deepness and horrors of which we can hardly imagine, a world inhabited by repellant creatures so unlike those of *terra firma* and conveying dread and fear to land people. In South Europe water means also unstoppable rafts, rubber boats, make-shift floats carrying eighty, one hundred, one hundred and eighty unnamed and unidentified refugees looking for Europe, many of whom sink into that cold blackness that strikes terror into our hearts. No wonder their watery bodies rising to the water surface on cold Mediterranean nights and ending up on a deserted beach somewhere infect the landworld people with an unmanageable plague of guilt and sin. In recent days another phenomenon occurred in the Mediterranean and Adriatic seas: warships are playing deadly serious war games, games that land people cannot grasp. We stopped to watch the gray line of heavy ships several kilometers out to sea passing from one fog bank to another slowly, unaware and unknowing of the turmoil under the restlessly rolling and impartial seas they sailed, as oblivious to the fog and the churning waves as they were to the creatures in the world below. Obviously warships, but whose, we wondered, as they became smaller and smaller in the watery immensity. What were they doing here so near Venice? We watched the gray ships pass but we were thinking of the wild and untamable Venetian seas—and also about the killer, Bernard.

"John, do you think occurrences like Bernard's return before the one year is up and the arrival of those American criminals are coincidence or pattern?"

"Well, as a writer I have to believe in coincidences, even though they don't prove the existence of a relationship between the parallel events occurring around us. Still—and that's also a part of fantasy—I tend to believe that often there is a relationship—if only psychic. They relate directly to the problem of probability; it was both possible and probable that Bernard would come looking for you. I would've done the same. I saw you across the room of a bar and I saw you through a cut glass window and then we somehow merged. Our relationship could've been predicted even though it seems like pure coincidence—and it makes Bernard the improbable outsider."

So there on Italy's Adriatic coastal highway, speaking of one thing and the other, Maxime's mention of probability reminded me of a book my friend and shrink, Karl Zetkin, gave me, in the hope it would help me in facing my problems. In *The Mirror and the Lamp*, Meyer Abrams tackles the intriguing subject Maxime raised. Meyer's point is that just because a thing is possible doesn't mean it's necessarily probable. Yet, in the example of a U.S. attack on Russia, we have the following realities to assist us: America's possession of—in the words of the nation's President—"the best military in the world", a huge nuclear stock pile and the possibility-capacity to deliver a nuclear bomb wherever it desires, combined with the unknown X factor of the nature of man and his propensity to harm others and himself make nuking powerful Russia more than possible and in the opinion of many analysts in the long run probable. So you see, as Meyer writes, improbabilities do occur. And he doesn't forget that man has always had that unpredictable evil stain. Therefore, the devastation brought by a nuclear attack must be considered not only a distinct possibility—but probable. Foucault shows that fresh possibilities are nearly always present from which successive comparisons indicate increasing probability—even though it is not certain that the event will happen. So the convicted murderer can go to the gas chamber even if the one-billionth DNA comparison-possibility might have proved him innocent. Possibility can be measured and quantified but despites theories of mathematicians and statisticians, the thinking of Aristotle himself, no one really knows the meaning of probability. The duality of possibility-probability is an eye opener in comprehension and evaluation of daily news and the shortcomings of the lying, propaganda-ridden mainstream press; in that sense the question plays a major role in our lives. Some people consider probability merely a feeling or a hunch, an expression of something that might or might not happen, In fact, probability is in reality nothing more than the estimated measure of the possibility that an event will occur. We see it in police films, the decisive "probability" that fingerprints or DNA match which can even clinch a death sentence. Still, since *apparent* impossibilities sometimes happen, another approach is to distinguish probability from what is possible and what is plausible, but not forgetting the terrifying consequences if the improbable does occur. Moreover, we know that under certain conditions man is capable of almost any good or any evil act. Man can be peace-loving and warlike at the same time. Depending on his culture and ethic and environment and mood and the very nature of man, each characteristic is both possible and probable. Which completes the circle, and we are drawn back to the lodestone of the socio-political question, to the struggle that has gone on since private property emerged in ancient societies. We know the story. The proprietor-capitalist lords it over the wage earner who to change his situation is obligated to rebel. But of course the capitalist still doesn't change; the capitalist is capable of any act he can get away with. He can torture or nuke or imperialize as he pleases showing that within the realm of possibilities the most abominable improbabilities can occur. In our times pragmatism and the fact that a hostile odious act is possible becomes its ethical justification."

I will interrupt both my impromptu musings and this narration to reassure readers that the people in this story are not representative of the thirty-three thousand people of the population of the micro-Republic of San Marino. Nor are they intended to be. They *are* representative of the small percentage—the same as in every other place on Earth—of the different, of the diffident representatives of the existing social order of those who don't know where they belong or whom they represent; they are always in search of answers. They live their fragile and precarious lives in search of themselves. They err, fall, stand up and try again. And again and again. Dissatisfied with where they started out, they go out into the world in search of answers; but then, disillusioned, they return and join others like themselves gathered at the top of barren Mount Titano in a kind of exile. In that respect, they *do* form a sort of, well, if not exactly a sect, then a cult, as Sammarinese people farther down the mountain suspect. Because of the lack of answers to our questions and doubts as to who we are and where we belong, we hold onto our mountaintop overhanging the ancient sea over which humans before us have traveled, searching and hoping to discover the secrets of the mysteries of life, time and space.

***

Bernard Kristinsson was actually more like the others on Mount Titano than anyone imagined. Nonetheless, before he ever laid eyes on him, John had concluded that there were deadly voids in that man. And though he doubted the psychotic killer image Maxime painted of him, her *infidelity* in Bernard's sick eyes, the presence of her new lover, me, John Sutton, and a homicidal pistol ready in a potential killer's pocket were a dangerous combination. Christened Bernardo by his Sammarinese mother on his birth in San Marino City, his name itself was an eternal subject of dispute between his parents who separated soon after his birth. His Icelandic father, Kristin, called him Bernard, which he made official when he returned to Reykjavik and gained partial custody of the seven-year old boy. So as the Icelandic part of Bernard matured he was torn in his two lives between "Smoky Bay" Reykjavik and lofty San Marino: because of the clash between his lingering feelings for his native homeland in San Marino and his professional successes in Iceland, he couldn't live peacefully in either place. His father who was an expert piano tuner wanted his musically talented son to become a classical pianist. So Bernard studied music and became a gifted pianist; but father and son were at loggerheads over how his gift was to be used. Bernard loved jazz and blues more than classical music. And later he named his musical group the San Marino Blues Band, which made a name in Iceland performing in the *Harpa* concert hall and starring at three editions of the Reykjavik Blues Festival. The popularity of his band in Denmark and throughout Scandinavia did not satisfy his Sammarinese soul; he yearned for the same recognition in the South of Europe where he remained an unknown. Thus, the existence in him of an infinity of determination and dedication to the achievement of his goal: recognition.

Bernard has been waiting at Hank's Bar since late afternoon, alternately making his ghostly presence known or maintaining a careful low profile. Bernard: tall, skinny, gaunt face, long coal-black hair and live alert eyes. For the third or fourth time he caught the disconnected words of Hank's favorite song—the fragment of a song, half remembered names and faces and again noted the faces staring at him from a table across the room, dark faces, other world faces on Mount Titano. It's around eleven. He feels a current of cold air and again looks toward the great door. Not Max. The golden-skinned woman behind the bar who calls him Bernardo tells him that Maxime and John have been away but that they come nearly every night and always at midnight. Bernard knew Max was a night person; she would gladly go all night and sleep all day in an upside down, topsy-turvy life like she did in Beirut when the San Marino Blues Band was going strong at four in the morning and she wide awake and drinking indiscriminately. Those were good times: music and he madly in love with Max even though she'd loved him such a short time, he thought, and even though she came to claim she'd never loved him at all. In any case, Max was present in his life even if in the long run one-way love proved to be more painful than no love life at all. It could never be enough. And that dichotomy nurtured his jealous nature; he'd forbidden members of his band to speak with her or even look at her too much, too often or too long. But then came her Arabic studies in a downtown language school, a territory out of his control. What did she do there? Who were her friends? Who did she know there? She'd insisted on her school where for those long painful afternoon hours she escaped from him. Once she mentioned an English language teacher, not an Arab, she said, like that mattered. But at the mere mention of another man Bernard saw red and green flashes. What man wouldn't be jealous of provocative Max in her short mini-skirts, careless legs and that come-on look in her eyes and out God knows where in sensual Beirut, alone? Sometimes he wanted to strangle her. Or better, take her and the band back to Reykjavik and tame her once and for all. 'What the fuck! Am I a real musician or just the failed lover I feel I am? Well, I shot that Caucasian looking man—German maybe. A German spy? God knows why my thinking goes haywire like this. Wrong way on a one-way track. Onto the shunt I go. And the way that son-of-a-bitch leered at Max expressed clearly his intentions. Besides the detective reported he was reputed to be a spy for someone— most likely the French, or the USA. He took money from anyone. And he wanted to fuck my Max. Not on your life. He had it coming. Mine was a spontaneous reaction to the way he undressed her with his dirty fucking Levantine eyes that day I killed him...or could've killed him...or might've killed him. He just went too far in the pretense I paid him for. Yes, the son-of-a-bitch had it coming. *Si, l'ammazzarei volontieri, quel figlio di puttana,'* switching from French to Italian in his thinking. He realized that half the time he forgot in what language he was thinking. 'Do normal people do that? Was I crazy enough to kill him right there in public and only because of a drizzle nobody was on the street? Still, that little flirt ended abruptly. And killing him would be a crime of passion anyway. Does that count as a real crime? Not really. Mine would be an honor killing in Beirut, carried out in a sudden rage when I saw the man who dishonored my fiancée speaking to her on the street. But Max was terrified anyway. Because I carry this pistol. You just never know. But now I can't simply shoot this guy John here in San Marino and carry her off like a Sabine woman.' He drank another beer. No strong stuff tonight. Sober as a judge. He listened intently to the words of a song. *If You Go Away* with Stan Getz and thought Jacques Brel in French. He listened to the words of *Endless Love* and thought Max: *there's only you in my life.* 'I shouldn't listen to this sweet stuff, no wonder some musicians stick to hard rock and reject any pleasurable, soothing shit. Still, that song gets to you. Hank knows something I don't and he's not ashamed of it. Bah, *chacun son goùt.* He's the overtly romantic that I must be at heart. '*There's only you in my life...you will always be*...he whispered and again examined the two dark guys at a wall table across the room.

It's midnight. His head lowered, his eyes are fixated on the door. Then, right on schedule, there they are: promiscuous Max and her cool looking lover. Max leads the way to a table in a shallow niche along the far wall on the other side of the room. She reaches across their table for his hand. 'It's John. I remember his name and how Hank always called him Jack. He's not the small guy I imagined. As tall as me, but powerful looking, strong neck and shoulders. Long hair, short beard. Looks good in that black turtleneck under the short raincoat. Not handsome, but a strong man who knows what's what in life. You can see he has lived life! And that he adores her! But is there not *un je ne sais quoi* of sadness in his expression too? Yes, most definitely, like Max in that. They resemble each other. Objectively, I could like him. In other circumstances we'd probably be friends. Oh, fuck it all! Don't think such thoughts that don't advance one whit my grand monomaniacal project! That's why I'm here with this pistol in my pocket and wondering how it would be to kill him. To kill both of them if I have to.' Mad, ever uglier thoughts passed through his burning mind. Max turned her head to look around the bar; the first thing she saw was him. He waved. She reddened, pushed at her table and stood up shouting, "Hank! Hank! He's here. The killer is sitting right over there." Instantly, Hank was at her side, speaking softly, almost lovingly. telling her not to worry, that Bernard was just looking for an engagement for his band. As she calmed down, he saw her sadness return in full force. Suddenly, she and John stood up, waved to Hank and Juanita and left without glancing at him but leaving behind a contagious turmoil in the room filled with its usual assortment of late night drinkers and music lovers. Shortly after, he too saluted Hank and rushed out the great door.

The following night the same scene, Bernard on one side of the room, Maxime and John on the other. From time to time, John cast a discreet glance toward Bernard, while unspoken, unformulated words and thoughts passed between them. Again, John and Maxime drank a nightcap and left. After an hour of tension on the third night, Bernard gathered his courage and made his way uncertainly across the room toward Maxime. She observed his approach furtively. Again, Hank was at her side and all eyes in the sprawling barroom of art deco lamps, multi-colored candles and soft music were glued on the scene unfolding before them.

"Hello, Max," Bernard said hesitantly.

Without raising her eyes Maxime replied: "Fuck off, Killer,"

In the same instant, John leapt to his feet and the three men seemed to measure each other.

After some seconds of silence, Hank posed a hand on Maxime's shoulder and said in a soft voice: "Goodnight, Maxime. Goodnight, John."

Bernard backed off without a word.

For ten days straight, Hank dined regularly at his private table near the bar with the two dark men Bernard now knew were in San Marino concerning offshore banking for New Orleans mafia black money. Max and John didn't show up at all, but when he caught Hank alone he never missed an occasion to repeat a proposal of a trial gig of two or three nights for his Blues Band whose music he had come to believe in perfect harmony with Hank's musical tastes which were one of the charms of Hank's Bar: no musical crap of any kind or category, chiefly quality artists and music. No night at Hank's passed without *Ne Me Quite Pas* or its English version, *If You Go Away, Windmills In Your Mind* and *The End of a Love Affair*—Bernard felt the last was for him. Since many of the world's cult jazz musicians who came to Italy performed also at Hank's Bar in the Republic of San Marino, then why not the original San Marino Blues Band of native son Bernardo Kristinsson? Slapping his forehead with the palm of a hand, he said to himself over and over, why didn't I think of my own place? A tavern like this, my studio, my music hall and my music? Let people come to me instead of me tramping around the world asking for their approval. Like my painter friend in Denmark, who worked and sold his work to his admirers in his own studio-art gallery. My own music, a mecca for music lovers. There's nothing art lovers like more than to watch the painter or sculptor at work in his own place where they can participate in the creation of a work of art, art that will live in their own homes. People are curious. Some are discerning. They want to witness the act of creation. Creation of something from nothing is the great mystery, the expression of the great secret hidden inside us. I can still do it. It's possible. I know my music is good. It has quality. It's too good to waste on a bunch of hysterical kids. I'm already old for hopping around a stage like kids do. I've made my name in that milieu. Got to set my sights higher. Become a real artist.

Bernard spent those same ten evenings reviewing his own career: though he'd regretted shattering his dad's hopes and not becoming **a** concert pianist, his musical nature, his taste, his proclivities, and his raison d'être carried him into jazz. Not only did he found a successful band without degenerating into cheap music of compromise performed before crowds of screaming kids whose cheers and singing the text overshadow the singer and his song. He knew he wrote good music. He was the song writer-singer, the modern troubadour, poet and philosopher who reduce**d** essentials to a few memorable words. *Say goodbye to loneliness...restless heart why be lonely, stay with me.* In Bernard's view one good song was worth dozens of the piano recitals he never gave. His dad never understood the poetry in him. The magnificent sounds emitted by the pianos his father tuned for the great performers of the world would never equal the poetry in Hank's favorite song: *And the world is like an apple whirling silently in space, Like the circles that you find in the windmills of your mind.* What else could better describe man and the universe? What piano recital could reflect him, Bernard Kristinsson, searching through his life for a reflection that would show him who he is? One thought tumbling after the other led him straight back to Max—and to his madness. For what piano recital could adequately represent his hopeless attempt to tame untamable Maxime Novak and still call his relationship love when in the circles of his maddened mind flashed scenes of lashing the traitorous loved one? Poor writers. Poor fiction writers. Striving for the reductive, they're limited to the meanings of words. John Sutton in his San Marino love story can't be more reductive than words allow him. But I, Bernard Kristinsson, can achieve what he strives for because of the medium of music—the rhythm and rhyme and the limited time—and the obligatory reduction of words to the marrow, to the very heart, to the quintessence of the meaning of love gone, never to return. *Now I see you running round, in love again/the weight of the world of living without her, living at all.*

December rain. Day in, day out, rain. The *tramontana* winds and intense cold descended on Mount Titano. And Bernard felt himself changing. He chuckled at himself, at his easy threats to kill Max, or John, or both, his childish past, the tragedy of existence of the poet that he considered himself. The months in

Australia and New Zealand should have had a calming effect on his indeterminate nature, his sham violence, his childish bullying of Max and his band members and his passion for killing that son-of-bitch in Beirut for messing around with his Max. To be truthful to myself, he thought, and though I regret it today, I'm also glad I had the courage to do what I did. Still, I've always thought that if it hadn't been raining in Beirut, if the air hadn't turned suddenly chilly and I wasn't wearing that raincoat with the deep pockets in which the gun rested so comfortably I would never have even pulled the trigger. Now that's really crazy; I could never have told Max that I shot him because it was raining. I didn't say that to the psychiatrist either. The Swiss shrink I went to after that ugly business was a Jungian. He pushed Jung's theories on what's wrong within our deepest selves—the devil we create inside us by first overstepping all our bad qualities and then denying them—yeah, then projecting them onto others as scapegoats, the reason we have conflicts. The solution that is more elusive than we imagine is to recognize our flaws emerging from our unconscious. And then make peace with them and create a balance that makes you whole. Discovering our shadow self should be a goal in life, he repeated dreamily, because that self is different from what you think it is. Maybe it is our better self but still it's also a devilish killer. I'm the proof— my desires are the proof. We have to aim at understanding and coexisting with other troubled individuals too. What an idealist, my shrink! According to him, one day those other troubled selves may also identify their own shadow selves, and only then can we build a better world. When the educated ignorant learn to stop projecting their fears and bad habits onto others then we'll know peace and prosperity. Ah, that dreamer, Jung. A shadow world, he wanted. I ditched him in short order. I can't claim I've discovered my inner self but my hope was that in the long run Max would've helped me pull myself together. Still, though my inner devil smacked her around and took care of that pompous guy, it also alienated her—for forever, I fear. Maybe if instead of running around the world searching for more and more and more, I'd followed my dad's advice and stayed in Iceland, just maybe my life would be more peaceful today, me in accord with that shadow self my shrink believed in—he might've been right after all, he could've been right, he was supposed to be right, his job was to be right in matters like my unconscious—if it even exists. Still, I've got the music I love, my own and the music of all the others. Just listen to those three jazz geniuses up there on the stage. Great stuff. Hank really knows quality, so maybe he'll recognize me soon and I'll finally play for me—and for my shadow self.

In that moment of his spiritual ruminations, John came in, alone. He spoke a few minutes with Hank, turned, glanced at Bernard, and went out again. Bernard watched him and on a sudden impulse to do something to break the stall and set things in motion, he followed John out the great door. The regulars observed the scene curiously and shook their heads. The killer, some thought. And Hank, as he had all evening, as he did most evenings of late, watched Bernard run out the door with concern, uncertain about what the man was up to. Why his stubborn invasive presence in San Marino at all? Was it all about the engagement for his band which Hank, despite Bernard's disturbing presence, was now convinced was a good idea? A band lead by a born Sammarinese playing the kind of music he loved would add fame to his Mount Titano Hank's Bar—the lovers' tavern of Europe. Yet the unknown factor of Bernard's crazy monomaniacal attachment-attraction to Maxime hung in the mountain air. He was a trouble-maker: Was he here to kill as he'd warned? Or were his words just an expression of his romantic nature?

It was a few minutes short of midnight. The cold wind had returned. Bernard pulled his jacket collar tight. No one else was on the cobblestone walkway. John was about a hundred meters ahead when he stopped at the great bend. He spread his hands on the parapet and pressed his body against the ledge and stared toward the lights of Rimini, his thoughts bouncing back and forth between the Bernard-Maxime-John Sutton situation and his novel in the works. He was nearly convinced that the Bernard problem was gradually solving itself. This guy was not really a killer even if in his heart John's novelist side believed that a potential killer lay dormant in our innermost being. The human tragedy since Cain, he thought. In fact, he mused, his mind wandering, his novel of pure fiction, make-believe, was no longer the pure love story he had intended and that the publisher had commissioned. Nor was it written in the easy flowing style that John preferred. He'd texted the publisher that instead of the simple narrative flowing from first meeting to nascent love, to full- bloom love, then withering to little betrayals and loss of trust one in the other, and inexorably to tragic separation—the end of the love affair—had become more mysterious and complex. A work that should've been already finished, his book was becoming a construction which he secretly feared he would never be capable of completing. He was thinking that the reality was the old idea he'd once bantered around that every written work was a draft, a first draft, a second draft, even the published book remained forever a draft in the mind of its creator—or was that just lack of self-confidence on his part? When he suddenly heard steps on the cobbles, he snapped around and started: Bernard stood just behind him.

"You know, John, I pictured you very different."

"And I imagined you a sadistic killer who would haunt our every step. Are you a sadistic killer?"

"Well, I am a killer in the sense that I've killed or have wanted to kill. Not a pleasant feeling, I assure you. Not at all. But I've got a lot more to do in life than killing people."

"Hmm. I think so too. But Maxime said you gave her one year before you'd come back to get her or to kill someone—her, or me in this case. A pretty dramatic threat."

"It was supposed to sound like a prediction of what could happen but it transformed into something dangerous and mean. Anyway that was my subconscious speaking. Not the me standing here before you. I'm still trying to get used to the idea, I mean, well, you know. John, you can't see it in this light but I'm blushing. And the reason is that I've begun to think that on another level you and I are becoming friends."

"What the fuck does that mean? What other level?" Another life? After you've killed me?"

Bernard shrugged. "Oh, maybe I mean in another place. In another time. It's unimportant anyway. We're here now and I have no intention or desire to kill you."

Although Bernard's words were as unexpected as surprising, John for some artistic reason was suddenly struck by his lack of accent. No trace of the local accent. In fact no accent at all. Little things like that count even though they cause his frequent digressions. Yet, he'd noted that uprooted people wandering around the world are like that. People of Underground are like that. They speak like people from nowhere, like people in some utopist world.

"Your subconscious, you said. Have you by chance been reading Jung?" John asked, feeling some link between Jung and the lack of accent. "Subconscious self indeed! Shadow self! Seems to me that blaming your shadow self is like blaming someone else because you don't know your other self—your shadow self."

"Or if it even exists. You writer guys always know a little about everything. So you have experience in psychiatry, do you?"

"I went to one some years ago. A Freudian. Drove me crazy about my dreams. Made me think that if I didn't remember my dreams, I was a hopeless failure. Eventually I dropped him—as a therapist, I mean. Maybe I should've tried a Jungian. But anyway nearly all psychoanalysts claim some sort of dominion over the mysteries in a writer's unconscious—up there or down there where his shadow-self resides. And they have the gall to inform the writer what he is really saying with his words. Then after all that interference they want to be paid for it. The truth is the writer is lonely, squashed between science and literary criticism," John said, quoting himself. "Psychoanalysts interpret even the interpretations of critics; they delve into what happens in the story—the surprising and amazing things that happen to the characters and the persona of the author who thinks it was just his genius that dreamed up the whole thing."

"Fuck'em all. I prefer my music. I learn more about life from it than from shrinks of any school. But you spoke of loneliness. Curious. I too have those moments. Terrible moments. For me the loneliest moment in life is when you stand in front of an audience and sing one of your own songs—when you want to hide behind the microphone. That's one reason songwriter-singers like to sing covers."

"Yes, that sounds like about the same thing. But truth really is elusive. Anyway, I'm afraid that what I'd really like to write is impossible to achieve. So I stick to fiction where I can let my characters say what they think."

"The thing is, John…hey, you know, we've got a lot in common."

"You mean Maxime? "

"Come on! Creation, I mean. Besides, that Arab was a criminal, a fucking fascist, neither Islamic nor Copt. And he was armed that day. I checked. I believed he was about to shoot me there…we were alone in the Muslim part of the city. Max didn't see that part, nor would she listen to my explanation. She'd made up her mind that I was a killer and *basta*."

"But she said you killed another man before that."

"Oh Christ! I just made up that crazy story to impress her. Or so I thought. Why, I'd never held a gun in my hand before Beirut. Bought it on the black market and took lessons on how to shoot it. I didn't even know how to load it. And I was as surprised as the Arab when it even fired."

"But you still carry it?"

"Until now," Bernard said, reaching into his pocket and pulling out a small pistol that looked more like a toy than a weapon that killed people. He held it high in the air, examining it as though seeing it for the first time.

John backed off and started to yell to people coming out of Hank's when Bernard threw back his arm and hurled the gun over the wall and straight down onto the rocks hundreds of meters below. They were both peering over the parapet, surprised at Bernard's compulsive act, when they heard a muffled crack like a pistol shot.

"Well, so you did have it with you all the time! And it's not a toy. Maxime was right."

"Oh, John, that's my shadow self again. Just teasing. That little pistol down on the rocks was just a toy. A cap gun. A fake. Or, or, maybe it was real but not loaded. The difference is that the one I used in Beirut fired and maybe killed a man. But who knows?"

"For Chrissakes, Bernard. You make everything ambiguous. And you scared the shit out of me."

"Forgive me. It won't happen again. My other self is always with me, you know. Always dramatic…trying to impress you too. I just can't seem to escape it. Sometimes my life seems like one great swerve. That's why I've never understood myself and why I do the things I do. You know, that guy Jung must have been right. Sometimes my unconscious does direct my life so that afterwards I don't know which of my selves did it. You know, like Doctor Jekyll and Mr. Hyde."

"*Maybe* you killed the man in Beirut? Did you or didn't you shoot him? And why all this charade?"

"No, I mean yes. That Beirut affair *was* a charade. She—Max—was my monomania. The madness drove me crazier and crazier. I really did try to get over it. Sometimes when I wrote some good songs and the band did well I would think I'd overcome it, and then suddenly wham, I'd do something stupid and hit her because of my craziness. I mean I only sometimes seem sane but

John my fixation on a woman who didn't love me was terrible and also real."

"Yeah, that would be a terrible thing," John said ironically, Martha on his mind.

"The reality is that after she stopped loving me and her first sense of adventure wore off, she prayed that I'd walk out the door and leave her alone in Beirut. She wanted to be alone there. In fact, one time she just disappeared for two long weeks and I still don't know where! But with somebody—and not that Arab. That was the last straw. So where was she? She had always spoken of her international girlfriends there, their freedom, the things they did. Travel to Damascus or Cairo, to the mountains. One thing on the top of the other—so you can understand that I still don't know. I just don't know what lies still deeper in me than the madness that caused my illusion of killing for her. John, the truth is I've never killed anybody in my life. That whole shooting scene was make-believe; I paid Omar for his part in it. All he had to do was speak to Max on the street and then fall like dead when I shot the caps."

"For Chrissakes! Maxime has been sad and scared crazy about that one-year deadline you gave her; it limited her freedom to love me—or anyone. That's the way she puts it."

As he often did here at the bend with Maxime, John boosted himself to a sitting position on the wall, looked back down into the abyss and had the crazy thought that he should be like Bernard. Entice him to join him on the wall and then wait for the chance to simply push him over. At the same time he realized he'd never had such a thought in his life. Their whole conversation was crazy. He almost understood Bernard. Now furthermore, I, the writer of this story, know that Bernard watched John sitting on the wall, looked down into the horrendous hell pit of a chasm, and thought how easy it would be to push him into it. Instead he repeated his childish remark that they could be friends.

"Yeah," Bernard continued. "That mad threat is what I've wanted to make amends for. And it affects me worse. Me, torn apart. Either I ruin what's beautiful or let a beauty like hers destroy me. Doubly bad because— well, after this confession you won't believe that in reality I'm highly sensitive to beauty, to the romantic and the melancholy. On the other hand, I seem unable to appreciate fully beauty. Did you know that I was once on my way to becoming a concert pianist—that Chopin was my life? Instead, my life has been insane, John! If I didn't really kill Omar that rainy day in Beirut, I killed part of myself. And worse than that, I arranged the whole stupid tragedy with Max because I'm unlovable. No, wait a minute, that's not what I mean. Why, I can't even blame my shadow self. You know, I should love Jung! It's not that I swerved off onto a shunt or something. Into a temporary kind of behavior with Maxime—There, now I've pronounced it, her perfect name—No, the monster was the real me all the time, Bernard Kristinsson."

"Dramatic, Bernard. Too dramatic! Anyway, while you've been analyzing yourself, I've been wondering why you even came back. Do you somehow still think you have rights to her? You seem to want to say because of love, but you yourself said that's not true. Love? I once read a lot of Rilke—now that was a poet for you! He wrote that love is hard and in high demand—it's unlimited ambition. A unique opportunity to become another world for the love of the one you love. But carrying a pistol doesn't promise love."

"No, it doesn't. But throwing it into the abyss like I just did is progress, don't you think?"

18.

Fisher Fools on the Mountain

By some twist of genetics, bald people are as rare at Hank's Bar on Mount Titano in San Marino as is the bald eagle in the trees of Central Park in New York City. Therefore, Roland's anthracite hair, neatly trimmed and combed, and Caribbean-colored Marcel's long and unruly mane fit in perfectly with the others. Since their arrival, Hank seemed to relive his youth of decades ago in Algiers-New Orleans. When nights he sat with them in the penumbra of the bar on Mount Titano there was a lot of laughing, back-slapping, Cajun- speaking, the quiet singing of Cajun songs and drinking of the Pernod that Juanita rationed strictly according to Marcel's instructions: no more than three in one session for Roland. Hank had related how back in Algiers when the older Roland drank too much, Marcel walked the tipsy low-level Mafioso home to wife and children. And so it was in San Marino nearly three decades later that Marcel still laid down the law: three drinks, three, and not a drop more. And I, the observer, found the three fifty-year olds of the same beauty as the other late-night Hank's Bar people: the scene was like the Captain's table on a luxurious ocean liner in the days of the Normandie and Queen Elizabeth or in the Captain's cabin of a nineteenth century Nantucket whaling ship. An invitation to dinner at Captain Hank's table was the highest honor among Hank's Bar regulars: one by one, most had had that honor.

Hank later filled in the parts I hadn't overheard of their dinner talk on the Cajuns' last night before their departure to see the wonders of Venice where—to his friend's disillusionment, Hank had sworn that no alligators had ever been spotted in a Venetian canal—and that the recent pictures in the national press of crocodiles frolicking in the waters of the lagoon turned out to be fake news.

"Their denial is the fucking bad fake news, *mon ami*," Marcel muttered: "You can take it from me, a Louisiana swamp expert, that sea level canals and swamps are not livable without alligators and crocodiles. It's their nature to live in the swamps and swamps without alligators dry up and become wasteland. Hank, did you know they're close to the dinosaurs? A breed seven million years old. Anyway I'd bet there are crocodiles hidden away somewhere in Venetian waters."

"Ok, ok, so you two take some *vaporetto* rides back and forth, San Marco-Lido, Lido-San Marco and text me about the crocodiles."

"A Cajun's word," Roland added, raising his hand for another drink, then lowering it when Marcel countered his order.no.

"I know and I take your word for it," Hank said. "Just keep us informed. My friend John, our in-house writer will then do an exposé about the strange disappearance of Venice's ancient crocodiles. So anyway, *mes amis*, down to your business. I now have from San Marino's two best banks the full account details, money transfer numbers, passwords, IBANs and SWIFT codes, and all the necessary confirmations. Both of you are now official account holders: Roland R. Smith and Marcel M. Jones and the banks are awaiting your deposits. Moreover, you have the right to assign up to three co-account holders. So your bosses should be pleased considering the fiscal restrictions reigning in the banking world of today. I suspect that the low capitalization of San Marino banks is the reason they bent regulations—nearly illegally—to make you and the Fools eligible. By the way, they were impressed by your flowery signatures everywhere—I told them it was New Orleans style which seemed to flatter their egos. You know, New Orleans businessmen in their bank!"

"Hooray! Hooray!" Roland said toward Juanita with gleeful enthusiasm. I, the watcher, laughed. I understood him. It was not just the bank accounts or crocodiles and alligators in Venice that so enthused Roland, it was the Hank's Bar effect. You sit there, you have to drink. Otherwise, you might as well go look at castles or visit exotic museums or search for crocodiles in Venice.

"As you must know, banking is tightly controlled today so the waiver of the usual restrictions for new account holders and any residence requirements at all is of super importance to the Fisher Fools…unless you are interested only in small individual accounts, or you plan on staying here and establishing residency in the Republic of San Marino which would make me happy. By the way, in our favor—or disfavor—San Marino is also a member of the United Nations, UNESCO and since 1983 a partner of the European Union. The best news however is that the EU frowns on our Communist government."

"Well, I couldn't live on this mountain," Marcel said, a vague look in his eyes. He had no opinions on the UN, had probably never heard of UNESCO and the EU could've been on Mars as far as he was concerned. His were third world perceptions. "As for Venezia, as I said, no swamps and canals are healthy without alligators. They eat mosquitoes and prevent malaria, you know."

"Never heard of that either, Marcel."

"Everybody in Louisiana knows."

"Nonsense, you crazy Cajun. Alligators eating mosquitoes is just swamp lore."

"Why, there are even songs about it. Something like *Ali ali, ali ga tor, never desert my beloved swamp shore…la la la…where we have mosquitoes galore.* We used to sing it in that cellar local I once took you to."

***

I was not surprised when Bernard joined me at the table near Hank and the Cajuns; he'd been on my mind since our crazy conversation at the great bend and he threw his pistol into the chasm and we'd thought of pushing one another over the wall. I'd been thinking about the complexities of the putative Icelandic killer, who after threatening my life had abandoned his murderous intents and now wanted to become friends. In a way I was flattered because of my admiration for song writers who are able to pack so much of life into the few words of a song.

"Bernard, after you threw away your unloaded pistol that night down there at the belvedere, you then unloaded yourself on me. So now it's my turn to do the same and unload myself on you."

"The all is all," Bernard said. "That's the title of a new song. Giordano Bruno! Remember him? I'll sing it some night…if Hank ever gives me the chance. Goes something like this:

> No transcending
> No bending
> No ending
> There's nothing out there

Nothing out there
All is fantasy, even me
I miss you most
I, the ghost
Still behind my wall.

"Oh, yeah. I miss someone too. For me, separation from my former life was my great failure. So I distance myself from my life of before San Marino and Maxime so that I feel my failure less. Parts of my life in Paris are fading; Germany is beginning to fade too, and I have to hang on so that I don't lose everything and just fall off into the chasm, alone. The things I miss most were at the heart of my old life. Time remains constant but then life keeps on changing—whatever I do. Big things change. And I feel the changes coming over me, you know what I mean? One after the other. Changes and the separations too. Each time it's like…like a new algorithm circulating in my genetic circuits. Things sputter and stall. Then life starts up again and I feel it…that something budding. Flashes of the new about to happen, even though still unknown, the future new life presses. Memories are all that remain of the past, but memories weaken too—a little each day—but I hang onto them even though I don't know what to make of the transformation underway. The situation is confusing, don't you think? You want to change, but still you're afraid of it. You don't know what you'll transform into. Yet, you change anyway. You know the song, *Come si cambia per non morire.* How one changes not to die."

"Yet that feeling of transformation in the air itself is worth dying for," Bernard muttered.

"Yes, although many of the changes are external, only the start of transformation. But sometimes I do perceive another *me—alive*. It's like feeling the essence of myself. That perception of *wanting* to feel alive. And to feel and not forget my former tension of reality of when I always had to be present. Do you know that feeling too?"

"Somewhat. Or yes, I think so. But it happens rarely—practically never."

"But now *big* memory remains fixed. It's always there, although sometimes old memories come back just to disturb like June flies. But those big old memories continue to haunt you, like those of Underground still haunt me."

"Underground? Did you live in the Underground?"

"Not the London one. A figurative Underground. With my father. If we surfaced, they would kill us. We were outsiders. Pariahs"

Bernard shook his head: 'This man really does need Jung.'

"It was the isolation I once felt in the dark of Underground. My father took me there. But he warned me first. For a long time he warned me that we'd go underground if things didn't change. Things didn't change and we went there. Aboveground, he said, was only destruction. Rotterdam, Rotterdam. Everything once destroyed by the war's bombs, he said. The old men, in the old port of Rotterdam, in Hoogvliet, in The Hedges as he called The Hague. Flattened. Underground was the only secure place for people like us. Revolutionaries. Underground meant safety—if you were careful. It was always dark there and I was five and alone and full of anxiety when he was Aboveground. The five-year old panic when he returned with turned-down mouth; the rejoicing when he came back in smiles. He was building, he said. Rebuilding the whole cell, he said. But living like that in the dark and the dampness of Underground, I ungrew. Time passed; I remained five. Isolated and helpless, alone in the darkness. I adored him; he was God and must be right. But I wanted to see. A compliant five-year old, I had to develop my own strategies so I could go up and at least take a look at the Aboveground. And if they were waiting for me to show my face up there, I would have to either bow down to them or take one of my father's guns and kill them. But then when he finally said the rebuilding was done and took me back up, I kept my distance. Detached and resigned that they were the enemies and I would fight another day. Another way. I interpreted my action as my revolt—or I did until Zetkin came along "

"Zetkin? What the fuck are you talking about. You're crazier than me."

"That's why I went to Zetkin. Karl Zetkin! A Freudian who read my dreams and wondered if my revolt was a surrogate. But no, it was my rebellion against myself, the five-year old. Against my essence. Zetkin suggested that though suppressed, my very existence had become an act of rebellion. Against the terrifying Underground where we once lived."

"Also against your father who took you there? Did Zetkin ask you that?"

"Against God, my father? Why, he always knew best. I was only five. But while I cowered down there in the dark, he rebuilt everything and took me back up. And I grew until they killed him."

"They? They who?"

"That's the mystery about fathers and gods, who kills them? I faced them. But not head-on. Sometimes in fear and trembling in my alienation. And Zetkin said that while I was hating those above me who'd never been in Underground, down there where my unconscious met my conscious emerged my fiction about love in which I—in reality the offended one, the victim—who'd lived all that time as a five-year old in Underground, decided to make peace with the Aboveground people and to make amends for my wayward father who died in an automobile accident right in the center of Munich.

"But then, Bernard, there's the panic that comes over you when you can't find your way out of a labyrinth-like Underground Reading Jung never helped me there. Time passes but you can't get away from yourself. You don't get away from all those little memories. They sting, the little memories. The stings burn and swell and leave welts and sores. You don't get away from former loves either and especially not from the pain of when someone is ripped from you. I took Giordano Bruno's quip that 'time is the father of truth' painfully personal. For there's always memory."

I didn't mention Martha to Bernard. There's still Martha. Always, Martha. Distant—but fixed. Martha means Samantha. The big memory. Maybe I'll never get away. My obsession. I perceive the loss and accept the awareness that I'll never have them again; so the old and the new exist side-by-side in me but not peacefully. Loving Maxime and at the same time loving the shadow of Martha. At times, those two loves are actually interdependent— then, one trying to absorb or ignore the other. The what-if questions hold me. What if we'd stayed together despite our loss? We'd gone too far to be able to leave it all behind us completely and painlessly. A shadow of her remains. A shadow of a memory. Something always remains. But what can I possibly mean? Martha is much more than a mere fragment of my life. I'd never felt so secure as with her. She is a whole. But then each time I think the what-ifs: Samantha and all the other returns and the suffering goes on. I was too immature for Martha. She had to keep an eye on me, afraid I might go berserk after Samantha–the landmark of my life. Samantha! I never suspected the existence of such metaphysical landmarks. Yes, metaphysical. For at times I had the wild thought that just letting go would lead me to a place of freedom from pain, a conclusion I'd drawn from my nightmares—so wild, but so free. Or, I thought that true freedom lay in madness. Unfettered. No holds. No binds. You just let go and leave all controls and sanity behind you. The step seemed so easy. What a joy to just break out. Fantasy! But not pointless. But even if I wasn't ready for that kind of pain and suffering, *IT* remains inside you, incurable, irremovable, forever. I would hear the echo of her two-year old hops and skips running through the house, forever. Time passes, but you never really forget. Success and failure are not the point. No longer the point. Never again the point. And you hurt. The pain also of your awareness of how impossible it is to forget. And your suffering makes you more and more aware of yourself. Self-awareness, I came to understand, comes directly from suffering, not from joy and pleasure. But what if we *had* adapted and survived together? Maybe we separated because of our incapacity to understand the other's pain; we were together, we were one in everything except in our suffering. And now each of us suffers alone. I was right to wonder where our love would've gone afterwards—after the pain calmed; but I was wrong to think we could survive the suffering together; we were reminders of Samantha, one to the other. Then, I was too weak when our relationship crumbled into painlessness and thoughtlessness. And that's the catch. Because as Maxime reminds me, things do end. Passion has a limited duration, as does suffering. And new things happen and happen again and again. Oh, I know, we could have survived our loss and gone on at least for a while yet. But Martha understood the reality better than I: I felt the passion of our unbearable reality; she, the reality of our passion. Our great passion was kaput. It would never return. That's why our long-distance togetherness came to seem preferable to nothing and we simply hung onto love—if only in word. Or would a have-had-her totally-and-lost-her-completely not have been better? A cleaner cut?

"Bernard, coherence is truly missing in me. No continuity whatsoever. At times, I seem to be someone else. Torn down the middle. According to my symptoms you'd think I'm afflicted with the infamous DDD, Depersonalization-Derealization-Disorder. I really do wonder who I am. Maxime says I fall too easily into daydreams—as if it were an incurable disease. No treatment available. Not even specialists agree on a proper name for my disorder. Stress? Trauma? Alcohol gives immediate relief but my nature once limited the alcohol route; it's like being weighed down to unfeeling dirt. Self-control at all costs! I wonder why they don't just hypnotize me and experiment on my vertically split personality. Despite my panic attacks, my claustrophobia and the shoulder burnings, after examinations and testing *they* concluded that I'm perfectly normal. But they know nothing of the

Underground in me. For some reason I've never revealed that time. So I have to live with my perfectly normal DDD."

19.

John Sutton

John's ideal of a well-lived life was one that proceeded naturally from one stage to the next, gradually maturing from one life and time and merging smoothly into the next. Into a new present of a new life in a harmonious relationship with the life of the past from which he carried over the positive aspects on which was then constructed a higher stage of existence. However, his own different real life stages were partitioned and sectioned by abrupt and unforeseen interruptions; each new life meant that a new person had been born to replace the former. In each new life, he had to start over again. Since he was a kid, he'd felt it odd when on arrival in another country his Dutch passport—EUROPESE *UNIE/KONINKRIJK DER NEDERLANDEN*—was accepted as proof of his true identity. He wondered why controllers didn't suspect its falsity. His father, Oliver J. Sutton, was English and had taught English language and literature in The Hague for so many years that for bureaucratic reasons he became a Dutch citizen; thus his son, John Howard Sutton, was Dutch on his birth in nearby Wassenaar. Then when John was five, Oliver accepted a dream job offer in Germany and they moved to Munich where John, for a certain period, lived another life and another culture and in his fantasy in the dreaded Underground; then, afterwards, when his parents divorced when he was fourteen, he returned with his mother to her native San Marino and his third life. At the same time, the Sutton couple's private life, about which their son knew surprisingly little, was a stormy and passionate up-and-down affair: his parents remarried and so at seventeen John was back in Munich which despite his Dutch passport he vaguely thought of as home. His father, who was then teaching ethics and morality at a private international institute, continued to exercise a powerful influence on his life until a banal and therefore suspicious automobile accident on a Munich city street took the lives of both parents. It was then that John began to feel the homelessness and uncertainty of who he was, creature-like feelings that found a permanent place deep in his being which he masked with pretense—and lie. Prevarication was his middle name. Nonetheless, his father's legacy continued to determine the zigzag flow of his life: his first language—English—and his social-political views remained constant: John had always written in English and like his father he felt he was born a Communist.

Observing Hank and his Cajun friends, he wondered if they too felt the kind of uprootedness that lived in him. He had never felt with any certainty his true identity: who was he, a survivor of the Underground? Displaced permanently? But deracination was not the real issue; the real issue was how he dealt with it. Evasion and equivocation, falsehood and prevarication became a way of life, his modus operandi, which, it seemed to him, guaranteed a seamless relationship with others—especially with his loved ones. Although he projected an image of solidity and decisiveness, John was irresolute and vacillating, traits which were the most obscure and disguised part of him. Traits that Martha however had seen. Characteristics that clashed with the persona who professed undying love also for Maxime, who—he thought—considered him her first real love. All the time, however, as compensation for the great lie of his life, he proudly never told those little white lies that are so forgivable, but that he considered despicable and vulgar, that unresolved could make cohabitation with another person a parody of respect and civility.

In that moment, Hank clapped the older Roland's shoulder and called out to Juanita for another round of Pernod. Juanita was leaning on the grand piano and waiting for the Egyptian pianist-singer who would soon relieve the jazz trio; he had taken a shine to her and arrived sooner and sooner each evening for his presentation of westernized love songs of the Near East. The trio's vocalist was singing a second time their theme song, *The End of A Love Affair*. Bernard was standing at the window peering out into the blackness of the Mount Titano night. It had become Bernard's habit to spend evenings at Hank's, conscious that he was learning that habit can truly accomplish wonders: he had nearly overcome his Max monomania and he had begun thinking in new directions since the night Hank more or less consented to a three-day trial gig for the San Marino Blues Band.

Now the reader will understand from the frequent grammatical swerves from third to first person that my role here is more than the narrator of the stories about the people on Mount Titano, all of whom are present now that Maxime has just entered through the great door of which Hank is so proud: Modest 'Hank' Gamper and his Cajun friends, Maxime Novak, Bernard Kristinsson, and—even though my distaste for biography equals my mistrust of autobiography—of course myself in the guise of John Sutton. Here I have permitted myself a few words about literary genres before the main story continues. I must emphasize my mistrust of biographies; I mistrust historical writings in general in which the compiler can never attain completeness and which consequently are less than true and I think there will always be valid reasons to doubt the truth in biographic history —at least anything resembling the essential truth. As Virginia Wolfe said, there is no such thing as objective biography: 'Positions have been taken, myths have been made.' Now, of course, true scholars do not make up facts, but they do choose which facts to use. That's their job. And one reality is that there are just too many facts—contradictory facts—to choose from. And each choice is conditioned by the writer's own experience and values and hopes. But autobiography? Well, we all should know that subjective honesty is impossible, for how can we be transparent to ourselves? We easily lie and we betray—even ourselves. In that sense, nostalgia too is a great liar, or, as someone once quipped, it only serves to remove the rough edges from the good old days. Besides, the very shock of subjective honesty would be too great—I use the conditional because as a rule we do think we're loyal to ourselves; moreover, because of my tendency to fictionalize my life and personalize my fiction I've experienced also how fine the line between autobiography and fiction, the confusion between where reality ends and fiction begins. Yes, the temptation to fictionalize one's own life is a power to be constantly reckoned with, especially when you look backwards but still wonder about your future. Some writers at the end of their lives consider their diaries—that is, autobiographies—their most important works; such a claim, in my opinion, is pure egotism. Such diaries might reveal something unknown about the writer, his flaws, some great moral transgression, or simply unachieved ambitions, all of which contradict the writer's creative genius. Besides, the attempt to mold your life objectively in words is a hopeless undertaking from the start because you know that during the writing you can add or subtract at will and you are moreover aware that you can never finish it. Walter Benjamin wrote the truism that we seek in fiction the knowledge of death which in our own lives is denied us. Well, that's one way of looking at it. But still it's no wonder to me that autobiographies are largely misrepresentation or exaggeration, prevarication, or outright lie, that is, a sort of fiction disguised as autobiography. Thus, at the very start of his work about himself, the autobiographer is already on the path pointed toward the lie; never in this world the full truth about ourselves! It seems that prevarication and lie are essential to living life—for most people, anyway. Nonetheless, I must admit that the attempt to be honest with ourselves is a good exercise; after all we pay psychiatrists in an attempt to see our true selves.

Now, I have no proclivity for interpreting the past, nor do I have prescient qualities for foretelling the future. Yet I do keep a sharp lookout on the occurrences of both the past and present, of who does what and how and when, of how these characters interact with and influence the others. Moreover, my role here is multiple: I am not the mere narrator of the actions and lives of these characters on Mount Titano in the Republic of San Marino as it might seem in my story. Not by a long shot. No. It so happens that in my John role I'm also the author of a novel, a love story about the end of a love affair also set in San Marino. Moreover, at the same time, I, John Sutton, am myself engaged in a love affair with a woman also named Maxime, a story in which my role is mangled and likely mendacious based as it is on one of my shadow selves that refuses to be integrated into one or the other roles or into a false morality play my father could have written. There are just too many marionettes and too many strings for one operator to manage.

When Maxime enters the tavern she looks longer than usual at Hank and the Cajuns, glances at Bernard and finally turns to me. In that seemingly endless moment in which I watched her regarding Hank, I pushed aside normal human doubts and petit signs of jealousy and perceived a sensation of what might have been divine intuition suggesting a process of love mutations in the air so startling that I am unable to record them even here. However, I must remark that this midnight she is exceptionally beautiful; some resistant snowflakes in her hair sparkle blue in the reflection from the overhead lamp; and she seems to have carried inside wisps of the Siberian wind lashing the flanks of Mount Titano. My eyes squint and blink in an attempt to clear my mind of the confusion of my complex roles represented here in Hank's Bar before I pursue further the question of truth as powerful as an early viral mutation, at the same time thinking of the deviation from the idea of truth inherent in the word "prevarication"; a word which in my narration may determine a hidden intention of so confusing the truth that it becomes difficult to recall what real lie is.

"Maxime," I ask, "I've wondered if Bernard lied to you about shooting the Arab…and if his threat to kill you too was not also a lie."

"John, you know now that he didn't even have to lie since he just playacted the shooting that day."

"But what did he say after the so-called shooting? He had to say something!"

"He was evasive and refused to talk about it," she says, looking at me funny. "But what does it matter now? That seems like another life—so long ago. *E quindi comunque, me ne sono scappata subito.*"

I look back at her in mild surprise—not at her words—but because she has never spoken to me in Italian and has always claimed that she doesn't want to speak it anywhere, I think for political reasons because of the Italian imperialistic occupation of her father's native lands—but of course, well, I don't know every minute detail that happens in the minds of the characters in this story; I don't even understand what happens in my own. Nor am I ubiquitous or, as I said before, prescient; in fact, at times I seem to lack any foresight at all.

"You mean to say that in the end he simply prevaricated?"

"You could say that, I guess. Yes, like in the Latin *praevaricati.*"

"Well, you're the expert; I'm just the poor writer always searching for the right word."

"And you're also strange. What is it you really want to know?" she asks hesitantly and turning slightly red. From anger or embarrassment? I wonder. Perhaps neither. Or both. In any case, I do know something is in the air, and she knows that I know something.

"I'm truly sorry. While waiting for you I was observing the same persons you did when you came in and the question of Bernard led to the subject of truth and lie. And besides I have some news—both good and bad news. I sent the first hundred pages of my novel to the publisher in London. After his initial enthusiasm, he's now rather noncommittal. He only said that the book's editor in their Paris office is not convinced; he's evasive, the publisher wrote. They want me to spend a few days with him in Paris to review the first part and if necessary convince him of the second part that I have in mind, that is, again as the end of another love affair. My ideas were not clear after the first love affair but you convinced me when you said that we must keep in mind that things do end."

"Oh, I see. So when are you leaving?"

"*Tout de suite, Cherie.* It's indeed a perplexing situation. Uh, I don't suppose you want to come with me?"

"Confusing indeed. But no, John, I'd just be in the way there so I'll stay here and mind the tavern."

"Yes, I can imagine. You have to keep your eye on Bernard too while I'm gone. I think he's accepted the reality that you're no longer part of his life. But who knows what happens in the recesses of a man's mind? His new calm might be worse than the storm itself. Sometimes I think his talk about pistols and killing people reflects his real self. Still, maybe everyone has similar pretenses. But then you should know the answer better. Still, in my view, his calm is pretense too; storm the reality. He told me once about his shadow selves; he says that because of them, he never knows what he'll do next."

"John, many people are like that," she says, now looking intently toward the cut glass window. "But don't worry, he's not the, uh, he's not a problem for me—not any longer."

Instead of asking what she meant, I look directly at her evasive eyes and recall the composer's words that *la donna é mobile*. But not so Maxime, I know. She's not flighty; yet love itself is capricious and precarious and easily changeable. Verdi's

Duke of Mantua sings of the emptiness and inscrutability of woman who can change thoughts and words as easily as a feather in the wind, according to her mood; but the composer's point is not the female character—but love and prevarication: the Duke himself is getting ready to meet the street woman, Magdalena. In stories love can be like the butterfly fluttering from one flower to the next, sucking its gift before searching for another, so that a romantic reader can think that love itself is the lie and the sadness it brings. That love today is not necessarily the same love of tomorrow. Therefore, I *am* perplexed by Maxime's insouciance about my abrupt departure. Or is it perhaps my own inconstancy like that of the Duke of Mantua that disturbs? My embarrassing Dutch passport lying invisible in its bureau drawer is emblematic of my own falsified identity. Maxime, if you only knew how my false identities weigh! My vacillations. And my tendency to prevaricate about my annual pilgrimage in Paris where *she* might be waiting— not, however, a Magdalena. But, after all, Maxime is Maxime. She knows as well I do the Latin roots of prevarication.

END part two

Part Three

20.

Back To the Future

It was September again. Nearly the seventeenth. And the Rue Fabert apartment felt more foreign each time I came. Yet it seemed to me the place where my uncertain situation with Martha could be resolved one way or the other. At the same time, my invented editorial meetings with the Paris publisher's agent were increasingly hard to explain to Maxime who clammed up at the mere mention of Paris. And as for Martha, my life on a barren mountain in San Marino was as alien to her as this luxury apartment on the Esplanade had come to seem to me.

On my arrival this time, haunted by shadows of *that* September and forever fearful of a return of my old symptoms, I felt a minor satisfaction that the monarchist stool pigeon concierge, Maurice, had been replaced by a middle-aged man named Anton. When I stopped at his loge in the entrance hall to introduce myself, he immediately knew who I was; my wife had become friendly with him, as had Comrade-Monsieur Ivaan. Comrade? It turned out that Anton was a lifetime member of the still surviving French Communist Party, which must make his life among these king-lovers in Rue Fabert precarious. When I asked about his predecessor, he shrugged, grinned and said they might have exiled him to the Island of Elba. Still, despite his quip, living alone in the cellar tomb the generous condominium allotted him and faced with the reality that his political party was dying an agonizing death, Anton must be a very lonely man. I embraced him.

On the now smooth but still snail-slow elevator up to our third floor, I perceived only minor trepidation about the possibility of a sudden attack of claustrophobia which I held at bay with distracting memories held in reserve for such occasions: once again the Café Coupole bombing of years ago, the DGSE secret agents who hounded me afterwards, the Chartres labyrinth walk, Zetkin the shrink, Pére François the good priest. Memory, I've always thought, is truly a rover. They are life. Though I couldn't help but agree with Ivaan that return to a place you once thought of as home can be a bitter disappointment indeed; on the other hand, it also has the capacity of making the spirit of your past live again. After all, a blocked elevator did resemble my childhood Underground. Still, as usual, I perceived an involuntary twinge at the expected sense of being adrift and out of place, I believed because of the tangle of good memories and the half memories that also plague me: like those wide chairs and the blankets and the tall tropical plant waving in the winds outside the Necker Hospital windows that September night, the stalks of which beat a danse macabre against the glass of the veranda while we waited in its permanent penumbra for the verdict—and while the everlasting rain poured down on Necker Hospital. Was there only one wide chair and one wool blanket that we huddled under together? Or were there two of both? Whether or not we were already separated there seems of vital significance now. My return, my eternal return here, seemed like a quest for the forgotten memories, a forlorn hope for a new awakening to nearly forgotten emotions, an optimistic hope too for a different outcome than the unjust one that had fallen on our heads. Return to Rue

Fabert was also a question of time. Since my last year's visit, my distance from the city itself had widened, my detachment deepened. Everything here said Samantha. Return was ambiguous, an equivocal undertaking based on ambivalent hopes that excluded the whole idea of celestial justice. Yet, this time, return did not lack in anticipation and some elation about the possibilities available. My return this year was disregard for the warnings of my detached self that this was not my place any longer. For that reason, I suppose, I felt that return should reward me in some way with fulfillment, although the mere act of stepping into the apartment house dampened my hopes for any kind of real intimacy: my elation nose-dived into pessimism in the same way the time I saw her Missoni scarf hanging in the Embassy cloakroom and I knew that in reality I had come back to Paris this time to observe and to collect the evidence of reality based on which I hoped to be able to decide conscientiously, psychologically and scientifically the rest of my life. For now there was Maxime. But on the other hand, there was the possibility of Ivaan too—an unsettling conundrum to consider.

The elevator door slid open soundlessly and I stepped out into what seemed more like a conceptual space created in the mind of some alien species than it did a residence for humans, a residence now as haunted as was my own mind. Grasping for a destination, I looked at the hardwood floor extending down the long corridor of my dreams and I reminded myself that though I had laid this flooring in place of its former ghastly sky blue-tinted Carrara marble, all the while I faced the real reality that this immense space was just the former residence of two no longer existent persons, a space that now seemed ghostly and uninhabited despite the disparate pieces of our former life, Martha's and mine, from our former home in Rue Saint-Dominique: couches and tables and chairs, unused and lonely, pushed helter-skelter into the corners of the immensity of these alien spaces. It seemed they too yearned to return to the real world, to their family, to their place.

Strange sensation! Since the last period of Underground when I was around seven or eight I've always been fascinated by those poets my father read to me who were convinced of a relationship between man's eyes and the objects of his gaze—that the things we really see, see us as much as we see them. I came to love Baudelaire's words in *Fleurs du Mal*:

> *Man wends his way through forests of symbols*
> *Which look at him with their familiar glances.*

And I too have come to believe that the so-called inanimate objects around us—a table, a stool, a glass we stare into, yellow wine bubbles—also see us—as Rilke writes in *Archaic Torso of Apollo* in admiration of the beauty of the Ancient Greek headless torso in the Louvre:

> *'for there is no part of the sculpture which does not see you.*
> *You must change your life.'*

In my more spiritual mode, a new world opens when I convince myself that every object around me is hiding secrets, secrets that can reveal its true nature. The secret that everything that passes between the spiritual and the material worlds is connected by vision and words, words perhaps speaking to me. When I think of communication with inanimate objects, I wonder if they are truly inanimate. Or if they too are not filled with the passion and inspiration of what in the world of humans is called *Duende*. Standing in the phantasmal hallway, as the real present began to return, I reached out and touched gingerly the table near the entrance; the shiny table Samantha had loved and shared her secrets with was unsullied by so much as a speck of dust. I stopped. I listened. I seemed to hear Garcia Lorca's "dark sounds" of the mystery from which comes the substance of art, the *duende*. 'Not a force, not a thought, the *duende* surges up from the soles of the feet, not a question of skill, but of a style that lives. It's in the veins.' It's creation, the spirit of the earth, which Goethe described as 'a mysterious force that everyone feels and no philosopher has explained.'

Martha's doing. It had to be Martha who couldn't bear dust on its surface. The question was: Why did she hang onto this huge place? Nostalgia? Allegiance to our past together? Guilt and misguided loyalty to Samantha, which made no sense for our daughter never lived here? It must be because of the shiny table Samantha conversed with.

Or did she perhaps hang on to the Rue Fabert place because of doubts about our future together that we both knew would never take place? And there, I knew, I was grasping at straws. For after these years of separation and vacillation, I had no idea of what was happening in her mind. For what am I to think of our togetherness after the years of this strange apartness which we share? How am I to respond to her supplications that I never leave her? Year after year, she in London—or wherever she has been—she still repeats the same old refrain: "John, don't you dare ever leave me."

Shit, shit, shit, Martha. She just won't let go...of me...of us. I love Maxime; yes, I do. I do love her—but I still love you too, Martha, my first great love. Can you ever unlove your first genuine love? Can I not not love you?' Can you leave behind something so joyous and precious, something so tragic and sad as our togetherness was? Or does it not remain like late-afternoon shadows against a white-washed wall which pursue you, follow you—relentlessly—until at least one shadow becomes part of you?

On the spur of the moment, I thought I should ask Zetkin; maybe he was as curious about me as I was about the validity of his vague diagnosis of my former phobias. According to Pére François, his friend Zetkin was fascinated by my *case*. 'Another case of too much conscience,' the shrink had said—which corresponds to my self-analysis.

He answered the phone in the same German way I remembered: "Zetkin". After my confused words about secrecy and mystery, he suggested in a likewise confused manner that I come on over to his place, we'd have a drink together—and talk about matters. Matters? I hadn't seen him since shortly after the Chartres labyrinth walk: after my voyage that day from Montparnasse surely fraught with the dark tunnels that so terrorized me in those times, after my painful half-kilometer walk on the medieval flagstones in the center nave of the great cathedral, and after the still unexplained disappearance of Martha and Ivaan while I staggered around the concentric labyrinthine circles. So without even touring the entire flat—as Ivaan called the huge silent space that didn't suggest even one fucking solution of the puzzle—I rushed over to his place, on the way carelessly, fondly, recalling my incapacitating leg weakness of those times and how on my way home I would stop to rest near Napoleon's tomb.

No wonder Zetkin's unquenchable curiosity. Were I the psychiatrist, I'd be curious about me too; I know myself, or should know myself, at least as well as he does, or perhaps better.

I know I'm an emotionally sick man. But I've long suspected that he has remained under the illusion that he cured me since I abandoned his strange therapy as soon as my symptoms abated—just as he'd predicted they would. In that, he was right after all. Actually, that was all I'd hoped for—the elimination of those God-awful symptoms that plagued me: the shoulder burnings that made desk work impossible; the weakness in my legs that made walking more than fifty meters inhuman torture; my animal panic in the Défense elevator the day it was blocked between floors; when the metro nearly stopped at the sharp curve on the Sèvres-Babylon metro line; or even when I chose to use the stairs at Rue Fabert despite Maurice's sneers.

Today, I could honestly report to him that those phobias had all nearly vanished. But, as I've long understood, something always remains: in my case, the fear of their return. For August 15 and September 17 return each year. Though the shoulder burnings have passed, if an elevator door opens a fraction of time too slowly, sweat fills my armpits; if a metro train stops between stations, I go internally berserk. But I don't do those things anymore. Thank heavens we have neither metros nor elevators in San Marino, a highly recommendable place to live for sick persons like me.

Zetkin only briefly appeared the same as I remembered him: I soon saw that his once fashionable jeans now just looked old, and the slipshod way he poured the martini cocktails into water glasses revealed he was not at all the same person he used to be.

The big room that had been his studio where he listened to stories and dreams like mine and handed out his occasional evaluations and interpretations like priceless gold nuggets was just a big room. There were no longer framed diplomas hanging on the walls behind his desk, no well-ordered bookcases, no more art deco lamps—and the cubist painting I'd liked so much had vanished. I looked him closely in the eyes and concluded that he was in this moment also sloshed. My shrink who'd cured me of the symptoms! My psychiatrist who knew how Martha and I made love, who interpreted my dreams, who found me 'an interesting case', and who attended learned conferences on esoteric matters, was already drunk before noon. But I liked that in him and thought it a good basis for real friendship. Nothing like a good non-fatal flaw or two to inspire confidence and fondness! *Hamartia* has a long, long reach—though shorter than *hubris*, another of those chilling, thrilling Greek words. Peering around the room, it occurred to me that he would love Hank's Bar, but that closer to home he would be totally bewildered by beautiful Martha in person.

Maybe because of the drinks on my empty stomach or because he once cured my symptoms—I switched spontaneously to the familiar *Du* in the German we'd always spoken together and asked what he'd meant when he told Pére François that I was 'a case of too much conscience'?

Zetkin laughed and slapped his legs and muttered also in the second person singular something that sounded like, 'How the fuck should I know?' Before adding in an ironical tipsy way, "Maybe I meant remorse. Not the same thing, eh, Sutton?"

"No, not the same thing at all," I agreed, no longer interested in the question of conscience, on which my drunken psychotherapist lurched into another key question to which I didn't know the real answer: "So what brought you back to Paris?"

"Martha."

Martha's always in my life…and at the same time she's not. She's also absent. Martha's like a ghost who flits in out of the past, says a few words, and vanishes until the next time. "But, Zetkin, she won't let me go. Over and over she says, 'Sutton, don't you ever leave me.'"

"Hmm, now that does sound like a case of too much conscience—on your part," he repeated grimly his former diagnosis, and poured himself a triple portion of straight gin, added a drop of vermouth and downed it. Looking around his studio room searching for something to do, he carelessly-purposely pushed a stack of books off the table to the floor on which a contented look returned to his eyes and he sat back in his rickety chair and looked at me in his therapist mode.

We were silent for a few seconds until the gin hitting his stomach unclenched his teeth and a brief smile of sublimity filled his blue German eyes. "Or is it after all remorse?" he asked me rhetorically, as he would if I were still his patient. "Conscience, as we're using it, is destined to become first bad conscience—then remorse."

"Time has passed, Doc. Things change. I live in another world. And anyway I have someone else now…on the mountain in San Marino."

"Mountains girls are the best in the world," he slurred, as if he in his madness knew anything about mountain girls.

"But Doc, there's a dream I keep having—wrote it out, saved it for you."

Zetkin giggled and looked at the bottle of gin fondly before shrugging dismissively.

"Shoot!" he said.

"Shoot?"

"The dream, *los*, tell it to me."

"Remember that I dreamt this on Mount Titano, ok? So in the dream, I dream that while I was in Paris the last time I again had a dream I've had many times before. I'm trying to return from an obscure somewhere to another no less obscure somewhere. I wander on leaden legs over rural roads, up and down steep hills in a labyrinthine suburbia searching for the safest and shortest road to that indefinite place I must reach that is perhaps a town. In my dream, I'm aware that I've searched for the right road in past dreams but that I always go astray and end up on roads infested with ferocious country dogs. Or I stumble into a neighborhood where strangers are methodically robbed and beaten. There is a safe high road but for some reason it's forbidden to me. I have to take the low road, the roundabout road, the dangerous road. I stand at the entrance to a village through which I must pass to reach my destination. The passage is blocked by a lowered barrier. The road is of dirt. Signs warn to be careful of children and of dogs. I pass the barrier and see two animals in front of the first wooden house. I slow but I continue. They seem to be dogs but have long thin necks and flattened black heads like pythons, with wide white eyes. Their necks or their thin bodies weave and dance menacingly, warning me to turn back. I'm afraid but I plod ahead temerariously. I wave and agitate my arms to beat them off. I'm disgusted and terrified. But I have to break through. I must get to that other place. At that point, I woke up in a sweat wondering where I wanted to go. Did I turn back? Or am I standing still? Fully awake, perhaps awake, I prolong the dream and for a moment consider the dilemma and can't decide whether to turn back or to continue despite the dangers. Was that the mythological home I was—am—striving for? The unobtainable home?"

"Dream state! That's the magic of dreams," Zetkin says in a sober way. "Everything is permitted. Everything is possible, but difficult to achieve. I suppose you never got there, the place you had to reach, eh? In your dreams, you might protest that this or that is not right, that it's impossible, forbidden, but your dream conductor mocks you and reminds you that you can do anything you like in your dreams. But that doesn't mean you succeed. In your dreams, you might hold onto safe persons or secure objects but for the most part, you flee. You try to escape—though on your leaden legs."

"Ah, you remember my leaden legs? I wonder if everyone has leaden-leg dreams? In one dream moment, I'm capable of extraordinary feats and in the next I'm fearful and cowardly. I want to say certain things, to warn, to complain, to explain, and to confess but I can't make myself understood. I suddenly speak a different language, a language incomprehensible to others. And I hope the dream will end and save me and I also hope it will last forever and I will succeed and escape. They're never laughable, my dreams. No comedy. They're terrible. In another one, I'm in a horrid prison in a strange land. I'm a prisoner. Then I'm a journalist admitted to interview prisoners. One of them is my son. My son, or myself, was brought here young. My son is terror-stricken and fat, masked in a bulky hood. I can see his uncovered fat face and fearful eyes. He has pimples. His little brother and sister are prisoners too. Wearing a long black topcoat, I'm in a waiting room with other visitors. The guards are returning for them, for my son. Who is it? The fat face does not look like my son—and his brother and sister are in some terrible violation, the consequences of which could be dreadful. I shout warnings but I can't save them. I remember that Borges wrote that dreams belong to God and recalled that Maimonedes had written that 'the words of a dream are divine when they are distinct and clear and you cannot tell who said them.'"

What the fuck! Is it irony or ridicule I see in the depths of Zetkin's mock candid eyes? What's so funny here? My situation is serious and my drunken shrink laughs.

"You find that amusing, Doc. *Ist das wirklich zum lachen?* I'm half crazy and you laugh at me."

"Sorry, Sutton. You're right that life is hard," he said apologetically and beginning to slur his words again. "But your situation is as old as Meffshe, Meshla, uh, Me-thus-e-lah. I once had a patient in the same situation. But in the end it was resolved. Anyway, since you had it, have had it, keep having it, you might as well tell me it."

"How?"

"How what?"

"How was your patient's problem resolved?"

"Ethically, I shouldn't tell you this...but he, uh, hanged himself in his studio. He was, *heh*, *heh*, a Jungian, and was recognized as one of the best psychotherapists in all gay Paris. He had two, maybe three loves all at once—and all were his patients. But he was so involved with his shadow self and his unconscious that he forgot reality until it was too late to go back: while he was loving his three women patients, he so completely convinced one of his few male patients, also a psychiatrist—all of whom he instinctively disliked because of their sex— that the life he was living—his wayward wife and his Jungian theories—as the wise Solomon said, was meaningless, so the man said he saw no alternative to jumping from the top of the Montparnasse skyscraper: but he didn't jump at all; he hung. Ironically it was one of my patient's lovers who found him the next day hanging from the rafters of his studio, dead as a door nail. In real life, my patient's patient's wife was his mistress. Unwittingly I got involved in a very confusing story."

"I don't understand a fucking thing, and no, you shouldn't have told me that, Zetkin. This is the last time I'll turn to a shrink for help!"

"Right you are! That's why I quit while I still could," Zetkin said, suddenly sober, proving my conviction that drunkenness is also a psychological state of mind—like a non-drinker I knew in Munich who would get roaring, amusing drunk just spending an evening with a group of drinkers.

"That man was my patient—in full analysis. To take that one shstep, uh, one step, farther, after one of his patients jumped from the Montparnasse skyscraper, he assumed the guilt—first he had a bad conscious, then remorse, then the void. He wanted to get to the very bottom of himself. He did. And he didn't like what he found there: he posed the question of the amoral person he thought he was becoming and pointing out that at birth the human being has no concept of right or wrong—a pure example of amorality—and that those who don't evolve from that early state remain emotional children. From that base, he convinced himself that he'd remained one of the underdeveloped amoral persons—that he only wore a mask of sanity. He, the prominent psychotherapist, was convinced he was an undetected psychopath who prompted his patients to jump off tall buildings."

"Remarkable, I must say. I've long thought therapists were chiefly a crowd of nuts…all except you, of course."

"Hmm, do you really think so?" Zetkin mumbled, trying to hide a crazy self-satisfied smile.

"It sounds like you were very involved with this patient."

"Very. You see I misdiagnosed him and it cost him his life."

"Did you show him his shadow self was a monster?"

" showed him he was innocent, only overly conscientious."

"Innocent! Wasn't it you who insisted nobody is innocent?"

"Me? Maybe. Anyway he interpreted my interpretation like a condemnation, that in the end his over-conscientiousness had transformed him. I meant it transformed him into an ally of his patients. He thought I meant it made him a monster. That he had an anal personality and all that implies. A good man died because of me—and because of this," Zetkin said, holding up and staring hard at his glass.

"I was drunk when I misdiagnosed him."

"Now you're back to bad conscience and remorse, Zetkin. But tell me anyway how you define conscientiousness…and why die for it?"

"Conscientiousness! No, it's not worth dying for. That's for sure. That was my patient's tragedy. He killed himself thinking he was a failure and also incompetent because another professional, me, saw into the real him and diagnosed him as overly conscientious. Actually, it's no tragedy to be conscientious. And he had the chief symptoms of conscientiousness. If you are very competent, you're likely to be also 'overly' conscientious. Not good for a therapist. And tragic for him. But anyway he thought it was worth dying for. In our profession the difference between morality and ethics plays an important role. That's what he feared: being judged immoral and unethical at the same time. He feared the death of his morality. That was my misdiagnosis. It's true that the overly conscientious are boring, even if it only means being responsible and reliable. The thing is you can overdo it. It's how you regulate your impulses. You formulate long-range goals. Psychologists list the traits of the anal personality as self-effi-effi-efficacy, orderliness, dutifulness, achievement-striving, that is, conscientiousness. CEOs of big companies and Presidents are overly conscientious—or criminal—or both. Mafia chieftains too."

"Anybody with all those traits has to be either crazy, suicidal or just trying their best to die like a hero or a scoundrel," John ventured. "Little difference. Like our political and social leaders, socially unethical and personally immoral, the two bonded against the subjugated colonized people. Ethicide! Most of them bearing the stain of servility at the same time. Still, your patient seemed to me like an overly sensitive person too. So what do you think he should've done? Can we just quit and leave at the slightest sign of the slightest painful or a mortifying experience? Just go far away and hide? In the desert? No, we can't. We have to stay. We must brave it out. Just look at me! Good example indeed! Another drunk. But I'm still here."

"Sticking it out, eh?" Zetkin said with a sharp flavor of irony.

"Unfortunately, I'm sticking it out. But I have an excuse: I don't know what the fuck I'm doing. Whatever I do, it's unintentional. As they say, nothing personal. "

"Well, anyway, yes!"

"Yes, what?"

"Yes, your layman's diagnosis is probably right. In any case I shouldn't have told him of all people the truth. Maybe I should try writing instead."

He looked shocked when I laughed and said that most writers deal with what's moral and what's ethical in one way or the other. "And writers diagnose and misdiagnose left and right but few jump off of skyscrapers or blow their brains out with shotguns like Hemingway or Russian poets. Instead they pose a lot of questions, like why there's no universal ethic for the respect of all life or a morality that backs a struggle for equality and justice for all. But they don't offer solutions."

"Oh, that kind of thing, I put the didactic behind me long ago," Zetkin said, looking at me like I was crazy, then poured us huge glasses of martini cocktail, and again downed his in a few seconds. With my one and only therapist leading the way, I was getting sloshed too.

But Zetkin! Zetkin was turned inside out, raging and weeping at the same time and again looking around the room this time as if searching for exoneration. He refilled his glass and we stared toward the window. A hard, wind-driven rain splashed against it creating curious aqueous patterns in which he might have seen cryptic messages and was trying to interpret them. A couple of times he muttered something that sounded like 'skyscrapers'.

In that quiet moment, we both started at the loud ring of his phone. *"François, quelle surprise!"* Suddenly sober again: "Yes, yes. In fact he's here now. Yes, join us…for drinks of course, as usual, as you well know. Ok, ok, *a toute a l'heure*."

"Pére François?"

"He lives just around the corner. A real reunion. How'd he know you were in Paris?"

"That's what I'd like to know."

Zetkin poured mammoth drinks, took off his shoes and zigzagged around the room examining the plants and shifting the chairs into a drunken semblance of order which only then made me aware that everything in the room was somehow disarranged and displaced: the etchings were crooked; uncomplaining chairs were out of place and maybe drunk too; his once perfectly ordered desk was covered with used paper plates and empty bottles; the Persian carpets lay at distorted angles; the dumped books were still scattered over the floor; an African mask on a wall near a window was hanging upside down. Zetkin himself seemed the totally non-conscientious person. How did he get his diploma anyway? Maybe he took it off the wall because of his doubts that he didn't merit it. And he took to drink instead. God knows how he cured my old symptoms. Or did he?

While waiting for the priest, I recounted a dream I've had over and over for years and that visited me again, I think last night: "There's a fabulous city with a powerful cathedral that I know well in my wake dimension. Maybe it's the cathedral in Strasbourg. Maybe Cologne, or Ulm. Or the towers of the Nieuwe Kerk or the Oude Kerk in Delft. Of course it could be Chartres. I thought of the cities and cathedrals of my boyhood. The dream is more an image than events. A tall gray cathedral—it is dark and enigmatic—stands at one end of the old town. All the town's congested streets lead to it and flow into a wide avenue divided in the center by parallel tram tracks circling the cathedral. The town itself is a labyrinth of twisting streets, loud and bustling, filled with noisy traffic. Yet when the traffic arrives at the cathedral it thins and the silence is total as cars glide silently and peacefully and methodically along the broad circular avenue around the dark and shadowy cathedral whose spires reach for the sky and fade into the clouds. It dominates the town and is visible from everywhere. I walk through the alleys of the town. I enter a nightclub. I wander from room to room. The rooms are filled with tables with white tablecloths and sparkling crystal glasses and laughing women in beautiful gowns. Then I walk out a rear door and find myself again facing the tenebrous cathedral. The fabulous town and the gray cathedral with the tall spires entice me. The cathedral, somber and threatening, the center of the universe, ruling and judging and chastising and rewarding weak man. Its force is a terrible thing. I struggle to imagine a loving god residing there."

I looked hard at Zetkin.

"So what?" he said, looking back at me it seemed cross-eyed.

"But what does it mean?"

"It doesn't mean anything, just a memory of a place you once saw and forgot."

"That's it? It means nothing? Besides, I didn't forget it. I just told you about it. And you guys get paid for this—for just listening to this supposedly meaningful shit!"

"Some people call us prostitutes: We get paid for listening. Sort of like getting laid—but still not exactly the same thing."

"For Chrissakes, Zetkin! You demean yourself. Writers can learn a lot from you. I do…or used to."

"Until you fled, eh?"

"Touché.

In that moment the door bell sounded and the door opened. Zetkin looked at his watch:

"Four minutes flat!"

"What?" I said, still stunned by the last martini.

"Our contest of who can get to the other's place the fastest," he said. "Four minutes, François. You just set a new record."

"How generous of you to admit it, Karl." Pére François was wearing jeans, a pale blue work shirt and a black leather jacket; he was soaking wet, his hair plastered flat and his beard glistening waterously Venetian. He looked like a construction foreman on a work site unimpressed by the heavenly elements. Nor did he have the priestly look about him as do most priests dressed in non-clerical attire. The priest took out from under his jacket a bag of sandwiches and slid it onto the table.

"To absorb the alcohol," he said, "but I see I'm too late!"

"And Monsieur Sutton, a real pleasure to see you again after such a long time…let's see, since we met at Ivaan's Embassy, just before the Paris events."

"Also for me, Pére, a pleasure," I said, wolfing down a ham on croissant sandwich—the first solid food in my stomach since San Marino.

"Please call me François. And I know your name is John. I heard you were in Paris and hoped to see you again, so this is a double pleasure—off duty, so to speak, at our friend Karl's place."

"Strange, I arrived only a few hours ago and everybody I know already knows I'm here. Even God must know I'm here…even though I hardly know Him. You must have spoken to

Him or to our secret agent friends…they too seem to know everything. "

"That's their job after all. And they still believe I have secret contacts with Islamic terrorists through my little church in the Goutte d'Or. Actually, I learned you were coming from two sources, yes, the secret agents and then your wife, dear Martha."

"That's another crazy thing. Everybody sees Martha but me and Zetkin. And technically, she's not even my wife. But holy Christ—oh, sorry for that, Pére."

With my hunger partially slaked, I examined the priest and thought *Pére* François: yet, again, just as that time in the Embassy, he seemed apart from the mainstream, unorthodox and off-center: still, though dressed in jeans, he nonetheless did retain something indefinable of the priest; but when in black and the stiff white collar as I recalled him, he'd seemed costumed. He was truly a man of two worlds: the spiritual and the secular. This man so at ease between us two drunks possessed the nearly indefinable quality that is grace. In that instant of sobriety, a Heinrich von Kleist story flashed across my dulled mind, a story purportedly about puppets like the ones I used to visit in Munich at the Marionette Theater. Magical, the graceful movements of the puppets—the more lightly they touch the boards of the stage, the more graceful they appear. I wondered how the puppeteers create that magic: the puppets just graze the boards, or don't touch them at all.

"Speaking of grace," I said drunkenly and thinking my thoughts, I related the Kleist story about an expert fencer and a bear—but really a story about grace. The recounting of the story sobered me up immediately. "The fencer was dared to try to touch a chained bear with his rapier. The bear parried each of his thrusts with the slightest of movements and didn't react at all to his feints. Its every move was graceful, free of wasted movements. A studied grace. Kleist said that grace appears most easily in people and animals that are unaware of their grace, that grace is a consciousness which those without grace cannot grasp. I came to think that grace is the same as goodness."

I looked at François—priest or healer, savior of souls or heretic—and thought that there stands a good man. And that Zetkin was fortunate to have him as a friend.

"Sorry for that," I added when they both looked at me for the rest of the story. "That's the end."

"No problem," Zetkin said. "He's used to it. In my view, this man should be defrocked because of the people he frequents and the way he lives and the language he justifies as the human stain that makes man, man. Pére, sometimes I think I should analyze you! I've gotten to know you somewhat, but only superficially—and you know that's true. But I wonder about your real passions, your dreams—the old dreams of all those years before you took the vows—your real joys and the secular things you conceal behind that black and white costume you sometimes wear. You know—your inner you."

"Karl, that's *your* real job. And mine is only a little different. So no, no analysis is called for. Besides, after all these years, just the thought of me even psychologically defrocked is as bizarre as you debarred."

"François! Pére François! In our years of friendship, you've already confessed to me more than I have to you. On the other hand, after all my listening to the confessions of others, I'm still unable to see myself, much less own up to anything—except my misdiagnosis of a colleague which not only debars me but prompts me—as only fair—to examine the skyscraper situation myself."

"What?" I yelled, Kleist still on my mind. "This is a house of lunatics. Graceless. Are you fucking mad? You healed *me*, now heal yourself."

"Heal?" Zetkin said ironically, "That's François's field. Healing the sick! I just listen to confessions of flaws and weaknesses…and sometimes comment."

"Ok, so listen to the priest's sage advice and get the fuck back to your job," I said, pointedly looking over the shambles of his studio. "And I still think you should walk the labyrinth at Chartres. It would do you a world of good –certainly it could do you no damage. Anyway, I've gotta go to the Goutte d'Or before I'm too drunk to ride the metro. Ciao, soldiers of the faith and thanks for the free analysis—and the entertainment," I added maliciously.

"But before I get on a metro train would you pour one of your martinis into my loyal Russian flask, just in case?" I said taking the flask out of my jacket pocket. It's empty now. No more will it be so neglected."

"What's this, Johann? You, with a flask? You don't normally drink!"

"Only since I became your patient. At last I can show off my father's trusty Russian flask. He gave it to me a few days before his fatal accident as though he'd had a foreboding of tragedy. You want to know where he got it, don't you? He told me the flask was a gift from a strange Russian stranded in Europe after the war. He was living in former army barracks on the edge of Rotterdam on the River Maas where that great river is wide and unpredictable as it rushes toward the North Sea. It's the Meuse, you know. My father was a poet too and very sensitive to time and place and especially changing circumstances, so that the relation of his memory of the origin of the flask was so vivid that I can feel it myself: It's the coldest winter in decades. Low wattage light bulbs hang here and there in the barracks. A coal stove burns red hot. Heavy felt tarpaulins separate his living area from others exactly like his. I can almost see the man before me now—the way I once described him in a short story: long thin blond hair, deep-set pale eyes under high Slavic cheekbones set in an angular somewhat tubercular face reflecting astonishment at his being there—but with a deceptively powerful body. They are sitting on orange crates, wearing scarves over their greatcoats. I love that descriptive old word my father always used for overcoat—like soldiers in the trenches at the Battle on the Marne. They're eating pelmeni and drinking vodka and beer when the Russian extracts from a box under the bed this wonderful present: a Russian flask. They were a little drunk, I'm sure, but my dad said that was not why he gave him the flask."

"No, I don't think so either," François said. "I think it was an expression of love for his fellow humans. That's just the way Russian are. I wonder what happened to him. Did he go home, or did he stay?"

"Those were difficult times, wherever you were or whatever you did," Zetkin said. "Some stayed since they'd been gone for so long they were afraid to go back. Just hung on—still in exile."

"But they at least knew what and where they were exiled from. I mean, they knew where home was. Anyway, my dad never saw him again. But his flask remains. So fill it up, Doc!"

Despite all my best intentions, in my newly discovered emotional escape of drunkenness, I momentarily forgot Martha, forgot Ivaan, forgot the Goutte d'Or, and even forgot the Russian flask full of Zetkin's martini cocktail in my jacket pocket. I instead fell asleep on the same couch we'd brought from Rue Saint-Dominique. I woke up and found it was five in the morning. For a time, I didn't know where I was or hardly my own name. At seven, I went to a café in Rue Saint-Dominique for coffee and again croissants, the only thing I ate yesterday at Zetkin's. Sitting at a table in the rear, I was half nursing my misery and trying to pull things together and half-listening to the morning news on a radio near me on the counter, when I heard a newsflash about a series of mysterious suicides in Paris:

'This morning at four a.m. a still unidentified man fell to his death from the fifteenth floor of a skyscraper in La Défense in Paris. Stay tuned for details.'

La Défense! Fifteenth floor! I alerted Pére François at once. He called me back a few minutes later. On Zetkin's desk he'd found a note scribbled on the back of a white envelope which he read to me:

Dear François Dear John
My final act in this Theaterstück seems like justice
Moral or immoral or amoral justice has been done
The labyrinth walk will have to wait till the next life
With affection
Karl Z. Zetkin Psy.D, Ph.D Clinical Psychology

That afternoon, *Le Monde* carried a strange and inconclusive story of "The Series of Suicides of Three Prominent Psychotherapists." Police were still trying to disentangle the apparent connections between the suicides. It was natural for investigators to believe it was not a coincidence that two of the three jumped from high buildings. On the other hand, it did not escape the attention of a thoughtful journalist at Libération that two of the jumpers were Freudians and one a Jungian. In the minds of queried psychiatrists, the Jungians won; in the minds of suspicious policemen, things didn't add up: the missing Jungian was either guilty or his life was in danger.

21.

Separation

I am only mildly surprised when Martha opens the door at the Embassy. I'd had a premonition, I suppose, but then, of late, my every move, my every reaction, every thought, every germ of thought and most of the things I do—like my being here now—surprise me less than they should. So what *am* I doing here? But then, why not now? If not now, when? Yet I know that the crazy things happening in my life today have less impact today than they will tomorrow. Still, such less than surprising events are driving me batty as they would anyone like me. Yet I feel certain that Karl Zetkin would've chuckled in delight at my first words to Martha: "My friend and shrink just jumped off a high building because he was overly conscientious."

Martha's mouth falls open and she stares at me as if she'd never known me—or as she'd once said about what I hope I will never be for her: just someone she used to know. I look into her eyes, I see her extraordinarily beautiful face, I admire her elegant being, and as each time I again try to get into her mind, I wonder who this person is whom I seem destined 'never ever to leave'. I stand there on her doorstep, so to speak, and wonder where our story is to go from here. I have no idea. And I doubt she knows either—hopefully the creator of our story does. Still, I can't accept Maxime's idea that every love story has to end. Most, maybe. But not all. Surely not ours. I take one short step in one direction or the other, unthinking, unreasoning, following unpredictable instincts, often in self-defeating directions. Then, before crossing the doorway, I pull back a step and ponder what to do. For in this moment, I feel the temptation coming over me to make again one of my purely instinctual decisions: I ask myself if this time I should not just turn and walk away, away, away? She's not going to change; she's no longer merged in me—she now belongs to somebody else. Zetkin once spoke of the fleeting nature of life, its precariousness, its uncertainty, its ever changing nature; he believed that short-term choices were of relative unimportance—'h, yes, Zetkin! Ok! But most certainly not relative to jumping off the top of skyscrapers. Ah, no! Overly conscientious Zetkin!' *Absolut nicht.* In recent years, back and forth between San Marino and Paris, I've lived with the illusion that I could continue loving two women simultaneously, forever: Maxime, in flesh and blood, in my arms on Mount Titano; and Martha, mother of my daughter Samantha, distant, a conceptual and by now almost a fictional love. Until this moment I've acted like this untenable situation could endure until the end of my time: I, on Mount Titano and Martha somewhere, anywhere but San Marino, forever absent from my physical life—Maxime merged into me; Martha, a fata morgana, like the Tartar who never arrives from the desert. From the moment Samantha left us, Martha's and my love one for the other began its descent, down, down, down our daughter's lonely river until its evaporation back into the tunnel train it came from. Still, the moment on the Paris train remains as vivid as then, now years ago, and the Gare du Nord looms up in my consciousness like a non-determinant fate, indifferent to Aunt Thérèse and her twenty cannons, to Rue Saint-Dominique, to the slippery rain-swept stairs in London and my swollen ankle, to Necker Hospital and Martha's infected breasts; live memories that ignite my symptoms—the panic, the terror, the burning shoulders, followed by the omnipresent sadness. Fleeting memories, Karl. You were so right: fleeting life.

"Martha!" I exclaim, and feel the anxiety, the pain of...of what? Of the unknowing? Of losing her? Of losing her before she let me go? Before she was instead torn from me too like Samantha? "So you're here! No, it's not surprising. It couldn't continue as it was, a long distance relationship held together by memories of her."

"No, it couldn't go on that way, John. And yes, her memory lives. But memories are part of life—a big, a major part. But still only a part. John, you don't really need me to let you go. You've never wanted to be free of us, no more than I've desired to be without you. You *are* Samantha. How could I let you and her go?"

"Sometimes, I thought you wanted to hold me as a keepsake. But you're right. We've always been three, not two."

"John, I can't see you without seeing her. I can't bear it any longer. I don't want to lose the pain. Above all, I don't want to lose the sadness that you've explained as the lower stage of pain. But I can't bear that constant threat. I try to imagine how our staying together would've been. If we'd stayed together, perhaps it would have gotten better, then less and less, but John that would've been losing her completely. I've loved you since the moment we met on that train. I still love you like I will never be able to love again but..."

"But you're here with Ivaan."

"Yes, did you not know?"

"Not completely. But once I saw your Missoni scarf hanging there in the cloakroom and wondered. Uh, where is he now? In hiding?"

"Oh, John Sutton, that's beneath you. He loves you, his best friend, so you can imagine his perplexity about the situation."

"Just my memory, again. A writer I like wrote that the working of memory collapses time?"

"What does that mean?"

"That memory is not an instrument for surveying the past, but that memory is the past's theater."

"Sounds like a bitter person, but his words do seem true. In a way it separates you from the past. Gives you more time."

"Not enough—not enough time or distance."

"He's in the kitchen, waiting for us, I suppose. You were always right about Ivaan; he is a good person. And he is good to me, John. We are good friends. And he'll be happy to see you. You're his friend too. Come with me."

Ivaan stood up from the table and embraced me—though not quite in the old way. Yes, we were friends—but not quite in the old way. We sat at the now modern kitchen table. The three of us, in these different times. We drank Arab coffee. Ivaan didn't display his usual savoir faire. Awkwardness fell over us—more over me than over Ivaan; the so-called situation was less sudden for him than it was for me. Though awkward, there was surprisingly no rancor. I couldn't accuse him for his attraction to Martha. Anyone would be. Still, my best friend? Should he not have closed the door between him and her? Took a distance from her? From us? Would that have alleviated and changed Martha's and my alienation? Did he betray my total trust? Yet, after all it was Ivaan who got Martha to the hospital while I was a prisoner on the tunnel train from London; Ivaan was at the Necker for her birth and became Uncle Ivaan; Uncle Ivaan held Samantha close and brought her presents. And he too suffered her loss—but not like us. Though now he taught Martha secrets of Egyptian cuisine, he couldn't suffer like us. Still, it was Ivaan again who arranged our affairs when Martha and I were both incapacitated. And finally, willy-nilly Ivaan became both a witness of and participant in our second calamity: the end of a great love affair—when, at that moment, however, should he not have been absent? I don't know the proper answer.

At the kitchen table in the Embassy of the Arab peoples in the Goutte d'Or district of Paris, the expected pain of the end had not yet struck me when Martha put a slender hand on each of our arms on the table. She sighed. And for the first time in the years since Samantha, an expression of peace filled her eyes.

When later, I stepped out of the Embassy door, I felt I was stepping out of Martha's life definitively. I felt a double sadness: she had once said an unspoken goodbye to me; now I was saying mine to her. Also only now did I perceive the premonition of the new pain to come—the pain of final separation like the new-born Samantha must have felt unconsciously when they clipped the umbilical cord linking her to Martha and she found herself alone in the world. I knew that my deepest pains, the worst kind you must endure as proper justice—the penance—would arrive later, in the theater of time and memory, as per Zetkin. In that truth theater in which also Ivaan would again be present.

On my way back to the airport, my fixation returns: I still don't want her to let me go. I still don't want to become her past. I still don't want to become just a memory. When the plane's heavy door closes with that familiar deep *thunk* , the first part of that past remains outside on the tarmac to be rolled over by winged giants millions and millions of times gradually reducing it to nothingness, while I hold close to myself the memories that past contains.

22.

Return to Mount Titano

In one coordinated movement, I drop my handbag from one hand and with the other take down a water glass from a shelf and pour it half full of the cognac bought at the Orly Aiport. I chugalug most of it. The glass still in hand, I look out the window over the flat rooftops of San Marino. The sky over the mountain is gray. I observe people strolling along the narrow streets. They have all the time in the world. It is seven in the evening, but these people are in no hurry. They are good people, gentle people, Communists all, Hank claims. The cognac feeling comes over me that I would like to do something for them. I can do what I do: I can write about them so that they will know they existed, that they lived good lives and as Hank says voted red. I glance across the room at the miscellany piled on my desktop and know I have to get back to work tomorrow. The wind from the northeast rattles the shutters in the other room and the house itself seems to waver. When I again perceive the mere suggestion of the impact of the reality of our final separation, the pain returns; I drink the rest of the cognac and refill the glass. Only recently have I come to appreciate just how good liquor is. Rejection is not the end of the world, I tell myself, but the final goodbye to your youth and to a woman you love is nonetheless a step closer to the ultimate nothingness. Hmm, yes. Now that's a sobering thought. I sit down again on the couch, and out the window I observe the mountain rising up sharply. Now and then sipping the cognac, I remind myself that a whole world lies beyond those mountains, which, if I am what I believe I am, I will investigate—sailing the seven seas. I'm not a prisoner. The wind suddenly picks up and the creaking of the shutters and of something or other on the roof sounds like music to my drunken ears. I think of Maxime; she should be back soon. Anyway, Maxime or no Maxime, it's goodbye to youth, I mutter and smack the side of my glass splashing a bit on my pants, and then smile at the assurance that there's more cognac where that came from, and I reassure myself aloud: 'though I feel older, I'm just thirty-five after all. That's not old. Not exactly young, but not old either. Not at all.' Then uneasiness sets in when I note the bottle is nearly empty. I feel like throwing up. Instead, I take the blanket covering a chair, stretch out on the couch, and it begins again. I hear the voices of the past; but not hers. The voices, mine too, speak of her, but she is silent. After her words "poor Poppy", not another word has she spoken. Never. Only I repeat them. Nor does she appear in my rich dream world. Never. I only dream of myself or Martha or Ivaan speaking of her. Unidentified voices speak of her too. But Samantha never speaks. She never even appears. Only the voices, voices speaking of her. Samantha and her voice disappeared into that little white casket. Why did it have to be little? Why?

The grand finale of my maniacal night on the couch is an incubus on the fifteenth floor of the skyscraper in Paris-Défence that I seem to know so well in my dream, but which evanesces in the morning. Drunken dreams don't last as do the sober dreams recorded in my dream log. In the nightmare, I keep asking people walking up and down the marble halls about a man in jeans torn at the knees but no one understands my language. I ask about such a man in German, then in Italian. No one even stops walking up and down the corridor to hear me out. They just walk up and down, up and down the corridor, wordlessly, no curiosity whatsoever. No one wants to know about psychotherapists in jeans. And I am asking myself if it really matters, when Zetkin beckons to me from an open window at the end of the corridor. He is looking at the view. He points out Chartres. See the cathedral, the medieval masterpiece. See the labyrinth. There you are, walking it. On the eighth or ninth circle. And there are Martha and Ivaan going out the door to do you'll never know what. Now Johnny Boy, he says, I must leave you. I'm hysterical. I perceive my unquenchable desire to know the truth. Doc, you can't go before you tell me where they went. You didn't know that I've learned to fly, did you, John? Admit you didn't know. Have a good flight anyway, Johnny Boy says—in my nightmare. And Zetkin flies out the window as he said he would without telling me what they did or where they went. And beginning to wake but trying to hold onto the dream, I keep repeating that he can't fly. Humans can only walk the labyrinth.

When I wake up, Maxime is still not back. Not back—from Hank's, I presume. Strange though that she's not here. It's nearly noon. Everything is strange today. Still, I really need to work after those forty-eight lost hours—but Maxime is not back. But what can I possibly mean? Not back? She obviously didn't come home. Everything is strange in my life too. Challenges left and right. No morality anywhere. Ethics eliminated in the great ethicide. So many things I don't think about anymore. I go to Paris and find that the love of my life now lives in the Embassy with my best friend. I return to San Marino and my new love, Maxime, is somewhere else. Hopefully not back with the killer, Bernard, who is now my friend too. All my friends! Bernard, for God's sake, whom she says she never loved even though she lived with him—she only "cared for him". But Martha says the same. Now what the fuck is this "care for" that they feel. My *situation* is indeed complicated as situations tend to be. They both claim to love me, but both live with somebody else and "care for" them…and they don't come home at night. But Bernard? If not Bernard, then maybe it's Hank—my best friend in San Marino? In any case, again today I have to face the truth—whatever the truth here is. Enough prevarications in my life. Better to face it today while I still feel more invulnerable than I will later when I'll have to confront the new realities that I sense in arrival. Someone or the other will begin to take punitive measures. That seems for certain.

I trudge up Mount Titano unwillingly, intermittently tempted to turn back—straight to my desk—or to the bottle. Yet anxious curiosity drives me upwards. Curiosity as to what awaits me inside Hank's Bar. The great oaken door is still locked. It's just shortly after three. I circle the stone building, trying side doors and peering through the windows. All the entrances are locked. I see no one. A few minutes later, two figures round the bend below and start up the hundred meters to where I stand. The wind has intensified and the shade following the bright sun descending toward Bologna is cold. I raise the collar of my jacket, conscious that I'm becoming more cold-natured with each passing year. Still, I'm not old yet, I remind myself as I shade my eyes and distinguish the two women: Maxime and, and yes, Juanita. They're holding hands and haven't noticed me standing along the wall near the entrance. So that's where she was! At Juanita's apartment on a parallel street only one block below ours. But if she was that near, why didn't she come home? Well, well, John! My naiveté surprises me, as ingenuous as the five-year old I once was blinking in the bright lights of the Aboveworld. I step away from the wall and greet them in as natural way as possible.

Now I'm of a jealous nature too. But mine is a different jealousy from Bernard's. I don't carry a pistol and stage shootings. But jealous of Juanita? Yes, but in what way? It doesn't seem the same if it's a woman. Maxime and I sometimes fantasized about a threesome—another woman between us. Who could she be, we wondered? How would it take place? Who would do what to whom and such details, repeated over and again in exacting detail? Aphrodisiacal thoughts: Maxime hers; I, mine. Strange that the formula of a threesome with another man hadn't entered into my mindscape; something to do with penis issues and penetration on my part. Male chauvinism, I know. No, it had always been another woman between us.

When still hand in hand the couple reaches me at the main door, the Cuban seductress doesn't blink an eye, but Maxime's sad look has returned.

"So how was your, uh, your book business visit to Paris, lover boy?" Juanita says in her usual joyful and ambiguous Latin manner. "Hopefully you got what you went for." I examine her eyes in a hopeless attempt to grasp the true intent of her words. Though elusive by nature, she has always been a friend, loyal and gentle toward me. Moreover, I'd believed, she was together with Hank in every possible way, his lover and manager, the center of the private part of his life: contrary to me and Maxime, to me and Martha. It seemed she and Hank had resolved the conundrum of one man and one woman genuinely merged one into the other as I had so deceitfully and hypocritically believed of both my overlapping and simultaneous relationships in which nothing was ever really certain or everlastingly secure—nor even sincere. Though Hank and Juanita seemed to have grasped the reality that as beautiful and perfect as an emotive, sensual relationship like theirs may seem, they had both accepted the reality that permanence was just a romantic illusion. My case—if it had any practical or exemplary value at all—was in truth the most wildly exaggerated example of the grand illusion of permanence. For how could Maxime and I be truly merged one into the other—as I the eternal romantic imagined—if I was still merged into Martha? Only bad faith on my part had spawned such ambiguous and destructive falsehoods. Now I stood face to face with a bizarre variation of reality.

"Hopefully, my editorial suggestions were satisfactory," I reply to Juanita while examining closely Maxime's eyes. "Now, I just have to finish the story. The end is the difficult part. Enduring love is a pleasant ending but the sad truth is that things don't end the way we hope."

"Then maybe the end of your invented love affair is the end of the story," Juanita says suggestively and smiles.

"Anything to avoid marriage or death to end a story. Like my friend Zetkin in Paris whose story ended when he jumped from a skyscraper and whose insane last words were that he could fly."

When both women look at me with half smiles as though I were teasing them, I explain that he was a psychiatrist who cured me of my symptoms at a bad time in my life but who also started me on the road to drinking as 'a panacea for various and sundry ills', as he said, 'the kind that can befall anyone in life.'

"Sounds like a wise man."

"In his way, yes. But he couldn't fly—yet. He fell from the window."

"Like some angels!"

"Yes, but maybe he got used to the idea and somewhere around the fifth floor his wings began working, too late to save him, but in time to carry him on his voyage."

"Very romantic idea, John."

During my brief and ironic exchange with her friend, Maxime's eyes and mouth remain indelibly marked by the faintest of smiles that seems to be asking me how I feel about them now. I hold her gaze a moment before asking Juanita:

"Where's Hank?"

"Still at home. He wanted to sleep a little longer today so I'm opening…that is, we're opening," she says looking—it seems to me—tenderly at Maxime and says in Italian: "Look, food and beverage deliveries will arrive soon so we'd better open the doors."

"Va bene, t'aiuto," Maxime agrees, a new tone in her voice. I was away only two days, just two fucking days, and Mount Titano seems inhabited by strangers. And she hasn't even asked about my Paris trip; she's hardly seen me at all. What the fuck! In only two days she's transformed. After the vanquishing of her barroom sadness, after the revelation of the secret of Bernard and Beirut, after the great rains, after our Venice of love, the MOSE rising and sinking back into lagoon waters, the board walking and cocktail drinking on Piazza San Marco, the three days and three nights in the Hotel Prince—part of the foundation for our imaginary merger one into the other—now another Maxime has materialized. Not the woman who escaped Bernard's Beirut, but the Maxime who burst forth and flourished in it. Oh, just for a whiff of truth! In my life,

the true truth is forever truant. I feel I'm still in the Underground world my father led me into. I stare at Maxime's profile and realize I'm seeing only one side of the person I'd merged into—that is, the one part of her that the Underground part of me—the non-Paris part—had merged into. For Chrissakes, am I never to be whole? No longer the vanquished, the defeated? Only shadows of the past slipping through the fingers of my hand. Like the winds of China. Like the nothing I felt after the labyrinth walk. Nothing. Prevarication truly reigns over my life. The end of the story has been written for me. Only pitiless readers can say that I have what I deserve.

I followed them into the tavern and went directly to Juanita's bar. Juana handed me what appeared to be a triple vodka and smiled in the way I knew so well. I drank off the vodka, put money on the counter, touched her hand and walked out the great oaken door, down the mountain, past the bend, past my apartment and into the village where I bought two bottles of Moskovskaya. No plans for work today. I sat on the couch and put a bottle of the vodka and a water glass on a side table. I poured myself a modest drink, discarded the idea of adding a bit of juice, and sipped it prissily for a moment. My head was empty of ideas but I perceived things turning and grinding noisily in the hippocampus like the metro train at the ninety degree turn after the Sèvres-Babylon station: memory was gearing up. Something was surfacing. Scared me, as it should. I finished that drink and poured a real one. The real one—another debt I owe to Zetkin. Now, my new plan was to think everything through with a mind flushed clean of clashing ideas by alcohol and to attempt to ascertain the connectedness of the isolated events that have occurred since the day I met Martha on the London-Paris tunnel train now so many years ago. But my very first thought sufficed to turn my ambitious plan upside down: to my surprise my first image was of Zetkin purposefully showing me that he couldn't fly, so how could I not wonder why my subconscious chose to begin things there in the ugliest and most disquieting link in the chain. Why start my mental rambling at the top of a skyscraper? Oh, that ever deceitful subconscious! And moreover, that skyscraper suggested a link with Underground—the true guilty party. So above, so below. Zetkin and my father. Now that is a truly mysterious association. I'd come to love crazy Zetkin like I adored that enigmatic man with his dark-suited friends, my father, who exuded the same cult-like mystery concealed within the walls of Hank's Bar and Tavern and some days in Zetkin's studio when the rain beat against at picture windows, and now —as if that were not the connection—also the wind and rain and those wild bushes beating against the windows in the Necker Hospital porch while we waited in the penumbra for the verdict. Thus, all the time my destiny was to end up in a sect on Mount Titano. But nonetheless, the question of Underground remains: Does such a place really exist? Or was it back then only the first conceptual appearance of my fertile imagination? And my father? Was he criminal or spy? I've always wondered. Maybe both. Much of me, much of the rest, I suspect was/is hidden in him. I pour another triple, slam it back like the first, aware that though I don't really love the taste, the immediate effect is magnificently magical. In that same instant, I recall Kierkegaard's father-son relationship. There was the story of Soren the Dane and the mirror. The son is like a mirror, the Dane noted, in which the father sees himself as he once was; for the son the father too is like a mirror in which he sees himself as he will become. But hadn't I broken that chain when I stepped out of Underground and began revealing parts of myself in my writing? With the realization however that the real revelation was that the limitation 'only parts of myself' was the real issue: compartmentalization. Maybe crazed by conscientiousness, Zetkin had nearly grasped that about me intuitively, but I escaped his hold first—or rather he escaped me. Evaded me. Deceived me. That other part of myself, the concealed part, slipped away even though some of me—I suspect—flew away with Zetkin now somewhere on his solo flight into the bright sunlight hanging over the skyscraper. So here's to my old friend and shrink, Karl "Icarus" Zetkin, I think deliriously, and tip another and note that all the triple shots have demolished the bottle. Having sworn that he was my last—and only—shrink, I'd convinced myself that I could analyze myself. I would doctor my own self and soul. My symptoms are mine, I thought, and I can treat them as I like, as the writer said of his Russian language: It's my language and I can do with it what I like. Now some of my symptoms are normal, I suppose; others are pathological. I'd understood that terminology is central: So does that mean my symptoms are pathologically normal, perhaps? For Chrissakes! At times, I do feel deranged. Unlike others—or, I think consoling myself—were their faces also façades as mine must seem to them? Is it not madness to reflect on every emotion, every mood, and every ordinary thought that comes into my mind? At which point I realize I'm in Zetkin's head. I merely anticipate his unspoken thoughts as he rambles along his Kierkegardian route; I dwell on the Dane's Journal of September 10, 1839 in which S. K. reflects that 'foresight is really hind-sight, a reflection of the future which is revealed to the eye when it looks back upon the past, as if he were reviewing the past in order to glimpse his future.' The Dane's observation makes me wonder if he, and most likely Zetkin too, had studied Italy's ancient Etruscan civilization. The comparison occurs to me because of the Etruscan belief that everything that happened was to announce a future event, or it was the realization of a sign the gods had sent earlier. For the Etruscans, facts were not important because they happened but because they arrived in order to have a meaning in the future—like Kierkegaard's son's view that his father's present is his future. But to get back to my personal conundrum, Zetkin, 'Is it your/my diagnosis that I am normal, but nonetheless feel just a little mad? And do you/I think that deep nuanced reflection begets madness? Yes, or no? You might say as Maxime said one day about feelings, *Le sfumature della pazzia*. The nuances of madness. Otherwise, to what extent can I too construct the pathological from the normal?' For am I not master of my madness? I ask; and though from afar the answer comes back unhesitatingly—maybe from that scary Underground…if it really existed: 'you're not a madman; you only imagine that state would be bliss.' Anyway, S.K. said that no man is entirely sane. And his life was the proof. A madman in life and thought. Crazed by words, words, words—and by Christianity. Nothing old Soren liked better than posing unanswerable ontological propositions: If you do it, you're wrong; if you don't do it, you're wrong. On appreciation or lack thereof for his home country, Denmark, he writes: *There is no such great difference between one generation and another; precisely the generation (he) censors finds itself in the position of praising what an earlier generation of contemporaries failed to appreciate.* And then he writes of links, like his link to his language, bound to it as Adam was to Eve first because there was no other woman. Ah, that Zetkin! He armored himself in such ideas and then took them away with him on his flight. And to think I instead took the Chartres labyrinth walk in search of epistemological solutions that the master seemed to have at his personal disposition and applied so freely. Kierkegaard's words sound exactly like him. Nevertheless, Shrink, at times I've found that if from day to day I go on doing the same things—wake in the morning, wash my face, dress, and breakfast, sit at my desk and stare at a blank and untitled document—I feel like I'm on the verge of going insane. Then, I spend the night at Hank's, drink in my former moderate way, sleep till noon, stagger to my desk and the disparate crazy ideas first cohere then spill from my brain, through my fingers and the keys and fill page after page. Dangerous thoughts, those. Explosive thoughts. But romantically false. In every sense wrong. Only nightmare garbage. Dream state raving. Like the rare recordings of the Welsh rock band, *Dream State*, the little known music Hank dared play only afternoons when the tavern was empty except for me—he said he was trying to wrap his brain around the concept of dream state…not the band but the trance, he called it. Stretched out on a cot behind the bar and covered with a green sheet, Hank was training himself to enter the dream state. *Dream State* recordings like *The Plot Is In You-Feel Nothing, Trauma, Suicide Silence* echoed from the great door to the bar. Provocative, unlistenable stuff. Like late-period Zetkin would conclude, Hank said he had to alter his consciousness to the point that his life seemed like a dream. I told him I do that every night, awake but still in the dream. When you're between sleep and awake and the dream continues, you know you're in the dream state. Condition your dreams, hang onto your dreams, don't let them escape and evanesce into nowhere before you lose them completely. That's the crooked winding route to what I like to imagine as creation. Reality is the first route—the crazy route. It is real mental derangement that is, always was and always will be compulsory artificial discipline: to know just where you stand, where to search your mind for ideas, and create artificially the time and space for imagination. The discipline alone drives you and everyone around you insane. The sleep till noon schedule is comfortable normality in which you are partially lost, but you are loved by all. Yet, yet, nothing is fixed. Nothing is determined. Hank, I whisper to myself, creative life is a circle. What happens, happens: Martha, Rue Fabert, Rue Saint-Dominique, Latin America, the Coupole and Ivaan number one, Samantha, Uncle Ivaan, secret service agents, the Paris false flag riots, state of emergency, Samantha tragedy, Martha to London, I to San Marino, distance gradually transforming into separation, Maxime and I, Martha and Ivaan number two, now Maxime and Juanita and Hank. And I, headed back into Underground. Destiny? I doubt it. Penance? Hardly. But depression, panic, fear and anxiety, my maniacal exaltation and the clouds of symptoms passing, drifting and re-passing overhead. Again they afflict me. They're my life companions, my Zetkin-free self-diagnosis. On which I empty the bottle, feel queasy only a moment, lie down on the couch and sleep like an angel.

23.

Premonitions

Before I left for Paris, I'd felt that something was not right in my relationship with Maxime, that some new factor had entered her life. I couldn't pin it down to anything more than a presentiment. In any case, I'd perceived a premonition like the foreboding that often precedes major changes in our lives. In a time when your life and relationships seem as calm as southern sea waters and you have no inkling of anything amiss, such creeping emotions may arrive as a result of the most minor of occurrences— a certain look of one person at another or the touch of a hand. Even a silence may suffice to set off a life-changing chain of consequences. Although I couldn't determine what had changed, Maxime herself seemed insecure and uncertain, as though she were trying to comprehend and resolve unidentified entangled aspects of her life. Sometimes she withheld her usual warmth, her expressions of joy at what she still called her first real love, her declared conviction that we were destined for each other, her ultimate trust in me and in the *thing* that was us, just as I had thought of Martha's and my relationship. So, although I was not conscious of anything specifically wrong, from the very start our togetherness was so close that even minor issues made their mark and gradually added fuel to my presentiment that change was in the air. I recalled the many times Hank stood with his arms around Maxime's shoulders; I remembered her long melancholy look at him the evening she told me she wouldn't go with me to Paris. At the same time, my Paris jaunt was my great-little lie, my prevarication: I had hoped she wouldn't want to go with me so I would be free for Martha. Then, I felt the foreboding all the more because she said I shouldn't worry, that Bernard was no longer the problem and that she would stay and mind things in San Marino. In hindsight, I reasoned that if she said Bernard was no longer her problem, then she intimated that there was a problem; and naturally I extrapolated that the problem was *another* person. And my presentiment was that her problem—and mine—was that the other person could only be Hank. So in that light, my shock yesterday evening at the threesome image of Maxime, Hank and Juanita that flashed across my mind, the consequence of which was my newly acquired reliance on alcohol as a quick panacea. The price of which however was the disillusionment you feel when it passes: the Lord Gives, and the Lord Takes away.

It was around seven when I walked back up the hill to Hank's. Where else would I go? I felt like shit. Maxime was behind the bar helping Juanita prepare for the evening. Hank was still absent. I stood at the bar and looked at the placard with a photograph of Bernardo Kristinsson and his six-man San Marino Blues Band hanging on the wall behind the bandstand. I snickered at the word *blues* because Bernard had once told me that his band played very little blues—he'd added the name only because it sounded good. When Maxime noticed me examining the placard, she blushed and said they would play tonight at eleven. I asked her for a double vodka. I carried the drink to our old table and sat down to consider my presentiment of things that were likely to happen now that the jinn were out in the open and among us, and that somebody was likely talking with them. Crazy things could happen, over which I had no control—especially not me. In fact, I relegated my earlier sensation of presentiment itself to one of the things destined to happen—things that were bound to happen; I could only duck for cover. It had been much easier in the Embassy where a laid-back Ivaan made the change almost tender and comprehensible—I suppose the real reason Martha was there. Her destiny had been pressing her gently in Ivaan's direction since he took her to Necker Hospital to bring Samantha into the world, since he became Uncle Ivaan. From that moment Martha was to some degree his. Strangely, I couldn't bring myself around to thinking Ivaan had betrayed our friendship which remained. Somehow Ivaan made me conscious of the absence of an *Egyptian* air on Mount Titano. We here who live the sect-like life we live are of a more pragmatic nature and submit to the interference of the jinn as nothing more than the goings-on in a parallel life.

I felt like a male jinn must feel. I was only partially inside human life. I kept my Paris and San Marino loves and lives compartmentalized and secret; my life with Martha was a secret in San Marino—I'd only revealed to Maxime that I'd once loved. Samantha was taboo. Martha only knew I had someone in San Marino; the rest of my life there was withheld. In my defense, I should say that the secrecy was not actually planned or the result of a tightly woven scheme; it came about because I simply felt no need to try to explain. I doubt the jinn explained their separate lives either, though they too might have liked to. I've read a bit about this intriguing race who in the times before God created Adam roamed the world as invisible entities. Now that was a quality we humans envy: invisibility. What a missing quality that is in us! You know, just push the INVISIILITY button when you need it. An invisible secret entity that can discover the secret lives of others. According to one legend, God created angels on Wednesday, then, a thousand years later, on a Thursday, he created the jinn, before, one Friday after another thousand years, he made man. I suppose such lazy displacing of his creations was to avoid confusion as to their identity and their roles. More about that in a minute. Now, the thing I like about the jinn—or the genie, as some people call them—and the curiosity they arouse is their parallel relationship with one thousand year-and-one-day-younger humans who are superior to them in strength and could defeat them in combat—I suppose as long as the jinn choose to be visible. In any case, though there are similarities between jinn and humans, they are different in that jinn could appear in many forms, the most feared of which was that terrifying invisibility state. Still, the jinn were not gods, and neither were they angels; in fact they were inferior to humans—or so thought early pre-Islamic humans, who however like Achilles and his heel had a terrible weakness: if they showed fear of jinn they became dependent on them and had to submit. The jinn had to be aware of that weakness and knew how to exploit it. Zetkin would have gone along with that analysis: show no fear of symptoms of sickness for that is what the jinn may have been: mere symptoms. Symptoms of a virus, like reflections of a wrinkled human face in clear water or in a broken mirror. But to continue the race theory, though they were physically stronger than angels they were weaker than the humans who could defeat them as long as they had no self-defeating fears and no mysterious symptomatic, virus-like illness—for example—fear of the jinn invisibility. Otherwise, they were just a parallel race living in a parallel world that I personally like to imagine and speculate about. Most certainly they were/are a race living in a parallel world; they once ate and drank and had children and were mortal and might have used their invisibility to defeat the human race but since in my imagination they were spiritual beings and had a subconscious, they had an ethic and besides, since they were physically weaker they decided it wasn't worth the risk: it was evident that humans were eradicating themselves. The final solution however was different than they imagined—unfortunately for the jinn—like humans they could be either angels or devils, but since they were not God either, they too fell and they had to face death and eventual extinction. I wonder and ponder one fundamental aspect: What if they had used their invisibility when they still could and defeated the humans. OR, even more, what if they did exactly that and won the battle and we are not humans at all but the weak jinn, who in order to achieve victory over humans and survive had to pay a price: their invisibility. Yet, yet the fear remains. Whether human or jinn. Fear has its time too—a lifetime. Unstoppable. It's a time thing too. When your mind fears too long, it moves to the body and becomes panic. You can reason with fear; it's a mindscape affair. Not so, panic. The mind is helpless after the transformation to panic. Panic is a body thing; you can't think it away. Fear time. Panic time. The two cohere, separately, one after the other.

When the great oaken door opened and Hank stepped in, the clock at the bar showed midnight. Hank stood with his back pressed against the door and looked over the room like a stranger arriving from Hyperborea. I smiled to myself and remembered Zetkin looking up at me over his lowered spectacles after I'd made some stupid remark and saying I sometimes spoke like an ancient Greek legendary Hyperborean and before giving me time to ask,

Who? he added I should look them up and that they too lived at the very edge of the world, up in the far north, north even of the Northwind.

A few last notes sounded on the piano and with a wry smile in his eyes Bernard finished Hank's song:
Like the circles that you find in the windmills of
your mind!

Hank clapped silently, nodded left and right, went straight to the bar and, after acknowledging Juanita and Maxime with a strange movement of his lips, thrusting both out in a pucker and then withdrawing them over his gums, locking inside his mouth words not to be spoken, he poured himself a finger of Pernod, added mineral water and carried his drink directly to my table.

"*Bentornato*," he pronounced his welcome back in a cynical voice at the same time glancing over his shoulder at the two women behind the bar. "As you can see, things got out of hand while you were gone."

"You seem to be sleeping well," I replied in his same playful manner.

"Maxime's arrival made Juanita's house too crowded for me so I moved back to my place and decided on a short vacation and I read your novel, *The End of a Love Affair*. I liked your words that sexual love is as different from marriage as spirit is from flesh and that falling in love is harmless unless you make the mistake of marrying the person you're in love with."

"Thanks so much. Maybe that's just false cynicism thrown in to tickle the fantasy of certain readers. You make my going away and my return worth the pain…and to learn that I'm not destined to live in total licentiousness."

"Not yet, you aren't. But still, John, those two women we love seem to prefer the new arrangement. So who knows what the future holds? You yourself say somewhere that anything is allowed."

"I didn't say that, Hank. And don't forget my dark background. "

"I read that in your article about the imaginative Jorge Borges and his crazy short story, 'The Theologians', about a fictional sect on the banks of the Danube known as the *Monotonous* who professed that history is a circle and there is nothing that has not been before and there will never be anything new. I read that part several times. The part where the Wheel and the Serpent replaced the cross. The wheel formed by the image of serpent eating its tail—the cycle of life—was a heresy, your Borges declared. His protagonist however decided that the thesis of circular time was too different to be dangerous; the most fearful heresies are those nearest orthodoxy. So the Carpocratians were on the right track. Before he invented the theologians Borges obviously discovered that the agnostics of Carpocrates of Alexandria believed that in order to leave this world, your eternal soul must pass through every possible good and evil—and the Carpocratians in good faith did all those unspeakable things so that when they died, they wouldn't have to reincarnate and try again but would return to God forever. Man, John lad, you're dealing in dangerous stuff. Do you live life like that sometimes? Maybe we all subconsciously would like to feel like a Carpocratian."

"That's Borges, not me. But still, I warned you I had a dark background. Really really dark—like being underground. And Hank, I don't plan to go back there."

Though I felt *enormously* relieved by Hank's clarification of the Maxime-Juanita scenario and it revitalized our friendship, bringing us closer together than before, I remained in the same no-man's land which resembled Underground from which I thought I'd escaped—first with Martha and Samantha, and, I'd believed, with Maxime. So even though I understood better the jinn in their godless world somewhere between angels and men, I knew I would have to search diligently for my place—either with the Carpocratians or the angels.

Words were falling smoothly into place the next afternoon when Maxime came. A faraway look on her face and exceptionally beautiful, she stood hesitantly barely inside the door like a timid visitor. "Sorry to interrupt your work hours, John, but I need to pick up a few of my things. You might know that Hank has moved back to his house, so I think I'll stay with Nita for a while to help her out in this difficult moment"—she prevaricated outrageously—"and give her a hand in much of the management of Hank's Bar and Tavern."

"It's not a bother," I replied nonchalantly, turning back to my text and waving a hand in the air and pretending to still be in deep thought. Actually, I couldn't concentrate on the Carpocratians, whom I kept calling Procarpatians, and free will. "Feel free to come and go as you please and by all means take all of your things, if you like."

"Oh, John, don't say it like that. It's just…well, it's just me. There are things about ourselves we can't change at will. Sometimes we never learn who we really are in life. I'm fortunate to learn something about myself even this late—and so are you—fortunate that I am learning who I am."

"Yes, Maxime. You're right and I was wrong. And I too am somebody other than the person either of us imagined."

"Juana had a hard life in Santiago because of the strict domination of her father. So she became a bartender and had relationships, everything he opposed. Then she slipped away with Hank, leaving father, Santiago and Cuba behind only to find herself again a bartender, this time in San Marino. And again she wanted to rebel. But against what? Against whom? Hank cared for her. Then you and I appeared, I truly loved you, John, but in another way, as you yourself say of your love. Everything with you was perfect—but different. In that sense, I lied to myself about my past, about us. As I suspect you lie to me about Paris. You and I know the truth about each other and we accept that truth. But Nita—our beloved Juana—does not. She wants to kill Bernard for what she thinks he did to me. It's revenge—also against her father. That's her state of mind in this moment. And she wants to say it in public and make Bernard pay proper penance for his crime—for his sin, she says, the source of all evil, she says. Her ideal of life is demoniacal, John. She said this morning that the next time he says Max to me publically, she will shoot him on the spot. This morning she said that since she has the power to kill him, then it is her duty to do it. I think that's a voodoo principle. She practices her form of Haitian vudu on him too. She made a doll, put some of his hair on it and mutters vows—she calls out to them—in Spanish vudu language. Also, somewhere she got a pistol. And John, she will kill him, I know she will. Because of what she believes he did to me, "he doesn't deserve to live on this earth," she says. "John loves you," she says. "Bernard did not love you: he wanted to kill you, so he must die."

"Maxime, she sounds nuts to me, and dangerous in her madness. Are you not in danger too? My God, who would have thought? That joyful and charming, Juanita! In fact, her very eroticism was a joy—as you know. The way she was with Bernard in the beginning. The way she was with that Iranian musician."

"Oh, yes! Yes, Nita is uncommonly erotic. Not at all what we thought she was. She claims she's a pagan. She says the Christian fanaticism of people like her father invented sensuality and eroticism. And for her the act of killing is of no importance at all. Nita doesn't even believe in jails and prison and courts and judges and trials; they exist for other people, she says. But no, John, I'm in no danger but Bernard Kristinsson is."

"If what you say is true, Maxime, then you're the one to guide her. You seem to be the only influence on her instincts and that's what they sound like: instincts—not convictions. Nor can Hank guide her; only you."

"You're right about Hank. He's out of the question. And I'm afraid the responsibility is too great for me. You make me aware of a strange aspect of her that I only realize now: Nita simply has no conscience—not a shred of conscience as we know it."

"My therapist friend in Paris would say she'd lost herself in her passion—lost every desire to control it. I mean, if she speaks of murder as though it were of no importance, she's lost. Murder means to kill. And according to that terrible Old Testament the Lord's commandment was written in stone; *Thou shalt not kill*. My Shrink taught me that not every mental derangement of passion or emotion of the heart can be resolved by cold reflection."

"Oh, John, you're able to reason your way through emergency matters like this. That's why I loved you—and love you as I still do." In that moment, John saw in her a brief flame of the sensuality that had fueled their relationship from the start: she was the purest statement of the sensual person he could imagine.

"If I were just not such a liar. If I could just be truthful, even with myself, you might not be here gathering your things to move elsewhere."

"Don't be too hard on yourself, John. We all have our secrets. And in my case, there are two things: my sexual nature and Nita. Now I'll make a little confession to you: there really was someone else in Beirut—and it wasn't a man."

"Maxime!"

"Are you shocked?"

"Of course I am. Well, shocked is not the word. It's too late for that. But perplexed, yes. Right now I'm so surprised that I don't yet know how I feel. Certainly I'm hurt but that doesn't reflect what I will likely feel as soon as I absorb that you *are* you. Maybe I feel as Bernard must've felt deep down: that there was nothing he could do to change things. But I'm not pissed and have no desire to kill you or anybody else. I suppose my true feelings will emerge slowly with time."

"I think Bernard guessed something like that and then reacted to the situation. But after all, John, he had a choice: he could just live with it."

"But killing the woman—or you or me—would be the act of a madman."

"So instead he faked the murder of that Arab to save face."

"Well, my choices are more limited. I'm not a madman—not yet. So, don't worry."

As the afternoon passed, the first stages of my old feelings of aloneness came over me. Though not a jinn, I've come to feel I'm living in someone else's dream or in the constant dream state of an interplanetary alien stepping out of his spacecraft onto an unbelievable Times Square on New Year's Eve. And I tell myself that there are alternatives to life on this barren mountain. But what alternatives do I mean? That's the question of questions. Zetkin would say my subconscious has been asking just that since I left the dark, tight and watery security of Underground—of course, his would be a peculiar and ambiguous manner of speaking of alternatives.

In the early evening, I stand at the window and watch the first rain drops fall. The usual fog and the rain enveloping San Marino have become even thicker than before Maxime. Later, after a bowl of pasta and a second bottle of San Marino red in the trattoria downstairs, I realize Mount Titano has become too crowded with shadows, and Paris too painful and teeming with memories. Of course, setting out for Mexico is a tempting alternative but it too would mean Martha and more loneliness. The reality of the missing home to return to is a bitter pill to swallow although I am not surprised when like a world appearing from the past, tried and true Munich comes to mind. After all, I lived there two times, why not again and, as Italians and Germans both say, *non c'è due senza tre*. All good things come in threes.

24.

Under Fire

Just one last time, I swore again, 9/17 in mind as always. One last check. One last time I returned to Rue Fabert to make sure. Again. The last time I was here, I still hoped. I still believed in us and our togetherness. After all we'd been through together, I couldn't believe that our separation was final, that it was over. Today, I'm no longer thinking of love, but in the entity that was once us. Part of me still hoped we would somehow recover from our suffering, maybe not whole, but more resistant, tougher and determined to hold together. Certainly not whole. Maybe only simulacra of Martha and John, who however together might find the spark of life to be able to start over again. I'd texted Ivaan that I would spend a few days in Paris. I didn't say where but Martha would understand. And she too might be waiting for a final clarification. She, just across town, I, here in our city. I went to the cemetery. I walked the streets. One day passed. On the second day I was still alone in the cavernous apartment when something most unexpected began. Twenty-four hours of internal struggle during which I was to have one of the most devastating panic attacks before I even knew exactly what a panic attack was or how to combat it. And my former shrink, Zetkin, no longer lived in nearby Rue Babylon. A psychological monster was raging in some uncertain place inside me. Then, after it was all over, I recorded as much of the gory details as I could retrieve from my synapses. Although I'm still uncertain if all the feelings and emotions happened in one time, or if my reconstruction is the sum reactions to different minor attacks that I then referred to as symptoms: first, the elevator episode in La Défense, then the metro terrors and the regular shoulder burnings sitting at the computer. This attack had begun slowly, silently before it struck me while I was peering at myself in the bathroom mirror and I alone in Rue Fabert, alone, alone, the only human being on earth and Zetkin unavailable to medicate me. Whatever happened on this occasion in Rue Fabert— or on that composite of several occasions lumped into one—it was another of the mysterious turning points in my life. Mysterious because we have so little control over such events; they just happen to us, willy-nilly, the way Destiny wills.

The afternoon of the day before, I'd felt relatively good and secure sitting at a sidewalk table of a café facing the Madeleine waiting for Martha and, drinking—I remember that distinctly—I was drinking Calvados—and not even excessively. I don't remember why I was at that particular café—it was the only time I was ever there, which didn't matter because I waited for Martha at all cafés. I don't recall why I was drinking Calvados either which is not one of my usual drinks. Probably some silly Hemingwayan idea struck me that day. Yet, since leaving Rue Fabert an occasional doubt had prickled me. Something was trying to remind me that I was not free, while at the same time and unbeknownst to my conscious self, that parasitic, incapacitating thing in my legs was all the time crawling insidiously, surreptitiously upwards though my tibia and the femur, along muscles and tendons and veins and nerves, ever upwards, aiming at my sensitive guts. I tried to ignore it as Zetkin had advised, admittedly drinking a bit more to suppress the caprices of my free-wheeling and impulsive psyche. Both distracted by and conscious of rising anxiety in attack mode, I stared back at a man about my age at the next table who kept speaking at me, his talk temporarily saving me from the advancing terror. It turned out he was the son of a White Russian émigré, a man I felt might know what Underground was and therefore put my trust in him. And thus began an elusive night in another trance-like dimension where uncertainty reigned: bloody Mary's at the George V bar run by a crazy Algerian my new friend knew, who later took us for whiskey to an improbable Playboy Club de Paris on the Champs d'Elysées, a band playing in rooms with wide open windows through which fog banks drifted in and out and among the bored and over-weight international Bunnies; repeated dinners in Restaurant Calvados for various and sundry chicken fricassées and bottles of Muscadet in alternation with piccolos of Moet et Chandon; during the night blinys and sour cream and vodka in a Russian bistro maybe somewhere in Montmartre and a young Russian who had never been to Russia singing ballads about Old Moscow. My Russian friend translated quite poetically I thought some of the words:

> *"softly oh so strange and gay*
> *that important little song*
> *the song that's still unsung"*

We made mysterious taxi rides in the night through narrow streets leading back and forth across the river; and at dawn to a railing on the Butte looking out over the gray slate roofs of Montnartre and the great urban bowl infused with the gray Parisian light. Under the gray sky of the worldscape pressing down on my head at the peak of Montmartre, I again felt totally exposed to disparate though uncertain dangers; the moment reminded me of the hated security my father sought for me in Underground, a dream state concept beyond my five-year old boy's comprehension.

The next morning, after a restless sort of sleep, I was brushing my teeth in one of the gigantic Rue Fabert bathrooms, surprisingly feeling no hangover but conscious that my mind was racing uncontrollably, my thoughts amorphous and confused, jumping from one thing to the other. I stared into the mirror; I imagined searching for the image of my father but saw only myself sneering back, for which I was just beginning to blame Kierkegaard for his father-son-mirror images when I perceived the frontal attack coming at me. It struck like a bolt of lightning out of a blue August sky. Oh, God, no! I'd almost forgotten you existed. Away! Get away from me! No, Zetkin! Don't let it happen! But when IT unleashed a terrific blow to my stomach, I was alone in Rue Fabert and Zetkin had flown. A vise clamped shut on my insides. The agitation spread. Veins pounded. Then, the fatal over-breathing overtook me. It was panic. Fear. Fear then panic. No answer at Zetkin's. No answer. I'd forgotten. Never again an answer at Zetkin's. Sweat started from my hands and flashed down my body. My stomach was a volcano ready to erupt. Ready to explode...or implode. Death, I knew, was the only release. Don't think! Think about not thinking. How did I stop it before? Go to the window. Look at the Invalides. Examine the twenty cannons. Count them again. Still twenty. No answer from François. Search for a good but old dream. No, not that! They're all bad, sad, incomprehensible. If I took a drink now? A drink? Are you mad? Don't even think such thoughts. If I have to take tranquilizers? If they give me an injection? Demerol? Have you drunk alcohol? they'll ask. After all

I've drunk! And tranquilizers! Oh, for a doctor and a shot. Have you drunk alcohol? he will ask again. Have I *drunk* alcohol! I am alcohol. Or just get the shot anyway and die of Demerol and alcohol like poor old what's his name at the Necker. Martha tried to calm me that time. Is that Martha again? What's she doing here? Go away, Martha. You're not even here anyway. In mind, rolling green pastures and geraniums in the windows of a village houses and how it would've been with Samantha too. But no! Don't think that! I'm in command. Don't think! Martha stroking my hand, my head. No, no, I can't stand to be touched. Can hardly bear a voice. Losing control. It will never stop. Only death! Call a doctor at the Necker! Momentary respite. Cancel the doctor. Then, another wave. Call the doctor. Try Zetkin-François again. Dress and elevator downstairs. A walk will calm me. Rush down the Esplanade. Rush back upstairs. Quick. Onto the bed. Find a position. Evanescent, ghostly, female jinn-like Martha is helpless. On my stomach, while the ghost of secret Martha speaks of London. I sink deeper into the mattress. Deeper, deeper. Until, finally, deep in the mattress and deep in the Adriatic where those gray warships passed so silently on the sea's horizon ignoring the swarming sea monsters deep, deep beneath the waters, I find that certain position that exists for every person. Find that spot. Hold it! Hold it just there! Yes, yes, yes, *it* is easing. I feel the release. The defeated parasite slides slowly down my leg, slowly, and out, out, out in search of other victims. Remember this position. The position, the position. What counts above all is the position. Courageously, I sit up. I look around me and find that it's gone. I smile at Martha's ghost which also vanishes.

As I might have noted earlier, my memory of these attacks is emblematic of my problem of writing non-fiction: in my own case, it is tempting and easy to leap from fact to a form of hyper-fiction, to fictionalize what in itself is actually even truer than fiction—which is it's justification—even though considered less accurate because it is supposed to be factual reporting, but in which you can't remember details of your all-important feelings and emotions about what happens. In memory I constantly resort to this lifesaving tactic: I group events, I skip over time and place and then select the event that best reflects my feelings and emotions and what suits me best—and oh, how I select! And after repeated reductions and cuts emerges the essence which is poetry! Yes, poetry. My poetic panic attacks. I mean to say, I really have those attacks. They are real. Therefore, for the sake of readers and writers, as E.L. Doctorow warned: "beware of sins against poets". He remarked: "Every book is an act of composition and if you happen to use memories or materials from your own mind, they are like any other resource; they have to be composed. And the act of composition has no regard for where the material comes from. So when it's all said and done it's all autobiographical and none of it is." His premise was that "the language of politics cannot accommodate the complexity of fiction, which as a mode of thought is intuitive, metaphysical, and mythic."

25.

The New City

From Bogenhausen on the hill across the River Isar I viewed again the city where I once lived and wondered if this was still my city. Surprising how I'd forgotten the layout in such a short time. Yet, maybe it's better that I start out anew. I'd lived in only a small part of Paris, a nearly forgotten childhood in the Netherlands and an endless period in Underground somewhere in Munich, early boyhood in San Marino, and, as a teenager, I returned to Munich. And since then: two lost loves and my child lost like my own childhood. Instead of a background of a tangible and well-defined life, I remained with my fictional world and painful memories. Now I want more. I want solidity. I want to move forward in life. In a real life, an everyday life. Now I want to participate and play a role in life. I could go elsewhere; but where else? Back to Argentina to pal around with Gustavo? No, for there was still that magnetic something about the city on the Isar, my first big city as an adult. The city that I still sometimes claim as my hometown. The city where still a kid I finally emerged from Underground. That was the city of the times when old walls were falling, new walls were rising, and the whole world was changing. And the sun there rose from over the Alps as it did from the great Adriatic Sea.

My childhood Underground and Ludwig Maxmilian University are one Munich. Not the whole Munich, I imagine now as a thirty-five-year old adult human. The Oktoberfest that Hank celebrates each year in San Marino is only a faint reflection of that

Munich foreigners know: the two weeks reign of Paulanerbräu, Löwenbräu, Hofbräu and Burgerbräu beer when Bavarians in lederhosen and dirndl's dance on massive floats yodeling and throwing bonbons to the crowds; when flag twirlers and bands and marchers from the entire Tyrolean world wind under the towers of the Frauenkirche in the capital of the Tyrol and rivers of beer flow in the Bierkellers until in the ugly light of the morning silent groups of men lean with their elbows on high, marble-topped tables near the departure platforms of the Main Station and sip a sour morning beer.

I know that Müncheners of today are not doing what I'd thought they were doing when I studied at the university. Not even their reality then was real reality. Their recent history had cancelled the national folly of Nazism that had come to seem only an unfortunate interlude in the city's history. Though certain memories still had to be banished in order to survive, another generation's war was already gestating. Theirs is more than just a German past. And their future is as fragile, euphemistic and futile as were the former attempts of some to grasp the real Teutonic past. What passed for real continued—economic boom, music, skiing, eating and drinking, BMWs, Carnival-Fasching and Oktoberfest and Lake Garda and the Italian Riviera. From the hill of the Angel of Peace monument, I see a tenacious people for whom only unreal reality counts. Everything seems fictive. Or wishful thinking. I sense that like the San Marino people no one here knows what they're really doing in their eternal present or even want to know what's really happening to them. Yet they do believe in duty and responsibility. As is often said: historically, Germans have distorted human values with their innate sense of conformity and their need for order. Therefore, they can never carry out a real revolution as suggested by their French neighbors that I had so recently experienced. Only among some youth in a substratum of Munich a revolutionary tradition survives, accompanied by a Protestant philosophy of no fun, no considerations, no excuses. Despite the fugitiveness of the times, despite the vagueness and ambivalence of what was happening in the world, the hot war in East Europe and the nuclear threat it nurtures, the times are still called a period of peace. Still, under the surface, nothing seems absolutely secure. And in the real present it's hard to know what is really happening anywhere.

In such ways Munich is much like any other city—even though it is indicated as the most livable city in Europe. Munich is inhabited by peoples much like others elsewhere: people yearning for other people, people filled with longing and ceaseless loneliness. Though I know I am marked by my strange origins and my not speaking as others speak and not thinking the thoughts others think, I fear I show the untrammeled rebellious stock of my father to whom the righteous upright others felt so inferior that we were obligated to that life in Underground. And they harbored such hate for him and fear of what he represented that they killed him. Somewhere, hidden in this perilous, poignantly dangerous city, still live those who conspired to kill him. But I will be here in my attempt to forget the rest: forget the time of Martha while holding close the memories of Samantha. While I wait for *them* to appear—*those others*—*I* will try to be like others and make my mark here.

I love Munich's river. Enough living on a barren mountainside. I want to live along the River Isar where, nights, embers of bonfires burn late. I've always loved river cities with their bridges and tunnels, the yellow lamps along their banks and old fishermen and the jumping fish; and I don't understand why people in some towns ignore their rivers. I love Paris for the role the wide rippling waters of the Seine play in the city. I love the homey multicolored barges, the mysterious house boats, the iron moorings, the wonderful lamp-lit bridges, the water birds, and if you are close enough, the nighttime sounds of the lapping of water against the embankments. When I resettle here, I will walk along the gushing Isar when there is high water from the weeks of Munich rains to watch the colorful jumping fish. The gushing river of sudden cascades and dams and sudden low water points and river islands and urban beaches for swimming—and many bridges and fishermen and jumping fish. Squadrons of lonely gulls fly low over the rushing current accompanying you downstream to the angel monument hanging over the green-white river and the throbbing multicolored city. Sundays, I will make the rounds of the downtown churches to hear the choral music —the Michaelskirche and the Theatinerkirche and the Peterskirche—in this city so fervently Catholic it was once called Germanic Rome. Sometimes in the summer, I and new friends will eat ice cream under the poplars on the boulevards or drink beer in the pubs or go to the Hofgarten and walk in the shadows under the arches around the park.

Super aware of NATO and Berlin's role in it, eager students at the university used to speak of turning history around and the triumph of human values over conformity even though the same dominant NATO was writing the only history they knew. In the minds of some the idea once churned that an attack on the heart of the state would rally the people and the capitalist regime would implode on itself; but they were a dreamy and forgetful student body that forgot that their state had two hearts: one in Brussels, the other across the Atlantic. Socialism would triumph, they said to each other, unaware that the socialist protagonist no longer existed. Still, I, who'd come from both Underground and the heights of Mount Titano, still liked the dangerous ring of such words that very few people speak today. They lay in the distant past. But from the Bogenhausen Hill and the Angel of Peace, I imagined this: the poor people in rich Munich seemed much less poor than the poor in southern Italy or in Saint-Denis in the Paris suburbs. Something was terribly out of whack in the upside down world. Yet, though I hadn't pursued the ontological matter back then, I knew one thing: I would always be on the side of the underdogs. I'd studied Lenin and Marx and, after all, I grew up with my revolutionary committed father and spent my childhood in his conceptual Underground. I too dreamed that the times of revolution in Europe were not over and done but I also accepted the idea that history did not repeat itself. On the other hand, it was crystal clear that U.S.-occupied Germany was an instrument of American power and that much authority in this new Germany that I was returning to was infested with a Nazi spirit.

It's raining, as expected. I drive down the winding street from Bogenhausen to the Widenmayerstrasse snaking along the riverbank and see almost immediately on a corner facing the river a real estate agency. I enter and wait until a curtain parts and out steps a gorgeous head of red hair.

"*Grüss Gott*," the magnificent woman says, holding her lighted cigarette at a distance from me and herself. "I'm Dorothea.

And you're looking for an apartment and I have just what you're looking for. Just next door, two beautiful furnished apartments go onto the market today. The house is excellent...if not unique. Though a little expensive, it offers a long lease—besides, what can you expect with this view of the river and the hills beyond—and after all it's right in the downtown."

I still hadn't said a word. I just stared at her, stunned. Smoke swirled around both of us and seemed to isolate us from the distant rumbling of traffic on Widemayerstrasse.

"I also live there on the top floor," Dorothea added.

"I'll take it," I said, in the German she had spoken to me without asking what language I spoke. How did she know? Hard to say about women folk. They know things. Was she a jinn? Could she disappear and observe me from her invisibility? I keep thinking of the jinn. Who knows if during those thousand years there was some cross-breeding? That would explain a lot of life's mysteries.

"Which? The one of the fourth floor? Or the one on the second."

"The second floor."

"Why not the fourth floor—just under me?" she said allusively, taking a final puff on her cigarette and squashing it on a saucer.

"I'm afraid of elevators...claustrophobia."

"*Ach, das ist ja albern!* Silly! Why that?"

"It's a long and complicated story."

"*Trotzdem*, your apartment on the second floor is bigger—four big rooms and a balcony. And you will tell me sometime about the elevators."

"I will tell you everything, Dorothea. Uh, my name is John."

"So what nationality are you then? Where are you coming from anyway? You speak good German. Are you being transferred by some company?"

"Uh, let's see. I'm a Dutch citizen, but I'm really English. I live in San Marino and in Paris. I work at home for myself."

"You work at home as what? And that Dutch-English business is not really clear."

"Well, I'm a writer. And I once lived in this city…went to the university here."

"So that's the story. Writers do live complicated lives. And I'm always meeting complicated men."

"I can well imagine you're always meeting men. But do I still get the apartment? And when can I see it?"

"Of course, you get it. It's yours. You can see it now. Let's go," she said, lighting another cigarette in a slow sensual way and looking me in the eyes at the same time. "Still, too bad about the claustrophobia! And that apartment just under mine. Who knows who'll take it?" Dorothea added, it seemed facetiously. Her come-on look, her here-I-am-take-me behavior was driving me nuts. I felt wanted—the last thing I should have wanted to feel. I, a man on the run, should be ignored, not acknowledged and catered to. Her whole demeanor said that she'd known me forever and had been waiting for my return.

Lithe and buoyant, she climbed the carpeted stairs alongside me, 'to help me get the proper feeling of it", she said ambiguously—like female jinn must have talked. The wall lamps, the dimmed ceiling lights, the variety of carpets and polished dark hardwood, the softness of things and our diverse doings of that precise moment on the embankment of the River Isar reminded me of the Embassy. Maybe someday I would tell this redheaded Circe long stories about the Goutte d'Or and of the terrifying elevators at La Défense and how my drunken psychiatrist Zetkin had a fixation on skyscrapers for jumping off of.

She opened the door and gracefully stepped two paces backwards so that I could enter first. While I gaped at the wide expanses and spontaneously exclaimed: "Rue Saint-Dominique!" she used the interval to light up, again, and said coyly, "I don't speak French." Pursing her lips, her eyes told me she hadn't finished with me.

The apartment did remind me of Rue Saint-Dominique in continuation of what seemed an unending series of new things that remind me of the old and I told myself that I had to get over this constant comparing my new life with the past. Or is it true that nothing in life is new? That life is a circle? I came out of Underground in Munich, went to San Marino with my mother and returned with her to Munich to my enigmatic father. I went to Paris and stayed for Martha, went back to San Marino and stayed for Maxime. And now I'm back in Munich and will hopefully be able to remain here with Dorothea and all her fancies and that everything will be clarified. I see portents that that's the way things are. Everything that has happened before will happen again and again. That book of Ecclesiastes is always so reductive—and as a rule so right. *"The thing that hath been, it is that which shall be; and that which is done is that which shall be done: and there is no new thing under the sun."* Life is truly a circle; round and round it goes—like memories. That's the way memory works. Only

Dorothea's explanations and her sparkling secular hair in this moment reflected in alternating rays of sunlight from a front window prevented me from dwelling longer on the Biblical aspects of memory. While she pointed out the qualities of the big double living room with a dining corner, I followed her hand with its graceful long fingers pointing toward the terrace looking out over the rushing, gushing Isar with its jumping fish of my dreams Spinning around, enthusiastically rushing here and there, she showed me the two bedrooms and a big kitchen and a storage room-study. "I want it as of today," I repeat, the vista of those speckled jumping fish and her red hair haunting my fertile mind. Ginger hair, some say. Dorothea's hair was not ginger. Not a deep burgundy nor auburn nor orange. Her hair was brilliant sensual mundane red. Though there was no reasonable haste to go back downstairs immediately and sign the lease and pay, and pay again—just to make sure—I felt pressed anyway. I perceived an unforeseeable catastrophe intent on ripping this particular apartment from me: a strange sensation, concerning an apartment, like my black car back then—yet it was already part of my life story. Hopefully, it was the fulfillment my destiny. Oh, if I only believed in *sud'ba* as did Hank. Yet, was it not to fate that I'd lost Martha and Samantha? Unlike Maxime who at one point just went missing, lost to her nature which as such was bearable and human. I thought that Zetkin—on the verge of his first and only solo flight— would laugh at my fear that a document left unsigned in this moment could deprive me of a new life: this specific apartment and maybe also Dorothea. I felt she was already part of the new world to come, the world of the River Isar and the speckled jumping fish in its white gushing waters. "Let's get the documents signed, I'll pay whatever you ask, then I have to leave for San Marino for about two weeks to wind up my affairs. I have only one request: Wait for me!"

Dorothea smiled purposefully, knowingly, took my hand and said, "John, I can show you other available apartments, bigger than this, some smaller, in high rises or in two family houses. Still, I wish you would take the one under mine."

"Dorothea, it's this apartment I want and, well, I confess I want to be near to you. It's just that elevator. From the ground floor, four floors up is a long ride during which anything can happen but from the second floor it's only a two- floor walk to you and…"

"What in heaven's name are you…? I didn't understand a word you're saying."

"Then there's also the question in the back of my mind about the singer, Sam, and this building. You know, he…"

"Sam Richardson, the baritone? You knew him? Why he and his wife lived in my apartment of today."

"He was my best friend at the Uni. My only real friend. Up there in your apartment by the piano in front of a window looking out over the river, he once sang his favorite aria: *Il Prologo* to *Pagliacci*. I remember the moment well. It was about noon and he was singing his aria and for the first time I noted that the fish in the Isar jump and that some are speckled—like your hair in this sunlight. Anyway, that's what got him the job at the Munich Opera. They liked his audition. That time he got the alternate languors and also the unexpected furies right. But not everybody did. At auditions he didn't always show his natural aplomb either. He usually tightened up, like once in Vienna when I sneaked in for his performance. But after the minor job here he made it bigtime. Sang at Covent Garden and the Met too…and then he… "

"Slow down, John, slow down!" Dorothea said as we walked back downstairs. I laughed to myself: she was holding my arm tight like Martha used to do, and also like people not used to walking on stairs.

"John, you keep getting lost in the particulars of the past or far ahead of yourself. You get lost in details. But yes, by all means, let's do get those documents signed. Those other things can wait, Sam, the Prologue and the speckled fish jumping in the river—and yes, John, I'll still be here when you get back and things will happen as they're supposed to, one after the other, and I'll teach you to ride elevators again and you can move and we can…Oh, you know! We can live."

I knew I was falling in love—for the third time. And no! I don't think three loves are too many in one lifetime."

26.

Falling off Walls

It was nearly midnight when I started up Mount Titano. Finally—possibly, probably, hopefully—one last time. Before reaching the great bend I was suddenly struck by a blinding spotlight. I stopped and shielded my eyes with both hands. And a voice rang out to turn that fucking thing off and for me to continue straight ahead. After the roar of the superhighways, the flashing and blinking of multicolored head and taillights of the caravans of eighteen wheelers monopolizing the autostrada, a spotlight in my face left me dazed and unable to move my legs forward until a man from behind the light came and took me by an arm and guided me forward. Men in police uniforms were milling around the bend in the pedestrian walkway leading to Hank's Bar and farther upwards toward the Castle topping the mountain.

"What's going on here?" I asked.

"What are you doing here?" asked the apparent boss, dressed in a dark suit and tie.

"I'm going up to Hank's Bar for dinner."

"Dinner at this hour?"

"That's usual at Hank's."

"Are you a regular there?" another asked suspiciously. Even San Marino police mistrusted anything connected with the Hank's Tavern sect.

"For years," I said sheepishly.

"Show me some identification," the chief said.

He examined my Dutch passport from cover to cover with obvious displeasure and almost disbelief—unhappy that I was even here, and at this late hour. "Where are you from anyway?"

"Uh, let's see. I lived here as a child, with my mother. But I was born in the Netherlands. And I live here now."

"Where were you earlier in the evening, say, an hour ago?"

"I just drove here from Munich, parked my car down there where the road ends without even unpacking anything. I was hungry. But wait a minute, why are you questioning me?"

"Now, you know the police ask the questions, but anyway a terrible thing happened here. Someone jumped or fell over that wall onto the rocks below."

"Or was pushed," another voce said.

"We don't know that," the chief said.

"Take a look down there. Maybe you recognize the person."

The spotlight lit up the parent oaks and their two children like the stage of the Moulin Rouge. On the rocks under the trees, lay the body. It was Bernard, clear as day. He seemed to be looking straight up at us. "Strange, his face seems intact. Of course, I know him. He's my friend, the singer and composer, Bernard Kristinsson. Like my mother, his mother too was Sanmarinese."

The cops looked at me funny when I added that Bernard could have been a great concert pianist and that his father was a piano tuner.

"Well, he won't be singing and playing the piano anymore," the chief said, frowning at me, I knew disgusted with my description of Bernard as a concert pianist. "Lads, let's get on up to that perverted tavern!"

The outcome of the police investigation lead nowhere; Bernard's death was ruled suicide and the case was closed. For the San Marino police, Bernard Kristinsson was soon forgotten. On Mount Titano, Bernard's death, however, became legendary.

Hank and I suspected the truth, a truth that in any case was to remain one of the darkest secrets of Hank's Bar and Tavern near the top of Mount Titano.

Actually, only Maxime and Juanita knew the real truth—and even *Juana* herself—the only witness, or perhaps the killer—seemed uncertain as to whether Bernard fell by pure accident, by choice, or if her playful shove—a mere hint of a push—sufficed to send him, as she said, 'flailing and screaming' down into the chasm.

The next day, Maxime related to me *Nita's* real version of the tragedy. Yet I am still uncertain whether Maxime and Juanita's story is lie, cover-up, or prevarication. In any case this is the way Maxime related it to me: After Bernard's first set of new songs performed on Hank's enlarged stage, he took a walk to digest the public's enthusiastic acclaim, humming and singing the fragment of a song and perhaps recollecting images of lovers walking along a shore and the way things could have been—Maxime elaborated—and seeing again the vaguely-remembered face of the Arab he pretended to shoot and the brutal moment, that unforgettable instant, in which he realized that his affair with Max was over.

Nonetheless, based on my understanding of this complex man gleaned from our open and frank but strange relationship, images of his alternative life began to unwind before my eyes. Unrequested though surviving in the half-closed niches of his artist's mind, Bernard might have seen and become obsessed by his

Jungian shadow self, the concert pianist that his artistic piano tuner father had so desired he become and, as it might have turned out, to the joy of the musical elect in the world at large: Bernard Kristinsson, the artistic symbol of an excellence achieved through the painful thoroughness of experience, combined with unrelenting ambition and the grinding torture of repetition, a "conscientious" life of the polished artist, could have produced a performer capable of perfect workmanlike execution of the world's greatest composers: Kristinsson playing the Tschaikowsky Piano Concerto in the Copenhagen Concert Hall, Grieg in Oslo, Brahms in Stockholm and to crown his father's dreams, the great Beethoven's Piano Concerto in Berlin. Dreaming, remembering, reminiscing and regretting, Bernard stopped at the great bend to admire the twinkling lights of Rimini, reassuring lights as regular, he might have thought, as the geyser somewhere in the expanses of exotic America. But the idea of his imaginary conscientiousness—I must have had in mind Zetkin's "overly conscientious" anal personality of those who strive for the top, some of whom, however, cannot bear the stigma and prefer to jump from high places.

Meanwhile, Juanita, following the dreamy man, was imagining other scenes passing through his mind: his brutish excesses, his crass extremes, his tardy regrets of his slave master relationship with Maxime. On her own admission, Juanita was furious and intent on punishing the real, down-to-earth Bernard Kristinsson for his treatment in Beirut of her beloved Maxime. When she saw him boost himself onto the wall down at the bend, her still rough, schematic plan for the execution of his merited punishment underwent a rapid escalation: in her mind, the chasm down below beckoned like the shiny watery gleam of the great white whale leaping for the body of the whaler-in-chief, Ahab. Although she had spent the past years with Hank and loved him as much as her nature permitted, at the same time, however, she often felt she was betraying her real self, just as she was betraying Cuba by her flight, which old friends back "home" interpreted as treason and considered her a traitor like a Miami *gusana* drinking cafecitos in Little Havana. Oh, she remembered and imagined. She and Maxime there together. Memories of the future. Such things happen. The spectacular vistas over the plains below with the sugarcane fields and the *macheteros* wearing tattered linens and straw sombreros slashing left and right with their blunt-nosed machetes. The familiar smells, the heat of the sun's blinding rays, or evenings the warm winds from the sea caressing their faces, a decades old Chrysler impervious to the mountainous terrain, passing them trudging in single file like ragged revolutionaries. Cuba's highest peaks within fingertip distance. All these heights and rare *mariposas*. And as light fades in the mountains, the warm lights of Santiago de Cuba will still beckon in the distance below. A rose radiance will color the mountains and sunlight paint Santiago's rooftops fiery red. And with Maxime, I will see the vermillion of Santiago rooftops from another perspective. In this moment, my breathing accelerates and the fever rises at the decision to return home. All Cubans think that way. On the one hand, I'd wanted to escape from the provinces where I'd been a prisoner since birth. But escape meant departure from Cuba. *Gracias a Dios,* Hank arrived to save me. Good Hank. Loving Communist Hank! Departure could have been exile, and betrayal. But thanks to Hank and San Marino Communists, mine was not. Now, how splendid it will be, Maxime and I back in Cuba together.

Nothing like the potential magnificence of memories to make the present and the future live. Meanwhile, she loved Mount Titano and San Marino—and Italy—which for her, despite San Marino's long history of independence, were one and the same. Also the Communist government of the Republic of San Marino filled her with pride, as did the professed Communism of practically everyone she knew here. But the sum of those positive aspects of her presence abroad was not enough. Now that she had discovered her true nature and since the explosion of her love for Maxime, her deepest regret was that she and Maxime were still in Europe and not in Santiago de Cuba where a real revolution was still in progress. Though such thoughts swept her in multiple directions, she nonetheless had projected Bernard into a role that perhaps was not completely his; yet the short period—a matter of days—that she and Maxime had been together, that period for her had come to reflect her real past—her past, present and future. Slovene Maxime Novak was the love she had dreamed of and thus was eternal. It always had been. Therefore, for her, Bernard was a brutish intruder and his treatment of Maxime in times past was the same as if it had occurred in the present. He must be punished. And she, as Maxime's other half, must execute it.

She sat on the ancient powdery and decaying wall at the bend and ranted at Bernard: he was a great *hijo de puta, pinche, hostia puta, pinche, puta madre, pinche, anda a cagar tu pendejo, puta madre.*

Bernard understood little but when he got the sense of her stream of Cuban abuse, he began giggling at her fury.

At which point, Juanita herself testified, she leapt to her feet on the parapet beside him still sitting on the wall. She admitted furthermore that his amused nonchalance and the way he carelessly splayed his hands on the plastered wall increased her fury.

Her curse words were still raining down on him when Bernard, rocking in laughter at the comedy of life, at the language people use and the time wasted, spinning and spinning and never ending nor re-beginning—slapped at the age-old mud brick wall, loosening several chunks of plaster and sending chips of stone into his face apparently causing him to lose his balance and simply tip over backwards into nothingness.

In Juanita's official testimony, she added that though he never said the words, it was her fervent but terrible belief that in that fatal moment, perhaps in an instantaneous flash of comprehension he perceived the uselessness, the futility of his life and that his San Marino Blues Band was not enough. That it would never be enough. Therefore, she claimed, his death was not entirely an accident; she believed he did it on purpose. And, as Maxime says, everything has to end.

But the real end was not to be found in Juana's official testimony: Yes, Maxime admitted, Juanita was deeply offended by Bernard's laughter; he didn't take the reality of Maxime's and her love seriously; he didn't even take seriously the Maxime he had so mistreated in Beirut. He had to die. And Juana considered it her duty to kill him.

While Bernard swayed back and forth on the crumbling wall, rocking in laughter, Juanita—our beloved Juana—placed both hands on his chest and pushed him backwards into the gaping chasm.

The End